THE
SECOND
SISTER

Claire Kendal was born in America and educated in England, where she has spent all of her adult life. Her first novel, *The Book of You*, was a Richard and Judy title and *Sunday Times* top ten bestseller. It has been translated into over twenty languages. Claire teaches English Literature and Creative Writing, and lives in the South West with her family. *The Second Sister* is her second novel.

🐦 @ClaireKendal
ƒ /ClaireKendalAuthor

Also by Claire Kendal

The Book of You

THE SECOND SISTER

CLAIRE KENDAL

HARPER

Harper
An imprint of HarperCollins*Publishers*
1 London Bridge Street,
London SE1 9GF

www.harpercollins.co.uk

Published by HarperCollins*Publishers* 2017
3

A catalogue record for this book
is available from the British Library

ISBN: 9780007531714

This novel is entirely a work of fiction.
The names, characters and incidents portrayed in it are
the work of the author's imagination. Any resemblance to
actual persons, living or dead, events or localities is
entirely coincidental.

Typeset in Lomba by
Palimpsest Book Production Ltd, Falkirk, Stirlingshire

Printed and bound in Great Britain by
Clays Ltd, St Ives plc

MIX
Paper from
responsible sources
FSC™ C007454
www.fsc.org

FSC™ is a non-profit international organisation established to promote
the responsible management of the world's forests. Products carrying the
FSC label are independently certified to assure consumers that they come
from forests that are managed to meet the social, economic and
ecological needs of present and future generations,
and other controlled sources.

Find out more about HarperCollins and the environment at
www.harpercollins.co.uk/green

For my Sister.
And for my Daughters.

She had no rest or peace until she set out secretly, and went forth into the wide world to trace out her brothers and set them free, let it cost what it might.

The Brothers Grimm, 'The Seven Ravens'

Contents

Late November

Eyes Like Yours

Somebody said recently that I have eyes like yours. Not just literally. Not just because they are blue. They said that I see like you too.

When I glimpse myself in the looking glass, your face looks out at me like a once-beautiful witch who is sickening under a curse. Those jewel eyes, losing their brightness. That pale skin and long black hair. It's only the little pit by your left brow that isn't there.

I see you everywhere.

If I really had eyes like yours, I wouldn't be about to ask a question that you are going to hate. I would already know the answer. But here it is. What would you do if the police wanted to talk to you? Because I need to follow where you lead.

Just forming these words makes me see what to do. The police ask their questions and I am supposed to give them the answers they are hoping to hear. I am almost sorry for them, with their innocent faith that they can capture you on an official form, kept to a page or at most a few.

We wish to seek the whole truth, they say. *You are a key witness*, they say. *We are concerned for your welfare*, they say. *We need to obtain the best evidence*, they say. *We will deal appropriately with the information you provide*, they say. *You can trust us*, they say. *The success of any subsequent prosecution will depend on accuracy and detail*, they say. *Other lives may be at stake*, they say.

Am I supposed to be impressed? Flattered? Grateful? Scared? Intimidated? All of the above is my guess. So I will allow them to think that they have had their desired effect, as they take their careful notes and talk their tick-box talk in the calm and reassuring style that they have obviously rehearsed.

I will *read the notes over to confirm their accuracy*. I will appear to *cooperate*. I will *sign the witness statement* they prepare for me. I will *date it* too, with their help, because I have lost track of time a little, lately. Still, these motions are easy to go through. They do not matter.

What matters is that I am quietly writing my own witness statement, my own way, day after day. Compelled not by them but by you. That is what this is, and I am pretending that you are asking the questions and I am telling it all to you. I am writing down the things you want to know. The real things.

I will say this, though, Miranda, in my one concession to police speak. *What follows comes from my personal knowledge of what I saw, heard and felt. I, Ella Allegra Brooke, believe that the facts in this witness statement are true.* This is your story, but it is mine too, and I am our best witness. Maybe I do have eyes like yours, after all.

There is one more important thing I must tell you

before I begin and it is this. It is that you mustn't worry. Because I haven't forgotten the confidentiality clause and I never will. You have taught me too well. What goes in this statement stays in this statement. It is for you alone. I am the sister of the sister and you are part of me. Wherever you are, I always will be. All my love, Melanie.

Saturday, 29 October

The Two Sisters

There is no visible sign that anything is out of place. But there is something wrong in the air, a mist of scent so faint I may be imagining it.

'I was wondering,' Luke says.

'Wondering what?' I am scanning every inch of our little clearing in the woods.

'Why are so many fairy tales about sisters saving their brothers? All the ones you told me last week were.'

He is right. 'Hansel and Gretel'. 'The Seven Ravens'. 'The Twelve Brothers'. Our mother seemed to know hundreds of them.

'We should write a different story,' I say.

'I want one with a sister who saves her sister.'

I touch his cheek. 'So do I.'

He marches straight into the centre of our clearing, dispersing any scent that might have lingered here.

This is where you and I used to make our own private house, playing together inside of walls made of tree trunks. We would eat the picnic lunches that Mum would bring out to us. We would plait each other's hair and tickle each other's backs.

When I think of your back, I see the milky skin beneath the tips of my fingers, my touch as light as a butterfly kiss. But this snapshot from our childhood disappears. Instead, I imagine your shoulder blade, and a flower drawn in blood. I hear you screaming. You are in a room below ground and I cannot get to you.

I blink several times in this weak autumn sun and remind myself of where I am and who I am with and that I cannot know that this is what happened.

I hear your voice. Even after ten years your words are with me. *Find a different picture*, you say. *Remember the things that are real.* This is what you used to tell me when I was scared that there was a monster underneath my bed.

I look around our clearing. This, I tell myself, is real. This is where Ted and I used to lie on a carpet of grass on summer days when we were children, holding hands and looking up through the gaps in the treetop roof. There would be snippets of blue sky and white cloud, and a pink snow of cherry blossom.

Your son is the most real thing of all. He bends down to scoop up a handful of papery leaves. 'Hold your hands out,' he says. When I do, he showers my palms with deep red. 'Fire leaves,' he says.

I shut out the flower made of blood. I manage to smile.

He cups a light orange pile. 'Sun leaves,' he says, throwing them high into the air and letting them rain upon us.

He finds green leaves, too. 'Spring leaves,' he says.

I lean over to choose some yellow leaves from our cherry tree, then offer them to Luke. 'What do you call these?'

'Summer leaves.' This is when he blurts it out. 'I want to live with you, Auntie Ella.'

I stare into Luke's clear blue eyes, which are exactly like yours. When I zero in on them I can almost fool myself that you are here. And it hits me again. I imagine your eyes, wide open in pain and fear, your lashes wet with tears.

For the last few years, my waking nightmares about you have mostly been dormant. It took me so long to be able to control them. But a spate of fresh headlines last week shattered the defences I'd built.

Unsolved Case – New Link Discovered Between Evil Jason Thorne and Missing Miranda.

Eight years ago, when Thorne was arrested for torturing and killing three women, there was speculation that you were one of his victims. We begged the police for information. They would neither confirm nor deny the rumours, just as they refused to comment on the stories about what he did to the women. Perhaps we were too eager to interpret this as a signal that the stories were empty tabloid air. We were desperate to know what happened, but we didn't want it to be Jason Thorne.

Dad spoke to the police again a few days ago, prompted by the fresh headlines. Once more they would neither confirm nor deny. Once more, Mum and Dad grabbed at anything which would let them believe that there was never any connection between you and Thorne. But I think they are only pretending to believe this to keep me calm, and their strategy isn't working.

The possibility that Thorne took you seems much more real this time round. Journalists are now claiming that there is telephone evidence of contact between the two of you. They are also saying that Thorne communicated with his victims before stalking and snatching them. If these things are true, the police must have known all along, but they have never admitted any of it.

'Don't you want me?' Luke says.

Thoughts of Jason Thorne have no business anywhere near your son.

'Luke,' I start to say.

He hears that something is wrong, though I reassure myself that he cannot guess what it really is. He walks in circles, kicking more leaves. They have dried in the lull we have had since yesterday's lunchtime rain. 'You don't,' he says.

Luke, you say. *Focus on Luke.*

I swallow hard. 'Of course I do. I have always wanted you.'

Don't think about my eyes, you say.

But everything is a trigger. I study Luke's dark hair, so like ours, and imagine yours in Thorne's hands, a tangle of black silk twining around his fingers.

How many times do I need to tell you to change the picture?

I try again to change the picture, but there is little in Luke that doesn't visually evoke you. I search his face, and I am struck by the honey tint of his skin. Luke can actually tan, while you and Mum and Dad and I burn crimson and then peel.

He must have got this from The Mystery Man. I once teased you by referring to Luke's father in this way, hoping it would provoke you into slipping out something about him. But all it provoked was a glare that I thought would vaporise me on the spot.

'Granny and Grandpa and I have always been happy that we share you,' I say. 'It's what your mummy wanted. You know that. She even made a will to make sure you'd be safe with us. She thought of that while you were still in her tummy.'

Luke wrinkles his nose to exaggerate his disdain. 'In her tummy? I'm ten, not two, Auntie Ella.'

'Sorry. When she was pregnant.'

But why? It is not the first time this question has nagged me. *What made you make that will then?* Were you simply being responsible? Do lots of people finally make a will when they are expecting a child? Or was it something more? Did you have a fear of dying while giving birth, however low pregnancy-related mortality may be in this country? If you did, you would have told me. I think you must have had other reasons for an increased sense of vulnerability. Jason Thorne is not the only possible solution to the puzzle of what happened to you.

Luke is waving a hand in front of my face. He is snapping his fingers. 'Hello. Hello hello. Anyone in there?'

Whatever questions I may have, I tell him what I absolutely know to be true. 'That was one of the many ways she showed how much she loved you, how much she considered you. But it's complicated, the question of where you live. It isn't the kind of decision you and I can make on our own.'

I don't tell him how much our parents would miss him if he weren't with them. *Too much information*, I hear you say.

He smiles in a way that makes me certain he knows the match is his, and he is amused that I am about to discover this. 'If you share me then it shouldn't make a difference if I live with you instead of them.'

'True.' There is nothing else I can say to that one, especially when I am enchanted by this new vision of having him with me all the time. I cannot help but smile and add, 'You will be a barrister someday.'

'No way. Policeman. Like Ted.' He kicks the leaves harder. Fire and sun and spring and summer fly in all directions. But nothing derails your son. 'I told Granny and Grandpa it's what I want. They said they'd talk about it with you. They said it might be possible. They're getting old, you know. And Grandpa could get sick again . . . '

'Your grandpa is setting a record for the longest remission in human history.'

'Okay.'

'And Granny sat there calmly while you said all this?'

'She cried a little, maybe.'

'Maybe?'

'Okay. Definitely. She tried not to let me see. But Grandpa said it might be better for me to be raised by someone younger.'

I'm sure our mother loved his saying that. No doubt Dad would have had several hours of silent treatment afterwards. Our mother is incapable of being straightforward at the best of times, and this is certainly not a topic she would want to pursue. She would have hoped it would go away if she didn't mention it to me.

'Then we will,' I say. 'Of course we'll talk about it.' He is not looking at me. 'Can you stay still for a minute please, Luke?'

There is a rustling in the trees at the edge of the woods, followed by a breeze that lifts my hair from my face, then gently drops it.

Luke doesn't notice, which makes me question my instinct that somebody is spying on us. Ever since we lost you I have imagined a man, hiding in the shadows, watching me, watching Luke. At least it cannot be Jason Thorne. He is locked away in a high-security psychiatric hospital.

I walk close to Luke, in case somebody really is ready to spring out at us. When the rustling grows nearer, he turns his head towards it. I am no longer in any doubt that I heard something. I put a hand on his shoulder and stand more squarely on both feet.

A doe pokes out her head, straightening her white throat and pricking up her ears to inspect us. She seems to be considering whether to turn back. All at once, she makes up her mind, crossing in front of us in two bounds, hardly seeming to touch the ground before she flees through the trees.

'Wow,' Luke says.

'She was beautiful. Granny would say that seeing her was a blessing. A moment of grace is what she would call it.'

'I can't wait to tell Grandpa,' Luke says.

I smooth Luke's hair. 'Happier now?' He nods. 'Are you going to tell me what brought on these new feelings about where you live?'

'I want to go to that secondary school in Bath next year. Why would Granny take me to the open day and then not let me go? She said my preference mattered. But I won't get in if she doesn't use your address.'

'Isn't the application due on Monday?'

'Yeah. But Granny keeps saying she's still thinking about it. It should be my choice.'

'With our guidance, Luke. It wouldn't be fair to you otherwise – it's too much of a responsibility for you to make this kind of decision by yourself. Granny never leaves things until the last minute, so she must still be weighing it all up very carefully. I'll raise it with her and Grandpa after breakfast – I can see it's urgent.'

'It's my life.'

'Is that why you wanted this private walk before Granny and Grandpa are up? To talk about this?'

'Yeah.' He kicks again. 'And before you say it, I don't mind that none of my friends are going there. As Granny keeps reminding me.'

The school is perfect for Luke. It is seriously academic, and sits beside the circular park I've been taking him to since he was five. It's also within reach of one of our favourite walks, along the clifftop overlooking the city. These are places he loves. Touchstones matter to Luke.

'I want to be in Bath with you,' he says. 'Everything's too far away from here.'

'Stinky little lost village,' I say.

He looks at me in surprise.

'That's what your mummy used to say.'

Would you be pleased by how hard I try to keep you present for him? How we all do?

I take his hand. 'The school's not as far away as it seems to you. It's only a twenty-five-minute journey from Granny and Grandpa's. Maybe you can live with me for half the week and Granny and Grandpa for the other half. I know we can work something out that everyone's happy with.'

I promised Luke when I finally got a mortgage and moved out of our parents' house that he would always have a room of his own with me. He was five then, and I nearly didn't go, but our mother made me. 'You need your own life,' she said, squaring those ballerina shoulders of hers. 'Your sister would want you to have a life. Miranda does not believe in self-sacrifice.'

I thought, then, that our mother was right. Because you certainly weren't – aren't – one for self-sacrifice.

Now, standing in our clearing with your son, I imagine you teasing me. *Yeah. Because it suits you to believe it. So you can do what you want. Since when do you think our mother is right?* Though the words are barbed, the voice is affectionate. The insight is there only because you apply the same filter to our mother that I use.

Luke turns back towards the woods. 'Did you hear that, Auntie Ella? Like somebody coughed but tried to muffle it? It didn't sound like our deer.'

I think of the interview I did a few months ago. Mum and Dad and I had always refused until then. But this was for a local newspaper, to publicise the charity. It seemed important to us, as the ten-year anniversary of your disappearance drew near. I talked about everything I do. The personal safety classes, the support group for family members of victims, the home safety visits, the risk assessment clinics.

There was no mention of you, but Mum and Dad were still worried by the caption that appeared beneath the photograph they snapped of me. *Ella Brooke – Making a Real Difference for Victims.* My arms are crossed and there is no smile on my face. My head is tilted to the side but my eyes are boring straight into the man behind the camera. I look like you, except for the severe ponytail and ready-for-action black T-shirt and leggings.

Could that photograph have set something off? Set someone off? Perhaps I hoped it would, and that was why I agreed to let them take it.

I catch Luke's hand and pull him back to me. 'Probably a rambler. It's morning. It's broad daylight. We are perfectly safe.'

'So you don't think it's an axe murderer.' He says this with relish, ever-hopeful.

'Not today, I'm afraid.'

'Well if it is, you'd kick their ass.'

'Don't let Granny hear you talk like that.' The sun stabs me in the head – warmth and pain together – and I squeeze my eyes shut on it for a few seconds, trying at the same time to squeeze out the worry that somebody is watching us. I am also trying – and failing yet again – to lock out the images of what you would have suffered if Thorne really did take you.

'Do you have a headache, Auntie Ella?'

Luke doesn't know he pronounces it 'head egg'. I find this charming, but I worry that he may be teased.

Should I correct him? I didn't imagine I'd be buying up parenting books when I was only twenty, and that they would become my bedtime reading for the next decade. They don't usually have the answers I need, but I know that you would.

'No headache. Thank you for asking.' I smile to show Luke that I mean it.

'I think Mummy would like me to live with you.'

I love how he calls you Mummy. That's how Mum and Dad and I speak of you to him. I wonder if we got stuck on Mummy because you never had time to outgrow it. Mummy is the name that people tend to use during the baby stage. You were never allowed to become Mum. Or mother, perhaps, though that always sounds slightly angry and over-formal.

'If I live with you part of the time, can we get more of her things in my room?'

'What things do you have in mind?'

'Granny put her doll's house up in the attic.'

'It's my doll's house too.' As soon as the words are out of my mouth, I realise that I sound like a little girl, fighting with you over a toy.

Luke smiles when he mimics our father's reasoned tone. 'Don't you share it?'

'Yes.' I lift an eyebrow. 'So you'd like a doll's house?'

'No. Of course not. I'm a boy. I don't like doll's houses.'

'There's nothing wrong with a boy liking doll's houses.'

'Well I don't. But why would Granny put it out of the way like that?'

'It hurt her to see it, Luke.'

He scowls. 'It shouldn't be hidden away in the attic. Get it back from her.' He sounds like you, issuing a command that must be obeyed.

Three crows lift from a tree, squawking. Luke and I snap our heads to watch them fly off, so glossy and black they appear to have brushed their feathers with oil.

'Do you think something startled them?' He takes a fire leaf from his pocket.

'Probably an animal.'

He is studying the leaf, tracing a finger over its veins. He doesn't look at me when he says, super casually, 'Can you make Granny give you that new box of Mummy's things?'

There's a funny little clutch in my stomach. I am not sure I heard him right. 'What things?'

'Don't know. Stuff the police returned to Granny a couple weeks ago.'

'Granny didn't tell me that. How do you know?'

'I'm a good spy. Like you. I heard her talking about them with Grandpa.'

'Did Granny open it? Did she look in it?'

'Not that she mentioned when I was listening.'

'Did she say anything about why the police finally returned Mummy's things?'

'Nope. Get the box too. Make Granny give it to you.'

Getting that box is exactly what I want to do. Very, very much. 'Okay,' I say, though I mumble secretly to myself about the challenge of making our mother do anything. Our mother gives orders. She does not take them.

'Auntie Ella?'

'Yes.'

'She would have come back for me if she could have, wouldn't she?'

I think of one of the headlines that appeared soon after you vanished, claiming you'd run away. I put my arms around him tightly. We have always tried to protect him from such stories. Since last week's spate of new headlines about Thorne, we have been monitoring Luke's Internet use even more carefully. But we can't know what he might have stumbled on, and I am nervous that a school friend has said something.

I kiss the top of his head and inhale. We have only been out for forty minutes but already he smells like a puppy who has run all the way back from a damp walk. 'She would have come back for you.' It is not raining but my cheeks are wet.

Luke wriggles out of my arms. He wipes at his cheeks too. 'Are you sure?'

'One hundred per cent. Nothing would have kept her from you if she had a choice.'

He bites his lower lip and looks down, scrunching his fists over his eyes.

Was I right to tell him these two true things, one beautiful and one too terrible to bear? That you were driven by your love for him, and that something unimaginably horrible happened to you?

Another thought creeps in, a guilty one. Is it easier for me to imagine you suffering a terrible death than to contemplate the possibility that you made a new life for yourself somewhere, as the police have sometimes suggested? I think of Thorne and shudder, absolutely clear that the answer is no.

'She wanted you so much.' It is extremely difficult to get these words out, but somehow I do, in a kind of croak.

'It's okay, Auntie Ella.' He has so much courage, this boy, as he takes his fists from his eyes and comforts me when I should be comforting him. He waits for me to catch my breath. 'I found a picture of her holding me,' he says. 'It's one I hadn't seen before. At first I thought it was you. You look like her.'

'I think maybe that's more true now than it used to be.'

'Because you're thirty now.'

'Thanks for reminding me.'

'I know. It's really old.'

I stifle a mock-sob.

'Sorry,' he says.

'You look stricken with remorse.'

'I'm just saying it because now you're her age. That's why you're looking so much more like her. You can see it in that newspaper picture of you too.' He clears his throat. 'Did you really try everything you could to find her?'

Did I? At first we barely functioned. Mum didn't leave her bed. Dad stumbled around trying to make sure we had what we needed, cooking and cleaning and shopping, trying to get Mum to eat. I lurched through the house, trying to care for a two-and-a-half-month-old baby. Mostly we were reactive, answering the police questions, giving them access to your things. But we got in touch with everyone we could think of, did the appeals.

I stuck pictures of your face to lampposts, between

the posters of missing cats and dogs. One of them stayed up for a year, fading as rain and wind and snow hit it, flapping at a bottom corner where the tape came off, dissolving at the edges but miraculously holding on.

I tell Luke as much of this as I can, as gently as I can, but he shakes his head.

'I need you to try again,' he says. 'I need you to. I need to know. Even if it's the worst thing, I need to.' His voice rises with each sentence.

I grab a bottle of water from my jacket pocket and pass it to him. He gulps down half.

'Is this why you want me to get her things from Granny?'

'Yes.' He wipes his mouth with the back of his hand. 'You have to. Tell me you will. You have to look at everything.'

'The police already did.'

'No they didn't. I hear much more than you think after I've gone to bed. I've heard all of you say how useless they are. Except Ted.'

I inhale slowly, then blow out air. 'Okay.'

'You'll do it?'

I nod. 'I will.' My stomach drops as if I am running and an abyss has suddenly opened in front of me. Because there *is* something I can do that we haven't tried before. I can request a visit with Jason Thorne. I reach for Luke's hand. 'But only on one condition.'

'What?'

'You will have to trust my judgement about what I can share with you.'

'If you mean you might have to wait a little while,

yeah. Like, until I'm a bit older. But you can't not ever tell me.'

Thinking about Jason Thorne makes it hard to breathe. The possibility of Luke knowing about him makes it even harder. But I manage to keep the pictures out of my head.

'I need to do what I think is best for you, Luke. It's going to depend on what I find out. And you need to be prepared for the possibility that this might be nothing at all – that's what's most likely.'

'I guess that's the best agreement I can get.'

'You guess right.'

His forehead creases. 'There's something else that bothers me,' he says.

I am beginning to think I may actually be sick. 'Tell me.' I realise I'm holding my breath.

'Granny says you didn't do well enough on your exams because you didn't go back to University afterwards.'

Afterwards. He never says 'after Mummy disappeared' or 'after Mummy vanished'. There is before. There is after. The thing in between is too big for him to name.

But at least he isn't worrying about Jason Thorne. This is easy, compared to that. 'I did go back,' I say. 'But they made special arrangements for me to do it from a distance so I could help Granny and Grandpa take care of you.'

'But Granny says you should have done better. She says you wanted to be a scientist, but I heard her telling Grandpa that Ted was distracting you even before you moved back home. It's not really Ted's fault, is it?'

'It's nobody's fault, and I wanted to be a biology teacher, not a scientist. But I don't any more. The charity work is important – it means so much to me.' I smooth his hair again, silky like yours, silky like mine. This time, I am not ambushed by an image of Thorne grabbing you by it.

'It was my fault,' Luke says. 'You wouldn't have messed up your degree if it weren't for me.'

'Luke,' I say. 'Look at me.' I tip up his face. 'Being your aunt is the best thing that has ever happened to me. That is definitely your fault.'

'And Mummy's,' he says.

'Yes. And Mummy's. I miss her so much and you are the only thing that makes it hurt less. Looking after you taught me more than those lecturers ever could. I wouldn't have wanted to do anything else. It's what I chose.'

His head whips round. 'There's that coughing noise again.' We both listen. 'And that's a different sound. Like somebody tripped in the leaves.'

'Probably someone on their morning walk. Someone clumsy with a cold.'

'Should we look?'

'They'll be gone before we get there.' I take his hand. 'If it's really a spy, he's not very good, is he?'

'Not as good as me. Plus he won't know what he's up against with you.'

'Let's go in. Granny promised to make pancakes for breakfast.'

'I'd better tell Granny and Grandpa about what we heard.'

'We can tell them together. And you know that if anybody comes near the house, one of the cameras will pick him up. I'll check the footage before I leave. You don't have to worry.'

He nods sagely. 'Can you stay for the afternoon and take me to my karate lesson?'

'I'd love to. I'll have to rush off as soon as you finish though. I promised Sadie I'd go to her party.'

'Is it her birthday?'

'It's to celebrate moving in with her new boyfriend.'

Luke wrinkles his nose. 'Ted says Mummy never liked Sadie.'

She thinks everyone is out to get her – she's the most bitter person ever born.

She talks behind everyone's back and it's just a matter of time before she turns on you.

She's always telling herself she's a victim but she's actually the aggressor.

These were your favourite warnings to me about Sadie. You made your assessment when she was four and never saw any reason to change it.

My friendship with Sadie has certainly lasted beyond its natural life. I try to explain why. 'I've known her since my first day at school.'

'Like Ted.'

'Yes. But she doesn't have many friends. She gets mad at people and drives them away.'

'So you feel sorry for her?'

'Kind of. I guess I always have.'

'What if she gets mad at you?'

'It's probably only a matter of time before she does. I'm too busy to see her much – I suppose that reduces the opportunities for her to find fault with me.'

'Don't go. Stay here with me and Granny and Grandpa.'

'That is tempting. But she's really nervous about the

party. She has hardly anyone of her own to invite and she's scared Brian will think that's weird. It'll be all his doctor friends.'

'Fun,' he says. 'Not.'

'Definitely not as fun as your karate lesson.'

'They'll let you watch me. I'm getting better. You'll be proud.'

'I'm already proud. Can I join in?'

He shakes his head no solemnly, partly not wanting to hurt my feelings, partly amazed by my silliness. 'It's for kids, Auntie Ella. Plus I'd have to pretend not to know you because you'd show off. You'd execute a flying spin and kick my teacher in the face with a knockout blow.'

'Never.'

'I don't believe you.'

'Well, maybe a little knifehand strike to the ribs.'

The Costume Party

Sadie is passionately kissing Brian. She is pressing her breasts against his chest. I am standing in front of the two of them in Brian's crowded kitchen, trying not to appear disconcerted – only a few seconds ago the three of us were politely talking.

'Autumn in New York' is playing, telling me about how new love mixes with pain, making me think of you as Sadie cups Brian's cheek with one hand and traces his lips with the index finger of the other. She stares into his handsome-in-a-geeky-way face and strokes his dark hair. 'You obsess me.' Her whisper is deadly serious.

'And you obsess me.' His whisper is a tease. She frowns, wondering where his eyes are darting to. The frown gets bigger when she sees they are darting to me.

I've never met anyone as sickly sweet on the outside and full of poison on the inside.

Your pronouncements on Sadie were endless.

Sadie is six feet tall, so perhaps one of the things she

likes about Brian is his great height. I am only five feet five. You always said that the thing Sadie likes best about me is that she can literally look down, though you pretended not to hear when I said she could do that with most people.

Sadie adjusts the rectangular frames of Brian's nerdy-cool spectacles, which have slipped down his nose. Brian is a dermatologist and I çannot help but imagine those spectacles falling off as he bends over a patient's head, smacking them on the forehead and leaving a bad blemish or maybe even interfering with the performance of some vital instrument.

She turns from Brian to examine me, though she curves his arm around her waist and holds it there in a way that makes my heart twinge for her. 'You're actually wearing a dress!' she says. 'I didn't think you owned any.'

'It was Miranda's.'

She motions me to turn around. I catch Brian watching me and I hope – though I am not quite sure – that he manages to tear his eyes away by the time Sadie glances at him to check.

Sadie has spent the last five years trying and failing to be in a serious relationship. She desperately wants Brian to be The One. She is sneakily buying wedding magazines already.

'Is that DVF?' She peeks at the label of your dress, scratching the back of my neck with a nail. 'Christ, Ella,' she says. 'These are £500 a pop in silk.'

How could you have afforded this kind of thing on your nurse's salary? This is a recurring question for me.

The police wondered about it too. Like so much else, it remains unanswered.

'Miranda had one in red as well,' I say. 'But red isn't really my colour.'

I imagine how furious you would be at my letting out one of your shopping secrets to Sadie. It was bad enough that I told the police. *But you signed the confidentiality clause, Melanie. The confidentiality clause never expires.*

Only you were allowed to call me Melanie, as if you wanted to make me yours alone. To name somebody is a powerful act, and you like powerful acts. You extracted Ella from the middle of my name, adding an extra L. You commanded everyone else to use it. Even Mum and Dad obeyed you. They still obey you. Was it out of guilt that they'd been careless and spoiled your decade as an only child by saddling you with an accidental baby sister?

'I'm not sure you're right about red,' Brian says.

My stomach tightens, but Sadie lets the comment pass. 'Those wrap dresses don't date,' she says. 'They're classic.'

'This one is a consolation prize, awarded by my mother.'

'For what?' Sadie asks.

For the box, I silently think.

Our mother actually grabbed me when I started towards the attic this afternoon to retrieve it. I was drawing strange men after me and Luke, she said. I was stirring up danger in my refusal to leave things alone, she said, especially after the newspaper article.

'Ignoring things, hiding them from each other, that's the real danger,' I said.

She didn't answer.

'The difficult things aren't going to go away because you pretend not to see them,' I said.

Stalemate is the rose-tinted view of where the two of us were when we parted, the box still up in the roof space beneath the eaves. But our mother took this midnight-blue dress from her shrine of your things and pressed it into my hands, along with a pair of strappy sandals you never even wore. She was horrified by the prospect of my going to a party in the jeans and sweat-shirt I'd been wearing all day.

Your dress flowed and swirled as I walked out their door in it. I even swished my hips like you used to, to try to jolt our mother into reacting, to try to shock her into giving me my way and handing over the box when she saw how like you I look.

Yeah, right. I imagine you rolling your eyes at the impossibility. *Like that's really going to work.*

I shrug away Sadie's question as if I am bewildered by it. I put a hand up to my neck, an unconscious reflex, near the place she scratched when she searched for the label. I'm startled when my finger pad comes away with blood. There is no doubt that she is being even spikier than usual, and that this heightening of her default state of resentment has something to do with Brian.

'Don't be such a baby, Ella – I was fixing your neckline.'

You follow me through this party like a sardonic ghost,

whispering in my ear. *Sadie's perfect at the can't-do-enough-for-you act. Every good deed is a little stab.*

'I have some extremely expensive overnight cream from a new line Brian recommends.' Sadie runs a beauty clinic. She first met Brian a few months ago, to discuss the possibility of his doing some treatments on her clients, the kinds of procedures she needs a proper dermatologist for. 'Would your mother like to try it?'

'That's nice of you. I'm sure she would,' I say.

'Evening, everyone.' The voice is talk-show host smooth and charming, and vaguely familiar. When I turn to its owner and realise who he is I want to sink into the floor because I had the misfortune of being assigned to Dr Blossom when our mother dragged me for tests to investigate why my periods vanished at the same time as you.

Sadie does not know this, so she feels the need to introduce me and Dr Blossom feels the need to pretend he has never seen me before in his life and certainly has never peered at my reproductive organs and pored over countless tests of my hormone levels only to diagnose the fact that my ovaries are in a decade-long and extremely mysterious coma. Something I could have told him myself.

Sadie is more agitated than usual, at this party full of doctors she barely knows. She is making lots of self-mocking jokes, which is what she always does when she is ill at ease. She glances under each of her arms and says, 'God, this room is hot. Good thing this dress is sleeveless.'

Dr Blossom says, 'Get Brian to inject you with some

Botox.' He points under Sadie's arms, in case there is any confusion about where the injections need to go. 'That'll stop the perspiration.' He touches the top of his absurdly flaxen head, as if to check that his hair has not flattened. 'Not sure it's available on the NHS, though. You'll probably need to do it privately.' He thinks he is being very funny.

But Sadie is funnier. 'Brian already injects me privately. Twice a day, morning and night.'

A laugh shoots out of me so fast I practically snort, and I am glad to be reminded of how quick and funny Sadie can be. But Brian flashes red, so I decide that this would be a good time to look for Ted.

I excuse myself and Dr Blossom nods understanding, making his shimmery curls bob.

Ted is not in the fake-gentleman's club of a living room. Barely any time has passed before Brian follows me in with Sadie close behind him. She cuts in front of him and sits next to me, wafting jasmine.

'Brian thinks you're pretty.' Sadie pulls him onto the sofa, keeping herself in the middle. 'He said so after lunch last month.'

I am at a complete loss about how to react, because Sadie sounds as if she is reporting a murder confession and Brian looks as if he has been sentenced to hang by the neck until dead. But at least I have more insight into why Sadie is out for blood.

'Does that please you, Ella?' Sadie says. 'Because you certainly looked pleased.'

'I'm sure you were being kind, Brian,' I say to Brian. 'Your dress is beautiful, Sadie,' I say to Sadie. It is jade satin, cut low without being too low, fitted at the bodice and slightly flared in the skirt.

'Thank you,' she says. 'Please don't change the subject.'

'I wasn't. I've been wanting to tell you since I got here how elegant you look.' I scan again for Ted, hoping against all reason for rescue, but his dark blond head and green eyes are nowhere to be seen.

Sadie notices me searching the room. 'Ted's not here,' she says. 'In case you were wondering.'

'I was a bit.'

'Have you and Brian ever met on your own?' Her eyes flick between the two of us.

'No,' we both say at once.

Sadie bites her bottom lip. 'Are you sure?' she says.

'Yes,' we both say at once.

I decide to reduce the amount of time before my getaway. 'Perhaps Ted is working?' I say, hoping very hard that there is no risk of his turning up only to find me gone – for him to be on his own at this party would not be a happy thing.

'He said he wasn't,' Sadie says. 'But he was cagey when I asked why he couldn't make it.'

Ted holding my hand in the playground when we were six, not caring that the other boys teased him.

She goes on. 'I think he's seeing someone. When exactly did he and his wife divorce?'

I inhale quickly, as if I have been kicked in the stomach. 'A year ago.' My voice is dull in my own dull head.

'Didn't last long on his own, did he?'

Stealing a kiss from me in the wooden playhouse on top of the climbing frame in the park when we were eight.

'How do you know that?'

Weeping in your arms when I was ten because Ted had appendicitis and I'd been terrified to see him so ill.

'From how he was when I asked him to the party,' she says. 'Definitely evasive. I wouldn't have invited him if you hadn't made me, Ella.'

Ted once told me that the antipathy between him and Sadie goes all the way back to reception class, when Sadie had a crush on him and couldn't forgive him for his complete lack of interest in her and his extremely big interest in me.

'Maybe he likes his privacy,' Brian says.

'Marrying one woman to get over another is never a good plan,' Sadie says. 'But you can't expect him to wait for you forever.'

Falling asleep on the phone with him when I was twelve and waking the next morning to hear his breath through the handset.

'I don't expect that.' This is a lie. I have expected exactly that. In recent months, since renewing what we both shyly call our 'friendship', I have thought that at last our time together would properly begin. I thought he felt this too.

Making love for the first time when we were sixteen.

We'd worried about pregnancy, then, like most teenagers. Not a worry I've needed to have for the last ten years.

As Dr Blossom knows. He is wearing his intelligent face as he studies me, posing by the chimney piece with every one of his gilded hairs in place, stroking his perfectly square chin. He looks as if he expects several

35

cameras to go off. Is he following me from room to room?

There is the ping of a text on Brian's phone. Sadie looks on as he reads. 'A kiss?' she says. 'That bitch. I want to kill her.'

Every once in a while Sadie loses control and has a social media meltdown. She is shrewd enough to cover it up quickly or delete madly, but she is perpetually in agony about who might have glimpsed or even filed away a screenshot of one of her public outbursts.

She turns to me, scowling. 'Did you put kisses on letters to Ted when he was still married?'

'We didn't have any contact while he was married.'

Brian plays with Sadie's honey-coloured hair, but he is looking at me.

'Right,' says Sadie, clearly meaning the opposite.

This insinuation that I am a marriage wrecker makes me recall one of the tabloid headlines from soon after your disappearance. It enraged our father, a man who is not given to rages.

Missing Nurse Spotted on Caribbean Yacht with Married Drug Lord Lover.

It seems a good idea to say, 'I would never go near a married man, or a man who has a girlfriend.'

Sadie tells Brian, 'Ella and Ted had a big fight because Ted was frustrated just being Ella's friend. So he started seeing this other woman, some police photographer. Then he married her. Ella cried for months.' She tears her attention from Brian and shoots it at me. 'But spare me the little fairy tale that you had nothing to do with him while he was with his wife.'

Ted and I saw each other or spoke every day from the time we were four years old until we were twenty-seven. Then nothing until we were thirty.

'There were three full years of absolute radio silence,' I say.

'Sadie tells me you're talking to him again now,' Brian says.

'Only recently. Ted came to my dad's seventieth birthday party this summer.'

'What made that happen?' Is it natural that this man should be so curious? Perhaps Sadie has reason to distrust him.

'My nephew invited him. I didn't know Ted was coming until he walked through the door.'

Ted and his wife were apart by then, but Ted never stopped checking up on Luke, even during his marriage. Luke has always idolised him.

Sadie cannot decide where to aim her surveillance. Her eyes dart to Brian's phone, then to me, then to Brian, then back to the phone, which seems to be pulsing with the contraband text. 'Who is she?' Sadie asks him.

'Someone I work with. A nurse. It's nothing, Sadie.' He kisses the tip of her nose. 'X is a letter of the alphabet. It doesn't mean anything.'

Sadie's hands are in fists. 'That's really unprofessional. To put a kiss on a message to anyone other than your true love is a betrayal.'

This makes me fantasise about emailing Brian with a string of kisses. xxxxxxxx. It's the kind of thing you would do. But of course I won't.

'You are not going to answer her,' Sadie says. 'That is the only message she deserves.' Sadie puts out a hand. 'No secrets,' Sadie says.

Brian hesitates, then silently hands over his phone. The first thing Sadie does is to check his contacts and his call log. 'You're not there,' she says to me.

'Of course I'm not.'

Brian shakes his head. 'Sadie. Can you stop.'

Sadie holds his phone out and makes a show of deleting the text. Her passion-induced craziness evokes another of the many headlines you inspired.

'*She was in love with love.' Missing Miranda's Romantic Obsessions.*

'I need some water,' I say.

'What are you doing, Ella? Seriously. What is with you?'

'Nothing.' I sound clipped and cool.

'Literally digging out your sister's dress?'

'Really, Sadie. I am just thirsty.' I sound dangerous.

'The crap you are. Are you opening up that stuff with Miranda again? After all this time? Why would you do that?'

'It doesn't affect you.' I sound like you practising icy dismissal. And like Mum.

'Is it the attention? Are you missing it? Is that what this is about, now that the fuss about her has properly died down? Is that why you gave that stupid interview about the charity, and let them run your photograph?'

'That doesn't deserve a response.' The sofa squelches embarrassingly when I stand up. Luke would make a joke about this.

'Don't you dare leave.' Sadie catches my wrist. 'You're always doing that when you don't like my questions.'

'She needs a drink.' Brian peels her fingers from my skin. 'Let her go.'

The Three Suitors

I head straight for the front door. I get as far as the entry hall when a man approaches me, standing too close. The alcohol fumes are coming off his skin so thickly I can practically see them, mixing with his sweat.

I step back and he steps forward. I step back again and stick my arm out, visibly warding him off.

His hair is silver, to the middle of his neck, and slick. 'Let me get you a drink,' he says.

I cannot believe this surreal nightmare of a party is actually getting worse. 'No thank you.'

'You sure, sweetheart?' Indiana Jones would get away with calling me sweetheart. This man cannot. His shirt is silk and purple and has way too many buttons undone.

'Completely certain.'

He doesn't even try to disguise the fact that his eyes are moving up and down my body, from the top of my head to the tips of my toes, lingering at my breasts. 'I'll go get us some mineral water. We need to keep hydrated. Trust me. I'm a doctor.'

I am all too aware of the verbal manoeuvre – this attempt to encroach upon me by speaking as if he and I are a team, followed by his bad joke. I begin to walk away but the man puts a hand on my waist.

'Take your hand off me now.' Anyone who knows me would hear the dead seriousness of my voice.

But this man does not know me. When he tightens his grip on my waist and starts to move the front of his body towards mine I unbalance him with exactly enough force to leave him two choices. Let go of me, or fall over. He takes option one.

'What the fuck is wrong with you?' The man shakes his head and squeezes his eyes and moves his mouth from side to side. Then he lurches upstairs.

I brush off my hands. Once. Twice. Firmly and completely done.

But there are two consequences of these mild physical exertions. The first is that a lock of hair has escaped the low knot at the nape of my neck. The second is that your stupid dress flew open without my noticing because when I look down I see that my skimpy black underwear is showing and I remember why I hate this wrap style that you love.

This is when I realise that another man has come into the hall. He has been watching the entire show, so unmoving in the shadow cast by the stairway I haven't noticed him. He must have seen the spectacle of the gaping dress before I readjusted it.

The man's black eyes are creased at the corners, I

think in amusement. Beyond that, his expression is neutral. My guess is that he is ten years older than I am. The age you would be. Maybe, just maybe, the age you are. Though his face is young, his hair is grey. It's peppered a little with black. He is one of those model-beautiful grey-haired men.

'I'd like to offer you a drink,' he says, 'but I can see that might be dangerous.'

'Well you would be correct,' I say. I double-check that there isn't even the slightest visible tremble in my fingers. There is not.

'I'm Adam,' he says.

I manage to incline my head slightly in response. It is not that I am trying to be rude to him, even though that is probably what he will think. It is that I need a few more seconds to collect myself before I can speak properly.

'And you, clearly, are the woman with no name. I'll call you the Kickboxer.'

'That wasn't remotely like kickboxing. That was gentle dissuasion.'

He actually smiles. 'And you've gently avoided telling me your name.'

'Ella.'

He repeats the word as if it were a question, as if he has decided he likes it.

I squint at him. 'Have I seen you somewhere before?'

'If I'd seen you before, I'd remember,' he says.

'Good one.' I start to walk away, only to be stopped by Brian, who has somehow extricated himself from Sadie to come in search of me.

'I wanted to check you're okay,' he says.

'Fine. Thank you.'

Brian looks uncertain, but he nods. 'Glad to see you've met Adam.' His frown is at odds with his words. 'I'll leave you two to talk.' He looks over his shoulder, then disappears upstairs, taking them two at a time.

'Brian seems . . . ' Adam falters.

'Throwing a party can be stressful,' I say.

'You're right. And I owe you an apology.'

'For what?'

'That line about how I'd remember you if I'd seen you before. It was cheesy.' He waits a beat. 'But true.'

For so long, I haven't properly grasped why you adored male attention. Your need for it bordered on mental illness. But this man's admiration makes me warm, which isn't something that happens to me very often.

'Let me guess,' I say. 'You're a doctor?'

He smiles again. 'You have the gift of mind reading.'

'My sister used to say that.' There really is something familiar about him. All at once, I see what it is. It is that he is a type. He is your type. The tall, dark and handsome type. This man is commanding, but he is restraining his power, a tension you always found irresistible. I am discovering that I like it too.

'I need to be somewhere,' I say. Somewhere as in, *not* this new love nest of Sadie and Brian's. Somewhere as in home, where there are no doctors to interrogate me. And where there is no supposed-friend to shoot barbs at me.

'Somewhere interesting, I hope,' he says.

Is he like this with patients, too? Does he make anybody he talks to feel as if they are the most fascinating person he has ever met? A lot of men couldn't do this without being sleazy, but this man is gentlemanly, urbane-seeming. The type of man Ted would hate and you would adore. But Ted, as I am all too aware, is not here.

'Lovely to meet you,' I say.

'Can I see you again? I have a fondness for the martial arts.'

'I am not in the habit of seeing strange men. Especially not strange men who tease me.'

'I'm not strange. But yes, I couldn't stop myself from teasing you. I'm sorry about that.'

'That was not a sincere apology.'

'Perhaps not.' He takes out a business card and offers it to me. I don't take the card and he lets his arm fall back to his side. 'We can meet at my place of work. Between clinics, so you wouldn't have to put up with me for too long if I bore you.' He raises his arm to offer the card again. 'It's not often that I invite women there.'

'How often is not often?'

'Not often as in never before. You'll see why if you look.'

Fuck you, Ted, I think. *Fuck your games and fuck your remoteness and fuck your impatience.*

I squint at Adam for a few seconds. To my surprise, my own arm rises and somehow the card is in my hand. I glance at it. *Dr Adam Holderness, Consultant Psychiatrist.* He is based in the secure mental hospital outside of town, where Jason Thorne is indefinitely confined. He probably thinks I ought to be an inmate. I suppose it's inevitable that in a house stuffed with doctors, at least one of them would work there.

'It's a great place to meet for coffee,' he says.

I am making silent fun of myself in a bad bleak way. I decided in the woods this morning that I would write a letter to one of the most horrifying serial killers in recent decades, asking if I can visit him. What normal woman thinks it is good news that she may have improved her chances of getting access to such a man?

I don't need Adam Holderness for that access, but having him behind me might help. It occurs to me that he probably knows who I am, but is being too polite to say. It is all too likely that Brian or Sadie told him. If so, he must guess that I will be drawn to his hospital by a more powerful force than a love of caffeine or a wish to date him.

I say, 'Do you find that your acquaintance with Jason Thorne is much of an inducement?'

'Only to an extremely select crowd. I tend to keep that one quiet.'

I fantasise a picture of Luke, proud of me, and happy, finding you at last, running into your arms, smiling at me over your shoulder. But I cannot stop a vision of what his response will be if the truth I discover is a dark one. And I cannot help but consider that if by some miracle we do find you alive, you will take Luke away from me.

The unexpected thing, though, since I made my promise to Luke this morning, is that the terrible visions of what Thorne might have done to you have stopped. Before that promise, nothing I tried would block them – last week's headlines brought them on with a relentlessness that I couldn't figure out how to fight.

'You know what I do,' Adam says. 'How about you? Or is your job classified?'

'Hardly mysterious. I'm a personal safety advisor and trainer. Mostly I work with victims, but also sometimes with family members of victims.'

'Oh yes,' he says. 'I remember Brian mentioning that. For a private charity your family founded?'

'Yes.'

'Sounds like important work. And difficult.'

'I get a lot of support from my mother. She does most of the admin, usually the helpline messages.'

'She must be very organised.'

'She has on occasion been described that way.' You would say, *If organised means control freak bossy, then yes*. But I have already confided more to this man than I do to most. 'Please excuse me. I need to go, Dr Holderness.' I use his title and surname to impose formality and distance, but it comes out like a flirtatious tease.

'What about that coffee?'

'I like coffee,' I say. This seems flirtatious too. It is a register I didn't know I had. It is not the register I was trying for. Again I sound like you.

'So do I. Goodbye for now, Ella.' With these words he steps away and disappears into the kitchen so I don't have to do any more work at extracting myself. It occurs to me that Adam Holderness has an instinct for doing many of the things that I like men to do. Most of them involve not invading my space bubble.

The Fight

Sadie makes her presence felt in the hallway, though I have been aware of her hovering at the edge of the kitchen, arms crossed and glaring at me, during the last minute of my talk with Adam Holderness.

I say, 'Why are you so angry? I'm trying to be understanding, but you're pushing it.'

'It is no longer possible to trust anything you say.' She swallows hard. 'You're so impulsive.'

'Sadie—'

She cuts me off. 'I never know what you're going to do next. When you're around I'm constantly on edge. Do you think it's normal to beat up my guests?'

'He deserved it.'

'My boyfriend's brother deserved for you to knock him over?'

'I didn't knock him over. I adjusted things to get him to take his hand off my ass. I didn't know who he was but it wouldn't have made a difference if I had.'

'It was embarrassing. So was watching you crawl all

over Adam Holderness. At least he got you to leave Brian alone.'

In a flash, Sadie has moved from ambivalent affection to naked hatred. I have seen her do this to other people. At last, after a period of grace that has lasted longer than I ever expected it to, Brian's wandering eye has triggered her rage at me.

'How much have you drunk tonight?' I say.

'Two glasses of wine. I don't need alcohol to see you clearly for what you are.'

'Are you ill?'

'Brian belongs to me. I should know by now how little such things mean to you. You never stopped running after Ted while he was married.'

'That was cruel. You know it's not true.'

'How dare you flirt with my boyfriend under my nose? How dare you meet up with him behind my back?' She steps towards me.

I step away, trying to keep space between us, repeating the manoeuvre I used a few minutes earlier with her would-be brother-in-law. 'You can't seriously believe that.'

'If it's not about your sister it's about making sure every man in the room is watching you. You'll do anything for attention.'

I am starting to shake, but with anger more than hurt. 'Get out of my way so I can leave.'

'Are you actually ashamed of the things you do? Do you know how sick you are? You're sick. Sick sick sick.'

'I told you to get out of my way,' I say. 'Don't make me make you.'

'Going to practise your self-defence on me? Or do you

only beat up boys?' She shoves me so hard I crash backwards into the door. I look up to see her towering over me. 'Get out of my face, you sick fraud.'

A tiny, disinterested part of me is fascinated by the question of whether I only beat up boys, because it is something I have never considered before. I have no doubt that I could send Sadie flying, despite her big advantage over me in height and weight. But could I push back at a woman? Everything about me centres on protecting women, but if my life depended on it, yes. Certainly if Luke's did.

Sadie does not deserve to know any of this. I choose not to shove back, but I close over, giving her nothing more than the silence she is now earning.

'You're so fake,' she says. 'Even what you have people call you is fake. You're not Ella. You're Melanie. Melanie, Melanie, Melanie.'

'You have no right to use that name.' I stand up smoothly. Our mother taught us to rise from the floor the way she used to when she was in the *corps de ballet*, before she got pregnant with you and gave up her dream of being principal ballerina. I face up to Sadie, taking command of the stage.

You have your mother's strength and single-mindedness. Dad has always said this to both of us. *That's why your love is so powerful. It's also why your arguments are so fierce.*

Sadie steps back. She actually looks afraid. Her voice trembles, despite her words. 'I know things about you. I know everything about you. Stay the fuck away from my boyfriend. Get the hell out of our house.'

And that is what I do. I get the hell out, not letting myself look back. I can hear the door slam behind me, followed by a kick and a scream of rage so loud they echo through the thick wood. But already I see the truth of Sadie. Not a new Sadie but the one who has been there all along, hiding from me in plain sight.

Another of your Sadie pronouncements is hurtling around in my head. *She's pathological in her concern for what people think of her. She must lie awake at night worrying about who knows the truth of what she's really like.*

Within ten seconds she will turn around and smile sweetly and remark on how violent and noisy the wind and rain are. And if any of her guests suspect the true source of the fury and noise, they will be too well mannered to say.

Monday, 31 October

The Scented Garden

The park keeper is waiting for us at the black iron gates of the scented garden. Already a *Closed to the Public* sign is dangling from them. I hang a second sign beside it – *Self-Defence Class Taking Place* – because I don't want passers-by to be alarmed by the noises we make. He ushers us in. All the while, I am looking over my shoulder, wondering where Ted is and triple-checking my phone in case I have missed a text from him.

Maybe he isn't going to turn up. Maybe he is busy with the new woman Sadie thinks he is seeing, though I have been wondering since Saturday if Sadie was lying.

Wishful thinking, you say.

While I clear away beer cans and cigarette butts and decide that this place ought to be renamed the Alcopop Garden, the women mill about in the late autumn sunshine, which has burnt away most of the wetness from the grass since Saturday night's rain. One woman crouches at the edge of the pond, watching the water lilies and goldfish as if they are the most fascinating things she has ever seen. Another has her nose buried in the climbing roses, her eyes closed as she inhales. The other two sit and whisper together on a wooden bench beneath a wisteria-covered bower.

As I slip my phone into my bag, it buzzes with a text from Ted, who tells me he is waiting at the gate.

Your voice is in my ear. *You are too forgiving. Too desperate. Don't make the same mistakes as me.*

'Do you want to gather over there on the grass?' I say to the women, gesturing towards the circle of towels I have set up at the far edge of the garden, off to the side and out of the sightline of anyone standing at the gate. 'I'm going to go and meet Ted so he and I can talk through what we'll be doing. We'll start in ten minutes.'

Ted is dressed like a football player this morning and it suits him, with his navy T-shirt untucked over the elastic waistband of his black shorts. I like the way this looks, like a little boy. He is not hiding or covering up, though – his stomach is as flat as it was when we were teenagers.

I say, 'I missed you Saturday night.'

He blows out air. 'Sadie's party. That can't have been fun.'

'She broke up with me.'

'More fun than I would have thought, then. Can't say I'm sorry. Or surprised.'

'She said you're seeing someone. She said that that's why you didn't come.'

He exaggerates a backwards stagger, as if I have thrown too much at him. 'Sadie's jumping to the wrong conclusions as usual and wanting to fuck things up for us.' He almost smiles. 'But did you dislike the idea?'

'Yes.' I say this softly. He gives me that melting look of his, so I feel a qualm at breaking the mood. My promise to Luke has taken me over and I am not going to have Ted alone for long – I need to ask him quickly, while I have a chance. 'You know your friend Mike, who you brought to Dad's birthday party?'

The melting look goes in an instant. He is as guarded as he would be talking to a drug dealer on the street. He has guessed what is coming. 'Obviously I know him. Since I brought him.'

'He was telling me how sorry he was for our family. You know how people get nervous about what to say. He seemed genuinely nice, though, Ted.'

'He's a good guy.'

'I think he really cared, that he was sad for us, sad that we still don't have answers. Maybe it's especially uncomfortable for a police officer when he's off duty and trying to be social.'

'Christ. That's why he's best kept in a room with machines and not let loose on actual human beings.'

'You're the one who took him out.'

'And I am kicking myself for that.'

'I asked him how he knew about her. He said he was in High Tech Crime when she disappeared. He still is.'

Ted crosses his arms. 'Making polite conversation, were you?'

'It got me thinking. He would have worked on her laptop. The police finally returned some of Miranda's things. My mother swears she hasn't opened the box yet.'

Ted makes a harrumph of scepticism at this. 'I know,' I say. 'She got Dad to put the box in the attic. He says from the weight and feel of it he doesn't think the laptop is inside. I wonder if you had any thoughts about why they might have kept it.'

'None. I'm Serious Crime, Ella, not High Tech, as you well know. Jesus – Luke had to teach me to work my smart phone. You know I've never had anything to do with Miranda's case because of my personal involvement with your family.'

'I know officially you know nothing, but I also know how all of you talk to each other.' He almost lets himself smirk but manages to hold it in. 'I thought maybe Mike said something.'

'No.'

'He did. I know you, Ted. I can read your expressions.'

'You can't ever let us have a moment, can you?'

'Yes I can.'

'You might think you can read my expressions but you can't read yourself.'

'I don't have a moment. Not for this. I need to know yesterday. I won't have peace until I do. Luke won't either.'

He shakes his head so vigorously I think of a puppy emerging from the sea. 'I wish I hadn't brought Mike to that party.'

'But you did.' My hand is on the bare skin of his wrist and I'm not even sure how it got there. The hairs are soft and feathery and dark gold.

'I saw you talking to him. I knew it would come back to bite me. You should work in Interrogation.'

'Despite your tone, I will take that as a compliment.'

'I was nervous going to that party, seeing you after so long. That's why I brought Mike.' His face flushes but I don't take my hand away. 'You can't let us be peaceful. You can't let things calm down enough for us to have a chance.'

My fingers slide up his arm, wrap around hard muscle. 'What is it they say? You had me at hello – that's it, isn't it? The minute you walked into Dad's party you had me. But the best way to create that kind of chance for us – for Luke – would be to find out what happened to her, to put all this behind us, finally.'

'That's more likely to destroy us than help.'

'Not knowing hasn't exactly done us wonders, has it?'

'I can't go through all of this with you again. I had enough of these arguments – I thought you'd finished with all that.'

'I never led you to believe that.'

'Luke is ten years old, Ella. He is a child. He has no understanding.'

'You know him better than that. How can you look me in the eye if you're withholding something crucial? That would always be between us.'

'Mike shouldn't have opened his mouth. It'll be a disciplinary for sure. He'd be lucky to escape with just a formal verbal warning.'

'I won't let anything come back to Mike.' My hand makes a broken circle around his bicep, with a very big gap between the end of my thumb and the tips of my other fingers.

'Don't.' He peels my fingers from his arm as if they

were leeches. 'You don't give a damn about the havoc you leave behind.' He has never broken physical contact with me before. It's normally me who breaks it first.

You always warned me about my temper. My bad EKGs, you called them, as if you could see the spikes in my emotions plotted on a graph. Yours are the same, though more frequent.

My EKG must be off the scale right now, fired by the adrenaline that makes me counter-attack. 'So where were you actually, then, on Saturday night?'

Ted glares at me, refusing to answer, and I have to stop myself from visibly doubling over as an old headline unexpectedly jabs me in the stomach.

Master Joiner Thorne Detained Indefinitely in High-Security Psychiatric Hospital.

I hit Ted from another direction. 'Since you're already angry at me, it's a perfect time to tell you that I am going to try to see Jason Thorne. I wrote to him. Now it's wait-and-see as to whether he accepts my request to visit, puts me on his list.'

Local Carpenter in Bodies-in-Basement Horror.

'Have fun with that.'

I cross my arms. 'He's a patient, not a prisoner.'

Thorne in Our Side. Families' Outrage as Suspect Deemed Unfit to Stand Trial.

Ted mirrors me and crosses his arms too. 'So they say of all the scumbags in that place. You're not up to seeing Thorne. You never will be.'

I think of the worst of the headlines from eight years ago, when Thorne was first captured.

Evil Sadist Thorne's Grisly Decorations: Flowers and Vines Carved onto Victims' Bodies.

That headline made me hyperventilate. It took hours for Dad to calm me down. Mum had to hurry Luke out of the house so he wouldn't witness my hysteria.

'There's no connection between her and Thorne, Ella,' Dad said. 'The police would tell us if there was. This story about the carvings is tabloid sensationalism – I'm not sure it's even physically possible to do that. And they've only just arrested him – no real details of what he did have been released by the investigators.'

'Are you listening to me, Ella?' Ted is saying. 'Try to remember what all of this did to you when they first got Thorne. You nearly had a breakdown.'

'That was eight years ago,' I say. 'I'm stronger now.'

Whatever happened to you, I will not turn from it. Whatever you faced, I will face. I brace myself for the pictures. For the sound of your screams. For tangled hair and frightened eyes. But the pictures do not come. I have now gone forty-eight hours without any.

'You were falling apart more recently than eight years ago.'

'I won't let fear and horror stop me, Ted. I owe her more than that.'

'Thorne has been compliant as a teddy bear since his arrest. He is a model of good behaviour but you will still be the object of his fantasies. You wouldn't want to imagine what they are.'

'I can live with that.'

'He has refused all visitor requests so far, but I am betting he will accept you.'

'I hope you're right.'

'I hope I'm wrong. You will be entertainment. He will consider you a toy.'

'I don't care how he considers me.'

'There's no point in letting yourself be Thorne's wet dream. There was a huge amount of evidence tying Thorne to those three women. There's nothing physical to connect him to your sister.'

'Really? Nothing? Those news stories last week saying there'd been phone calls between them are nothing? Those journalists were pretty specific. Phone calls are evidence.'

'Since when do you believe that tabloid shit?'

'There were reports that they were looking at Thorne for Miranda when he was first arrested. You know it. We asked the police back then but they wouldn't admit anything. Now the idea is surfacing again, and with much more detail.'

'It's a slow news month.'

'They're saying—'

'Journalists are saying, Ella. The police aren't saying.'

'Too right the police aren't saying. The police never say anything. We learn more from tabloid newspapers than we do from them.'

'There's a big difference in those sources. You know that.'

'The police have probably known all along that she talked to Thorne – we asked them eight years ago and they wouldn't comment.'

'You were a basket case eight years ago. Maybe they did confirm it and your dad didn't tell you. Your parents were trying to protect you then. So was I.'

'No way. My dad would never lie to me.'

He considers this. 'Probably true. Your mum would, not your dad.'

'Anyway, Dad asked them again a few days ago and again he got silence from them. They won't ever be straight with us.'

'You're not being fair.'

'Do you think I want it to be true?'

'Of course I don't.'

'The tabloids are saying she phoned Thorne from her landline a month before she vanished. That's more precise than eight years ago. Eight years ago there were just general rumours. If she talked to Thorne, would the police know for sure?' He doesn't answer. 'They have the phone records, don't they?' Again nothing. 'Do *you* know if she spoke to him?'

'How many times do I have to tell you? I have no information. I can tell you though that whatever those journalists are saying, the police aren't behaving as if they think it's a new breakthrough. They wouldn't have returned your sister's things if they thought the case was about to crack open. If there actually is evidence that she talked to Thorne, my guess is they've always known and decided it was irrelevant.'

'Then why wouldn't they admit it to us, if they knew? What would be the harm in telling us? Why is this new information coming out now?' I tug his wrist in exasperation. 'Ted! Can you please answer my questions?'

'Not if I don't know the answers.'

'Do you think a journalist got hold of the phone records?'

'Not possible.'

'Well someone told a journalist something. Who else if not the police?'

'Why now, Ella? Why this moment for this new story?'

'Shouldn't you and your buddies be figuring that out?'

'Not me.'

'So you keep saying. Whatever the reason, it made me remember something else. A little while before she disappeared she told me she was looking for a carpenter to build bookshelves for her living room. It makes sense that she called Thorne.' My voice is calmer than my pulse.

'Then why wasn't her body in his basement with the others?'

'Even if Thorne didn't take her, he may know something. Somebody may have bragged to him. These kinds of people do that.'

'In movies, maybe. He's clever. He doesn't reveal anything he doesn't want to.'

'Not that clever. They still found the women.'

'Okay. Let's say for argument's sake that she did talk to Thorne. That doesn't mean he's responsible for taking her. You accept that, don't you? Never assume. If you really want to think about what happened to her, you need to be open-minded.'

'You're right. I need to remember that more. I might sleep better if I do.'

'Good.' He pulls me into his arms. 'Don't go. Don't visit Thorne.'

'I still need to try to talk to him, Ted.'

'I don't want you near him.' I can feel him gulp into

the top of my head. 'I want to protect you. Why won't you let me?'

My anger has blown away. I disentangle myself from Ted as gently as I can. I touch his cheek lightly. 'I need to be able to protect myself. You know that.' Despite my speaking with what I thought was tenderness, he looks as if I have struck him.

'It's all I have ever wanted to do, protect you. Since the first time I saw you.'

His words take me back twenty-six years, to the day we met.

We were four years old and it was our first day of school. I fell in love with Ted during playtime for punching a boy who'd been teasing me about the birthmark on the underside of my chin.

I stood beneath the climbing frame beside my brand-new friend Sadie, but she was slowly moving away to watch the excitement from a safe distance. I was covering my face with my hand, blinking back tears as the boy jeered at me, laughing with some of the others. 'Look at the baby crying. Bet she still wears nappies.'

'Leave her alone,' Ted said. That was the first time I ever heard his voice. Even then it was calm but forceful, the policeman's tone already there.

But the bully boy didn't leave me alone. 'She's a witch,' the boy said. 'It's a witch's mark.' Looking back now, it was rather poetic for a child's taunt. I later learned his father was some sort of writer, so maybe they talked like that all the time at home. But I didn't think it was very poetic then. 'Let's see it again.' The boy made a lunge towards me and I jumped back. 'Take your hand away, witch.'

The boy moved again, reaching towards me. That was a mistake. His fingers only managed to brush my wrist before Ted grabbed the boy's arm and hit at his face. I don't know if Ted's childlike blows really sent the boy to the ground, or if the boy threw himself there to try to get Ted in trouble. But there was no mistaking the blood and tears and snot smeared over the boy's nose and mouth.

Ted ignored the boy's screams and sobs, coming from somewhere near our feet. He touched my hand and said, 'Don't cover it up.'

It was only a few seconds before a teacher was at Ted's side to scrape the mean boy up and drag him and Ted off to the headmaster. Ted looked over his shoulder as he moved, and I only vaguely noticed that Sadie had returned to my side to put her arm around me. All I could think about was Ted, and how glad I was that he could see me take my hand away from my chin.

That night, when you asked about my first day of school, I told you about Ted and the boy and my birthmark. 'Your magic is in it,' you said, kissing it.

The birthmark has faded now. It is almost invisible. A mottled pink shadow the size and shape of a small strawberry.

When it first started to diminish, not long after Ted's fight with the boy, I worried that my magic would dwindle away too.

'The magic goes more deeply inside you,' you said. 'It

grows more powerful because it's hidden so nobody knows it's there. It's your secret weapon.'

Remembering this, it strikes me that Ted has now been in my life for longer than you. So has Sadie.

I try to reassure him. 'There are guards everywhere in that hospital, Ted. Nurses. Syringes full of tranquillisers. Thorne must be drugged up to his eyeballs anyway as part of his daily routine, to keep him sluggish and slow and harmless.'

'Nothing can make Jason Thorne harmless. You know better.'

'They wouldn't let him have a visitor if they didn't think it was safe. They are constantly assessing him.'

'There's a gulf between what counts as safe behaviour for Thorne and safe behaviour for ordinary people.'

'He will need a long record of good behaviour before they let anyone near him. Not a few hours or days. I'm talking years of observing and treating him – they'll be confident that he's capable of civilised interaction. They know what they are doing.'

'Nice to see you put your faith in authority figures when it suits you.' He slings his bag over a shoulder. 'Luke will be hurt if you get his hopes up.' He starts to walk away but then he halts and turns. 'Have you thought about what it would do to him if something happened to you? There are real dangers.' He squeezes his eyes shut, then opens them with a jerk of his head, as if he does not really want to. 'The women are waiting. This conversation is over.'

'This conversation has only just begun.'

'You need to stop stirring things.'

'Stirring things is exactly what I want to do. It's what I should have done long ago. The ten-year timer is about to go off.' I push past him, determined to have the last word. If he has anything further to say, it will have to be to my retreating back.

Trick or Treat

The women shift around to make the circle wider and create an empty space for Ted on the grass beside my towel. Ted nods thanks and drops into place, saying hello.

This is the second time he has come to help the group – the first time was last month. The police think it is a good thing for officers to do volunteer work in the community, and I made sure that the women were all happy for him to join us.

'I want to thank Ted for being here. He has come on his day off to let us kick and punch him, which is extremely kind.' To my relief, everyone laughs, including Ted, who is doing a good job of pretending that we are not furious with each other.

I always worry about making jokes, even though the women and I agree that we must. Telling jokes is a way of defying the things that were done to them. They are all here because they have been victims of sexual assaults and they are determined not to lock themselves away forever in the aftermath of what happened to them.

'Ella's been beating me up since we were four,' Ted says, and they all laugh again, though my laugh is a half-hearted mask for sadness and guilt, as well as fury and distrust. He and I both hear the complex history behind this comment, including our recent argument, though thankfully they cannot.

Ted leans over to unzip his duffle bag, then pulls out what looks like a puffy astronaut suit. His predator costume. It is navy blue, a poor mimicry of a man's jeans and T-shirt. Only his forearms and hands remain bare – he will need to use those hands. He stands up, talking as he steps into the suit, and the others stand up too.

'Here's the thing,' Ted says. 'It's not about size. Ella's barely eight stone but she can floor a man more than twice her weight.

'Slap an assailant's jaw, he will smile. Punch his stomach, he will laugh.

'But jab his throat, he's going to clutch it with both hands and his eyes will water. Hook your thumb into his nose or mouth, he won't move for fear of your tearing his flesh.

'So you don't hesitate. You fight as hard as you can. You give me everything Ella taught you. You can't hurt me in this suit and I'm wearing protective shoes as well as the helmet over my head and face. So kick – I can see you all obeyed Ella's instructions to wear trainers and they can't do me any damage. Punch. Push. Scream. Stomp. Keep it going. Make noise. I am not going to hold back when I attack, so you are going to need to work hard. If your moves work on me, you can bet they are going to work on an assailant.

'The idea is muscle memory. If you can go through the motions physically, really fighting, then you are going to have the confidence you can do it. Your body is going to remember what to do.

'I want you awake,' Ted says. 'Not afraid. Awake. That is the point of all this.

'The thing about policemen is we know how scumbags think. Today I am the scumbag. Ella will talk you through the scenarios. But first, she and I are going to enact a new threat and response, so you can see what she wants you to work towards.'

I say his name in surprise. We had not agreed we would do this. We didn't when he came last month. But he only shoots me his hard villain look, which actually makes a shot of fear go through me.

He continues to talk to the women without pause, clearly not prepared to allow any interruption. 'You need to promise not to laugh once I've got this zipped up. I know it's Halloween but this is not my costume.'

And of course they do laugh as soon as he says this, because Ted has disappeared into the suit. But his head – that serious mouth, those green eyes, that ruffled hair – are all still visible as he cradles the giant silver helmet in his huge hands. He is a stuffed man, a creature made of dough. When he moves, he makes me think of a life-sized toy space explorer making his way through a gravity-free atmosphere.

'I'm going to be a bad guy,' he says. 'And I am going to approach you in lots of different ways, giving each of you a turn to fight me off. The best thing you can do is to avoid being in a dangerous situation. Avoid being in a position where you need to fight. I want you to deal with me with that in mind. But everyone here knows that avoidance is not always possible. Ready, Ella?'

I move towards Ted, not wanting to look reluctant in front of the women, but it feels like I am dragging myself through mud.

'You're in your bedroom asleep,' Ted says. 'It's the middle of the night and you're woken by an intruder.'

One of the women gives a little gasp in the background.

'I haven't gone through this kind of situation yet.' My whisper is a low hiss that I am pretty sure the women cannot hear. 'You know how fragile some of them are. We normally do the role play and talk it all through before a session so they're prepared. I – they – don't like surprises.'

'Better for them to see how it works while you've got me here.' Ted pulls me by the hand into the centre of the circle as they watch. 'I hate wasted opportunities.' There is an edge to his voice but the others cannot hear it. They must be thinking that this is what we have rehearsed and planned. 'Practice is always better than theory alone.' He points down at the grass.

'Fine.' I lie down and curl up on my left side.

'Close your eyes,' he says. 'I'm putting the helmet on now. Don't make me wear it any longer than I have to.'

'Don't tempt me.' The grass is tickling my left cheek and I am trying hard not to scratch it. There is a small pebble beneath my hip and I am not sure how much longer I can ignore it.

Ted puts on the giant silver helmet, which is lined with shock-absorbing material. He zips himself the rest of the way into the suit. His eyes are not the jewelled green of emeralds. They are the earthy green of moss, one of my favourite colours, and I wish I could see them but I can't. They are hidden beneath two squares of reinforced plastic that look black from outside.

A hand slams onto the ground only inches from my head. Ted is screaming, 'Wake up.' His voice is as muffled and scary as anyone's can be. He is grabbing my right shoulder and rolling me onto my back, pinning both of my arms down and pressing me onto the grass with the full weight of his body. Everything is in slow motion and my ears are buzzing and the sun is dazzling. One of the women cries out.

I have been turned to stone. Every trained reflex I have is paralysed. All that I have practised is dead. Is this what he really wants to do? How he really wants it to be?

I disappear from the park. I am somewhere else, in a city by the sea, and it is almost ten years ago, the last time Ted and I were lying in this position. And I want him on top of me, in this narrow single bed in this rambling old house that seems to come out of a dream and is full of twisting corridors and hidden bathrooms and seemingly vanishing loos as well as multiple other inhabitants I hardly ever see. Whenever he is able to visit, we spend all the time we can in this basement room, pressed against each other, the ocean in our ears. He is so beautiful as we kiss, his expression so soft and blurred, as if our kissing is all there is in the world, and he is lost in it, lost to himself. His eyes are closed but mine are open, wanting to see, unable to look away from his face, which I have loved since I first saw him in the playground sixteen years ago. He seems half asleep and half in a trance. All the time we make love I look at him, not knowing that this is the last time we ever will. Not knowing that as we kiss and I watch him, at this exact moment, you are vanishing.

·

There is a hissing in my ear, bringing me back. There is grass beneath me and sky above me and the scent of honeysuckle all around me though I am not sure how that can be possible and all I can think is that you loved honeysuckle.

There is a voice spitting questions and commands. *Are you scared? Spread your legs.* Were these the last ugly words you ever heard? There is a man squirming his feet between mine and using his knees to try to force my legs apart. There is a pebble bruising the small of my back, reminding me where I am.

But still I cannot move. There are women's voices and they are saying my name over and over again, as if urging me to do something, but I cannot understand what it is. I cannot think who they are.

There is a horror-film face above mine and I do not know who it belongs to. I hear my name. It is not a question, and even though it is still in that same strange voice, it is not said with hatred. Even beneath its static fizz there is a note of concern that brings me back and I remember that the face is behind a mask and it is Ted's face and I am glad I cannot see his expression. I am glad his murky green eyes are hidden beneath the tinted visor, and his hair is beneath the helmet so that I cannot be reminded of what it felt like ten years ago when I last cupped his head in my hands and pulled it towards me.

He is inching my knees farther apart and I am trying to keep my legs as fixed as marble but it isn't working. My name is getting louder but Ted isn't saying it. My name is a screamed chorus of female voices and it isn't coming from me but it goes through my bones like an electric shock and jolts me and jolts me and jolts me awake.

I let out a grunt and roll onto my left side, taking Ted with me, taking him by surprise and in one continuous motion kneeing his upper thigh once, twice, three times in quick succession. He is crouching now, coming at me again, and I am sitting up with my legs bent in front of me. I raise a leg and kick him hard in the face again and again, until he falls onto his back. I scoot closer to him and bring my heel down on the helmet-shaped cage that covers his mouth and nose. Again it is once, twice, three times. Always the magic number three. My movements are controlled and exact. The impact is precisely as I wish it to be.

He is completely still. Everything is silent. Slowly I stand up, knees bent, looking all around me, holding my hands in front of my face for protection in case he pops back up.

'Ted?' I say.

He sits, pulls off the helmet, gives his head a shake. When he speaks this time, there is no hint of the muzzled villain. 'Each and every one of you is going to be that good by the time she finishes with you,' he says to the women.

I offer a hand and he takes it to pull himself up. 'Then reward me,' I say, so quietly that only Ted can hear. 'Tell me what was on her laptop.'

'What you need to emulate in Ella,' he says to the women, 'is that she never gives up.'

I pick up my towel and thrust it at him to mop up the sweat. 'Too right.'

That snaps him back. He is beside me again. His mouth is near the side of my face so that his whisper whistles right down my eardrum. 'If you meet Thorne you're going to need to practise every move there is. And not just the physical ones. He's an expert at the mind fuck.' He turns to the women, restored to his usual relaxed and friendly stance. 'So. Who wants to beat me up next?'

Friday, 4 November

Small Explosions

I am driving away from Bath, where I now live and you used to live. I am driving away from the city that you and I love, to the house in the countryside that our parents brought both of us home to as babies. They will never leave it. They want you to be able to find them. We all want this.

It is only midday, but the dense branches of the trees on either side of this rural lane meet and tangle overhead, plunging me into near darkness for what seems to be an endless stretch. For many miles, I do not pass another car. There are still no cameras along this winding lane. There are still no mobile phone masts. This is the road you made your last known journey on, and it would be all too easy to intercept somebody along it.

He could have moved you under cover of woods, or over one of the many tracks, or through fields on some sort of farm vehicle. He could have got you into a building and hidden you. He could have wound along this narrow lane, then accessed the large road that circles this land before speeding you into another county.

I am working so hard to imagine the different possibilities I nearly overshoot the turning to our parents' village. It is a turning you and I have made countless times, and one I normally navigate on autopilot. I force myself to look around me more carefully, though I know this landscape so well it is the place I must always go to in my dreams. The old church and graveyard. The pub. The closed-down schoolhouse Dad converted several decades ago, now occupied by our parents' closest neighbours.

Five minutes after the nearly missed turn, I am sitting with Dad at the same scrubbed kitchen table you and I used to do our homework on. Your son uses it the same way these days, though not right now, because he is in school eating the sandwiches Mum packed for him. She and Dad and I are about to have some private bonding time over the lunch she has cooked for us, and is currently putting the finishing touches to.

I start with the easier thing. 'Luke wants me to take the doll's house,' I say. 'He wants to have something Miranda loved when he's with me.'

'I'm not sure Miranda loved it as much as you did,' our father says. 'Though she knew how much it meant to you.'

'Really?' I am seriously surprised.

'*Miranda loves it.*' It is our mother's usual correction of tense. '*She knows how much it meant* . . . But your father is right.' She puts a bowl of broccoli on the table. 'Cancer cells hate broccoli,' she says.

'They do,' I say. 'Can I take the doll's house, then?' I say. 'Seeing as you both agree that I love it most.'

'I suppose so.' She touches our father's bristly orange head, flitting away from the subject as she does. 'Only your father has a full head of hair at his age. And not a speck of grey. Look at him and then at his friends. Your father is still handsome. It's because I take such good care of him.'

Dad laughs. 'You certainly take good care of me, Rosamund.'

Our father's head still looks as if it is topped by a scouring pad that has rusted to dull copper. When Luke was six he drew a picture of Dad as one of the creatures from *Where the Wild Things Are*, snaggle-toothed and goggle-eyed. He drew another picture around that time, of you and me, in imitation of *Outside Over There*. How can I have forgotten this? I file the memory away, so I can remind Luke that there is a story of a sister searching for her lost sister. And finding her. He made me read him those exquisite books so many times I still know them both by heart.

'I'm with Mum,' I say.

'It's your mother who hasn't changed a bit since the very first time I saw her.'

'Yeah. Dancing that poor man to death during the *Giselle* rehearsal. Don't say you weren't warned, Dad.'

'Very funny, Ella.' But she is smiling. 'Your sister tells the same joke.'

'I was supposed to be working,' Dad says. 'Building something last-minute for the set. But the only thing I could see was your mother. She stood out from all those other *Wilis*. I nearly fell off my ladder, twisting around to watch her.'

How many times has our father told us this romantic tale? One of his tricks for pleasing Mum, who never tires of it. You used to circle your throat with your thumb and index finger and pretend to mock-choke yourself whenever he did.

'I love this story,' I say. 'And ten months later, Miranda was here.'

'Yes,' Mum says. 'Yes she was.' She closes her eyes and reaches out a hand. Dad grabs it.

'Your mother was an enchantress, Ella, from the first time I saw her,' Dad says.

Mum brushes the compliment away. 'Your father was the real enchanter,' she says. 'The three of us lived among the dust and rubble as he turned a crumbling old wreck of a house into the beautiful thing it is now.' She gestures her arms slowly out, a ballerina on the stage showing us the world. 'He made all of this for his family.'

'You are both magical,' I say, imagining you closing your eyes, yawning widely, and fainting your head sideways into your cupped hand with a slapping noise.

'What could the police have been doing with Miranda's things for the best part of a decade?' I try to sound casual, despite my abrupt change of subject. I pick up my water glass and lift it towards my lips before realising it is empty.

'Letting them gather dust in a store cupboard somewhere,' our mother says. She gives me her sharp look as she sits down. She knows where I am headed. She scoops fish pie from the casserole dish and onto our plates with studied grace and care. 'Eat your lunch,' she says.

'But why finally give them back now?' I say.

Dad fills my glass from the jug Mum has already put on the table.

'They probably wanted the space for more recent cases.' Mum can't stifle a laugh when Dad signals with a wordless frown that she hasn't given him enough fish pie, though he has four-times the bird-like quantity she took for herself.

'They made a big show of victim's rights when they returned the box, saying it was important that families had their loved ones' belongings returned as soon as was practicable,' Dad says.

'A decade is hardly soon,' I say. 'Do you think the timing means anything? So close to the ten-year anniversary, and the new stories about Jason Thorne?'

'I don't want you thinking about Thorne, Ella. It simply means that they'd forgotten about Miranda's things until now.' Our mother puts more food on Dad's plate. 'It's a mistake to credit them with any plan. It's all coincidence.'

Dad's eyes bulge. 'It's a confirmation that she no longer matters to them. They put the data into their fancy predictive analytics and the computer tells them where to focus their energy and funds, where the future dangers and risks are. Finding Miranda at this point in time isn't likely to save someone else. She will be at the bottom of their list.'

'Where did you get that term, Dad? Predictive analytics?'

'Ted. He doesn't like it much either.'

'It's just that – I wondered if one of you asked for her things?' I am searching for any flicker of a reaction from either of them. 'Maybe if one of you wrote to the police? I can't make sense of what else would have prompted this.'

'I certainly didn't,' our mother says. She pops out of her chair and turns her back on us to root around in a cupboard.

Dad stares down at the table, moves his glass an inch. His cheeks flush. He looks up and catches my eye before hastily shovelling food into his mouth.

Mum is still facing away, mumbling. 'Where is it? – Nobody in this family ever puts anything in the right place.'

I mouth the word, 'Why?' but Dad shakes his head in warning, a single slow movement to one side and back. When I get him alone I will find out.

Although bonfire night isn't until tomorrow, somebody in the village is already playing with fireworks. The first burst makes our mother whirl away from the cupboard clutching a grinder filled with black peppercorns. She huffs in irritation as she sits down. 'Probably some truanting kids.'

'Yes. Probably.' Dad watches me lift my glass in the silent toast to absent loved ones that he and I always make. I am looking at your empty chair as I do this. Only Luke ever sits in your chair. Mum and Dad and I always take the places we have occupied for as long as I can remember.

'You can't have the box, Ella,' our mother says. 'How many times do I need to repeat myself?'

'Why can't she have it?' Our father reaches out a hand but she leans out of reach. 'Rosamund?' He stretches farther, until his fingers brush hers.

'It's not the box,' she says. 'Ella is losing sight of her priorities.'

'Excuse me, but I am in the room. You don't need to talk about me in the third person. And I don't need predictive analytics to see where our priorities lie.'

'Reviving all of this will lead nowhere.' She gives our father's hand a brief squeeze before she slowly rises, her lunch barely touched.

'Can you say what you mean please, for once, Mum, in plain English? It's obvious that something's bothering you but it's not fair if you don't tell me what it is.'

'This isn't good for Luke.'

'What isn't?'

'Talking about his mother stirs up his feelings. Don't forget that he's only ten years old. I realise he is mature for his age, but don't treat him like a grown-up.'

'Maybe you shouldn't treat him like a baby.'

'How dare you speak to me like that, young lady?'

'I dare because I'm not young and I'm certainly no lady, that's how.'

There is another explosion. A plate slips from her hand and lands in the dishwasher with a clatter, but doesn't break. 'Damn,' she says. Your mouth would fall open, to hear her swear. If you were here, the two of us would cackle and mockingly scold her and threaten to wash her mouth out with soap as she used to threaten us, though she never actually went through with it.

Dad holds his hands out to both of us. 'Can we please

start the afternoon over? I don't usually get my two best girls on their own.'

Our mother looks like she is about to slap him. Or cry. 'Three best girls. You have three.'

'Of course,' he says. 'I'm sorry. That was careless but you know I never forget.'

She wipes her eyes. 'I do, Jacob. Of course I do.'

'We're all on the same side here,' he says.

I nod in agreement and say, 'Yes.' Then I say, 'I'm very sorry, Mum. I shouldn't have talked to you like that. I need to be more understanding and careful.'

'Be careful of yourself and be careful of my grandson.'

'I'm always careful of your grandson.' I try to hand her Dad's empty plate but she snatches it from me. 'I thought we promised each other to be open. Always. To share worries and information. We agreed that would be safest. We agreed that sticking our heads in the sand was the dangerous thing. That it was emotionally dangerous to do that and very possibly physically dangerous too.'

'Every new development needs to be evaluated. There is no single rule that can apply to all of it, Ella,' she says.

'I thought it was just a box of stuff that the police think is irrelevant.'

There is another explosion outside, which earns the window a death glare. 'Why can't they wait until tomorrow night?' She is still terrified of fireworks. You and I were never allowed near them, and she finds reasons to keep Luke away too. I know this would make you furious. I know I need to change this. *Don't let her coddle him, Melanie. Don't let her ruin him.* That is what you would say.

I catch Dad's eye. 'Are you afraid of what I might find in the box, Mum?'

'No. Because there's nothing there. What I am afraid of is raising Luke's expectations. Of churning up his feelings about all of this. Of frightening him.'

'Your mother makes a good point.'

'He's ten now. The impetus is coming from him. We can't ignore it.'

'You make a good point, too,' he says. Our father is still the family peacemaker.

'Always the diplomat,' I say.

'I do my best. You and your mother don't always make it easy.' But he is smiling, as if this is how he likes it.

Our mother stands behind her empty chair. 'It is not good for your soul, Ella. You're already too churned up. Remember how you were when it first happened. I don't want you falling apart again.'

'I'm not going to. I haven't come close to that for over seven years.'

'More like six,' she says.

'I'm much, much tougher. I am not the person I was then.'

'I liked that person,' she says.

'People need to change.'

'Not as much as you have,' she says.

'I'll tell you anything I uncover. We promised each other we'd do that and I will. I'll share anything and everything. Even if it's dangerous.'

'Especially if it's dangerous,' Dad says.

'What about Saturday morning?' She picks up my plate, slots it into the dishwasher. 'Do you really think someone was watching the two of you?'

'Possibly. But do you see how I really do tell you everything? Even the stuff I know will come back and bite me? Most likely it was some random walker out early. It's doubtful they could even see us through the trees.'

'Whatever you said to Luke that morning obviously disturbed him.'

'I don't think that's true. Or fair. And he was so happy about the doe. He keeps going on about it being magical.'

Dad looks solemn, which is not a look he readily does. 'Ella checked the footage from the outside cameras before she left for Sadie's party. There was nothing, Rosamund. But I did report it to the police.'

'I'm sure that pushed us right to the top of their predictive analytics list,' she says.

'I think we've talked enough about this,' Dad says. Mum glowers. It isn't often he shuts her down. 'Luke and I will bring the doll's house and the box tomorrow night,' he says. 'His consolation prize for missing another bonfire night.' I didn't think anything could make Mum's glower deepen, but this last comment does.

I am frightened of our father trying to move the doll's house with only Luke to help. It is far too large and heavy. I think of the tiny satellite of malignancy in his spine, shrunk down and kept dormant by the injections they give him each month to suppress the male hormones that the prostate cancer cells love. Our father's bones have weak points, but he refuses to act as if this is the case.

'Leave the doll's house for now,' I say. 'I'll come for it another time. Just bring Luke and the box.'

'No need,' he says. 'Luke and I can manage a doll's house.'

Our mother shoots me a sharp shrewd look that our father cannot see.

'Thanks but no.' I manage something more concrete. 'I need to clear some space for it first.'

What our mother says next is at odds with the small thumbs up she gives me behind Dad's back. 'I won't be coming with your father and Luke tomorrow.'

'I wish you would. We can order in pizza. Luke would like that. It would be fun.'

'I'll eat pizza.' Our father quickly turns to her. 'If your mother doesn't mind.'

'You do what you like, Jacob.' It is her martyred voice, the one that used to make you scream. She turns to me. 'You're not going to sneak Luke off to a fireworks display?'

'I wouldn't do something like that behind your back.'

'I let you take him out for Halloween on Monday even though it was a school night.' She makes it sound like this was the most extraordinary concession. 'Luke says you made a wonderful Catwoman. He was proud.'

'My everyday clothes,' I say.

'True.' She can't suppress a small smile. Then she gives me The Look. 'He mentioned that Ted came along. Dressed as the Joker.'

'He makes a great super-villain,' I say.

Ted and I were still furious with each other that night. The morning's self-defence class was still too fresh for both of us. All of our communication was to Luke, who was dressed as a policeman and too happy in his trick-or-treating to notice the stiffness between the two of us as we followed him from house to house.

'I promised Luke I'd take him to a fireworks display next year.' I'm shaking my left foot up and down in nervousness. 'Halloween and bonfire night aren't the same thing. He wants both.'

'Absolutely not. I've told you before. Bonfire night is dangerous.'

'He is a boy, Mum. He's not made of porcelain. He's going to be angry if you don't let him try things.'

'He's going to get hurt if you let him try too much. Your father and I may need to reconsider how much time he spends with you.'

'That's a bit hasty, Rosamund,' our father says.

Our father is the recipient of yet more glowering. 'Don't keep pushing, Ella,' our mother says. 'You're getting the box and the doll's house.'

My eyes are prickly with tears, but I know myself well enough to realise they are made of anger as much as sadness. 'Why are you being so mean? You still have me, you know. I'm still here.'

'And I want to make sure that doesn't change. Do you think about what it would do to us if we lost you too? Do you consider how terrified I am?' Her voice cracks. 'Imagine how you would feel if something happened to Luke.'

I wave for her to stop. I shake my head for her not to say another word. I cover my ears like a small superstitious child. Because to hear these words about Luke is too much for me.

'Yes. Exactly. And that is the best analogy I can give

you.' She takes the dessert from the oven. 'I worry about how far you will go to find out. I don't think you'll stop at anything.' She closes the door with a loud bang. 'You're like your sister.'

'I'm not.' I know you would agree.

She places a bowl in front of me with heightened care and precision, even for her. 'You have her determination.'

'She was the beautiful one.' I want to deflect our mother from a point that is too true and too frightening for me to contemplate.

'You look like her twin. You are equally beautiful.' Our father is still caught in his own loop of paternal fairness to daughters.

'Well I don't want to be.'

'That is where the real difference is,' our father says. 'Miranda turned the dazzle on. She sparkled because she wanted all eyes on her.'

'Jacob.' Our mother's voice is a warning and a command. It means, *Stop and go no farther.* It means, *Do not ever say anything that is critical of Miranda.*

He makes an attempt at appeasement. 'You both take after your mother. You have her beauty. But you keep the dimmer switch on, Ella. If you flicked it, those eyes would stick to you too.'

'I am more comfortable in poor lighting.'

'I know you are,' he says. 'But still you shine. The two of you were so alike, but so different.'

'Not *were*.' Our mother sits down and begins to scoop out apple-and-blackberry crumble. 'Are.' She manages a weak smile and leans closer to kiss my cheek, a serving spoon full of crumble still in her hand, dripping purple syrup. Our mother never drips anything, normally. She is not a woman who spills. The kiss makes me blink away tears. I kiss her back.

'Right,' my father says. 'The two of you are.'

'It's sweetened with apple juice concentrate,' our mother says. 'You know your father can't have sugar. Cancer cells love sugar.'

'You mentioned it once or twice before, Mum.'

'I am keeping your father alive, Ella.'

'I know you are.'

'You can't tell the difference,' she says.

Our father sneaks a tremor of disagreement and winks at me.

'I saw that, Jacob,' our mother says. She wanders to the side of the room, and turns her back on us to stare at a photograph hanging on the wall. It is the last one of you and Mum and me together. Dad snapped it. Mum and I are sitting side by side at a wedding. You are standing behind us, upright and elegant, the front section of your hair pulled back in a jewelled clasp.

The photograph is washed out despite Mum's care to hang it where the sunlight doesn't reach. Your dress is a perfect-fitting organza bleached into cream, its sprinkling of bright blue painted flowers drained into pale grey. Your made-up face is faded, the deep maroon lipstick now the lightest pink. Is all of this blanching a trick of the light? I do not want to see it as a sign.

Mum puts my thoughts into words. 'I look at that, and she is somehow already ghostly.' She cups the side of her face in her hand, her head tilted to the side. 'I think she is standing behind us, watching over us.' She clamps that hand to her mouth and straightens her head, realising that even though she is using the present tense, she has broken her own rule and spoken as if you are dead.

The Photograph

The email is anonymous and already I am betting it won't be easy to trace. It landed in the charity's inbox five minutes ago. The sender's name is 'An Interested Party'. The subject heading says, 'Lovers at a Café'. Attached is a single photograph, probably taken with a smartphone and certainly with the location services and time stamp turned on because it was snapped six minutes ago and the name of the café appears on it too.

I do not want our mother to see this, so I sit in my car in front of our parents' house and forward the email to my personal account. Then I wipe all traces of it from the charity's. As I am about to drop the phone into my bag, it rings, making me jump a little. It is a blocked number. Normally I don't answer blocked numbers, but this time I do.

'Hello?' My voice is weak. 'Hello,' I say again, forcing a strength I do not feel into the word. But there is only silence at the other end of the line, and it is a silence that is so perfect they must have muted the call. 'Sadie?'

Still there is nothing. I cannot shake the idea that it is her, but I will not give her the satisfaction of hearing a single syllable more of my uncertainty. I tap the red circle to make her go away. Immediately it rings again – once more from a blocked number – and I hit ignore before turning the phone to silent.

I force myself to study the photograph. I need to see in person. I need to know that this is no trick. I throw the phone into my bag with a kind of violence and reverse quickly out of our parents' driveway. I speed along the winding lane faster than I ever have before, dangerously fast, my wipers on full power but still not quick enough to clear the windscreen in the heavy rain.

Half an hour later, I run my nearside tyres over double yellow lines and stop the car on the corner, not caring if I get a ticket, indifferent even to the possibility of being towed through this Georgian Square that Jane Austen's characters sniffed at but I have always thought beautiful.

I am not sneaking. If he is still here, I don't care if he sees me seeing him. Seeing them. This is the only thought I am aware of as I push through the glass door of a café that he knows I have always hated. Is this why he chose it? Because he knows there is little risk of my running into him here?

This place gets rapturous praise for its artisan coffee. My taste buds seem to be the only ones on the planet to find it bitter. It is even more crowded than usual, because so many have rushed in to escape the rain.

Despite my initial bravado about whether he catches me here, I am glad to hide in the thick queue.

What has changed his feelings towards me so drastically? Has he finally decided that a decade is long enough to be patient? Is it work ambition? Some top secret new knowledge about you that he doesn't trust himself not to share? His pure fury that I won't take his advice and give up the idea of visiting Thorne?

A split second before I see him, a trickle of sweat runs down my back and my skin prickles and I think I am going to panic. Something in me, some sense somewhere, knows before I really know. A change in the air carried by his voice or scent. A glimpse in my peripheral vision. Simply his material presence in the building. My heart freezes. My stomach goes hollow.

Liar. I want to scream the word at him. But I don't. I swallow it back and feel as if it will choke me.

Ted is sitting at a small corner table with a woman whose face I cannot see, though the back of her head – her dark silky hair – is visible. That hair is so like my own my stomach seems to lurch up to my throat and there is a flame at the top of my head that rushes down my spine to my toes.

Is it you? I grab the arm of the stranger standing next to me to steady myself before he looks down and asks if I am okay, which shakes away my crazy split-second thought that you are actually here. I mumble that I am fine, I stumbled, I am so sorry.

The two of them haven't changed position since the photograph was taken. Ted is facing the room with his back to the wall of draughty glass, so he can keep watch.

But he isn't watching. He doesn't notice me, and not because of all the bodies between us. He doesn't notice me because he is looking at her with such deep interest.

I think of Sadie a year ago, when she and I ran into her latest ex-boyfriend. He was holding hands in a restaurant with his new girlfriend. Sadie marched right up to them. Her performance was received in stunned silence. There is no doubt it was memorable. I certainly have not forgotten it, and I doubt her audience ever will.

Hi. I'm the ex-girlfriend. Has he moved his mother in yet to give you lessons on how to clean and cook for him? You know, until I met Donald I thought it was a myth that all men wanted anal. If you haven't yet, you're about to learn from him that it's no myth. Do you enjoy it when that nasty brat of his wipes his snot all over you and screams until he gets his way? I hope the two of you get all the happiness you deserve.

I am not Sadie. I do not want to be anything like her. I do not want to go anywhere near Ted and this woman. I can taste bile, coming up from my stomach and into my throat. Did Sadie take the photo and send the anonymous email, following it up with her silent phone call to gloat? Who else could have done it?

I consider Ted's ex-wife. I have never properly met her. I haven't searched for her on the internet. I feared that even a glimpse of her face would be like staring down Medusa and I would be turned to stone. More than anything, I feared that once I started to look at her I wouldn't be able to stop.

Maybe his ex-wife suspects me of luring Ted away from her, of sleeping with him while they were still together.

Maybe she blames me for their failed marriage. She is a photographer. It is perfectly possible to imagine her sending me a carefully selected image.

I am faint and jumbled to the core as I continue to watch the woman sitting across from Ted. Her shoulders are slim and her back is straight. The fabric of whatever dress or blouse she is wearing is navy blue with black stripes, a kind of zebra print. I cannot help but be certain that her face is as lovely and interesting as her waterfall hair, and this is why Ted is staring at her so closely. This is why I am doubly and triply safe from him noticing me as I peek through the gaps between these coffee addicts' arms, over their damp handbags. Their closed umbrellas drip onto my boots and rub against my jumper so that the wet seeps through and into my skin – I hadn't bothered to grab my coat when I rushed from my illegally parked car.

Ted isn't on duty. He is wearing a Christmas jumper of all things. I bought it for him five years ago. Fair Isle, with small reindeer parading across its variously toned charcoal stripes. Why would Ted wear something I gave him if he were on a date? This thought makes my stomach unclench a tiny bit.

In that way I have of letting my mind open up to find out what it knows before I am conscious of it, I think of Ruby, from my personal safety class. She didn't come to class on Monday and hasn't returned the concerned message I left her the next day. In a rush of certainty, I know who the woman is, and my jealousy is complicated by worry. The worry grows bigger when she turns her head to look off to the side and I see that there are tears on her cheek. Has Ted made her cry? Or is he supporting her while she cries about something else? Six months ago, she was raped by a fake meter-reading man who tricked his way into her house. Ted reaches out and touches her hand, lightly and quickly, but doesn't keep it on top of hers. He frowns.

What is he doing with her? Could he have known her before last month's self-defence class? Could he be meeting her as part of the investigation into her assault? No – he wouldn't do that in a café.

Whatever the reason, what should disturb me most? That Ted is here with a woman when he swore to me he wasn't seeing anyone? That Ruby is vulnerable and he may hurt her? Or that somebody cared enough to clock their meeting and photograph them?

Whoever that somebody is, they know who I am, and who Ted is. They know what Ted and I are to each other. And they knew how to find me through the charity's website. Whether they are for me or against me remains to be seen, though if it is Sadie or Ted's ex-wife it is all too clear which group she is a member of.

Whoever sent it, whatever their reason, I am actually glad they did it. They gave me a gift even if they didn't mean to. I would rather know than not know. Always. My stance on everything. Because the information – the fact that Ted is in this café with Ruby – is louder than everything else. It is so loud it is drowning out the context. Even if my brain is asking the right questions about the circumstances which got that photograph to me, my emotions are engaged only by what it shows.

Saturday, 5 November

Bonfire Night

It is after seven by the time I have finished my daily run, followed by my usual sit-ups and presses and pull-ups and stretches. I have barely stepped out of the shower before I hear Luke's keys in the locks, then the front door of my little Victorian house crashing open and his shout, 'Stay out of the way, Auntie Ella. Back in a minute.'

I shrug off the oversized towelling bathrobe that Ted left with me shortly before you disappeared. It is navy blue. It is so big I used to wrap me and Luke in it together when he was a baby and I wandered through the house late at night, trying to lull him out of crying and into sleep. There are holes and loose threads from uncountable washes, but this old thing of Ted's is an object of comfort to me still.

I shimmy into a jumper and jeans, tie my wet hair into a ponytail, and fly down the stairs to the sight of Luke and our father, lurching sideways into the hall. They are each clutching one side of the doll's house, which is shaped like a medium-sized chest of drawers.

Ted is rear and centre, taking most of the weight. Above Ted's head, in the clear black night that followed the afternoon storm, there is an explosion of silver stars. They fall from the sky as if to announce him.

Luke cranes his neck to watch. 'Awesome,' he says.

'Luke asked me to help.' Ted says this like an apology. He looks at Luke, not me, when he speaks, and a wave of sickness moves through my body.

Somebody on my street has lit a bonfire. The air is thick with smoke. Ash floats into the house. My eyes are burning. I blink and rub them. I think of the disappointed embarrassment that coloured my parting from Ted on Monday night, after trick-or-treating and dinner, which I see now he only went through for Luke.

'Ted came out to Granny and Grandpa's tonight,' Luke says. 'He helped us get the doll's house down from the attic and into Grandpa's van. He followed us here.'

'That was kind.' I am moving backwards, up the stairs again, out of their way.

'Luke and I could have managed,' our father says. I wink at Luke without our father seeing.

Once the doll's house is in Luke's room, there is a great deal of whooping and high-fiving between our father and your son and my furtive ex-boyfriend.

'So what have you and your aunt got planned for tomorrow?' It is infinitely easier for Ted to talk to Luke than to me.

'How about the zoo?' I say.

'Yessssss,' Luke says. He puts out a hand for some more high-fiving with Ted.

'Luke and I will run to the van to get the box.' Our

father is trying to channel our mother's matchmaking impulses but not managing her social smoothness. Ted and I stand awkwardly in Luke's room after they are gone, looking at our own feet.

My heart is squeezing as if I were a teenaged girl about to ask a boy to a dance. But what I have to say is not at all romantic, and it hardly matters anyway because it doesn't seem possible to piss Ted off any more than I already have. Besides, it's not like I will lose him – I have been there and done that several times over – and it looks as if I am about to repeat the experience. Once that happens my chance of learning what I need to will vanish forever.

'Tell me about her laptop,' I say. 'Tell me what they found on it.'

He actually sighs. 'You will never stop.'

'No. But I am willing to say please if it helps.'

'I wouldn't want you to do something so unnatural.' He shakes his head slowly. 'You won't believe me.'

'Try me.'

'They found nothing. The laptop's empty.'

'Then why are they holding on to it? Why does it still matter to them?'

'I said you wouldn't believe me. It's lose-lose with you, no matter what I do.'

'I am not the one making it lose-lose for us.' My fingers are fidgety and nervous, brushing hair from my eyes that isn't there because it is already pulled into a ponytail.

'What the hell is that supposed to mean?'

'You know exactly what.'

'Is there something you want to get off your chest, Ella?'

105

'No.' For now, I want the power of having knowledge without his knowing that I do. 'So why did you make such a big deal of refusing to tell me about the laptop if there's nothing to tell? Was it some kind of power game for you?'

'Low blow. That was beneath you. When I say there was nothing, I mean that whatever is there is hidden. Tech have kept the laptop in the hope that some future tool might uncover something.'

'You're saying she used the laptop, but everything she ever did on it is invisible?'

'So far as I can understand, yes. One of the things they think she did was to use an onion router to mask all of her online activity.'

My amazement actually drives the photograph and the café and Ruby from my head. 'But that's impossible. She wouldn't know what an onion router is.' My head snaps up. 'What is an onion router?'

'You're talking deep web. That internet world where nothing leaves a trace anywhere. None of the search engines you'd recognise.'

'But she was seriously useless at technology.'

'Evidently not.'

'But she can't have done that. If MI5 gave her a spying device she wouldn't know how to turn it on.'

'Well she did. And it wasn't the kind of technology ordinary people have access to.'

'Then someone else set it up and taught her. We need to know who. And why.'

I spend my days warning women of the importance of guarding their privacy to keep safe. But your skill at doing this – your talent for secrets – might have been the very thing that put you in jeopardy. Did you continue your conversation with Jason Thorne that way, after the phone calls the tabloids said you made to him?

Ted is frowning. 'You're going dangerously quiet.'

'Just thinking. Thank you for telling me. I mean it.'

'Don't drop me or Mike in it.'

'I won't. I never would. You know that.'

'I know you wouldn't want to, but you might not be able to help yourself.'

'I'll be careful for you. I'd always be careful for you.' And of you, I silently add.

He doesn't look convinced. 'That's the end of it. Don't ask me for more.'

This is not a promise I can make, so I change the subject in the crudest way possible, mostly for Luke's sake, but partly for my own. 'Will you stay for pizza?'

'I'd like to but I have to be somewhere.' He glances at his watch and I imagine Ruby waiting for him in a French restaurant, or in her little house, where she has cooked him dinner and lit candles. 'Half an hour ago, actually.' Ted is wearing black jeans and a black shirt and something that smells of woods. Even yesterday, I might have secretly hoped these things were for me, but today I know they are not.

'Next time,' I say.

'Yeah,' Ted says.

'My dad . . . Thank you . . .'

'I know, Ella. You don't need to say.'

Pandora's Box

Dad leaves with his phone to his ear, talking to Mum in a hushed voice. Luke wants to get straight to the box, but he is still sweaty from his afternoon karate lesson so I make him take a shower first.

'Fastest shower ever,' I say, when I walk into his room to find him waiting for me. He is wearing the football club pyjamas I bought for him a few weeks ago, and they make him look achingly sweet and young. He is sitting in front of the giant oak wardrobe that used to be yours, cross-legged on carpet that was also yours. I had these moved here from your flat three years ago when our parents were finally able to sell it and close your bank accounts and put the money safely away for Luke.

The carpet is pale beige, with a white trellis pattern, and beautiful, like everything you choose. Luke loves the fact that it was in the Georgian flat where the two of you lived together for such a short time.

I sit across from Luke and lift the lid of the cardboard box between us. 'Should we start?'

'Have I told you lately that you're brilliant, Auntie Ella?'

I raise my arms and tilt my head to the side, an upper-body-only curtain call, careful at the same time not to spill any of the Mexican beer I'm holding in my right hand. I take a sip.

'I've heard Granny tell you that ladies should never drink from bottles.'

Even wet from the shower, Luke's funny cowlick is as unruly as ever, a tight swirl above his left temple. I poke a finger into its centre and twizzle it around until he laughs. 'I'm not a lady.'

'Granny told Grandpa before we left that he wasn't allowed to drink.'

'She worries about his health, Luke. And she knew he was driving.'

'*Beer is made of sugar. Cancer cells love sugar.*' Your son's imitation of our mother is terrifyingly good. I try not to laugh but I can't stop myself. I nearly spray Luke with a mouthful of liquid death.

'Can I have a sip?' he says.

'No! But nice try. Smoothly done.'

He pauses to watch a dazzling waterfall of blue pouring into the night, followed by a streak of red fire zinging upwards like a reverse comet and screaming all the way. 'Please will you take me next year?' He is still staring out the window.

'I hope so. I'll keep talking to Granny.'

Luke rolls his eyes and turns back to the box. The cardboard has thinned in places, where sticky tape ripped off layers. 'Do you think Granny's looked through it?'

109

'No – I asked – she said she didn't.' But I'm sure she has. I wouldn't be surprised if she's actually taken something out. I have already snuck a phone call to her to ask this very thing, but she will not depart from her little charade that she never even looked inside.

I am not sure what we are expecting. Some obvious clue the police missed? Presumably they have already combed it all for DNA.

'What's this?' Luke is holding a scrap of soft white wool, edged in silk and fraying.

I reach out a finger to touch it, smiling. 'The sole surviving piece of Mummy's baby blanket. She used to tuck it into your cot with you.'

He buries his face in it, then jumps up and sticks it beneath his pillow. 'Please know that I will have to kill you if you tell anyone.'

'Never.' I glance at the doll's house, half-expecting to see a spectral glow behind the paned windows. 'Will you mind having this if you bring friends back here? You won't be embarrassed?'

'Nah. I'll say it's yours and you insist on keeping it in my room.'

'Well that's true.'

'Part of the truth. Not all.' He gives me a look. 'I learned that from you. And Granny. Probably not from Grandpa, though.'

I think of our father's secret request for the police to return your things. Luke and I wouldn't have this box at all, if it weren't for him. 'Your grandpa is a man of many wonders. I think your grandpa is a visionary.'

'He's the master puppeteer.'

I look at him in surprise. 'He is, yes. Though few people guess. Which is why he is so effective.'

Luke picks up a pink plastic compact. 'What's this?'

'Some kind of travel mirror? Face powder or blush, maybe?' All of your make-up had designer labels on the containers, but this doesn't. 'Shall we see?'

'Yep.' He finds the clasp and it opens like a clam shell. Inside is a circle of pills, faded in colour. Each pill is numbered, to keep track of the days of a lunar month. Numbers 1 through 21 are pale yellow. Numbers 22 through 28 are light blue. The two of us squint at them. 'Same question, again, Auntie Ella. What is this?'

I gulp so much beer the bottle depletes by two inches. 'They're birth control pills. Women use them so they can have sex without getting pregnant.'

He makes a face and thrusts the container at me as if we were playing hot potato. 'Do you think Mummy used them?'

'Probably, but she must have taken a break from them. Which is an extremely lucky thing for all of us. Because she wanted to have you.'

All at once, he flushes. His nose begins to run. He looks down.

My heart begins to beat faster. 'What's wrong, Luke?'

But he can't speak. I scoot close to him and he climbs onto my lap and I cradle him as if he were a baby, though he is bony and gangly. He sniffles onto my shoulder while I hold him tighter and rock back and forth, kissing the top of his head. His hair smells like the shower gel Ted uses – he must have persuaded Ted to get some for him.

Luke pulls away to catch my eye. His own are red. 'You won't stop looking at things again because I got upset?' He wipes his nose on a pyjama sleeve.

'No. I won't do that.'

He climbs off my lap and sits opposite me, with the box between us again. He swallows hard. 'Maybe she wanted me but my father didn't. What I'm most scared of is that I'm the reason he hurt her.' He shakes his head. 'You wouldn't admit it if you thought so, though, would you?'

What should I do? What would you do with this tearful boy, asking such direct questions? My instinct is to be as straight with him as I can be, but I am worried about misjudging it. Am I treating him too much like a grown-up, as our mother says? I think again about the possibility that you were in contact with Jason Thorne. There is no etiquette book for talking to a child about such horrors.

I say, 'I'll always try to be honest with you about what I think, Luke.'

'I wish I could remember her.'

'I wish you could, too.' I take a deep breath. 'When she's in a room, you can't look anywhere else. She's the most charismatic person ever born.'

'I know,' he says.

'Why don't you go wash your face, sweet boy? I think we need a break. We can do some more of this another time.'

'I don't want to stop. I won't be able to sleep. I've been waiting too long.'

I know my stomach is lined with nerves. They must be the source of the punch in the gut that makes me take a deep breath. 'Okay then.' I reach into the box for a plastic file pocket. Specially chosen by me, it is cornflower blue and covered in ditsy flowers. When my fingertips brush it there is a small electric shock. I lift it out and hold it before me like a sacred document. I sit back on my heels and place it on my lap. 'I think this will help us.'

My hand floats to my belly. There is a piercing ache low down, on the left side. When I last touched this folder I was twenty and you were thirty and right next to me with Luke inside you.

'It's a bit girly, whatever it is,' Luke says.

'I didn't know you were a boy when I bought it. You were born a couple of days after that.' I manage a smile. 'Mummy always gave me the fun jobs.'

'So what's in it?'

'Her antenatal notes. She got me to photocopy them after her last midwife appointment. It took forever, standing at the machine in the library, feeding it coins.'

'Why did she make you do that?'

'For the memories. She knew the hospital would keep hold of her notes once she was admitted to the labour ward. She wanted duplicates.' I trail a finger around the neck of the beer bottle thoughtfully, then pick it up and take several sips. 'Give me a few minutes to check something.'

He shuffles next to me so he can read too. Your hospital number is top and centre on the first page. For *Next of Kin* you put Mum and Dad's names – of course you wouldn't be lured into telling us who Luke's father is that easily.

I begin to flip through the notes. There is your blood group. AB+, the same as mine. We liked to smile at our rareness. Luke is AB+ too, so his father could be type A, type B, or type AB. Those three types account for about 55 per cent of the population. When it comes to narrowing things down, Luke's blood group doesn't help much.

'What does this mean?' He touches the word Chlamydia, which has always struck me as a pretty word for an ugly thing. It is the first word in a box that includes other ugly things. Gonorrhoea. Herpes. HIV.

'There are certain diseases that can hurt a baby when it's inside the womb or while it's being born. They test all pregnant women for these. This shows that Mummy didn't have any of them.'

He touches my hand. 'What exactly are we looking for?'

I hastily skim through the list of every appointment you attended, each with a date, the number of weeks gestation, the height of your fundus, your blood pressure, repeated affirmations that there was no protein in your urine.

'I want to confirm something that isn't here. It will make you feel better.'

I already know more than I wish to about intimate partner violence and homicide. But there is conflicting evidence as to whether a woman's risk increases during pregnancy and when she is newly post-partum.

'It's as I thought.' I look up at Luke. 'There is nothing here to suggest that the people who cared for Mummy while she was pregnant thought she was at risk of violence or abuse.'

'But they wouldn't write it here. They'd worry that the person who was hurting her would snoop in her notes and see they were onto him.'

'God you're smart.'

'You're always saying that.'

'Because you are. And you're right again. They wouldn't have stated any worries explicitly, but they would have found excuses to keep a closer eye on her. They didn't do that. See how the medical staff filled it in after each appointment? There is nothing extra anywhere. Routine pregnancy. Routine visits. No additional scans or specialist treatments or bloodwork.'

I leaf through the pages some more. It is so quick. Only in my line of vision for a few seconds. A single note popping out after several blank boxes in a row. I have already turned the page before it registers. I see the brief entry through a kind of replay.

Amniocentesis. The word. The date. The gestation you were at that time – sixteen weeks – which I remember from my second-year Genetics class is the absolute earliest they would do such a test. So you must have been desperately eager to have it, and to know the result as soon as possible.

Some women want to make sure the baby is okay before they tell anyone, but you went well beyond the customary three-month cut-off. You announced your pregnancy at twenty weeks. You had the amniocentesis one month before that. I am in no doubt that you needed to know the findings before deciding to share the news.

Twenty weeks pregnant and taken by surprise, you said, laughing and claiming that you'd only just realised it. I remember looking at you in suspicion – you are so aware of your menstrual cycles you stick a tampon in an hour before you even start bleeding. You didn't meet my eye. Did the entry in this fat stack of papers slip past your notice? It must have. Because clearly you didn't want us to know.

My degree in Human Biology taught me so much about experiences I will never have. The irony isn't lost on me that my favourite module was the one I took on Human Reproduction during my third year – I did most of the work for it while looking after Luke.

I know amniocentesis is not routine. I know it is a test women opt for, either in response to medical advice or for reasons of their own. So why on earth did you have it? You were only thirty years old. Hardly the advanced maternal age that would make them want to screen you for genetic abnormalities. Twenty weeks is the usual time for an amnio. You must have pushed hard to have yours early. Few people can say no to you. Not even medical professionals.

Luke touches my arm. 'What are you thinking?'

'I'm thinking that I hope Mummy's hospital notes reassure you.'

'A bit. But I wish they said who my father is.'

I realise I am biting my lip. I make myself stop. 'So do I.'

'I thought maybe you knew.'

'Oh, Luke. Do you think I could keep something like that from you?' I pick a piece of fluff from his pyjama top. 'I know your mummy so well. I think he must have been a good man, and she must have loved him very much, and he would never hurt her.'

'Maybe he died or went away before she could tell him about me.'

'That's possible. I've wondered about that.' I close the box. 'Go blow your nose?'

'Okay.' He pops up and goes next door to the bathroom.

It seems only a few seconds before he is back, but he pauses to grab the bar I installed in his door frame. He knocks out two pull-ups. Three months ago he couldn't do a single one. I am in serious danger of crying with pride and happiness, but I manage to restrain myself. 'You make those look easy,' I say.

He hangs for a few seconds before he drops down casually to emphasise that it was nothing. He sits back down and opens the box again, giving me your just *you try to stop me* look. He peers inside, excitement and surprise moving across his face. 'We missed something.' He reaches in and pulls out a book.

The quilted cloth cover is dusty and faded. The fabric is an Art Nouveau design. The black background is sprinkled with drooping cream snowdrops and little cream dots. The spine is worn, the fabric coming away from its top and bottom.

'Oh,' I say, and I shiver.

Luke puts it in my hands. 'What is it?'

'Mummy's old address book.' I turn it over, then over again. A precious thing. 'Grandpa gave her this for her sixteenth birthday. She loved it. She never used anything else.'

The headlines seem to play themselves out in my head in an endless loop. I argue with almost every one of them, but that doesn't make them stop.

Runaway Theory in Nurse Disappearance.

You didn't run away. None of your clothes were missing. Your passport was still in your desk. And you'd left your address book, which was a kind of bible to you. You would never have gone anywhere without it.

Luke presses a finger onto the cover, testing the sponginess of the quilting. He does this several times, seeming to enjoy its texture. 'Do you think you'll find a clue in here?'

There is another explosion. The sky is erupting with giant dandelions in emerald and fuchsia and violet and sapphire. 'Maybe.' Each flower pops, then vaporises. 'I think though that you and I need a break from all of this. Okay?'

He looks disappointed, but nods. 'Yeah. Okay. But you can't forget your promise. You have to try to find her.'

'I'm going to try.'

'Why are you smiling, Auntie Ella?'

'I think I may say that a lot.'

'That you're going to try?'

'Sometimes when Ted catches me at it, he says, "Yes, you're very trying."'

'He's messing with you.'

I tap a finger beneath his chin, forcing a laugh from him that he doesn't want to release and making him protest that it tickles. 'Well he's good at that,' I say.

'So are you with him,' my nephew says wisely.

Monday, 7 November

The Doll's House

On Luke's bedside table is a photograph of you and me. We are sitting on a patchwork quilt in our garden. You are eleven and I am one. In every childhood photograph of the two of us, you are looking at the camera, smiling your closed-mouth secret smile, and I am looking at you, a flower following my sun. Your hands rest serenely in your lap. My chubby fingers grip your arm. Your posture is straight, your dress immaculate, while I lean into you with all of my baby weight, chewing a pink plastic plate.

I barely take my eyes from the photo as I sit on Luke's bed and dial our mother to ask if she knew about your amniocentesis.

'I'm sure you're wrong, Ella,' she says. 'Miranda would have told me if she was having one. What makes you think she did?'

'It's in her hospital notes. I don't know if you remember? I made copies for her. They were in the box.' *As if you didn't know.*

'I need to go. Your father's back from the school with Luke.'

'So you don't have any thoughts about why she might have had that test?'

'None.' She is happy to end the call and let the question of your amniocentesis blow away. For an instant, I find her incuriosity surprising. Then I remember that our mother's need to be the world expert on you is strong. She does not like to linger over mere details that might put this expertise in doubt.

But our mother is not the only potential source of information about the test. I grab my laptop from Luke's floor and fire off an email to the hospital, asking for a copy of all reports and data relating to your amniocentesis. I explain that I am allowed access because you were declared dead three years ago and I am one of the executors of your estate. I attach the paperwork to prove it.

At last, I turn to the doll's house. The outside walls are a honey-coloured wash of Bath stone. The front swings open in two parts, like a cupboard, for access to the rooms. The doll's house belonged to our grandmother when she was a little girl.

I feel like a giant peeping into an ordinary human house, squinting between the glazing bars and below the festoon blinds of a twelve-paned window.

The children's bedrooms are on the second floor, separated by the central staircase. In one of them, a teenaged Miranda doll and a little girl Melanie doll are sleeping on the same feather mattress, holding hands. I told Luke that you and I used to do this. I would sneak out of my room and into yours and you would grumble but never send me away. He must have set it all up early on Sunday morning.

Your doll's house bedroom is papered in an offcut from your childhood bedroom. Flowers in different shapes and colours entwine with berries on a cream background. I'd always wanted wallpaper like yours. I'd always wanted everything of yours.

In the living room, sitting on a greeny-blue sofa patterned with small gilt medallions, are the doll versions of our parents. The nursery's perfect replica of a rosewood cot now has a tiny baby Luke sleeping beneath its lace coverlet. I sit cross-legged on the carpet and open up this house that Luke has never known in real life, with all of us happily together in it.

I slip the tips of my fingers beneath the feather mattress that the doll versions of me and you sleep upon. I slide my hand from the top of the bed towards the bottom, waiting for the small bump. There it is. A dried green pea. Luke must have put it there for me, like you used to. I'd told him how I used to pretend that my doll self was too sensitive to sleep with a pea under the bed.

My fingers reach towards the Miranda doll, hover above her, and finally drop to her shiny black hair. My fingers remember when I pulled that hair in real life and wouldn't let go. You had to walk around for a full minute with me gripping on in a temper. What made me release it was your whispered promise to cut off my hair while I slept. I was terrified for weeks afterwards that you would do this anyway.

'Talk to me, Miranda.' I startle myself that I have spoken

these words out loud, casting a magic spell I don't believe in. 'Tell me where you are.' The miniaturised Miranda's eyes are closed in sleep. 'Tell me what happened.' If I were to stand the doll up, her eyes would fly open, but I don't do this because those painted doll eyes will tell me nothing. 'I'm sorry I pulled your hair,' I say. 'I'm sorry I lied to you,' I say.

It isn't just the news headlines that still waylay me. Phrases from the advice leaflets I pored over ten years ago do this too.

When someone goes missing, do not give up.

Our parents still say that with no proof of death, there must be life. I mumble my dissent but do not elaborate on the fallacious reasoning here. How can they say this when you have been declared dead? When they themselves pushed for this declaration, against all of my protests?

This is the double think of those of us who love the missing. We cannot help but cling to hope when there is no body. Yet this hope is in tension with demands to access property and dissolve estates and meet the needs of those left behind.

My last five words are a whisper. 'I miss you every day.' They are the truest and most obvious words I can say.

I don't quite know why what happens next happens. One doll's house disaster follows the other, domino-like and near-comic, if it weren't so deadly serious.

My fingers have messed up the Miranda doll's hair. When I try to smooth it back I only make it worse. I pluck her out of the bed, a monster grasping a fairy, but my hand is shaking so I drop her. When I pick her up my fist knocks into the bed and that shoves out of place too, making the doll version of me fall out of it to roll along the embroidered rug before halting on the polished floor. I put the mini-Miranda back. I put the mini-me beside her.

My hand wraps around the bed, my thumb on top of the fringed counterpane, which is the colour of weak tea because that is what you dipped it in to help me make it look antique. My finger pads grip the bedframe's wooden underside and find a bump that shouldn't be here. I turn the bed over, letting the miniaturised versions of you and me tumble once more to the floor, along with the satin coverlet.

The paper is a familiar faded gold. It is folded into a tiny square and held in place by tape that was once clear but is now yellowing.

I continue to speak aloud, as if you were in the room. 'I said, "Talk to me." Are you actually doing it? Since when do you follow my commands?'

You will not know that Mum and Dad and I check the post every day. We catch each other at it. Half-expecting a letter from the person who snatched you away. Living in hope of a clue. Perhaps even a card from you. But I wasn't looking for anything here, in this private postal system of your invention.

The tape has been applied exactly, with your nurse's skill, along each of the four sides. Carefully, carefully, my heart thumping so loudly it seems to be between my ears, I peel away a corner. The paper has been here so long the tape has lost most of its stickiness, so it comes away cleanly.

I imagine your voice. *What took you so long, Melanie?*

There is a hint of teasing laughter. *I was counting on you, Melanie.*

There is hurt and disappointment, too. *Really? Suicide? Running away? Me? You know I'm full of tricks and schemes, but running away has never been one of them. And my self-preservation instincts are strong.*

I unfold the tiny square you made. The blue forget-me-nots are no longer vivid but I recognise the paper, which is from a small notepad I bought when you were pregnant. I am moved that you used it, my cheap little gift on a student budget – you had to work hard to pretend to like it, and you weren't entirely convincing. The stuff you normally favoured was thick and handmade and pressed from fabric pulp.

It is as if your ghost has led me here. The thought is poetic more than supernatural. I do not believe in ghosts. I do believe our mother though, who says again and again, to me, to Luke, to our father, 'Love never dies.'

That's convenient, you say.

But this is what I say. You didn't want to be invisible. You didn't want every trace to disappear. Even if you were mostly willing to let that happen at the behest of someone else, you still wanted something material to remain.

I study your dear handwriting, made by your dear hand. It is perfect and delicate and considered. It is strangely like my own. My breath is coming very, very fast as I read.

M + N + ??

That is all you wrote, surrounded by a heart.

What did I expect? A warning that if anything ever happened to you I should suspect that Professor Plum did it with a candlestick in the drawing room?

Don't be so lazy, you say. *Get going on decoding. You're good at that.*

The likelihood is that M is for Miranda. It could be for Melanie but I don't think so. The question marks narrow the time frame of when you wrote it. It had to have been while you were pregnant but before Luke was born. In any note or card during that period you always designated the baby's signature with two question marks. *Lots of love from Miranda and ??* That is what you would always write, so happily and proudly.

But if my deductions are right, then who was N? Luke's father? The man who took his mother? Even if N were either or both of these things, there are countless male names that start with that letter.

For you to put this little love token under the bed of our doll's house must have had the force of a charm for you. A blessing or a wish. Maybe both. Certainly some kind of power you were trying to invoke.

Such an act is in keeping with your superstitious tendencies. There were mugs that you shunned, perhaps because a person you disliked had drunk from one, or it was a souvenir from an unhappy trip. You would tip steaming liquid into the sink if someone – never me – mistakenly forgot and made you a cup of tea in a forbidden vessel. You would not take a single sip.

Should I share this message with our parents? With the police? My first impulse, born of the sisterly habits of hushed confidences between me and you, is that the note is mine and mine alone, left in a place you knew I would eventually find.

I remember what Dad said about the doll's house. *She knew how much it meant to you.*

I jump up before I change my mind. I snap several shots of the note with my camera phone, then slip it into zippered plastic before stowing it in the side compartment of my handbag. I will take it to Mum and Dad and discuss it with them on Friday after Luke goes to bed. They can pass it on to the police if they want to. Assuming they think the police will care.

M + N + ?? Even with the note out of my sight, I keep seeing it. *Who was N? Who was N? Who was N?* This is a question I know I will ask again.

Tuesday, 8 November

The Address Book

As soon as I see the sender's name in my inbox, I know that something is wrong. Justice Administrator. They have written only one sentence. *You will pay for what you have done.* I think simply, *Sadie*, and imagine Ted saying, *Never assume.*

Whatever Ted may say, Sadie's mad new hatred ought to make me sick with distress and shock. But it hardly registers against the hurt of being without you. It is nothing compared to the tightening in my belly at the prospect of losing Ted all over again. Some loves matter much more than others.

Sadie was always jealous of you, you say. *I never trusted her*, you say.

So what made her turn on me so violently, so suddenly? What could have made her think that I was sneaking around with her boyfriend, who I had only met once, at her behest and with her in the room, before that nightmare party?

I know that for an offence of Harassment to be

committed, there must be a 'course of conduct'. This means I need at least two messages like the one from Justice Administrator before the police can do anything. Even then, they may not judge that a reasonable person would feel a sufficiently pressing sense of alarm, distress or torment for them to act. Still, I find myself wishing for a second message. That I should have such a wish makes me want to scream.

I do three things. One, I take a screenshot. Two, I send the letter to my printer. Three, I forward it to the special address my email provider lists for documenting abuse, though I know they get countless messages a day and are highly unlikely to reply.

It occurs to me that this message could also come under the offence of Malicious Communications. That offence only requires one piece of evidence. For the hell of it, I do a fourth thing, and send the details to the police using their online Report a Crime or Incident form. I am not holding my breath for a response – they are hardly likely to see me as being in imminent danger – but at least I now have it on file with them.

I want to scream when I consider how much of my morning this email has wasted. I close it down, determined not to let it sour my day, and glance at Luke's karate-pose wall clock. I am working out how much time I have before I need to leave for my day of individual home safety assessments. I actually have a full hour to explore a little more of what Ted bitterly refers to as the Museum of Miranda.

I pick my way through an assortment of Luke's wiggle

worms and glow slime and safari animals, all from Ted. To avoid crushing the wing of a model aeroplane Luke is building, I bring the side of my boot down onto some joke putty. There is an obscene squelching noise that Ted would find gratifying and I cannot help but laugh.

The wardrobe has three doors, each with a drawer beneath it. Until late Saturday night, the middle drawer was empty. But after Luke fell asleep, the room lit only by the landing light outside, I filled it with the things from your box. On the floor is another of Ted's presents for Luke, a secret message kit.

Again I hear your teasing voice, in your most over-dramatically comical tone, *It's a sign*, and I am struck by the thought that, as I grow older, you grow with me. Even without you here, my closeness to you hasn't stopped and our relationship hasn't frozen. In some weird way I can't yet understand, it is continuing to develop and change. This constellation of ideas makes me smile as I open your drawer.

The address book is at the top. Dust puffs from the fabric when I pick it up. Once more, your funny, sweet voice rings so clearly in my head I can almost fool myself into thinking you are really here. *I always wanted to talk to you. You weren't ready to listen properly until now.*

I find a puddle of carpet that isn't strewn with Luke's toys and curl my legs beneath me in your best mermaid pose. But instead of combing my hair and studying my looking glass, I open the book and flick through the pages in order.

The first entry to make me pause is under H. All I can see is heavy black marker. You have filled in every square millimetre of the box with the person's name, address and number. I am not sure even a forensic X-ray machine could uncover what was once beneath this. Did the police attempt it?

You would have used a trick our mother taught us. You would have written arbitrary words over the original, many different times, building layer upon layer of letters. It's unlikely that the police could have deciphered this even before you added the extra protection of the thick marker.

You must have felt this person's importance the first time you wrote their name. So why did you go to so much trouble to cover it up? Did you change your mind about them, perhaps coming to loathe them and not wanting to be reminded of their existence? Perhaps you were hiding them from somebody else?

Did the man who took you scrawl over his entry himself? Almost immediately I dismiss the idea. The cross-out is too Miranda-like. It is your technique all the way. Plus, any serious criminal who knew of the book's existence and managed to get his hands on it would have burnt it or dissolved it in acid or buried it in a very deep and intolerably smelly dungheap. He would not have simply overwritten his details and risked the book falling into the hands of a forensics expert.

You, on the other hand, loved this present from Dad too much to dispose of it. That is why you obliterated the entry rather than the entire book.

I study the other names under H. Your usual habit was to write in pencil, so you could easily erase an entry if you eradicated the person from your life. What draws

my attention to *N. Henrickson* is your rare use of ink –
this was someone you knew you wanted to keep. The
other odd thing is that you put only an initial rather than
the full first name. You didn't do this in any of the earlier
entries.

I flip quickly through the rest of the book. Ted's name
rushes past me, and Sadie's too, despite your dislike of
her, but that is no surprise and they are not what I am
looking for. What I want to see is if you've used a first
initial for any of the later entries. You haven't.

M + N + ??

Is this the same N? Is this entry some kind of code?
A record you wanted to preserve but in a form that
nobody else would notice, or even if they did, not be able
to identify?

It makes me remember a trick you and Mum used to
play. Whenever the two of you couldn't help but talk in
front of me, but wanted to disguise who you were talking
about, you would make up a silly name. The fake name
would always sound ridiculous, have the same number
of syllables as the real one, and start with the same letter
as the actual person. They would live in a preposterous
place extremely far away. And they would be a long-lost
distant relative I had never heard of.

I am four years old and I am sitting high up in my booster
seat in the rear of the car. Our mother is driving. You
are fourteen and sitting next to her and I am extremely
cross that I cannot sit in the front so I press my feet into
the back of your seat.

'Stop kicking, Melanie,' you say.

'Sorry.' I kick again.

'Stop it now,' you say, 'or I'll make you stop.' You twist around to try to grab my ankle but I dodge out of your reach, laughing as you strain in your seatbelt. 'God you're a brat,' you say.

I squish a shoe into what I think is your bottom.

You look straight at me. Your eyes are moody blue. 'Fine. Have it your way, Brat. No baking this afternoon.'

I picture the ingredients for chocolate-chip cookies that you arranged on the kitchen table before we left, promising what we would do if I behaved well on the shopping expedition for the many things you and I still need before starting school.

I don't know that tomorrow I will meet Ted for the first time. I don't know that I have only sixteen years left of a life that has you in it.

'Please, Miranda,' I say. 'Please make cookies with me. I'm really sorry.'

'No way. Too late. You don't deserve baking.'

'I promise I'll be good.'

You ignore me. Mum's knuckles are going white from squeezing the wheel.

'Please change your mind,' I say. 'I've stopped. Please.'

'No.'

'Please. Please, please, please.'

'If you promise not to talk for the next five minutes. Not even a whisper. Five absolutely perfect minutes of peace from you. That's the price you have to pay. Open your mouth once and no cookies.'

I nod my head, worried that this is a trick and even to say a word of agreement with you will mean no baking. I silently count pairs of magpies and pretend not to see any of the single ones. All the while, I am lulled by your voice and Mum's. You are both laughing, so I tune in. You are talking about somebody who has awful hair.

'Who has awful hair?' I say.

'It hasn't been five minutes,' you say.

'Yes it has. I was watching the clock. It changed one second before I talked.'

'I should have made it ten minutes,' you say. 'Or better yet, forever.'

I hate it when you leave me out. 'Tell me,' I say. 'Who?'

'Cousin Petunia from Cucamonga.' I can hear that you are trying not to laugh. 'That's who we were talking about. Her hair is really, really bad.'

Mum is pressing her lips together.

'Do we really have a cousin called Petunia? And is there really a place called Cucamonga and does our cousin really have awful hair?'

'Yes, yes and yes,' you say. But I can tell there is at least one lie in those three yeses of yours.

'Your friend Pamela has awful hair like Cousin Petunia, Mummy. Is Pamela really Petunia?'

'Of course not.' Mum purses her lips, as if trying to stop her face from doing what it really wants to do by distracting it with weird moves.

You snort and then complain that the snort made you get water up your nose.

'Why does Pamela make her hair so frizzled? Is it supposed to be like that? Does she mean for it to be green? It's not pretty green like a sea princess's.'

You are choking with laughter. 'We need to change the game,' you say.

I laugh too, to show I'm in on the joke, even though I am not. I say, 'Can I meet Cousin Petunia? I would like to go to Cucamonga.'

Is *N. Henrickson* a version of that trick you and Mum used to try to play, to reveal your secrets right in front of me in the hope that I wouldn't understand them?

It occurs to me that Henrickson fits neatly with the surname of the psychiatrist I met at Sadie's nightmare party. Holderness and Henrickson. Both have ten letters and begin with 'H'. Is it a variation of that silly name trick, but switched from first name to last? I quickly decide it cannot be a secret reference to Adam Holderness, because the first name of this entry begins with N, not A.

I use my phone to snap a picture of the double-page spread of H entries, so I will have N. Henrickson's details to hand as well as an image of the blocked-out box.

I dial our mother, who puts me on speakerphone so that she can go on clattering saucepans and dishes in the kitchen.

'Are you alone in there?' I ask.

'Your nephew's about to leave for school. He's sitting at the table doing some last-minute homework – he got behind after last weekend. You should have got him back to us earlier on Sunday.'

'That's not true, Granny,' Luke says. 'She made sure I did all of it. This is from yesterday.'

I smile at his defence of me but say nothing. He goes on. 'Granny says you need to bring crisps on Friday, Auntie Ella.'

'I said no such thing.'

'Sorry, Mum,' I say. 'I already bought them – your grandson got to me first. Luke, I need Granny on her own for a minute.'

'I'm so hurt.' He pretends to weep.

'Go tell Grandpa it's time to leave or you'll be late,' she says.

I wait until I hear a door slam. 'Take me off speakerphone, please, Mum.' I get right to the point. 'You know Miranda's address book?'

She thinks for a few seconds. 'The fabric-covered one?'

'The one Dad gave her. It was in the box with the stuff from the police.'

'Was it?'

'Yes.' The charade of absent-minded casualness suits our mother less than anyone I can imagine. 'Did the police ever ask you any questions about it?'

'Only to double-check a couple of the names. That was soon after she disappeared.'

'I've been looking at it. Did she ever mention someone called N. Henrickson?'

'She put just the initial?'

'Yes.'

'I remember the police asked about that. It's not someone I knew of.'

'There's another weird entry under H. One that's completely crossed out so you can't see what she originally wrote. Did the police mention that?'

'Not that I remember.'

'Can you think of anyone she might have wanted to obliterate any record of?'

'Lots of people. When Miranda is finished with you, she is finished. A switch flips and she turns off. That is how she is.'

You are like one of those terribly sweet and seemingly gentle little dinosaurs I once saw in a film. They are oh-so-pretty, making their squeaky cute noises to lure their victim close and hypnotise him with their charm and beauty before they tear him to pieces. Few people can survive getting close to you. I am not sure if I have.

'But not with you,' Mum says. 'Never with you.'

'Mostly not.'

'That's how you are, too. Someone can push and push, but then they push that final inch and you shut down forever on them.'

I think of Sadie, and know our mother is right, though Ted seems to have indefinite immunity. 'Maybe,' I say.

'Is that the best you can give me?'

'Definitely.'

Our mother misses nothing. 'Definitely the best you can give me, or definitely I'm right?'

'Definitely you're right, Mum.'

'Good. Now I need to go.' In her usual fashion, our mother clicks off on a last word that pleases her. She is more like you than she knows. And so am I.

Wednesday, 9 November

The Catalyst

The rational part of me is whispering that the police probably did this ten years ago. But the doubting part of me is louder. And the part of me that wants to stir things, to nudge anyone that may lead me to you, to find anything that isn't Jason Thorne, is practically screaming.

I think of what Mum said. *I worry about how far you will go.*

How far is that? Would I risk my life? Probably not. Have sex? Just possibly. Risk Luke? Never ever. It is unlikely I will ever be tested in any of these ways.

By the time I have driven the five minutes from my little house on the outskirts of Bath to the Georgian terraces in its centre, the night is about to close in. The arrangement of this street and its buildings makes me think of a gigantic bicycle wheel. The eighteenth-century houses are laid out as if on top of the rubber tyre, with parking places radiating from the outer parts of the spokes and a fountain at the hub.

Your old flat was on a side street that branches off

this road. It would take only a few minutes to walk to it from here. Was the proximity deliberate? You lived in it for two and a half years before you vanished.

I loop around the fountain, hoping a parking space will become vacant. The fountain is overflowing with bubbles. Students are always pouring liquid soap into it. They must have used something extra-powerful this time, because the bubbles are churning into a dense white foam. The breeze detaches small balls of the foam from the main body, then floats them through the air. I seem to be inside a snow globe.

I get lucky. Somebody jumps into a car and drives away. The space is right in front of the address you wrote down for N. Henrickson. As I walk towards the building, a cloud of jackdaws wheel and shriek slowly beneath a creeping grey sky. So many of them, teeming above the rooftops.

Four marble steps lead up to an outside landing and the green double doors that mark the entrance. There is a gold plaque to the right of the doors. *Henrietta Mansions*. To the left of the doors is a metal square with a camera, intercom, and numbered metal buttons for the flats. The occupants are clearly security savvy, because there are no names. I push the button for 'Flat 7' and wait. Nothing happens. I press it again, wondering if the occupant of Flat 7 is watching me. Still nothing.

I lean against the wall, my head against the gold plaque. A foam ball drops from the air and rolls around in front of my feet. I take out my phone. I dial the number listed by N. Henrickson's name and get through to an automated recording from a mobile network provider I have never heard of. The computerised voice invites me to leave a message.

I think of a scientific word I have always loved. Catalyst. That is what I hope to be. The spark to make things happen. But can I really remain unchanged?

I leave my message, an uncharacteristic one in which I reveal concrete information about myself. 'Hello. My name is Ella Brooke. My sister is Miranda Brooke. I think Miranda knows you. Can you please ring me? Hopefully my number will be on your phone, but just in case . . . '

I always turn my phone off at night. As I press end on the call I notice that I forgot to switch the sound back on this morning. When I look in the log of missed calls, I see that the most recent one is from Mum, from ten minutes ago, along with a message commanding me not to be late on Friday. There is a missed call and voicemail from Ted, too, left half an hour ago, asking me to phone him, and this makes my heart race as if I were a teenaged girl whose big crush has unexpectedly rung.

Four missed calls came in the middle of the night, all from a withheld number. The rational explanation is that these are from someone trying to sell me something. But my instinct tells me that this is personal. I think again of Sadie and the muted voice from five days ago. For now, though, I have more important things to worry about than Sadie.

I punch the bell for Flat 7 again. I use my phone to do some quick internet searches while I wait. First I try the unfamiliar mobile network provider, but there are no hits. Is it defunct? Or deliberately hidden? I try another search engine, but still nothing. I plug in the word Henrickson. Though several possibilities come up, none of them have first names beginning with N and they are not even based in the UK.

The sky is darkening rapidly. I do yet another search, this time for the marketing history of Flat 7. I don't expect to find anything, but I quickly learn that it hasn't changed hands for twenty-one years, when it was bought by a company called E.B. Property Services. I search for that too, but the results are more dead ends. Was the company dissolved? Why is there no trace of it, beyond the initial purchase?

There is an email address below N. Henrickson's number in the address book, with a provider I have never heard of. I search for the provider on the internet, only to discover it charges a high fee because it uses end-to-end encryption so that no third party can monitor it. Its servers are in Switzerland, so no government can shut it down or demand the data be handed over.

What kind of person chooses an email provider like this, and how did you know them? The answer is all too obvious – a person who is expert at staying invisible, and wanted you that way too, at least in relation to him. And you must have known this and not minded. It is in keeping with your seemingly empty laptop drive.

I type an email along the same lines as the telephone message and expect it to bounce back, but when I check my inbox there is nothing there to tell me it failed to deliver.

As I consider what else I might do, a woman approaches the building, probably in her late eighties. She is wearing shell-pink trousers, a shell-pink blouse and a shell-pink tailored jacket, all in the same fabric and visible beneath her lavender tweed coat. She is pulling a navy-blue shopping bag on wheels. Practically every old lady I have ever seen tugs one of these bags, but our mother swears I must kill her before allowing her to own one. I hurry down to ask this woman if I can carry it up the steps for her.

When she looks at me she startles and blinks several times, as if to clear her vision. 'I'm afraid the bag is heavy.' Her skin is blanched but her voice is calm.

I lift it and see she is right. When we are both standing before the building's entrance, she takes a key card from a side pocket of the bag and waves it over an electronic pad. A light flashes green and the right-hand door pops open with a click.

'Would you like me to take your bag up to your flat for you?' I am not being a good Samaritan. I want to get into the building. But the personal safety expert part of me hopes she is smart enough to refuse.

She hesitates. For an instant, I think she really is going to invite me in. Instead she says, 'I am afraid we need to be careful not to let even charming strangers into the building. Resident Association rules.'

'That's wise.' I push the door open wider and look inside as I hold it for her.

There is an elegant carpeted foyer with a chandelier, several mock-eighteenth-century chairs, and a dark wood coffee table stacked with the sort of magazines read by people who own both town flats and country houses. The building you lived in was similarly grand.

The smell of furniture polish wafts towards me. 'Can I ask you a quick question or two?' I say.

She moves past me and stands in the doorway, blocking any further view of the interior but smiling permission.

'Have you lived here a long time?'

She is studying me as intently as I am studying her building. 'Twenty-one years. Since my husband died.'

She is lonely, this woman. She is steely and careful, but her need for talk and companionship is working against this. How hard will it be to get her to let me in?

I decide to be blunt, imagining Ted laughing at my doing so crudely what he does so smoothly. 'I'm trying to find Mr Henrickson in Flat 7. Do you know him?'

There is a flash of surprise, then calculation, that she tries to mask. 'I need to respect my neighbours' privacy.'

'I only want to know if you've seen him here lately.'

She waves a hand and shakes her head, a helpless non-committal gesture.

I write my name and number on a scrap of paper and hand it to her. 'If he comes back, will you call me? I can ring the bell to his flat and he can choose whether or not to let me in. Surely that would be okay?'

'No. It would not.' She presses the paper back into my palm.

I decide to tell her what I don't readily tell. 'My sister went missing ten years ago. This is her.' I write your name below my own, on the paper scrap, and underline it with my finger.

'I'm very sorry.'

I take out a framed photograph of you that the press never got hold of. We are sitting on our parents' living room sofa a few months before you got pregnant with

Luke. We are both holding glasses and cracking up, clinging to each other and in real danger of spilling red wine. Our faces are creased in the hysterical, unstoppable laugh that was almost always at our mother's expense, which she says she never minded from the two of us. She says she misses our conspiracies against her.

The woman looks carefully at me, then the photograph. 'She's beautiful. How very like you she is.'

I study the photograph along with her, wondering what secret plans were in your head, and already in play, even then.

She touches my arm. 'Tissue?'

'Thank you.' I take the tissue and blow my nose with an extremely unpretty noise. 'We're approaching the anniversary of her disappearance. It's always a difficult time for my family.' The near-welling with tears is not fake, but I know I could control it if I chose to. I know I am letting it happen to manipulate this woman.

And it works. 'Come inside for a few minutes.' I follow her into the foyer, sit beside her on an ivory sofa with my boots resting on the thick gold rug arranged before it. She pats my knee. 'Better?'

'Yes. You didn't tell me your name,' I say.

'I'm Mrs Buenrostro.'

'That's lovely.'

'My husband was Spanish. It means good face. Handsome face.' She smiles. 'It suited him.'

'Do you have any children?'

She spends too long considering the answer to a question that ought to be straightforward.

'No.' She gathers herself as if that word has hurt her and I wonder at the untold story here. A long period of trying for a child but never managing it? A child who died? There is something, but I do not dare press it. At last, she takes a breath. 'I don't know much about the man in Flat 7.' She fidgets with her hair, a long grey plait coiled and pinned low, just above her neck.

'Has the flat been occupied by anyone else since you've lived here?'

'No.'

'Can you describe Mr Henrickson?'

'I would say tall, dark hair. You'd probably call him handsome.' She sounds proud when she says this. She speaks of this man as if she cannot help herself, as if she knows she should not but is impelled to partake of a guilty pleasure.

'Does he ever have visitors?'

She weighs up whether to say more, but then does, again in the manner of someone who is visibly saying something she shouldn't, but cannot stop herself. 'I once saw a woman and a baby go in.'

When did this encounter turn round, so that she is the one probing for information, rather than me? When did she start watching my reactions as carefully as I have been watching hers? Has it been from the start?

'How long ago?' My voice is sharper than I mean it to be.

She shakes her head, as if perplexed.

'Could it have been ten years ago?'

'I can't be sure.' Once more she is stroking that grey coil. 'You must understand, these flats are owned by the very rich. Many of them are investment properties. People are happy to leave them empty for long periods.'

'Can you remember if the baby was a boy or a girl?'

'It was swaddled. Nothing memorably pink or blue. I approve of that. I don't hold with all that gendering by colour. Don't you agree?'

I imagine Luke's horror if I were to buy him something pink. But I say, 'I do.'

'The woman rushed past me. I do remember that, because I'd hoped to look at the baby but she clearly didn't want me to. I like babies. Do you like babies?'

'Very much.'

'Do you have one?'

'I have a nephew. My sister's son.'

'Do you have a photo of him?'

The question makes the top of my scalp tingle. 'Not with me.' My phone is filled with pictures of Luke, but I am not about to show one of them to this stranger. Am I right in my instinct that her interest in Luke goes beyond the simply polite? I say, 'Can you remember anything else about the baby? How old it was, maybe?'

'It was very small. No more than a few weeks.'

'What about the time of year? The month or season?'

'Late summer. Maybe early autumn? I remember worrying that the baby might be too hot for the weather. It was so wrapped up.'

'And the woman? Can you remember what she looked like?'

'It was barely a glimpse. I remember though that she had long dark hair, your sort of colour, but a bit longer.' She places a hand on top of mine. 'You've gone pale.'

'Can you remember what she was wearing?'

'Just that it was pretty. Like her. Something floaty, I think. Let me see your sister's photograph again.'

I hold it out. Unlike Luke's image, yours is all over the internet. 'Are you thinking that she was the woman you saw go into Flat 7?'

She peers at it, more carefully this time. She turns it to a different angle and looks some more. 'Possibly.'

I tuck the picture safely back into my bag and again offer her the paper scrap. Your name flashes at me, below my own. 'Please ring me if the man in Flat 7 comes back. Or the woman. They might help me find my sister.'

'Shouldn't the police be doing that?'

I hesitate before what I say next. 'Did they ever talk to you?'

'No.'

'Were you aware of them talking to anyone here about Mr Henrickson? Or maybe talking to him?'

'Not that I know of. But that doesn't mean they didn't. Don't you have – what is it they're called – a family liaison officer? Don't you have one of those to update you on what they've done, what they're doing?'

'The police never got anywhere and we were never assigned a family liaison officer. Not everyone is. But did you not hear of the case?'

Her mouth dips before she speaks, as if she is getting ready to tell a lie. 'No. I'm sorry.' I am still holding out the paper scrap. She takes it from me. 'I will phone you if anybody returns to Flat 7.'

'Thank you.' I have another thought. 'Is there CCTV in the building?'

'I'm afraid there isn't.'

'What about when someone rings your doorbell? I know you get a live visual of the outside landing so you can see who it is. I don't suppose those images are recorded?'

'Again no. The majority of residents value privacy over security.'

'I see.' I stand up. 'You have been so kind, Mrs Buenrostro, and generous with your time. I must leave you in peace.'

She watches me make my way to the door. I can see her through its slit of stained glass. She checks that the wood swings shut and locks before she turns away.

Thursday, 10 November

The Woman in the Chair

The first person at my morning risk assessment clinic is sitting in a cracked vinyl chair and sobbing so hard she can barely speak. Her eye is red and swollen – it will be purple in a day or two – with another large bruise below it. There is an open cut where the skin above her cheekbone split like ripe fruit upon impact.

I am holding her baby, who is screaming as I walk up and down the room to try to soothe him while his mother gets a chance to calm down. This woman makes me puzzle even harder over the things that your medical notes could not tell me. Did I miss the physical signs that someone was hurting you?

You were always lifting your dress or top to show me the progress of your bump, pressing my hand against your tummy to feel him kick, pulling my ear to your belly in the hope that I would hear his heart. You would make me inspect every inch of your body and swear under oath that you were not gaining weight anywhere besides your bump. I know I was right to lie when I said again and again that you weren't. Your skin was unblemished but for the small blossom of stretch marks that appeared at the top of your left thigh at thirty-seven weeks, making you swear against cruel fate.

I need to shake you away and concentrate on the screaming baby. I bounce him gently on my shoulder, managing at the same time to grab my unopened bottle of water and set it down near his mother. I scoot the box of tissues closer to her too. The movement makes her visibly startle.

On the floor is the woman's massive tote bag. When I cross the room to retrieve my first aid kit, my shoe bumps the bag, making the blue plastic crackle. Baby clothes and nappies spill onto the grubby carpet, which is ugly beige to match the ugly chairs and ugly walls of this furnished office whose only virtue is the cheap rent and the fact that they are willing to let me have it for just one day a week.

At last, the baby is quiet. His mother is finally quiet too. I hand him to her and when she flinches I see that her wrist is swollen.

Eye, cheek, wrist – and these are the injuries I can see. I want to photograph them. If I can't get her to go to the police herself, at least I will be able to provide them with the medical evidence for an assault investigation and potential Actual Bodily Harm charge.

She consents to the photographs in a flat voice, adjusting her body as I snap away with my camera phone, wincing in a way that makes me suspect she has been kicked or punched in the ribs. Her shallow breaths go with this, so I ask if she can concentrate on trying to breathe more evenly. The two of us inhale and exhale together for a few minutes, until she is calmer. Afterwards, she lets me clean the cut on her cheek with saline and apply wound glue to hold it together and protect it from infection.

'You're good at that,' the woman says.

'My sister was a nurse.'

Was. As ever, I hear our mother's quiet fury.

I activate an ice pack with a snap, wrap it in a cloth, and ask the woman to hold it against her eye, which she does with a zombie's indifference.

Were you in this kind of trouble? Was I too young then to see, not yet doing the work that your vanishing turned me to? Wouldn't Mum and Dad have noticed? As an orthopaedic nurse, you knew too much about the signs of abuse. You had seen too many bones broken accidentally-on-purpose.

I decide to confide something personal, in the hope she will be more comfortable with me. And because talking about you is something I like to do. 'Our father had prostate cancer,' I say. 'That's why my sister wanted to be a nurse.'

This is your official story of why you came to do what you did, and one that I have always, at least partly, been puzzled by. For the first time, I envision other motives for your choice of a life as Florence Nightingale. Not just because you wanted to help people like Dad. But because it was part of your disguise. Part of what made people trust you. Made them let you in.

More than anything, it brought you into contact with all kinds of different men. Rich doctors you could assist in their heroic orthopaedic efforts. Male patients with manly sports injuries for whom you could perform your beautiful angel routine. You knew what you were doing when you chose a job in the private sector – where there is plenty of money and the work is not quite so punishing.

'Is she still a nurse?' The woman is more alert than I first thought.

'Not any more, no.' This is where any talk of you must stop. 'Do you feel able to tell me what happened?' My voice is very soft.

As I expect, she is at last fleeing from domestic abuse – a story I have heard more times than I would wish. This is why I have a lone worker safety device built into my wristwatch, with GPS tracking and an SOS button wired straight to the provider's emergency centre. I always activate and wear it when I'm working. If her husband follows her here, there are measures I can take to protect us both.

With her consent, I begin making phone calls and arrangements. 'There are so many of us out here, wanting to help you. Wanting to make sure you don't slip through the net. There are so many places you can turn. You only have to ask.'

'I said no police.'

'The police are starting to make domestic violence a priority. They have had a lot of criticism, so they are really trying to respond to that.' Ted would faint if he heard me saying this.

'He'll take my baby away if I leave him. He says I'm not a fit mother. The police will see that. They'll see I'm mentally unstable and depressed – I've had pills before. They'll see I can't support a child by myself.'

'Depression can be situational.' My voice is so calm I am amazed to hear it, as if it belongs to somebody else. 'Depression doesn't make you an unfit parent.' I need to be neutral, but I worry that you will make me mess this up badly. Because neutral is the last thing I am. 'Have you considered that if the police have his violence on record, then it will help your legal position?'

'They already have a voicemail. I went to my mum's last year and he said he knew where I was and he was going to do me in. But I withdrew my statement that it was his voice and number on the recording. I think the police were angry, because it meant they couldn't prosecute him. And because I went back to him.'

'Why?'

'I still loved him. He was drunk when he left that voicemail. He didn't mean it.' She veers to another thought. 'The house is in his name. He said if I leave again he'll take the house and take the baby.'

'You have rights too. There are some excellent helplines where you can get free legal advice. I've written a couple of them down for you.' I put my hand on top of hers and squeeze, then wrap her fingers round the paper. 'I'll book a taxi for you. I'll arrange for the driver to take you to the doctor's. You need more medical attention than I can give. When you're finished there, the taxi will get you to the shelter.'

She looks at the baby, asleep at last across her lap. Tears roll down her cheeks and plop onto his tummy. When the paper slips from her hand I pick it up and reach over and drop it into her big crinkly bag. She watches me do this. I hope this is a symptom of canny self-preservation, the hidden resilience of the secret street fighter in all of us. She shifts her eyes to her feet. 'You must think I'm pathetic.'

'What I think is that you are amazingly brave and strong to come here. You were clever to get out as soon as he left for work this morning, in the biggest window you had. Your son is lucky to have a mother who loves him so much.'

She shakes her head in denial that this could be true. 'I don't have any money for the taxi. He doesn't let me have money of my own.'

'The charity will pay for that. I'll give the driver cash in advance.'

I type a text to order the taxi. She grabs my hand just after I hit Send.

'No,' she says. 'Cancel it.'

'Why?'

'I can't. I can't do this to him. It's not all his fault.'

'Sitting where I am, it's difficult to see that.'

'But I provoke him.'

I can't stop pushing her. 'What was different about what he did to you this morning? There must have been something to make you take action.'

There is a clicking noise, deep in her throat. 'It was in front of the baby. That's never happened before.'

My face is hot. 'You came to me for my assessment of your risk. My assessment is that you are at considerable risk and you need to get safe. Now. Your baby is at risk too.'

'He has so much on his mind, trying to make a living for us. I make too many demands.'

My heart is beating faster.

'What about the injury to your wrist? And your eye and your cheek? There is no possible way to justify those. If he was happy to leave visible evidence of violence on your face I think it's highly likely there are bruises beneath your clothes. He punched you in the upper body, too, didn't he? Am I right?'

'He might kill himself if he comes home and finds us gone. I can't leave.'

The heat on my skin and the speed of my heart are signs that I should keep quiet. Signs that you have finally blown away my ability to do the job you carved for me. But I cannot stop myself. I am looking at her baby and thinking of your son.

Thinking of what it means for a baby to lose his mother. Remembering what it means in the flesh.

Walking up and down with Luke. Bouncing him. Singing to him. Trying to get him to drink from the new bottle he hated. Buying up teats in every size and shape and material ever made. Taking him into bed with me. Hours and hours of being useless as he screamed all night and every night after you were gone. Driving around at three a.m. to try to lull him to sleep. So tired myself I wasn't safe behind the wheel.

A friend of Ted's pulled me over for careless driving during one of those aimless journeys. Who was crying louder, then? Me or Luke?

'I promise if you don't write that ticket I will go straight

163

home and never do this again. I swear it. I'll take an advanced driving course, too.' How did I manage to get those words out? How did he even understand me through the sobs?

He didn't write the ticket. He followed me back to our parents' house and watched me carry your baby inside. All Luke wanted was your smell, your milk, your voice. Your way of holding him. The two of us fell into an exhausted sleep, Luke on my chest, both of us hot and flushed and sticky, our cheeks stained with tears.

Ted's policeman friend reported it all to him, and Ted was there early the next morning to check on us. What room could there have been for Ted in all of that? Always understanding. Always agreeing that Luke was what mattered most.

'You're doing what she would want. You're doing everything you can.' That is what Ted said, again and again. At least at first. Before the fights started. Over you. Always over you. Still over you. No wonder he is moving on to Ruby. My message to him hasn't changed. You and Luke are first, last and always.

Even as the words shoot out at this woman I know they are the wrong ones and I shouldn't say them. 'That's fine. You go home. Next time I come across your name it will be because you've been murdered or you've gone missing.'

Her mouth drops open into a perfect O, then shuts again like a fish's.

I am about to say I'm sorry. I am about to say I shouldn't have said what I did.

But she speaks first. 'You're right,' she says. 'I actually hate him. Hate him.'

So I remain silent and decide to forgive myself for saying the wrong things and not being perfect. You used to tell me that it was okay not to be perfect. You used to say that perfection was terrible. You used to say that you were not perfect and I must always forgive you for it.

My phone buzzes with a text announcing the arrival of the taxi. I look out of the grimy window and see the driver next to his car.

When the woman and I stand up I take in the sack-like floral dress she is wearing. There are holes in the thin fabric and it is faded from being laundered too many times. She is shivering with cold – she doesn't have a coat. I drape my own over her back, the two of us juggling the baby as I help her to fit each arm into a sleeve. I heave up her huge bag, which contains only baby things. 'They'll provide you with what you need at the shelter,' I say before I open the door and lead her into the corridor. She is limping. He must have done something to her leg or hip, too.

Most of the people who come to my risk assessment clinic are women. But this morning there is a familiar-looking man sitting outside the office, on one of the stained, cloth-covered chairs. He has the discretion to look intently at his telephone screen when the battered woman passes him.

I guide her into the grey rain and the grey air beneath the grey sky and settle her in the back of the grey taxi with her son in her arms. She holds out a hand. For a split second I imagine that her hand is grey too. I squeeze the hand, which is not grey after all, but is reddened and coarse and flaky with dry skin. I lean into the taxi and put my arms around her, then kiss the top of the baby's head, a mix of silk and cradle cap.

I press banknotes into the driver's hand – he and I have been through this routine many times before – and let him shut her in. I stand on the pavement, not caring that I am getting soaked as I watch the woman bend her face over her baby. I do not move until the car turns the corner and glides out of my sight.

The Man in the Corridor

When I re-enter the building, the man in the corridor stands and says hello, greeting me by name and putting out his hand.

Other than his hair, there is nothing grey about Adam Holderness. His jumper is black and his jeans are black. His eyes are black too. His skin is pale, like mine, but there is a shadow of dark stubble wanting to break through.

You used to call me Snow White. Though I could have said the same of you. *As white as snow, and as red as blood, and her hair was as black as ebony.*

This man could be Snow White's male counterpart. Though it strikes me that gentleman vampire is a better description. While Ted is sturdy and muscled from weightlifting in the police gym and weekend rugby whenever he can, Adam Holderness is an inch taller and a stone lighter but looks equally strong beneath his expensive clothes. I wonder if there will ever be a man I don't compare to Ted.

I am struck again by the thought that Adam Holderness really is the kind of man you liked. I feel a clutch low in my stomach and I cannot decide if it is excitement or fear. Perhaps it is both.

I am still holding the main door open. 'It's nice to see you again,' I say. I manage to stick out an awkward hand to shake his briefly. The rain is growing so heavy it is slanting in and hitting me. 'I'm running my walk-in clinic this morning.' I look outside, as if to suggest that that is where he should go.

But he doesn't. 'That's why I'm here.'

I remind myself that anybody can be a victim, or love somebody who has been one, or feel that they are at risk. So I say, as carefully as I can, 'Do you need my help?'

'Not personally. I'm here for professional reasons. Can I come into your office to talk to you?' He moves his head slightly, taking in the empty corridor. 'If there were anyone else here, I'd let them go first. I won't take much of your time.' It is a bedside manner. Friendly courtesy but with confident firmness behind it. 'You're getting wet, Ella.' He sounds sincerely concerned. More of that extremely practised courtesy.

I let the main door fall closed and motion him to follow me into the office, gesturing for him to take the chair so recently vacated by the mother and her baby.

He says, 'I'd like to support the work you're doing.'

'How did you know I'd be here this morning, Mr Holderness?' Again I fail in my attempt to impose formality with his title and surname. I end up sounding like a woman whispering to her lover in bed, playing at a distance that is patently not there.

'You talked about the charity.' He says this mildly and I begin to see that he is imperturbable. I must look puzzled, because he adds, 'At Brian's party.'

'Oh yes – I'd forgotten.'

'I rang the number on the website a couple of times but it kept going to voicemail.'

I don't explain that we almost never answer that number. Our mother picks up the messages as soon as she can, though she occasionally diverts them to my phone.

He goes on. 'I thought coming here would be easier than leaving a message.'

'Isn't coming here a lot more trouble than speaking for a few seconds into a recording?'

'I wanted to see you.' He pauses. 'Sadie and Brian told me about your sister.'

He says this with such neutrality I cannot infer what tone Sadie used to speak about me, and what defamation of my character she almost certainly unleashed. She has moved so irrevocably from friend to enemy. Our mother was right – when I am done I am done. Just like you.

'As soon as they mentioned your sister's case, I realised I'd heard of it.'

'Most people have.' I had guessed that Sadie and Brian told him, but I still have to adjust to knowing that he knows, something that gets easier but never feels normal. I sit back and cross my legs. 'When did you last talk to Sadie?'

'I dropped by on Sunday to see Brian.' He is squinting at me. A slight squint, but a squint nonetheless, as if he thinks he will be able to see inside my head and into my brain if he only looks hard enough. 'He wasn't there but Sadie was.'

'Oh,' I say.

'You don't know, do you?'

I lift my shoulders, puzzled.

'He'd put her things outside and changed the locks. He tried to end it gently, but it seems that gentle doesn't work with Sadie. He thinks she's crazy – his word, not mine – and she managed to hide it until she moved in with him. She was packing her car when I turned up.'

I realise that I now have even more reason to look out for a Sadie hurricane blowing my way.

'Is that why you came here? To warn me about her?' I think of the email from 'Justice Administrator'. It seems likely that Brian's rejection has pushed her over the edge.

'Her rage is . . . How to put it politely? Disturbing. You seem to be the target.'

'Did she mention where she was going?'

'To her mother's, she said.'

'Then that's a neighbourhood I will avoid.'

'I was concerned. But I can see that you have enough expertise to manage someone like Sadie.' He thinks for a few seconds. 'Why do you do what you do?'

Your disappearance changed everything. Our mother and Ted are right to say it changed me. But I give Adam Holderness the public script. The one he will already have read on the website. 'There are lots of support services in London. But there's nothing hands-on in smaller cities like Bath for people who need help. Not unless they can pay huge sums of money for advice and protection.'

'It says on the website that you run a support group for families of victims. I'd like to come along to help.' He pulls out his wallet and extracts a laminated card, a photo ID with his name and title. 'In case you're worried that I'm not who I say I am.'

It is an expressionless photograph, mouth straight, eyes serious, hair shorter and even more extremely military than it is now. I know from the internet searches I did after Sadie's party that he is ex-army. I found a photo online, taken fifteen years ago, during his final few months as a medical officer in Iraq. It is certainly him, but different. His pale, pale skin is actually tanned. And his hair is still pure black.

Did something happen, some stress event, to change it overnight? I know he left the army to become a civilian doctor after his minimum four-year commitment. I know he worked in the psychiatric unit of the same private hospital you worked at, though you were over in Orthopaedics.

I decide I have nothing to lose by asking blunt questions. 'Did you know my sister?' I want to catch him off guard, though my voice is casual.

But he is as smooth as ever. 'I can see you have good reason to be wary of everyone you meet.' He looks right into my eyes. 'Even when you actually like them.'

'True,' I say, not making it clear which of the two points I am ratifying.

'Do you suspect every man you meet of your sister's disappearance?'

'Pretty much.'

'If I had anything to do with that, do you think I'd come here and make myself known to you?'

'That's the sort of thing people like that do. You should know that in your line of work.'

'Only in films and novels. Not in real life.'

I remember Ted saying something like that to me about Thorne. 'I think you and my sister worked at the same hospital.'

'Not in the same area of medicine.' He speaks as if he is disappointed that he cannot provide me with stronger evidence of a connection between the two of you. 'There are scores of people who work in the same place but don't know each other.'

'I wondered if there was anywhere else she could have run into you?'

'Not unless she spent time in Iraqi field hospitals.'

I consider the types of things this man would have learned in officer training. Leadership. Weapons handling. Knots. Survival. And much more than this in conflict zones. All transferable skills. He would know how to hide, how to spy, how not to leave traces. Probably even how to make someone vanish.

'Where do you live?' I am thinking of the countryside that surrounds the winding lane where you made your last known journey.

My questions and changes of tack don't ruffle him. 'Near Brian,' he says. 'A lot of doctors own houses in those villages.' Is he over-explaining? He says, 'I think I saw you talking to Jonathan Blossom, didn't I?'

'Yes,' I say.

'John lives around there too. So does Brian's brother.' There is a glint in his eye with this last one. 'You'd be welcome to visit me.'

The photograph of Ted and Ruby was emailed via the charity's contact page, and Adam has just told me that he used the charity website to find me. 'Can you remember what you were doing on Friday of last week?'

He gives me a confused but tolerant smile. 'Only because I was in the hospital so much I barely saw any natural light. Why do you ask?'

If this is the truth, he could not have taken that picture. I tell a calculated fib. 'I thought perhaps I glimpsed you in a café that day.'

'That wouldn't have been possible,' he says, 'but I'd have liked bumping into you.' There is no tell. There is no sign. There is nothing to signal that he is lying.

I consider Ted's contempt for psychiatrists. He thinks they thwart justice when they advise judges that murderers and predators are not fit to stand trial. He is disgusted by their hospitals for criminals, which he regards as hotels. Ted would not love Adam Holderness.

I realise I am still holding his identification card. I hand it back to him, then try to say the passionate words I am about to utter in the most dispassionate tone I can. 'Given the fact that you spend most of your time trying to help the men who hurt their loved ones, why would my support group want anything to do with you?'

'Insight.'

'Are you willing to give me any insight into Jason Thorne?'

His voice is very gentle when he says, 'I think you know I can't discuss patients with you. At least let me help where I can. Let me help with your group.'

'Perhaps.'

'If a single one of them reaches a new level of understanding, isn't that worth it? What you do and what I do are on a continuum. We're closer than you allow. I already made an online donation.' He looks almost tired after he finishes this speech, and a little embarrassed that he isn't above telling me he has given money. But it is the kind of abashed demeanour that extremely well-bred people deploy when they have been complimented for an exceptional achievement.

It occurs to me that he is used to people trying to persuade him. Trying to convince him they are not dangerous. Trying to explain that their actions were justifiable. Trying to persuade him not to medicate them, not to take away their privileges. Trying above all to argue that he should let them out. Perhaps it is even the reverse sometimes, and they try to persuade him to keep them in, seeing the locked ward as preferable to a real prison.

Whatever the case, it is not supposed to be this way round, with him trying to sell himself. This powerful man who works hard to appear gentle and kind but also strong and reasonable. He is in charge of some of the most dangerous human beings alive. Thorne is only one of many.

There is the creak of the outer door to the building opening and shutting, then a sigh and a rustle in the corridor. He stands. 'Full disclosure. If you're wondering whether I came here because I'm interested in you or in your charity, the answer is both.'

My face is warm. It has been ten years, I tell myself. Ten years since Ted and I were together. Ten years since you were taken. Ten years since I have been to bed with anybody, which is a mortifying thing to admit even if it is just to myself. I am thirty years old and I have only ever slept with my childhood sweetheart. And now Ted is moving on and will probably cut me off and I am not sure I can endure it again. It isn't criminal to be pleased that this handsome, intelligent man likes me. Is it?

The kind of man you liked likes me. And I like him too. This silent admission pinches my chest.

'Incidentally,' he says, 'there's something on your shoulder.'

I look down at a splodge of what appears to be congealed cream. I know from my experience with Luke that it is baby sick. He passes me the box of tissues and I do my best to wipe it off. Then I cross the room to the door and open it wide. Neither of us says another word.

I wait until he exits the building, then turn to the two people who arrived while he and I were speaking. There is a slim woman in a professional navy skirt and white blouse in one of the chairs. Beside her is a man, but his face is entirely hidden by the open newspaper he holds in front of it. Only his long, suited legs and expensive leather shoes are visible.

I ask if they can please bear with me for a few minutes. The woman gives me a stiff nod. The man does not lower the paper.

'Sir?' I say. 'Is that okay?'

He puts the paper on his lap. Dark hair slicked back. Serious mouth. A nose that looks as if it was broken sometime in his past, and stops his face from being perfect, which is a good thing. Designer stubble that

175

would actually be a beard if it were a millimetre or two longer. Black shirt beneath his jacket. No tie.

'No problem,' he says. His brown eyes hold mine.

I vanish into the office to check the charity bank account. Adam Holderness's donation is at the top of the transaction list: £100. Generous but not excessive. Like him, somehow.

I return to the corridor to beckon in the waiting woman, only to find that two more have appeared in the chairs either side of her. But the man with the newspaper is gone.

As the woman settles herself where Adam Holderness was sitting only five minutes ago, I glance once more out of the smudged window and I am surprised by what I see. A thing that somehow doesn't belong in this room, in this month. It is only a tiny ray, but it is really there. Sun.

The Letters

I am in Luke's room, at the end of a long and challenging day. What draws me here is you. Tomorrow, the people who most love you will gather together to comfort each other and think of you. You'd never have deliberately left us to this. Would you?

I sit at the edge of Luke's bed and stare at our doll's house, puzzling over hidden messages. You and I never tired of playing with the doll's house together, despite the ten-year age gap. Or at least that is what I thought until recently, when Mum admitted that she used to bribe you with 'babysitting' money to entertain me.

My phone is on the bed, sinking into Luke's blue-striped quilt. It pings to alert me that a voicemail has been left on the charity helpline. I think of Sadie, whipped into a fury that she will want to blame me for, and feel a sick pang that it may be her, trying to trick herself through to me by using the charity number instead of my own.

But the message is not from Sadie. It is from a journalist, who wonders if this charity is indeed run by

Miranda Brooke's family, and if the Ella Brooke from the recent newspaper article is actually Miranda's sister, and if so, would she like to meet with him for an interview to mark the decade since Miranda's disappearance.

It occurs to me that this man may not be a journalist at all. He may be someone connected with you, trying to get hold of me but not wanting to disclose his real identity. Maybe in response to the messages I have been firing off, or my visit to Mrs Buenrostro. I wanted to be a catalyst. Perhaps I really have become one.

I close the voicemail screen and open my personal email. I am so distracted by my murderous thoughts towards the journalist that I have to look once, twice, three times, before I properly take in the two messages sitting at the top of my inbox.

Like most longed-for letters, these arrived when I stopped checking for them. What confuses me at first is that both of them are from hospitals. It takes me a few seconds to grasp that they are two different institutions. One email is a response from the hospital where you had your amniocentesis and gave birth to Luke. The other is from the psychiatric hospital where Jason Thorne is imprisoned.

It is easy to choose which one to read first. The letter about Thorne will be a yes or no to my request to visit him. It will require no complex analysis from me. So this is where I begin. My heart beats faster as the message pops open and I squeeze my eyes shut for a few seconds, too nervous to look at it.

I am not certain if I am more frightened of the prospect of coming face-to-face with Thorne, or the possibility that I will not be allowed to. The latter is more likely, given what Ted said about Thorne's refusal to grant the wishes of those who want to come and gawp at a human monster.

I make myself look. The letter is short and to the point. Jason Thorne has accepted my request to see him. I inhale, several jagged breaths.

There is an attachment that I need to print off and bring with me. They have scheduled an appointment for the afternoon of Tuesday, 15 November, in just five days. Seven hours have passed since Adam Holderness's visit this morning. The timing of this message is unlikely to be an accident. He couldn't discuss Thorne, but he must have at least done this for me.

I do a quick reconnaissance of the other attachment Thorne's keepers have tagged to the email. Pages and pages of rules and regulations and instructions. I close the message and open the one from the hospital where you had your obstetric care.

The body of the email contains only one sentence. *Please see attached letter.* I immediately tap on the small grey box and watch it bloom into a document. I read it over and over again, squinting at the tiny type, as if by doing so I will somehow discover a coded secret hidden inside these clinical words.

Dear Miss Brooke,
Thank you for your request for access to the medical records pertaining to your sister MIRANDA CHARLOTTE BROOKE. Your application to view the results of her amniocentesis test was considered by the undersigned.

There are a number of grounds upon which information should not be disclosed. Your request is being denied in accordance with the following exemption[s]:

- *the information you have asked for relates to a third party who has not given consent to disclosure (where that third party is not a health professional who has cared for the patient).*

We take our duty to safeguard the confidentiality and security of personal information extremely seriously. We regret that we are unable to assist you on this occasion.

Yours sincerely,

Miss M. J. Atworth

Medical Records Officer and Data Controller

I put the phone on Luke's bedside table, my heart beating faster.

There is a message here and Miss M. J. Atworth has not made any attempt to hide it. Miss M. J. Atworth's regret is not appropriate, because she has, in fact, *assisted me on this occasion.*

The information you have asked for relates to a third party who has not given consent to disclosure.

First, I make myself run through an obvious point. The third party cannot be Luke. Luke's identity is already known. And in legal terms, sixteen weeks into the pregnancy, he was regarded as part of you. He was not a third party.

Even without seeing your medical records, I now understand. You must have been desperate, given how paranoid you were about anything that could cause miscarriage. You would have been terrified of the risk to the foetus from that needle. But there was no other way to do a paternity test.

The hospital would have required the DNA of one of the two possible fathers so they could compare it with your unborn baby's. Whoever's DNA it was, he would have needed to consent to their testing it, though not to their revealing his identity. This means at least one of those men knew about the test, and the result.

I am guessing it was the man you didn't want. You would have been horrified by the prospect of the man you loved discovering you'd slept with someone else. You would not have wanted him to know that the paternity could be in doubt. Either of these men could have hurt you in the wake of his jealousy and anger.

How did you hide all of this from me? I am imagining your panic, feeling in my own bones what it must have been like to live with this secret for so many months. I see now why you didn't tell us about the pregnancy until you were twenty weeks, once the genetic tests gave you the answer you'd been praying for.

If the answer had been otherwise, I think you would have ended the pregnancy. You'd had months to steel yourself to do this. You would have been prepared to add another secret to your collection.

It occurs to me that you could have had an early abortion, then tried again with the man whose baby you wanted, in circumstances where there would be no doubt. But you didn't. Was this because the opportunities to become pregnant by him were limited? *M + N + ??* I think you couldn't bear to lose the child if there was even a slim chance of his belonging to the man you loved. And you wanted to give the baby every chance.

You talked so often about finding your true love, and that is what Luke's father must have been to you. So why did you sleep with someone else? This question makes my stomach drop – perhaps you didn't want to and he made you.

There is another question, too, a more obvious one. Why on earth didn't you let us meet the man who must have been your life's great passion? Surely you were bursting to introduce him to your family? But every question I answer only breeds countless more that I cannot.

Friday, 11 November

The Anniversary

I stand at my bedroom window, squinting out at the sodden graveyard as the light fades. I replay what I was doing the day you vanished, trying to map my every minute against yours. Will I notice something new, something important that I have forgotten, if I continue to go over it? Does the man who took you do this too?

Exactly ten years ago, when I was twenty and in the final year of my undergraduate degree in Biology, you dropped your ten-week-old son off with our mother. It was a Friday morning. It was 8.30 a.m. It was *that morning.*

You and Luke should have been visiting me, making a long weekend of it. You were going to stay in an extremely grand seafront hotel near my student room. It was to be your first real trip with Luke. But a few days earlier, I'd phoned to put you off. All because Ted discovered he could be with me that weekend.

. . .

'So your boyfriend's more important than your sister and nephew?' you said.

And I lied. I said it wasn't Ted, that I was behind with coursework, that I had to work day and night to catch up or they would kick me out of university.

'So Ted won't be coming to stay with you in Brighton then?'

'No.'

'Don't kid a kidder, Melanie. Lie to anybody but never to me. I am the one person who will always know.'

I hardly ever lie. I don't know why I did then. 'I'm not lying,' I said, which was a big lie.

'Just tell the truth. It's me you're talking to.'

'I know that.'

'I know what it's like to love someone and not be able to see them anything like as much as you want to. I'll understand. But fess up now. I hate you lying to me.'

I learned then what you already knew well. That once you lie, it is hard to admit you have done it and even harder to dig your way out. Instead, I used a Miranda technique right back at you. 'I can't believe you don't believe me.'

'Good one. Taught by a master. But remember this. Whatever mistakes I make, I never choose *anybody* over my family. And I never choose *anybody* over you.'

'Really?'

'When the coin drops, it always comes up with your face on top.'

'Miranda—'

'Don't lie about men. Don't ever do that. I promise it's not worth it.'

I thought of something our mother once said. *If you lie, make it simple or you will catch yourself out. You will forget what you said.* But I deteriorated, in the grip of my lie. 'I'm not—'

'Ted's not worth it. You're way too good for him and I haven't got time for this crap, Melanie.'

'Please—'

'The baby's crying.'

'Let me explain—'

'I can't do this.' And the phone slammed down on the last thing you ever said to me. Our last conversation and one of the worst we ever had.

Never say goodbye in anger. Our mother cautioned us about this over and over again. My last memory of you is that you were furious with me. And I will never stop being furious with myself. I chose Ted over you and Luke. If I hadn't done that, everything would have been different.

That morning – the two words creep in again and again – you parked your metallic black BMW in our parents' driveway and carried Luke into the house.

A-List Tastes of Missing Nurse.

This is one of the few headlines that actually had a ring of truth. How did you afford that shiny new BMW on your nurse's salary? We asked you this. Of course we did. But I never believed anything you ever said on the subject of money and even Dad used to joke that you were never to be given the keys to the family vault.

You just said the car was 'baby friendly' and they'd

offered you an 'amazing deal' because they could see that someone like you would bring them extra customers because anyone who saw you driving that car would have to have one too.

Nobody could argue with you when you talked like this, especially when your lies were at their most preposterous. Our mother didn't dare. Was it because she feared your huffing away forever if the charade was exposed? Or that you would fall apart? Then again, there is a chance you were actually telling the truth. If anybody could charm a salesman into giving them a luxury car at a preposterously huge discount, it is you. But whenever our father uttered even the tiniest sceptical question our mother would shut him up and you would happily pretend he hadn't spoken.

Is this why he went behind Mum's back to ask the police to return your things? Knowing that I wouldn't let it rest? That I would do the work for him, so he could have a peaceful time with Mum?

The police asked about your finances, after learning you paid cash for the car, but we didn't have a reasonable answer. The new practices to stamp out money laundering were not in place ten years ago. It was easier to spend large amounts of cash, then, and to deposit them, completely without trace. The police were intensely curious about your money at first. But all at once, they seemed to lose interest. I wonder now if they did discover something, but deliberately let it go.

That morning, our mother held Luke up to the living room window and waved his little baby hand as you walked back to your shiny car. Your leaving Luke with Mum was a last-minute thing. You rang her the night before to arrange it. You didn't, of course, tell her where you were going. And she, of course, did not dare to ask.

As I stare out at the graveyard and try to reconstruct your last known movements, I think again of the advice leaflets I read when you vanished.

When someone goes missing, make a note of the clothing they were wearing when they were last seen.

You were wearing a smoky blue shirt dress that fell to just above your knees.

'Was she wearing a poppy?' the police asked.

'No.' Our mother was anxious that they disapproved of your lack of patriotism, fearing that they wouldn't try as hard to find you if they didn't like you.

The dress was silky, bought with cash the afternoon before you vanished. The salesgirl remembers that you took the dress in both the colours it came in without even trying it on.

I picture the covered buttons, torn from the front of the dress as the man who stole you ripped it away. I imagine the tie. Around your wrists instead of your waist. Around your throat. I try not to give credence to the rumours about what Jason Thorne did. I fail at this.

The second dress was brown, a colour you seldom wear, and still hanging with its tags dangling in your wardrobe. Above it was a shelf on which you stored a handful of designer bags, costing tens of thousands of pounds. Below it were several pairs of film-star worthy shoes. There is no record of your ever having bought these things. It seems likely they were gifts from Luke's father.

You left these glitzy objects to me. Three years ago, when you were declared dead, I had the bags auctioned and donated the funds to the charity. The Birkin bag was made of teal-coloured crocodile skin and I could hardly bear to touch it, though I made myself examine it as I did with each and every thing, in case you'd hidden a note in a pocket or sewn a secret into a lining.

'Where did you get that?' I would occasionally ask you, which also meant *How* did you get that. The answer would always begin with the words 'You wouldn't believe what happened . . . ' and a laugh, then the phrase 'Long story short . . . ' though the story would always be the complete opposite of short. You would invariably recount a series of events so complex and strange I could barely remember the beginning by the time you reached the end.

'You're making that silly smirk face,' I'd say. 'It's your lying face. I know you're lying. You always make that ridiculous fish mouth when you lie.'

You would laugh, and give it away even more. 'You need to teach me to lie, Melanie,' you'd say. 'You're the best liar I ever met. To everybody but me.' Then you'd say, 'You'd never bust me, would you? You'd never tell if you caught me in a lie?'

That morning, you were wearing a platinum locket on a platinum chain around your neck. You always wore that locket, with my photograph on one side and Luke's on the other. You gave me one exactly like it. Even our mother frowned to consider what they must have cost. In mine, it is your photograph that accompanies Luke's. I never take it off. The locket's existence is something the police withheld from the public.

Because there is no physical evidence that someone took you, the police have told us that we need to allow for the possibility that you chose to die on your own somewhere or that you ran off with a rich lover.

When someone goes missing, follow your intuition.

My intuition is that there is no way you were depressed. You didn't do depression. You would never have killed yourself. You never would have left Luke. Not even for a fortune. He is the only thing you would have passed over a fortune for.

But I hear Ted's voice again, which seems to be on a loop these days. *Are you sure about that? Are you sure you really knew her?*

My answer to both questions, the single word a hiss, is *Yes.*

I fear that whoever stole you kept you for a time. Jason Thorne did that to the women he took.

What must it have been like for you as your breasts filled, reminding you how badly Luke needed you? You might have got a fever, unable to release the milk. You'd already had a course of antibiotics for mastitis, only finishing it a few days before you disappeared. The mastitis could have recurred. Your disappearance meant you missed a doctor's appointment you'd set up for late that afternoon.

Is it any wonder the blood froze in my body? I can hear Dr Blossom, giving me my diagnosis as if he were reading poetry. *Temporary alteration of the function of the hypothalamus. Stress-induced Amenorrhea.*

Although 'temporary' has stretched to ten years, Dr Blossom tells me cheerfully that it is not premature menopause. He says that my ovarian reserve is normal for my age, and not diminished. However many eggs I may have, they sit there, undeveloped and going nowhere. Month after month after month.

Ted wants children. He wants lots of children to make up for the loneliness of growing up with just his mother, a woman he always seemed to want to keep as far away from me as he could. I used to tease him that he only loved me for my father, but I was right to perceive how much Dad means to him.

Ted used to say we would have at least a dozen children because we wouldn't be able to keep our hands off each other. How could I have tied him to me, when his great wish was for a huge family?

That is probably why he has given up on me so quickly, so readily falling back into our old fighting ways. Despite a brief renewal of his fantasies about me, he wants a woman he can have a child of his own with. It is all too easy for him to repeat the same old grievance that I am too obsessed with finding you.

Stop living with the dead, he once said. And like our mother I shot back, *Don't you call her dead.*

How can the life-making part of you not turn to ice when you are imagining the worst possible things happening to someone you love?

Whatever diagnosis Dr Blossom makes, I think something inside my body froze in the face of the pictures I was living with during the first few years of your absence. The pictures were like a slideshow. It made no difference whether my eyes were open or closed, however hard I tried to turn from them.

When Ted and I woke up late on your last morning, we took a bath together in a huge old iron tub, soaping each other's bodies, laughing. Afterwards, Ted planted tiny kisses all over my chest. He trailed a finger over my shoulder and down my arm.

When someone goes missing, do not delay in searching.

By 2 p.m. you were an hour late to collect Luke. You were not famous for punctuality but where Luke was concerned you were uncharacteristically dependable. Especially when your breasts were filling with milk for his next feed.

When someone goes missing, contact friends and family to see if they are aware of the person's whereabouts.

The calls to you and me that our parents started making at 3 p.m. went nowhere. Your battery was already out of charge and my phone was off.

Our parents had a major crisis on their hands – you were missing. And a minor crisis too – your son was starving. The emergency breast milk you'd stored in their freezer defrosted perfectly but there was a flaw in the plan. After three hours of nonstop crying, they couldn't persuade Luke to drink it from a bottle.

At 5 p.m. there was a knock on the door of my basement room. I later learned it was someone from the housing office. They were trying to find me at the request of our parents, who were hoping that I knew where you were.

As the knocking continued, Ted and I pulled the covers over our heads and ignored whoever it was until they went away.

When someone goes missing, it is never too soon to tell the police, especially if the disappearance is out of character.

At 6 p.m. our parents alerted the police.

When someone goes missing, do not panic.

At 8 p.m. your car was found.

When someone goes missing, do not blame yourself.

At 10 p.m. there were more knocks on the door. Ted put his hand over my mouth to stop the noise of my laughing as he tickled me. Then there was my name, repeated several times in the kind of stern male voice Ted uses when he is working and has to deliver bad news, and an announcement that this was the police, and the knock became an incessant pounding that wouldn't stop, and Ted and I pulled apart and everything went into slow motion as he wrapped a towel around his hips and went to answer the door and we learned that we were living *that day*.

I was sure – I am still sure – that an evil magician made you disappear. I spend my life imagining the tricks he used, and trying to stop other people falling for them, and figuring out how I can fight them, if my own time ever comes.

The light is almost gone. I must leave soon if I am not to be late for the dinnertime start of my weekend with Mum and Dad and Luke, but I can't make myself move.

I am playing shadow tricks with myself as I peer out of my bedroom window.

If I am quick enough, I will catch sight of you in the graveyard, raven-haired and pale-faced as Giselle's ghost, flitting between the broken stones. You are searching for me, as you did when I was a little girl. You seeking me. It seems an impossibility that that was how it used to be.

Something makes me freeze. A man, dressed all in black, presses himself against a small tomb the size and shape of a gingerbread house, then disappears behind it.

I consider rushing outside to search. Your cries are ringing in my ears. *Don't you dare.* What stops me, though, is the futility of the chase, rather than the danger. He would be gone before I could get there. And it is already too dark to see.

I imagine what Ted would say. *Just someone on a walk. Nothing to do with you.* But I cannot shake the feeling that that man was everything to do with me, and he deliberately positioned himself with a perfect view of my bedroom window.

Never ignore your instincts. This is one of the precepts that I drum into the women who come to my self-defence class. I am not about to discount my own advice. There is no need to catch him now. If my instincts are right, he will be back.

Saturday, 12 November

Yellow Roses

I am traipsing after Luke through the woods, chattering and smiling, though my head is pounding from all the wine I got through last night.

After Luke went to bed, I sat in your little wooden chair by the side of the fireplace as if I were keeping it warm for you. I fiddled with the yellow roses I'd brought for Mum because they are your favourite. They were arranged within my reach, on a low table.

I tried not to see it as a curse when I pricked my finger. I tried not to regard it as a bad omen that the roses were drying out so quickly and browning at the edges of the petals. I so wished they would stop dropping off. But despite the sachet of liquid nutrients I'd tipped into the vase, the petals seemed to be falling even faster. And though I tinkered and tinkered, I couldn't get the roses to stay in a pleasing shape. One would always tilt away, leaving a gap.

You didn't know when you fell in love with yellow

roses that yellow is the colour of the missing. You didn't imagine that yellow was to become your colour. Most families of the missing tie yellow ribbons to trees or fences. We do that too, but we also fill the house with yellow roses.

So I played with your roses and sucked on my bleeding finger and poured glass after glass of wine, trying to drive out all thoughts of Jason Thorne and the roses he supposedly prefers. But all I could do was count down the hours to my seeing him. Mum frowned at the drinking and the obvious cause. Her frown deepened when I handed over your hidden forget-me-not note and told them about Mrs Buenrostro.

Dad left early this morning to deliver the note to the police. He will probably have to wait there for hours while they decide what to do with it. Lose it accidentally-on-purpose, most likely.

As ever, Luke is drawn to the split oak that you always loved. He keeps a photograph by his bed of you sitting in it a few days after he was born, holding him in the late summer sun of the brand-new September. You are so completely beautiful, smiling at the swaddled lump in your arms.

As Luke and I approach your tree, I put a hand on his shoulder and pull him closer. In the soft earth at the base of the trunk is a man's partial shoeprint. Only the front of the shoe, but there is no doubting what it is.

I think of the man in the graveyard yesterday and continue to study the landscape, trying to work out what it is that is bothering me so much about this print. That is when I realise. It is because there is just the one and it is incomplete. Whoever left it made an effort not to leave any others. Nothing leads to or from it.

How did he do this? Maybe by placing something on the ground with each step? But he got careless with the one he did leave. Was he interrupted? Startled into a lapse from habitual carefulness? I keep my hand on Luke's shoulder, lightly and casually, as I check and double-check until I am absolutely certain that whoever left that print is now gone.

All the while, I am watching the sky. Smoky black clouds are rushing towards us. A damp, old-newspaper smell is rising from the earth. Any minute and the sun will disappear. Soon after, the rain will start and the shoeprint will melt away. The police are hardly likely to send out a crack team of crime scene investigators for this, let alone order them to race here ahead of the clouds.

I let my hand drop away. 'Can you run into the house for my phone, Luke?'

'Sure sure.'

I love the way he always doubles this word. As he moves off I think of something else. 'Wait a sec.'

I have a vision of me and Luke when he was much smaller, filling moulds with plaster of Paris and then painting them. Entire seas of fantastical creatures. Enough animals to fill a miniature zoo. 'Can you also bring me your school ruler? And Granny's hairspray? It's the matt-gold aerosol on her dressing table.'

He raises an eyebrow. 'Do you wear hairspray? I didn't think you did that kind of stuff.'

'I thought we could embark on some consumer testing. How strong a hold does Brand A have on soil . . . '

'Intriguing.' He says this like the master spy he wants to be and makes me laugh. 'Don't worry. I'm super-fast.' I like that he still defaults to ten-year-old-boy mode, mixed in with all that maturity. Right now he is too excited about having an adventure with me to consider being frightened. He is already moving and I see that I don't need to worry about scaring him. At least for the moment.

I watch him run, a clumsy run that I love, his arms waving. Not a natural athlete's run. Until he started primary school, whenever Luke ran, he'd do what I called his happy laugh. It came out of him like breath. But the teasing he got for it in the playground made the happy laugh disappear. I am not sure when I first noticed its absence. I am still hoping he will let it out again someday.

I return to your tree and crouch on the other side of it, away from the shoeprint. I am looking at the stones that Luke and I arranged in an M after his birthday party on the last day of August. M for Miranda. M for Mummy. M for me.

Luke and I collected the stones from the beach at Norfolk when I took him there for a little holiday earlier that month. The stones are not as we left them. The left side of the M is shorter than the right, though we had taken great care to make them both the same length, using Luke's arm as a measuring stick. The pink-shaded stones are gone. We had started at the lower left tip of the M with the earth-stained pinks, then used purples, then blues, then greys, until we got to the lower right tip.

They are too heavy to have blown away. The earth, though moist, is too solid to have swallowed them. I do not see any strewn pebbles to indicate that an animal disturbed them, and an animal would not carry them away. The pinks have been removed neatly, without any of the rest of the M being affected. Only a human being could have done this so systematically, but there are no footsteps anywhere close.

I study the next oak tree over. The nearby weeds are bent. Did he pause there too, after circling through the woods and around the house? After deciding that the cameras I put on each of its four sides would not penetrate the thick trees he hid in?

Did he watch us as if we were human-sized dolls in their house of green sandstone? Did he hear our mother at the piano and our father at the double bass as Luke and I whooped and laughed and trumpeted? Did he see our silhouettes through the gauzy curtains as the two of us lunged in and out of view, huge then small, dancing a wild rumpus that could only be elephants?

It seems hardly any time has passed, but already Luke is back. 'You're so muddy, Auntie Ella. Granny's gonna kill you.'

I look down at my jeans and see that he is right. Even the bottom of my jumper is sticky and smeared. 'I'm about to get muddier. So are you.'

'Cool.'

I take the things from Luke. 'Can you run back in and get one of your old plaster of Paris kits?'

Luke rolls his eyes exactly as he did after our mother last gave him one.

'I know. We all sometimes forget how grown-up you're getting. But trust me – you're going to like this – you'll thank Granny. Go stir up the powder and water – you're better at that than I am.'

'It never sets when you do it. It stays gooey or it cracks as soon as you take it out of the mould.'

'I know. I'm a disgrace of a builder's daughter. Use Granny's glass jug.'

'She'll go crazy if we put plaster in it.'

'I'll wash it, after – bring the mixture out as soon as it's ready.'

Again he is already running his special Luke run. 'On it.'

A drop of water hits me splat on the nose and I crouch by the shoeprint, crossing fingers and toes that it won't soon be splashed away. I aim the aerosol towards the depression and pump one dose of spray at it. I hold my breath and pump again. The theory I am going on is that it will firm things up and help to hold the print in place in the damp earth for a little longer, despite the rain.

I lay the ruler along the sides and top and bottom of the print and snap pictures with my phone. I get up and repeat the process with the damaged M. It's while I'm aiming the phone at the subtle disturbances on the forest floor that I hear Luke, rustling through leaves, his steps uncharacteristically slow and careful. When I look up, he is only a few feet away, holding a jug of grey gloop.

'Yummy,' I say. 'I'm hungry.'

He laughs.

'Over here.' I motion for him to join me near the

shoeprint. Another drop of rain hits me, this time in the eye. 'Crap.'

'Granny said ladies don't swear.'

'It's the usual problem with that little piece of etiquette.'

'You're not a lady?' He grins, never tiring of this old joke between us.

'Exactly.' I point at the small depression in the ground. 'Here. This is what we're going to cast.' Luke drops to his knees beside me and we pour the mixture in.

After we set the jug aside, he hands me his waterproof coat, school regulation navy. 'I thought this might help,' he says.

The two of us lie on our stomachs with the cold damp of the earth seeping into our clothes and beneath our skin. We are propped on our elbows with the shoeprint between us, holding the coat over it together, shielding it from the rain, which is now coming down properly from a sky the colour of pewter.

'I can hold the coat myself if you're tired,' he says, heroic as ever. 'Give you a rest.'

'I like doing it as a team.'

'So do I.' He smudges his nose with a muddy finger. 'I forgot to tell you, the directions say it dries in half an hour, but it won't be properly strong for two days.'

'That's really helpful.'

He looks hard at me. 'Is this to do with your promise about Mum?'

Mum. The word punches the air out of my stomach. He has never called you that before. It is a progression from the babyish Mummy that we have all clung to for him, probably for too long. Does he know he has done this, to signal to himself and to me that he is growing up? I remember him crying in my arms on Bonfire Night, thinking that whatever happened to you happened because of his very existence. So many declarations of his loss of innocence.

How should I answer his extremely direct question? He is way too smart for evasiveness or lies. As he reminded me only two weeks ago, he is ten, not two. *But ten*, I hear you say, *is still a child.* Something you forgot too readily with me.

'Remember that show you watched about police investigators?' I say. 'They were talking about the transience of crime scenes?'

'Yeah. How you can't count on evidence being preserved, especially outside. The elements can get to it.'

'Exactly. And you want to be a policeman. So I thought it would be fun to try to document this footprint.' Because, I silently add, I'm pretty sure the police will not be inclined to spend time and money doing it themselves. And even if they were, it will be gone before they get here.

'Cool,' he says.

'Yep.'

He laughs at my imitation of him and I laugh too, though my thoughts are dark as I consider what this anniversary may mean. So much has changed. There is the fresh and sickening possibility of Jason Thorne, but that isn't the only potential source of information. Someone new could come forward. Perhaps a friend of the man who took you. Maybe they were loyal to him then but hate him now.

People fall out. That's what you used to say about Sadie, ever-hopeful that the end of my friendship with her was imminent.

'Can you help me with my maths when we go in?' Luke says. 'I want to do really well on my test on Monday. Mum used to help you, didn't she?'

Mum. That new word again. It is your son's right to decide how to name you. It is natural for me to follow his lead. I say, 'Do you think Granny will pay me? She used to pay Mum.'

'Very funny.'

'I'm not joking.'

'Auntie Ella.' He sounds genuinely exasperated.

'Of course I'll help.'

He moves his arms, to try to get more comfortable holding the coat over the shoeprint. 'What are you going to do with the cast?'

'If it doesn't break, I'll put it in the living room as a souvenir of time with you.' I am already plotting to tell Luke a tragic tale of a fate like Humpty Dumpty's for the cast. In reality, I will be giving it to Ted, even though I have a mild fear that he will take it to the tip rather than risk the scorn of the property clerk.

'Will you stay tonight, too?'

'I'll stay for lunch and help you with your maths, but I have stuff I need to do at home after.' He doesn't need to know that I want to have a look at the graveyard before nightfall.

'I like Saturday mornings with you, Auntie Ella.'

'I like them with you too, Luke.'

Sunday, 13 November

Hide and Seek

The graveyard is filled with mist. The sun is only just beginning to rise. There has been no frost but it is so cold Ted is wearing his black knitted hat and I have on that old one of yours, made of cream-coloured wool and pulled over my ears.

Ted checks his watch. The white numbers and dials on the illuminated face are huge and clear even from where I am standing: 6.05. He needs to be at work at 7.00.

The moss is spongy beneath my wellington boots and Ted's solid black shoes. I look more closely at his trousers, then notice the white shirt and epaulettes beneath his civilian coat. 'You're in half blues off-duty,' I say. 'That's not safe.'

'Wouldn't have had time to meet you otherwise.'

I imagine Ted taking his turn in the succession of images of the recently fallen on the police roll of honour. Ted's picture would be the snapshot I took of him after a rugby match eleven years ago, and I feel sick and guilty at how vividly I see it.

'I want you to be safe,' I say. A cross looms above us, seeming to materialise out of the fog. It sits on top of multiple squares of granite that are stacked like a child's super-sized building blocks. I halt a few inches short of crashing into them.

My abrupt stop causes Ted to bump into me. His arms go round my waist to stop me falling over. A row of winged angels tower over us in their flowing gowns, hands clasped over their hearts, clutching passion lilies and seeming to watch us through their lowered eyes.

We look at each other for an instant. Ted's face is so close to mine I can smell the coffee on his breath. It makes me wish I could drink some coffee. It makes me wish I could kiss the coffee from his lips.

But I don't. We quickly break the contact, and I think – I am not sure, but I think – that he moves away a split second before I do.

I tuck a strand of hair behind my ear and pull your hat back down over it. 'Do you know, Luke still has that knitted doll you gave him when he was a baby, the little police constable? He sneaks it into bed every night. We all pretend not to see.'

Ted smiles, the first whole-hearted smile I have seen this morning. 'He's a great kid.' The smile fades as he considers. 'How did he do on Friday?'

'He did great,' I say. 'He keeps the rest of us strong.'

There's a cut on Ted's cheek from shaving. A drop of blood blooms out and I pull a tissue from my jacket pocket to clean it away. I kiss my middle three fingers and lightly, briefly, touch them to his cheek, smiling faintly.

Ted's face softens. His eyes seem to cloud. 'Thank you.'

'I'm always happy to tend your wounds.'

'You know exactly where they are – you made most of them.'

I scrunch the tissue up and hide it away. 'Luke's with me part of next weekend. Do you want to come for Sunday lunch? Maybe kick a ball around with him?'

He pauses before answering. It is slight, but definitely a pause. 'I'm away.'

I picture him and Ruby in that café. I feel weak and sick, as if my blood sugar has dropped. But I know it hasn't.

'Another time, then.' I try to sound casual, but I don't think I do.

'Where will you be at eleven?' he says.

'The Remembrance Day service. Luke tried to stow-away in my car when I was leaving yesterday. He made me promise to meet them in church.'

He doesn't laugh in fond commiseration as I expect him to. 'She wasn't perfect, you know.'

'Sorry?'

'Your sister wasn't perfect. Stop idealising her.'

'She didn't need to be perfect. You can still love imper-fect things.'

'I should know better than anybody how true that is.' He is looking hard at me.

'You can make mistakes and have all sorts of faults and still deserve to be loved, deserve to be missed.' His face tightens as I say this.

'We need to be careful of Luke, Ella. He's at an age where we can mix him up.'

'You've lost interest in me and you're using Luke as an excuse. Sadie warned me you'd do this.'

'Sadie's—' He stops himself. 'Why would you listen to her? She hates you. Always has. Her greatest wish is to fuck up your life.'

'That doesn't mean every word she ever said is untrue.'

'I haven't lost interest in you. That appears to be a biological impossibility.'

'I thought you were seeing Ruby.'

'From your self-defence class? Why would you think that?'

I shrug. 'Why do you think I might think that?'

'Stop playing games, Ella.'

'So you're saying you haven't seen her at all? Except for the class?'

He pauses for a beat too long. 'Yes. That's what I'm saying. Can we move on now, please? Why am I here?'

'You'll see.' When I pass a tomb topped with a bird, I jolt and halt in my steps. Am I really seeing a vulture? I blink, and the stone shapes itself into an eagle. Even my vision is distorted.

A minute later, we reach the tomb where I saw the man. It is the size and shape of a playhouse with its triangular roof. I point in front of me and upwards. 'The mist is in the way, but this is a perfect vantage point for my bedroom window.'

Ted frowns. 'You checked all of your video footage? House and dash cam?'

'There's nothing. But there are blind spots – he could be exploiting them deliberately.' I turn back to the vault and drop to my knees. 'Look.'

He doesn't look. He crosses his arms. He says nothing.

'I actually saw a man here, Ted.'

'When?'

'Friday. As the sun was going down. I'm pretty sure he was watching me.'

'Pretty sure? Listen to yourself, Ella. You saw a man in a graveyard. Men walk in graveyards. All the time. You found a shoeprint in the woods. People walk in those too – there's a public footpath through them.'

I whirl at him. 'Why are you dismissing me? Why have you always tried to stop me looking at all of this?' His face flushes. 'Is there something you don't want me to know, Ted?' The thought has never crossed my mind before, but now it blocks out everything else. 'Something about you I might uncover if I look at all of this afresh?'

His flush deepens. However controlled a man Ted is, he is not in command of his blood supply. 'Do I need to remind you where I was when she disappeared, Ella? Don't you see how all of this damages your ability to think and act rationally?'

'No. I don't. Plus there's something else. There's this man I met. Adam Holderness. He works in the hospital where they've locked up Jason Thorne—'

'Are you trying to make me jealous?' His face is twisted in rage. 'Trying to make me see that another man is clearly interested in you?'

I am so shocked, and so ashamed he could think this, and so outraged by his hypocrisy, that my mouth opens and closes with nothing coming out.

He is practically growling at me. 'In case you were in

any doubt, it wouldn't be hard for you to do that. Does that make you happy?'

'You should know me better than that.' I think of his blatant falsehood about Ruby. You and I were uniquely schooled in our mother's principles for lying and not getting caught. Ted clearly was not. 'How could you be so self-righteous?'

'This has been ruining your life for ten years. It nearly ruined mine. It's ruined us. I thought I'd escaped it when I got married but even that got fucked up by it.'

'Are you actually blaming me for your fucked-up marriage?' My heart is pounding. My blood is thrumming in my ears. 'Given what you've done?'

His face completely drains of colour. 'What do you mean?'

'You're a liar, Ted. You lied to my face. I saw you and Ruby.' I say each of these five words with deadly quiet clarity but somehow hear them as a scream.

A tremor passes through his mouth and jaw. 'You what?'

'You heard me. I saw you in that café.'

'What the hell were you doing there?' He is clearly furious that he has been the object of surveillance. He can do that to others but nobody can do it to him.

I glare and shake my head in disgust and say that I needed coffee.

He grabs both of my arms. 'Were you following me?'

I knock him away. 'Somebody sent me a photo of you. It was location and time-stamped.' I take out my phone and flash the email and photograph at him.

'The fucking bastard. Forward it to me. Tell me if you get another one.'

'Fine.'

'It's not what you think, Ella, with Ruby. It's work.'

'How convenient. Is that supposed to excuse your lying?' The leaves of an old cedar tree lift gently in the still air as if moved by a ghost. 'I don't trust you, Ted.'

'That's a mistake. I hope you'll change your mind.' His voice is measured again, even if his circulation is not.

'Can I ask you something?'

'What.' It's not a question.

'If I disappeared off the face of the earth, would you ever stop looking for me?'

His voice is choked. 'You know I wouldn't. I'd never stop.'

'Well I can't stop looking for her. I won't let her go. She wouldn't if it was me. Ten years and absolutely nothing. Then all of these things start happening.'

'Ten years doesn't mean it's time to go back, Ella. It means it's time to move on. To take stock. I have and you should too. The police did everything they should.'

Can I love a man who keeps secrets from me? Who lies? What kind of a life would that be? I suspect that you could offer some expert advice on this one.

'You talk all the time about the police family.' I am startled by the bitterness in my voice. 'They're your family, not mine. Our loyalties aren't the same.'

'That's why I need to stay out of it. Why I need to stay objective and talk you down.' His murky green eyes are fixed on the grass.

'See how the twigs just there are broken, as if some-body's stepped on them?' I say.

'That could have been anybody. And even if some creep is watching you, it doesn't mean he had anything to do with Miranda.'

I startle when Ted says your name, realising for the first time that he rarely does. For now, I file the observation away.

'Look how the dust is a little thinner here.' I point to the side of the vault's ornate double doors, beneath the roof's overhang. 'Like somebody's shoulders and head rubbed against it. He sat here for some time and leaned back.' I squat down. 'The moss is compressed in front of it, too. See? From his weight while he was sitting.'

'Why do you assume it was a man? It could have been Sadie. The photo too.'

'The person was all in black, but they were tall.' I point to where their heels dug in. 'If it wasn't a man it was a big woman. So yes – it could have been Sadie.'

He gets onto his knees beside me. 'You came here on your own?'

'I did. It's my neighbourhood, Ted. It's hardly a war zone.'

'The gravestones are all falling over. None of these structures are safe.'

'They've been here hundreds of years. I doubt they're going to crumble to powder today.' I stand up. 'I want to look inside.'

Ted stands too. He crosses his arms. 'Why did you ask me to come here if you don't want to listen to anything I say?'

'Because I want to know the counterarguments.' I look straight at him. 'And because I wanted to see you.' I have really messed with his blood flow this morning, but whether this new flush is in gladness or alarm, I cannot tell. I push open one of the iron doors with a horror-movie creak. 'I'm going in with or without you. I doubt the roof is about to fall in.' And with that I squash myself through the opening.

It is difficult to see much, with only the crack of misted daylight from outside. But then Ted is beside me, crouched low so his head doesn't hit the roof. 'Here,' he says, scanning the little chamber with a torch that he must have had in his coat pocket. 'I hope we don't get buried alive.'

I fumble for his hand, let my fingers brush his skin, notice the usual shiver. Even though I fear that he no longer feels this too, I can't resist the impulse to send him little reminders, in case they ping something in him. 'Thank you,' I say. He lets his fingers entwine in mine, making me think of Hansel and Gretel clutching on to each other in the gingerbread cottage. But his touch is fleeting.

There are two gigantic rectangular boxes. They sit on either side of the room and rise to half its height. He is systematic, moving the torch's beam over every inch of the stone slabs beneath our feet. He guides it over the top of the boxes too.

There is no disturbance that I can see. There is nothing in this little house. No clue. It is damp and dusty and earthy smelling, but there is nothing in the air to suggest anyone was in here for any length of time. No residue of smoke from a portable stove. No smell of urine or faeces. This place hasn't been used to camp in.

'Wait a minute. Just inside the doorway, Ted. You didn't shine it here.'

He groans but aims the torch where I have commanded. That is when I see it. Something black. A button. So small and flat and average a button, lying in these shadows, it is a miracle we spotted it at all. I fall onto my knees to peer more closely.

Ted sees too, and guesses what I am thinking in his quickness to dismantle it. 'That could have come from anyone who's passed through this place.'

'Yes, but most of them don't go into the tombs.'

'We have no way of knowing how long it's been here. Plastic doesn't weather quickly. It doesn't rust or tarnish.'

'Maybe.' I snap a few quick pics of the button in situ, using the flash. 'Hand me an evidence bag.' I know he always carries one.

'Did you hear what I said, Ella? It's not something we need to call in the crime scene team for.'

'I heard you. But he could have left DNA on it. Or maybe, if we can finally identify a suspect, he'll have the shirt it came from. It will show he was here.'

'There's no way Jason Thorne left that button. You do admit that?' He speaks as if he is trying to establish whether I was the vandal who spray-painted graffiti on a church.

'Yes.' I stick out a hand. 'Evidence bag, please.'

'I'm not supposed to get involved.'

'If you don't then you're neglecting your duty in serving the public. I am a member of the public and I need you to serve me.'

He says something about how he's been serving me

for as long as he can remember but he still pulls a plastic bag from one of the huge pockets at the bottom of his jacket. He ignores my outstretched hand. Instead, he swoops the bag down and swallows the button up with it himself, avoiding any contact between the button and his own skin. Then he squeezes himself out of the building and I follow.

'Let me have it for a minute,' I say, once we are fully out in the light. 'I'll give it back.'

He drapes it over my palm, making sure that the transparent side faces up, and the side with the opaque white box and blue writing faces down. I snap a few more pictures with my phone, so I can have a record of the button to scale. Then I give the bag back to Ted and stand up. 'You'll write up all the information on it later?'

'Yep.'

Yep. I see now why Luke always says that, imitating the idol otherwise known as Ted. 'You're going to drop it in a bin as soon as I'm out of sight, aren't you?'

'Nope.'

'You're worrying about what the property clerk will say, aren't you?'

'You want to know what he's going to say? He's going to say, "I'm booking in a fucking button? You're asking me to book in a fucking button?" I'll pass this one on, then I'm done. Anything else, deliver it to the station yourself or get your dad to.'

He walks away, not looking back, not caring whether I stay or follow him out. He moves steadily through the fog towards the archway through which all the dead bodies in this graveyard passed, then he melts out of my view.

It actually hurts to breathe and I feel like I might throw up – as if I have somehow ingested his disgust with me and need to expel it. I stand near this mockery of a playhouse, hoping he will call something to me over his shoulder. In all of the countless fights since you vanished, he has never before walked away so angrily, at least not without relenting within minutes. But if he does call back, the words are lost in the mist.

Monday, 14 November

Never Climb Down

I am wandering through the cobbled lanes in search of something to wear for my meeting with Jason Thorne tomorrow. I forwarded the hospital's official advice about suitable dress to our mother, deciding that including her in the preparations would be the best way to manage her.

As ever, though, she is managing me. She has hijacked this excursion to make sure I do it right. She is walking beside me, reading bits of the leaflet aloud from her phone. 'The rules are there for a reason, Ella,' she says. She looks up, seduced by the windows of one of the small but extremely expensive boutiques the two of you love.

I, by contrast, cannot tear my eyes from the gigantic plane tree in the middle of the square. 'Remember when I made all four of us reach round the trunk to hold hands?' I say.

'You must have been about four.' Mum smiles. 'We had to strain, but we did it. It's a good thing we had Dad with us that day or we wouldn't have made it.'

'Miranda only did it under sufferance,' I say.

'You used to imagine when the tree was a baby. You once drew a picture of a tiny girl from the eighteenth century. You put her in a perfect miniature Georgian dress so she was the same height as the tree, all those centuries ago.'

'I've always loved this tree.' I pull Mum beneath it.

'Come on,' Mum says, and drags me away and around a corner to another cobbled street. Each time Mum points to a shop I shake my head no, grab her arm, and keep walking.

'I passed Sadie's clinic on my way to meet you,' Mum says. 'It was closed. Isn't that odd at this time of year? No lights. No sign. But it's the season when women want manicures and facials and hair removal.'

'I suppose,' I say. 'All of the parties.'

'Exactly. I peeked through the letter box. There was a pile of post on the floor. Perhaps she's gone away with her new boyfriend? But wouldn't it be a busy period for him right now too?'

'Probably,' I say.

'It makes me see how thoughtful she is,' Mum says.

I look up sharply. 'What does?'

'Well, she's gone away, but she still took the trouble to send chocolates and a card before she went.'

My cheeks are burning and the tips of my fingers are tingling, little spears circling the nail beds. 'When exactly did she send them?'

Mum thinks. 'Thursday, I think. Because of the anniversary. She said she wanted us to know she was thinking of us. It was kind.'

'Tell me exactly what she said.'

'It was just a card. *Thinking of you* was printed on the front, with red chrysanthemums. She signed her name inside.'

'So a condolence card?'

'I suppose it was, yes.'

I picture Sadie, furious and distraught after losing Brian. All the while, she is blaming me for everything that has gone wrong for her. But she takes the time and trouble to send our mother a card and some chocolates. There is a big big problem with this picture. Sadie and kind are not two words that should ever be used together. *Thinking of you*, on a card chosen by Sadie, is a threat, not an act of love.

'You can't keep those things, Mum.'

'What?'

'Sadie is . . . ' I don't know what Sadie is, or why. A functional psychopath? Adam could probably give her a diagnosis. 'Miranda always said she's full of poison. She's not our friend. She didn't send those things to be kind.'

'You need to be specific, Ella.'

'I don't want to upset you with the details, but I don't want her anywhere near you or Luke or Dad.'

'You're acting as if you think she put cyanide in those chocolates.'

'Probably not, but there is a small risk.'

'The box is sealed in plastic.' Mum sighs. You know that sigh. I seem to push the button for it a lot. 'Do you think you're being paranoid? That going over and over what happened to your sister is winding you up?'

'No.' I try not to make the word sound like a hiss.

227

'Fine.' There is another sigh. 'I'll get rid of the chocolates and recycle the card.'

'Sorry. I wasn't clear. I don't mean for you to throw them away. I want them, in case I need to go to the police. I'll collect them when I see you on Thursday.'

'Is that really necessary?'

'Hopefully not, but I want to be prepared.' I take her hand in mine. 'If you hear from her again, please tell me. And keep anything she sends. You will, won't you?'

'Yes,' she says.

I suspect she only agrees because I have reminded her that you never liked Sadie. She wouldn't listen to me, but we both still listen to you. She also agrees because she wants to shut me up. But that will never happen.

'Good,' I say. 'No more Sadie. Shall we walk on? Find some more shops?' The last sentence is calculated to please Mum.

I cannot tear my eyes from the arches of twinkling Christmas decorations. It is only the middle of November and already they are up.

Mum has her phone out again. She has returned to the hospital leaflet. She is reading something about 'modest dress'.

'They actually wrote that?' I say. '"Modest"?'

'Modest isn't a dirty word.' She peers at me. 'Your father and I are really not happy about this business of visiting Thorne.'

'I'm hardly happy about it myself. But we said we'd try not to argue, didn't we? We promised each other.'

'Yes. Yes, we did.' She points up, at the strands of waterfall lights. 'They are like shooting stars.'

'Why do the bells and snowflakes look like they're made of frosted barbed wire?'

'I give up,' she says. 'Perhaps they are.' And then she shocks me, which is something she loves to do. Just like you. 'There are a few things we need to talk about. The first is that I have made a discovery about Mr Henrickson.'

I halt so abruptly another pedestrian has to swerve to avoid me. 'You what?'

'I believe I spoke clearly, Ella.' She looks like a snow-drop in her white coat and hat, which she makes careful adjustments to, using a shop window as her looking glass. Only you and Mum could wear these colours without worrying about getting them dirty.

'But you keep saying you don't want me doing any of this.'

'I don't. But I must confess that I was curious.'

'"Must confess" isn't usually part of your vocabulary.'

'Do you want me to share or not?'

'I want you to share.' I steer her out of the lanes and into the courtyard on the side of the Abbey, searching for an empty bench. There is already a scattering of temporary wooden chalets trimmed with greenery, selling Christmas things. I notice one with a display of gingerbread-house kits, another with sachets of mulled wine.

'Please tell me what you found out.' I try to pull her beside me, onto a bench, but she won't let me until she has taken out a packet of tissues and wiped it.

'You have your sister's patience.' She shakes her head as if I am exhausting her beyond endurance. 'I phoned up Henrietta Mansions Management Company, who run the building. I said, "Hello, this is Mrs Buenrostro from Flat 6."'

'You what?!'

'Please do not interrupt. The woman on the line said, "Hello, Mrs Buenrostro." I hung up without saying anything else. But there is no question of the flat number Mrs Buenrostro lives in. The woman confirmed my guess about that, because 6 is definitely next door to 7 – I checked a building plan I found online.'

'Impressive,' I say.

'Isn't it?' Our mother looks deservedly proud of herself. 'So Mrs Buenrostro and N. Henrickson are close neighbours. One wall between them.'

'You withheld your telephone number?'

'Of course. But here is the really significant thing. When E.B. Property Services bought Flat 7 twenty-one years ago, they also bought Flat 6.'

My excitement and perplexity at this intelligence is competing with my admiration for her sneaky cleverness. 'You searched the Land Registry?'

'Yes.' She pauses. 'The likelihood is that both flats are investment properties owned by the same company.'

'Mrs Buenrostro said she bought her flat.' I am thinking aloud. 'Perhaps she's behind E.B. Property Services? The B could be for Buenrostro. But it's odd that she didn't admit any connection with the flat next door. I asked her again and again about its occupier.'

'There's one more thing, still. It's the thing that seems most important.'

'You're better at this than I am, Mum.'

'Of course.' We both smile.

'When did you do all this?'

'Friday morning. But I didn't want to talk about it on the anniversary. You had enough of your own to say – it made me wish I hadn't opened all of this up. I thought of not telling you at all.'

'You were right to tell me. And it's only fair. I'm telling you everything. What's the other thing you found?'

'It's to do with Miranda's flat.' She touches my fingers lightly, giving me an electric shock. 'Something made me look through the old paperwork. She bought it from E.B. Property Services. They owned it before she did.'

We had assumed you rented your flat. You were happy to let us think that. Only after you disappeared did we discover you owned it. You wouldn't have been able to come up with an explanation for that one – even Mum wouldn't have been able to sit quietly and pretend to believe you'd managed it on your nurse's salary. No mortgage for a first-floor Georgian flat. Nobody normal does that. There was no payment trail but all of the papers were in your name.

Now we have a likely explanation. 'Oh,' I say. 'Wow,' I say. 'There's no question, then, of a link between Miranda and Henrickson that she kept off our radar. It's as if E.B. Property Services made it over to her.'

'Why would they do that?'

I look hard at her. 'As payment for something. Or out of love. A love gift. Maybe from Luke's father.'

'No.' She shakes her head, too, for emphasis. 'No. I don't want anything to bring him out of the woodwork.'

'Did you really not consider the possibility, when you found all of this out?'

'No. I did not. Don't you dare open that up, Ella.'

'I'm not sure I'm the one who did.'

'No more.'

'Okay.'

She touches my cheek with the back of her freezing hand and I turn my head to kiss it. 'Shall we walk on?' she says. 'It's starting to drizzle. It may turn heavy.'

'Good plan,' I say, and we step onto grey paving stones that are already spattered with dark spots. 'Why did you help, Mum? It can't have been mere curiosity.'

'Once you know you can't un-know. You can't not act. You can't not share. But I am feeling more and more that this is going to pull you down, Ella. Especially after last night.' Uncharacteristically, our ballerina mother slips a little and I steady her.

'What happened last night?'

'That's what I need to discuss with you.' She bites her lip in that way she has when she is about to deliver bad news. She did it when she told us Grandma died.

'Should I be scared?'

She doesn't answer.

'Let's get some lunch,' I say. 'It's later than I realised and you were right – it's getting wetter – we should be inside.'

'I'm not hungry. Just a cup of tea, please.'

The Abbey's stones usually look like honey, but today they are grey. We skirt the side of the building, beneath Gothic rows of arched stained-glass windows. I steer her into another cobbled lane, where there is a cosy, old-fashioned café that Mum likes. I open the door for her and she glides in like the queen.

The furniture is dark wood and draped in white cloths. Reproduction prints of eighteenth-century portraits hang on walls papered in blue damask. There are displays of sweet things on lace doilies that you would scorn. Coffee walnut and chocolate fudge and lemon drizzle cakes. Scones and Florentines and treacle tarts.

We sit in a corner and Mum delays whatever it is that she really wants to tell me with chatter about the little girls in the ballet class she teaches once a week. At last she says, 'Things aren't right with you, Ella. You're looking tired. Is it Ted?'

This is the big thing she wants to talk about? 'No.'

The waitress puts peppermint tea in front of Mum and black coffee in front of me. I take a sip and feel physically sick.

She looks shrewdly at me. 'I knew you'd make things hard on yourself, with all of this. Whatever is going on between you and Ted, you should trust him.'

'I didn't think you were a great fan of his.'

'People change, Ella. Things aren't always as they appear. You have to forgive them their mistakes.'

I reach across the table to give her arm a little squeeze. 'I'm in a plain old bad mood. It'll pass. I'll try not to be so bah humbug.'

'You will be careful with Thorne, won't you?'

'Of course. And I'll call you as soon as I'm safely home. But can you tell me what happened last night? You've worried me.'

She considers for a few seconds. 'Perhaps now isn't the time.'

'Maybe if I go first with a tricky subject, you can feel better about going next?'

She inclines her head slightly but says nothing.

'You have always said how twirly and happy Miranda was on that last morning. But she seemed' – I fumble for the right words – 'more of a mix of moods, around then. So I wondered – were there maybe other things you noticed?'

She frowns. 'Of course not. How can you ask me that?'

Our mother would never want to climb down from the evidence she gave the police as the last known person to see you. She would never want to be found out. Especially not by our father, who would not understand, perhaps would not even forgive, if she'd kept something important back that might have helped us to find you. Her pride would be involved too. She cares about what she looks like to others. Whatever our mother really saw in you that morning, she will take it to her grave.

But I still have to press her, however futile it may be. 'Memory is difficult. Sometimes things come to us over time. We were all in such shock and distress, then. It's understandable if some detail slipped your mind. But maybe it's resurfaced?'

'There is nothing to resurface. You're the one who should be asking yourself about what you may be failing to notice.'

Something about her tone makes my heart start to beat faster.

She goes on. 'Your father didn't want me to say anything to you but Luke had a nightmare last night. I think you may be sharing too much with him.'

234

I take a sip of coffee and it goes down like a hard lump. When cornered, our mother can counter-attack very quickly. 'Did he say what the nightmare was about?'

'Just that you were being hurt. Your father went to him.'

'I'll be more careful.'

'It's too late, Ella. I warned you but you didn't listen. Your father and I are going to have to consider whether it's still appropriate for him to visit you.'

I try to speak lightly, though I feel as if there's a boulder in my stomach. 'Isn't that a bit of an overreaction to a bad dream?'

'He doesn't normally have them. Your father and I have no choice.'

'You can't be serious. You can't do that.'

'I am and I can.'

'He's living with me at least half the week from next year. We agreed he would go to school in Bath.'

'School choices can be changed.' Her voice is brisk no-nonsense.

'You're fucking joking. Is this some kind of revenge because I got too close to something you don't want to admit about the morning she disappeared? Too close to the truth about how and why she got her flat?'

'Don't you speak to me that way.'

'This is what Miranda hated about you. You can't change these decisions on a whim. Not for next year and not for now. He's spending Saturday night with me – it's all arranged. And I said I'd come to his football match on Thursday afternoon.'

'I don't think it's wise for you to be near his school

right now. My priority is what's best for Luke. You never appreciate how much it means to me to keep him safe.' She is blinking those grey eyes of hers so fast I think of hummingbird wings, as if she is in the REM stage of sleep, though she is as awake as she has ever been. 'I have no power to do that for you any more, but I do for him.'

'I would never put him in danger. I don't understand how finding out what happened to her isn't the most powerful force there is for you.'

She seems not to hear me. 'And your father. You don't see when he gets a twinge and thinks his cancer has woken up. He doesn't let you see. You're not the one who has to calm him down.'

'I know that. I know how hard that must be for you.' I clasp her hand in mine. When she bats it away I feel a small stab in my heart.

'And you never support me over making sure he eats right.'

'Oh my Lord. So the real reason you're punishing me is because I think you're a control freak about Dad's diet? Have you been listening to a word I say?'

'Of course I have. Of course I want to know about your sister, Ella. But I can't lose the rest of you. The fear of that is stronger than anything else.'

'I understand that. I'm sorry if I'm not sensitive enough about that. But I think if you knew what happened to Miranda it would release you. It would release all of us.'

'I don't want you to find Luke's father. I don't want some strange man coming into our lives and trying to take him from us.'

'It's not fair to Luke to keep him in the dark. What

would he feel if he knew it was in our power to find his father but we chose not to?'

'He's not going to know.'

'There's little risk of us losing him. No judge is going to remove a ten-year-old boy from the only family he has ever known and give him to some stranger.'

'Even if they share the same DNA?'

'Even then. Not at this stage of his life. We'd have to face the fact that the courts would want to consider if contact is appropriate. But they would put Luke first. As we do. And we share his DNA too.'

'The best compromise I can offer is that when you see Luke, Dad or I will need to be there too. And only at home. You can't take him out or go near his school.'

I try again to put my hand over hers, as if touching her will stop this war between us, but I half-wonder if I am holding a monster's claw. 'Luke needs time on his own with me as well as with you and Dad.'

She pulls her hand from mine. 'There's no alternative. What you're doing is affecting his well-being.'

'No. What I'm doing is good for him. And I'm not involving him in any way that puts him at risk. You can't put people in prison to keep them safe.'

'Well I don't agree.'

'Whether you agree or not doesn't matter. You aren't the God of Luke. I'm thirty now. I'm not a child. I'm a responsible consenting adult.'

'I'm not sure about responsible.'

'Then it's a good thing you have no official status as judge and jury. Dad won't tolerate you doing this.'

'You're wrong. Your father's with me.'

'No way. Did you know that Dad asked the police for her things? That that's why they finally returned them? He's sick of you shutting all of us up about her.'

'Do you really think you could possibly tell me something about your father that I don't already know?'

'I think I just did, but you're too self-obsessed and controlling to admit it.'

Her eyes fill with tears but they don't leak out and I can't help but wonder if it is some old theatrical trick from her ballet days to get herself in character. 'It isn't easy for me to say these things to you,' she says.

'Well you make it look effortless. Do you realise that, if it came to it, the court would ask Luke what he felt, at his age? They wouldn't let you take him for yourself.' How can I get through to her? Appeasement and anger have failed. Perhaps I need to try harder with reason. With facts. 'You're overestimating your legal power. You seem to have forgotten that I have shared custody.'

'Yes, but he still mostly lives with your father and me. No judge will want to upset that. And as you pointed out, the courts will always look again at child custody if circumstances change. What you are doing is changing the circumstances, so your rights with Luke may no longer be appropriate in the court's eyes.'

I want to shake her but I literally sit on my hands. 'Are you saying I'm unfit?' She doesn't answer. Her silence is her answer. 'Have you stopped to think about the moral rights and wrongs of this? Not just legal – clearly you've been busy with that.'

'Of course I have,' she says.

'Miranda would hate what you are suggesting.'

'Don't you presume to know my daughter better than I do.'

'Don't you presume to know my sister better than I do.' I croak out something that sounds like an evil cackle. 'And you wonder why she never told you anything? Why she was so secretive?'

'Your sister confided more to me than you could ever imagine.' She clamps her mouth shut as if I have provoked her into saying more than she intended.

'Easy for you to say that now. If you weren't the way you are, she wouldn't have made herself vulnerable by keeping everything hidden.' I stand up so fast the table rocks and my coffee sloshes from its china cup. Our mother's tea spills onto her fingers and when she winces I actually feel pleasure.

'Please calm down, Ella.'

'What do you expect?' I blink hard, refusing to cry. 'I've tried to reason with you but you are impossible. I can't talk to you. I can't even look at you. If you try to do this you will fail and your grandson will hate you and I will hate you and you will lose the only child you have left.'

'Don't talk about her as if she's dead.'

'That's all you have to say? That's your first thought? For the child who isn't here, rather than the one who actually is? Save your breath, Mother.'

I have never called her Mother before. If Luke can change the word for the woman who gave birth to him, so can I. The word is cold on my tongue. It makes me stand straighter.

I have one more point I must make. 'Do you think it's

good for Luke to have the three people he loves and depends on most fighting over him?'

'Sit down and lower your voice. People are looking.'

'Do you think I care?' I shake my head. 'When Luke said he wanted to live with me I told him the three of us shared him. I didn't for an instant exploit that, even though I'd love to have him with me all the time. I talked to you and Dad about it with total honesty and fairness and we negotiated. If you weren't such a monster I'd be sorry for you. You're not keeping anybody safe. You can't control the whole fucking world.'

I can hear our mother sob out a little gasp, but I don't look at her. I grab my coat and stomp from the café without turning back, slamming the door so hard I am surprised that the paned glass doesn't break.

The Masquerade Ball

I am so filled with rage and desolation and fear I hardly notice where I am going. I have deactivated my usual scanning of everything and everyone around me. It is only three in the afternoon, but already the dark is setting in as I stumble over the bridge, then the little side street that borders the scented garden where Ted helped with the self-defence class only two weeks ago.

I'm not sure how long I have been walking before a policeman materialises out of the shadows, like a ghost who has been waiting for me in a nightmare. 'Sorry to startle you.' He moves away from the wrought-iron gate that is meant to stop pedestrians falling off the pavement and smashing onto the mildewed grey slabs of the basement garden below. He positions himself between me and my little charcoal hatchback. All thoughts of our mother fly away.

He gestures towards the number plate. 'Is this your car?' He has the kind of bulky arms that men get when they work out too much and take steroids. He looks like a nightclub bouncer. He has a mole the size of a blueberry below his left eye, high on his cheek.

I don't answer. I stand more squarely on my feet. It is a stance. It is readiness.

'I'm PC Finn,' he says. PC Finn is not wearing a hat. Not a flat cap. Not a helmet. His dark brown hair is curly and close to his scalp. It is cold outside. Heads are vulnerable. Why is PC Finn not protecting his?

'Are you Miss Ella Brooke?' His hair continues into small, distinct sideburns, impeccably shaped to end above his earlobes in a point.

'How do you know my name?'

'Came up from your number plate when I called it in.'

Shouldn't he have asked if I was Melanie? I'm pretty sure my car is registered in the full version of my name.

His radio is stuck to his black vest above the breast, like a big ugly brooch. It looks authentic. So why do I keep thinking something is wrong about that radio?

'Someone was trying to break into your car. We want to make sure you're okay.'

I can't see any obvious evidence that anyone has tampered with my car. I think some more about the radio. PC Finn's radio is absolutely silent but Ted's is always on a mumbling low when he is interacting with the public, so he can listen out for a potentially urgent call. He never turns that radio off when he is on duty.

'Why is your radio off?' I say.

He looks up and down the road. 'I'm supposed to ask the questions.'

'Only of suspects and criminals. I'd appreciate it if you would answer my question.'

What he says is, 'So I can hear you properly.' What I hear is, *All the better to hear you with, my dear.*

'Are you a real policeman?' I say.

'Never been asked that one before. But we appreciate members of the public taking care. Can you please accompany me to the station in your car?'

He reaches for my arm and I pull away before he can touch it. 'I will not. And I know that I am under no obligation to do so.'

'I need to accompany you to the station, where we are holding the man who did this.'

The uniform looks real. Standard black trousers. A white shirt and dark tie peeking out from the high-visibility jacket. 'If the man who did this is at the station, then I'm quite safe on my own. I'll get myself there and meet you.'

Something is bothering me about the epaulettes. There's no collar number, but that's not necessarily a sign that anything is wrong. I say, 'I'd like to see your warrant card, please.'

'I can't let you touch my warrant card. No officer will allow a member of the public to do that.'

'I don't need to touch it. Hold it out for me. Then I can phone the station and check that you are who you say you are.'

I am looking at the scene as if from outside my own body. All of my practised responses are kicking in. I keep enough distance between us to move quickly. I open my bag and root around, so that my high-powered LED torch is towards the top and easily grasped. I am feeling more and more like Little Red Riding Hood trying to outsmart the wolf.

He puts a hand in a jacket pocket to search for the card. As he moves, one of the epaulettes glints into closer focus and I realise what the problem is. He has pinned two silvery Order of the Bath stars to one of the epaulettes but not the other. The man said he was a PC, but he is wearing the rank insignia of an inspector and only on one shoulder. Inspectors do not go on foot patrol. The uniform isn't fake but I'm certain it isn't his. And he has only been able to lay hands on some of it, hence the missing headwear and the single, wrong epaulette.

I take my phone out to wait for his warrant number, wondering how he is going to play this one. Using the buttons on the side of my phone, I snap pictures of his face, the birthmark high on his cheek, the pointy sideburns, his uniform, the epaulettes, all without his knowing it.

'I can't seem to find my warrant card.'

My adrenaline levels must be as high as when Ted buttonholed me into playing out the intruder-in-the-night scenario with him just a few metres away in the park. 'Tell me your collar number, then. I can phone the station and read it to them.'

'I really do need to talk to you. It's very important.'

'So you keep saying.'

He steps forward and as I move away I snatch the torch and engage the strobe function, temporarily blinding him. He gasps and sways. The hand he slaps over his eyes to shield them won't make the big white spots he is seeing disappear any time soon. I go from stillness to motion in a split second, imagining sparks flying from my heels as I speed back towards the town end of the street, plotting to bash him on the forehead with the torch if he catches me, though I doubt very much that he can.

I don't hear him behind me so I risk a quick glance over my shoulder. At last, the fake PC has recovered enough to run, veering off into the park. Does he have the faintest idea that I have his photograph? Whether or not he does, I know where I need to take it.

Despite my long history with Ted, I haven't spent much time in the police station. Wherever possible, our father has mediated between our family and the police. The insect-like buzz of the reception area's strip lights and its half-full vending machines are as strange and depressing to me as they would be to anyone.

I have needed to pee for the last half hour so I brave the small public loo. The walls and ceiling are snot green. I know from Ted that this is to stop drug addicts from using this murky little room as a place to inject – the colour stops them from being able to see their veins. As I pee – crouching rather than sitting, and thinking of our mother, who brainwashed us both to do this in public loos to avoid germs – I look around in dread for a camera. I can't see one but it isn't easy to see much in this sickly fluorescent glow. I wash my hands, examining my skin in the cloudy shatterproof mirror. Your face, tinted green, looks out at me.

Cold metal chairs are bolted to the waiting room floor. I don't sit for long before a real police constable calls my name and shows me through a steel door that leads directly from the reception area into a small consultation room with a green light on the outside to signal availability. Inside, there is a computer for digital capture of interviews, which he fiddles with before we begin.

I sit on yet another bolted chair, watched by yet more cameras. But I am startled by the seriousness of this man's interest in my story and the photographs I took of the fake policeman, by the care with which he writes down everything I tell him, despite the recording device. His primary concern seems to be to listen and talk openly to me.

I slide my telephone over to him. 'You don't recognise him, do you?' I ask.

'No. Not known to me. You were sharp to pick up on his using the wrong form of your name, and to see that the uniform doesn't add up.' I have liked this real policeman until now. But when he puts a thumb beneath his chin and glides his fingers back and forth over his mouth, I am no longer sure I trust him. All the while he peers at me, as if wanting an explanation for my insight. When I do not give it, he continues. 'It's high-order fakery. Most members of the public wouldn't clock it. It wouldn't have been easy to get hold of these items. I'd like to know how he did.'

'That thought occurred to me too.'

He intensifies his professional manner. 'We'll feed the images through our systems to see if we can get a hit on who he is.' He pushes a paper towards me with an email address. 'Can you please email them to our technical support unit?'

I do this instantly, then check my sent box. 'They seem to have got through.'

'Good. We'll post your images on our website and social media before the day is out. Let's hope someone can identify him.'

'You'll let me know if you discover anything?'

'If it is in our power to do so.' He is talking with his hand over his mouth again. 'We can't risk compromising any further investigation or charges.'

I have to strain not to roll my eyes at how many times I have heard this before, usually ventriloquised by our father. 'Do you have any ideas about what he was after?' I ask.

He only throws the question back at me. 'I wondered if you had a pulse on that.'

I shake my head. 'My first thought was that he was a predator, trying to lure a woman into getting in her car with him. I wanted as much information about him as I could get, so he wouldn't do it to anyone else. Another thought I had was that he's a journalist, and he wanted some sort of story about my reactions.' I pause to explain briefly about you, glad he doesn't know who I am until I do. I also tell him about my work with victims of violence.

'So you're saying it may have been some sort of test, and he could then write about the encounter?'

'I can see you think that sounds silly. I'm not confident about either of those explanations, but the ten-year anniversary of my sister's disappearance was on Friday. That could explain the interest, if he really is a journalist.'

'Was there any publicity?'

'No. But a journalist did leave a voicemail. I didn't call him back. Here. Listen.'

I play the message on speakerphone and he makes notes.

'Listening to that again, it could be the man I met today. I'm not sure.' I'm kicking myself that I didn't record as well as photograph him.

'I'd like you to share the voicemail with us. Use the same address you sent the photos to.'

A few taps on my phone and it is done.

'I apologise for what I'm about to ask,' he says, 'but do you have any enemies?'

I tell him about Sadie, followed by the anonymous silent phone calls as well as the email from Justice Administrator that I already logged with the police. I even mention the chocolates and the card to my parents, though I realise I'm probably unique in regarding the phrase *Thinking of You* as a threat, and that these won't count because they weren't sent to me.

'There isn't enough for us to do anything at this stage, but forward everything to us to log – we'll see if the sender can be identified. And if anything else happens, we'll pay her a visit,' he says.

I open my mouth to tell him about the photo of Ted and Ruby, but nothing comes out. Do I really want to risk getting Ted in trouble at work? Or at the very least embarrassing him? In any case, I forwarded the email and its attachment to Ted already, which is as good as logging it with the police. I am not about to suggest to this man that I don't trust Ted to do the right thing with it. My habits of protectiveness towards him cannot be broken.

So instead I say, 'It's just as well if you hold off on visiting her for now. It could make her angrier. Make her escalate things, if it actually is her behind those communications. She may calm down, now that she's let off steam.'

'And if she doesn't, you'll come straight back to us.'

'Yes.'

'Let's return to the man from earlier today. You will know that impersonating a police officer is an extremely serious offence.'

'I do know that,' I say. And then, 'I'm sure I wasn't a random target. He knew who I was and he planned that ambush. What I deeply want to know is why.'

The real police constable nods. His hand is not covering his mouth when he next speaks. 'I'd like to know that too,' he says. And to my great surprise, I actually believe him.

Tuesday, 15 November

The Tour

I have seen this place from the road many times before, driving along what locals still call Lucifer's Lane, though it has never officially been given that name. In the road atlas, it is just a numbered road skirting atop a sunken valley. Inside this valley sits the hospital for the criminally insane that Jason Thorne is unlikely ever to leave.

The hospital itself is an imposing Victorian building, typically beautiful and terrifying from the elevated road. It looks like something from a Gothic nightmare, despite the propaganda in the information leaflet. *Patients, not prisoners.* How many different ways did they manage to stress this?

There is a last glimpse of the whole complex before I follow the narrow slip-road down the hill and wind my way to the car park. When I emerge from my car, I can hear no screams from inside the building. At least nothing piercing enough to escape its thick red bricks and the high walls circling the entire grounds.

Hospital, not prison. Really? The walls are topped with razor wire.

I find my way to the main reception building and murmur my name into an intercom. The door clicks and swings open, and I step over the threshold and towards the barrier of safety glass that encloses the receptionist.

'I'm Ella Brooke.' I slide my passport into the shallow metal tunnel that runs beneath the safety window. My hands are visibly trembling and I hope she doesn't notice. 'I have an appointment with Jason Thorne, but I'm meeting Adam Holderness first.'

She shoots me a tight professional smile before extracting the passport from her side and examining it. 'It says your name is Melanie.'

'Melanie is on my birth certificate but I go by Ella.'

Do you see how much trouble you cause me?

Really? What about when I saved your ass yesterday because I changed your name?

The woman scrutinises the passport again, flicking her eyes between my face and the photograph. She puts the passport onto a photocopy bed, then returns it to the tunnel without comment, leaving me wondering if she will let me in.

'Is everything okay?' I ask.

'I suppose the image matches your face.' Her hair is so over bleached and over straightened and over long it seems to exemplify every warning you ever gave me about the things that cause hair to look and feel like straw.

'That's a relief.' She doesn't laugh. 'Here's my letter of invitation, to see Mr Thorne.' I slide it through.

She stretches her nose and purses her lips in the manner of a banker regarding a forged £10,000 note. But she seems to decide that I am not an imposter with a master plan to free all the inmates. She gives me a name badge and points me towards the search area, which is full of guards with guns on their belts.

Patients not prisoners. Did the people who wrote this really not mean it to become one of those ironic refrains you cannot get out of your head?

The guards X-ray my bag, then direct me to stow it in a locker. I shove my coat in too. A female guard takes my fingerprints and an image of my eye before snapping my photograph. She conducts a body search by patting my arms and legs and even my torso. She makes double sure by waving a wand over every inch of me. More security guards signal me to go through the body scan's archway. I pass through it and practically bump into Adam, who is waiting for me on the other side.

His pupils are so big in his black eyes that I cannot see where they begin and end. It occurs to me that he has watched the body search. I have walked into all of this in full knowledge of the fact that this man is pursuing me – it has happened before, but I have never had reason to play on it until now, sickeningly faithful to my lost true love for too many years.

Is our mother right to worry that whatever it takes, I will do? You would know the answer to this question. I do not. Do you remember that little note you once wrote me? I still have it, taped to the mirror over my dressing table.

I told you so.
Love, Your Intuition.

I'd never heard it before. Until last year, when I saw somebody wearing that slogan on a T-shirt, I thought you had invented it yourself.

I had planned to raid my wardrobe for my best approximation of the tasteful clothes I failed to buy during the disastrous expedition with our mother. But I went for a last-minute change of plan. My smoky blue shirt dress and block heel boots match the ones you were last seen in, though I have had to leave the fabric tie off the dress's waist because it is a potential weapon.

The space between my breasts is empty. I put a panicked hand to my chest, thinking I have lost my locket, only to remember that I left it at home in deference to their long list of proscribed items. Like the tie, a chain of precious metal could be used to strangle somebody.

I am not used to heels like these. How did you walk in them? I take a wobbly step and nearly fall on my face, only just catching myself. The preposterous entrance makes me blush.

Adam has the grace to pretend it never happened. 'I can show you some of the grounds if you'd like, before your appointment.' His well-mannered professionalism is exactly what I need, but there is warmth mixed in too.

I manage a half-smile. 'That would be good.' He knows how deeply curious I am about this place and its inhabitants.

He motions me to follow him through another door

into an airlocked, metal-lined room that reminds me of a space-capsule and makes me feel as if I can't breathe. He opens a second door, which spills us onto the other side of the perimeter wall, facing an elaborate arrangement of squat outbuildings around the towering main hospital. To access this complex, we walk through a corridor of grim steel fences with lock after lock that he opens so we can pass through barrier after barrier.

He sees me squinting at the wall-mounted cameras. 'You get used to them,' he says.

I have never seen so many, so ostentatiously close together, so obviously moving to survey us, either adjusted remotely by an army of unseen observers in a control room somewhere or triggered automatically by motion.

'I'm glad you came.' His voice is casual-friendly but his eyes are not.

I remind myself of his expertise. Figuring out people's thoughts, the way their minds work, so he can try to manipulate them. 'It was kind of you to invite me.'

He allows himself an ironic raised eyebrow. 'You're the first woman who has ever subjected herself to a full body search and biometrics to have coffee with me.'

'I find that difficult to believe.' *See Ted*, I think. *I can do flirting*.

His black eyes don't waver from mine. 'I'd like to think that Thorne wasn't your only inducement.'

'I have a general interest in criminal rehabilitation. And in talking to you.'

'Glad to hear it.' He frowns. 'And Sadie? Have you heard from her?'

'Not directly.' Literally truthful but also evasive. One of your best tricks.

Though I must not be as good at it as you. I can see from the seriousness of his expression that he hears something in my tone, but doesn't press it.

'This way,' he says, and leads me through an extremely well-manicured garden, though it is dull and unadorned. He motions around him. 'The patients do this. Cut the grass. Trim the hedges. We have kitchen gardens, where they plant vegetables. It's all part of their occupational therapy.'

'You're actually proud of them, aren't you?'

'Yes. I am.' He points to a large, single-storey outbuilding, built of more grey stucco with a flat black iron roof. 'They do woodwork in here. Primarily it's patients who've come a long way in their treatment. Want to see?'

'Very much.' We both know it is no accident that he is suggesting this particular workshop.

I am hugging myself, getting goosebumps out here, beneath a dark grey sky that seems to reflect the security fencing. All I have on is this filmy Miranda dress. Were you always freezing, skipping about in such things?

'You're cold,' he says.

'Not at all.' I lead him towards the woodwork studio as if this were my world rather than his. He unlocks the door by holding his identification card to a small scanner that flashes green. That is it. The only security there is for this building.

The studio is one large room. It is so light in here, with the walls made mostly of windows and the rows of rectangular fluorescent bulbs on the ceiling. There are large wooden workbenches and pieces of heavy metal equipment. Table saws and planers and vices and sanders, all of them potentially lethal weapons. Considering the warnings that visitors can't even bring in plastic cutlery due to the risk of it being turned into an instrument of death, I cannot help but appear surprised.

'These are human beings, Ella. They have talents. We need to help them develop those talents. The hospital is remedial in every way it can be. As I said, they only get access to this particular workshop when they're doing well.'

This man really does seem to read my mind, which isn't something many people can do. I give him an *I'm not convinced* look, feeling my face echo yours. 'Not well enough not to be in a secure mental hospital. They are confined here because they've done unspeakable things.'

'As you'll see shortly, there's heavy supervision. Patients need to develop their skills. They need stimulation. They have to feel the things they do are meaningful. That their lives have value.'

I think of Thorne's indefinite detention order. 'Even the ones who will never leave?'

He knows who I am talking about. 'Even those,' he says.

'All it takes is a blip in his good behaviour and you can end up with your wrist shoved between those blades,' I say.

'You're one of those people who is funny without meaning to be, aren't you?'

'Hilarious. Or your neck. Maybe get the skin of your arm sanded off with the planer or your fingers in the vice.'

'It's controlled. We train them in computer technology too, though everything they do is monitored and recorded.'

I am fixated on a rocking horse that is so exquisite it could be a gift for a baby prince. To be faced with evidence of Thorne's considerable carving skills makes me want to cry. I replay what Adam has said and look up from its intricate face. 'Do the patients know they are being spied on?'

He doesn't answer, but I persist. 'Do you ever learn anything useful?'

Again he doesn't answer.

'They must reveal things,' I say. 'When they've let their guard down. When they are immersed. Is that the real incentive for all of this skills development?'

'The education team report to us on how they're doing.'

'Not exactly what I was asking. I mean, do you discover more about the people they have hurt, the things they've done?'

'Occasionally.'

I am thinking of the onion router that made your laptop seem as clean and shiny as a brand-new machine. I am thinking also of the recent headlines linking you to Thorne, as well as the interview I did a few months before they appeared. Could Thorne have seen my interview, then somehow instigated those news stories himself?

'I bet some of them are clever enough to circumvent your computer spyware. Maybe visit websites or communicate in ways you don't know about.'

'No.'

'I wouldn't be so confident – they must be finding back doors.'

He moves his head to acknowledge the possibility, but only as a matter of politeness.

I run my hand over the smooth top rail of a perfectly carved chair.

Killer's Woodwork Fetches High Price at Auction.

'Whoever made that rocking horse is talented. And this chair.'

Murderer Donates Auction Proceeds to Hospital for Sick Children.

Thorne never hurt children. Just the three women whose frozen bodies were found in the room he'd dug and fitted beneath his house.

Adam touches the chair too. When his fingers bump into mine I let the contact stay for a few seconds before I pull them away to brush hair from my face.

Thorne Too Disturbed to Be Interviewed by Detectives.

I pick up a jewellery box. Its top and sides have been carved with tiny daisies and vines. Did he use this pattern on skin too? I turn it over, looking for his initials – he was rumoured to have engraved them on the women he tortured.

The two letters seem to blaze at me. *JT.* A man who was capable of the most terrible acts of ugliness made this breathtaking thing.

I cannot tear my eyes from the box as I say to Adam, 'I'd like your expertise.'

'I already offered you that.'

'Not for the people I help.' I'm still studying the box as if looking away from it would be the most impossible thing in the world. 'I want it for myself.'

'As a patient?' He takes the box from my hands as if

261

it were a deadly weapon. 'Because you must know that's not how it works.' He walks towards the door and I follow him.

I touch his hand, briefly, as he moves to open it. 'Of course not as a patient.'

He pauses to look at me. 'It doesn't take an expert to see that you're still traumatised by your sister's disappearance. That it was a deep stress event for you and you can't let her go. I have never seen anyone hold on as tightly as you do. Do you talk to her?'

I push past him to open the door and walk out but he quickly catches up.

'Please stop for a minute, Ella,' he says.

His emotional ambush makes me reel almost as violently as our mother's. My hand finds its way to the building and I lean on it, as if that will stop me from falling.

'Does she talk back to you?' he says. 'Do you hear her?'

I blink at him.

'Are there ever other voices than hers? I suspect yes, but that it's predominantly her. Am I right?'

I swallow and try to move my mouth to speak but nothing comes out.

'There isn't any treatment I would want to give you for these symptoms. They are situational. They arise from a specific trauma. They are not co-morbid. I'm inclined to think this private communication works for you, keeps you functioning and actually keeps you well. That these are your tools rather than any sort of pathology.'

I cannot speak at all. How does he know this? Nobody has ever guessed it.

'I'm sorry,' he says. 'I've upset you. I said too much. I want to know you as a person, not a patient, Ella. So let's close this subject.' His phone rings. He answers and talks in monosyllables before ringing off. 'I need to go,' he says. 'I'll take you back to Reception. You can wait there until your appointment with Jason Thorne.'

'I can find my way back.' My voice comes out as a croak.

He shakes his head. 'Visitors need to be escorted at all times.' He reaches over to brush my shoulder.

Despite the electric shock he gives me, and my small jump backwards into a flower border, his fingers seem to pause to test the silk of your dress between them.

'What are you doing?' My voice is shrill.

'Baby spider.' His voice is calm and unworried, a parent to a toddler who is in the grip of irrational fear. He holds out his hand and I can see the tiny creature dangling there by its fine strand. 'What did you think I was doing?'

'Nothing.' I sound like a child telling a ridiculous lie.

He continues with that chivalrous patience of his. He is concentrating. Gently, he moves his hand, floating the wisp of spider silk to a rose bush, letting it catch on a branch. The spider baby wafts into the green leaves and disappears.

The Door at the End

I stumble along in your clunky-heeled boots, following a beefy security man who probably moonlights as a nightclub bouncer. Soon, I am back at the glassed-in reception counter. Another encounter with the grumpy frazzle-haired woman is enough to shake away the near-paralysis induced by Adam's unasked-for diagnosis.

'I have an appointment with Jason Thorne at 2 p.m.,' I say.

She looks at me blankly.

'I gave you my letter of invitation when I first arrived,' I say.

Has Ted done something to stop the visit? Maybe he wanted to keep me away not just from Thorne but Adam too. I hear our mother's voice. *Paranoid.* Then I remember the intensity of Ted's eyes on Ruby, and the contempt of those same eyes when they were turned on me. I should not fool myself that Ted would care at all.

The woman starts click-clacking on her keyboard.

'I made the request two weeks ago and it was approved last Thursday,' I say. 'Mr Thorne consented to the visit and put me on his list. Dr Holderness knows about it.'

She is reading a series of notes on her computer screen, continuing to act as if I am a ghost she cannot see or hear. She sucks in air, grimacing as if she has come across something extremely disturbing, and I can see plum lipstick on her teeth.

'I was led to understand that there are no clinical grounds to deny my visit,' I say. 'Is there a problem?'

'No problem.' She pushes her spectacles down her nose so that she can give me a sharp look over the frames. 'Please be patient.'

Some people don't have much power, Melanie. So they exercise the little they do in the smallest, nastiest ways they can.

Were you thinking of someone in particular? I remember you coming home from the hospital in an especially bad mood when you made this pronouncement.

At last, the woman says, 'Dr Holderness will not be personally escorting you this time. That is not what he usually does.'

Maybe she has a crush on Adam and that is why she detests me. 'Of course,' I say. 'I don't mind who escorts me.' I smile sweetly and she pretends not to notice.

Jason Thorne lives in the main hospital building, in a ward for patients with dangerous and severe personality disorders. I am sitting on a red upholstered chair, part of a row of six that are linked together like the snap-apart pieces of a cereal box prize. I was deposited in this secure area by a security guard after retracing the route through the tunnel of locked gates, then yet another silvery airlock.

A door swings open and Adam walks through it, despite the grumpy woman's assertion that he would not be escorting me again. He looks confident and elegant in his dark suit. I cannot help but like him for the pink shirt he is wearing beneath it.

'I'm sorry I was called away,' he says. 'Emergency with another patient. I owe you a coffee.'

'It's fine. I understand.'

'I'll take you in,' he says. 'He's under my care.'

My knees are shaking so much I am pressing on them to try to keep them still. I say, 'Are you sure it's safe to expose him to someone you diagnosed with multiple personality disorder?'

'I haven't diagnosed you with anything. I said you are functioning well.'

I am not going to stop talking to you, even if this man has guessed that I do. If there is a name for it, even if it is a disease, I do not care.

He clears his throat, as if that will draw a line beneath the subject.

'Did you approve my request to see Jason Thorne?'

'I may have acted a bit more quickly when I saw your name. Sped the paperwork through – I wanted to do something to help.' He catches my eye. 'It would have still happened without me, just a bit slower.'

I stand to follow him. 'Thank you, Adam.'

He startles at my use of his Christian name for the first time. But this is no occasion for him to smile. 'He's taking his meds. He's stable. His behaviour has been satisfactory for several years now.'

'Will he be in restraints?' My voice is trembling, though I am trying to steady it.

'He's deemed to be low risk – he's made good progress since he first came here and the visit will be carefully supervised. There are security measures in place, but if he needed restraints you wouldn't be seeing him.'

I give up on trying to hide my anxiety. 'Will there be a barrier between us?'

He shakes his head. 'This isn't a prison, Ella. We want patients to have the most natural interactions possible with their guests. The Visitors' Centre is like a living room. It is as un-medical as it can be. But there will be staff quite close. They will be watching carefully. They are in a position to act quickly, if necessary. Does that make you feel better?'

'A little.'

'He has a legal and humanitarian right to visitors, but his ability to exercise that right is subject to quite stringent medical criteria. That approval is appropriate in his case, on clinical grounds, and has been for some time.'

Adam flashes a card at an electronic reader, punches in an access code, and opens the door. 'It was his choice to see you. If he had refused your request, I couldn't and wouldn't have done anything.'

The sight of the long corridor lined with locked metal doors makes my stomach drop.

'Ready?' Adam says.

I try to say yes but the word stops in my throat. I swallow. I manage a nod.

'Good. It's the door at the end. He's waiting.'

Jewels

It is more like a Victorian drawing room than a hospital visitors' area. It is big, but Jason Thorne is so huge he seems to be the only thing in it. He is also the only thing I can hear. A thunderous bellow erupts from his belly and I understand why the smell of cabbage and faeces is mixed with the lemony disinfectant they must use on every surface and spray into the air to try to disguise the scent of male sweat that is inescapable in this place.

All I see in the room is him. He is spilling over the single cushion of a sofa that is upholstered in gold fabric traced with vines and flowers in a deeper shade of the same colour. I know Adam said they'd designed the Visitors' Centre to be homey and unclinical, but it still seems an absurd piece of furniture for a secure mental hospital.

Thorne was tall and thin in the newspaper photographs published after they caught him. Now he is obese. The sofa is shaped into a perfect half-circle and reminds me of a piece of doll's house furniture. He is a giant atop a dainty toy that seems about to collapse beneath his enormous weight.

He stands to greet me, all six foot four of him, and it is clear that he wouldn't need to jump high or hard for his bald head to crash into the ceiling.

'Lovely to meet you.' He speaks like a politician greeting his guest of honour but his voice is such a bellow I have to resist the urge to slap a hand over my ear. The voice alone could knock me over. A few minutes of this and I will need to go into a decompression chamber to recover. His movement sets off another roar and an intensification of the smell that is so horrible it is a struggle not to bury my nose in my hair so that I can inhale my soapy-fresh shampoo to try to mask him. It is the same shampoo you used, and I like it because the scent reminds me of you. It occurs to me that this may be the case for Jason Thorne too.

He beams at me and puts out his huge paws, waiting to take mine between them. They look like normal hands, but for their giant size. How can a pair of hands have done what these did but not have a mark or a sign? I stare at them, as if searching for one. But there is nothing, of course.

My inability to move or speak or breathe goes on for an uncomfortably long time and I keep my own hands firmly at my sides. My feet are frozen on the ludicrously thick green carpet. My heart is thumping so loud I think he can hear it. All the while, he smiles understandingly, slightly amused, as if he is a movie star patronising an awestruck fan. His stomach does something that sounds exactly like a wolf's howl.

270

He shrugs and slowly lowers his arms. 'Thank you for bringing her,' he says to Adam, dismissing a servant. 'You can leave now. My visitor and I would like to speak privately.'

My normal inclination to correct a strange man for teaming himself with me is paralysed. Above all else I do not want to be left alone with Jason Thorne. I am groping for the right words to say so but Adam saves me from needing to.

'You know the rules, Jason. Ward staff need to be present. Today I'm one of them.'

'Interesting step down from your usual activities, Dr Doom.'

'If you're not happy with the arrangement, Miss Brooke will need to leave now.'

I still haven't moved or spoken. The room is starting to spin and there is a serious danger that my legs will buckle.

Two hulking male nurses who look more like body-guards than medical professionals are sitting at a shiny wood-veneered table, positioned five feet from Thorne's side of the sofa. Is their close-by table close enough? They appear to be working their way through papers, but I am certain they are listening to every word. I am certain they have perfected the art of seeming to read when in fact they are watching us, ready to punch tranquilliser needles into Jason Thorne's tree-trunk arms if he moves too quickly. I am certain that I am not deluding myself with this impression. Adam said that there would be carefully trained staff nearby. He said there were security measures in place, but I wish they were more obvious.

They must need to special order Thorne's jeans. The hospital kitchen probably tries to control his weight, but he has to be carrying an extra two hundred pounds at least. Why has this happened to him? Is it the medication? Comfort eating? They will be wheeling him out of this place some day in an industrial crate. Rolls of fat are visible beneath his red lumberjack shirt, but his sheer bulk makes him dangerously strong.

Thorne pats the thin sliver of sofa beside him. He really does love to play the genial host. 'Please sit here and make yourself comfortable, Melanie.'

My head whips up at my full name. Did he hear you use it?

I remind myself it is on the passport I showed the frazzle-haired woman. It has probably been transmitted all over the hospital since I arrived, perhaps repeated to Thorne. I imagine a ward nurse approaching him. 'Melanie Brooke has arrived for you, Jason,' the nurse would say.

Thorne reads my mind. His eyes flick to my chest. I look down and see the sticker the receptionist gave me, above my left breast. Melanie Brooke is written on it in permanent ink. I had forgotten about it.

At last, I speak. 'I'd be more comfortable in a chair, thank you.' I grab one, a small-scale version of the sofa that is clearly part of a set, and drag it across the room. I place the chair opposite Thorne, glad of the low coffee table between us, made of more of that unidentifiable blonde wood veneer they have used all over the room to make it look like a pseudo drawing room.

The cushion is slippery. It squeaks when I move but

I am relieved to be sitting down. It means I am no longer in danger of falling over. Already I am beginning to feel less faint. Adam takes a chair that matches mine and places it beside me.

'Good to know you can talk,' Thorne says.

How would I fight a man like Thorne? How quickly could he get to me? Could he grab me before one of the bouncer nurses got to him with knockout drugs and restraints? A big part of the strategy would involve making sure he couldn't possibly pin me down with his body, because once that happened the options would be limited. Small things would work best. Eye gouges. Breaking his pinky finger. Using his weight against him as he crashed down. The most important thing would be stunning him and getting out of his reach.

There are cameras everywhere. I suspect there are hidden microphones too. I am certain that Adam is listening intently, though he looks as if he is about to have a beer with an old friend in his living room. His legs are far out and he is slouching in his chair over his clipboard with unbelievable casualness. I have never seen him slouch before. Is he trying to be less visible? Less threatening to Thorne?

The only way to get through this, I realise, is to try to pretend that Thorne is normal. To speak to him as if this were an ordinary encounter. As far as possible, anyway. Because the alternative to tricking myself in this way is total shutdown.

'I saw some of the things you made, Mr Thorne,' I say. 'The rocking horse is beautiful.' My voice is steadier than I thought it would be.

He ignores the compliment with studied well-manneredness but his face lights up. 'I like to make things for children,' he says. 'I like children. Do you?'

'Yes.'

'I don't like people who hurt children,' he says.

'Nor do I.'

'Call me Jason.' He says this as if he is giving me a gift.

I move my head in acknowledgement but I do not call him Jason. It would be difficult to breathe, if you were too near him. There is a cloud of sour sweat in the air around him. Was this the last thing you ever smelled, obliterating your memories of fresh air and rain, making you forget your baby's milky-sweet skin? Bile is rising in my throat and I have to work hard to swallow it down.

'I thought you'd come.' His face is so fleshy, when he smiles. I do not like this politician's smile of his. 'I always thought you would. I've been waiting for you.'

Adam barely looks up from his clipboard. 'How long is always?' Thorne ignores him and Adam asks another question. 'What made you think that?'

'This is my party. You get to be a silent guest, if you insist on crashing it.' Thorne speaks as if he is in charge and Adam is the one locked in the mental ward for criminal psychopaths. Is this really 'satisfactory behaviour', as Adam called it? The standards of measurement are clearly different here.

Adam simply continues in his sleepy pose, while Thorne turns back to me, his face full of concern, enjoying the obvious difference in the way he is treating me and Adam. 'I'm deeply sorry about the disruption, dear Melanie.'

'How and when did you become aware of my existence, Mr Thorne?'

'It is too early in our relationship for us to be so personal.'

'Do you know something of interest to me, that made you think I would seek you?'

'Again, we are not yet ready for such confidences. You will need to be patient. Why don't we begin with your telling me why you wanted to come here.'

'I think you know why.'

He nods, as if proud of me for living up to his expectations. 'Do I repulse you?'

I don't answer this. I won't answer this. My refusal to answer is an answer.

He holds out his hands, shrugs, and looks down at his body. The series of theatrical gestures verges on comical, because they are so overdramatic. 'I mean this corporeal shell, lest there be any doubt.'

Corporeal shell. Where did he learn to talk? What does he read?

I don't acknowledge the words or the movement. He studies my face and I force myself not to squirm, not to move. Just to meet his gaze evenly.

'You're not a liar,' he says.

Little the fuck do you know, I think.

'I didn't take your sister,' he says. 'Have you been having bad dreams, Melanie, thinking that I did?'

I am not about to tell this man anything about my dreams. Or my nightmares.

'Was she much like you?' he says.

'A lot of people seem to think so.'

275

'Tea, Melanie. Allow me to make you a cup.' The offer isn't a question.

I can't help my surprise. 'They let you near boiling water?'

'You're funny. I like a sense of humour. But you don't have to worry. There is a maximum temperature. Never hot enough to injure. Everything is toddler-proof. I am afraid that the tea will not be as I would wish it for you.'

'No thank you.' He must guess that I will not drink anything he has touched.

'Then squash. I insist.' He pours orange liquid from a clear jug that looks like glass but is actually made of something shatterproof. Those sausage fingers of his are remarkably adroit and precise. When he places a blue tumbler in front of me something flakes from his wrist and into the drink.

That is when I notice his bracelet. It is a short string threaded with dead bluebottles. The centrepiece is a desiccated moth, shedding dust, with the corpse of a wasp on each side.

He holds out his wrist, smiling. 'Do you like it?'

'Were they already dead or did you make them dead?'

He looks at Adam, whose eyes flick up to watch his answer. 'Of course they were already dead.' He is practically laughing with the lie. 'If I killed living things I'd lose my privileges. I'd like to try a necklace but I am only allowed frustratingly short pieces of string.'

Yet they let you near saws and planers. I point to a dried slug, marbled black and curled through one of his buttonholes. 'That too?'

'More found art.' He opens his eyes wide in fake regret.

'Convenient that it died in that position. It's a perfect fit.'

'Before my repentance, I got excellent results by putting them in an oven alive and cooking them slowly.' He moves his expression into shocked innocence. 'One patient, far less well than I, has been known to trap them beneath a cup on his windowsill, when the sun is hot.

'Not to your taste, alas,' he says. 'You're very controlled, Melanie, but not perfectly – I can still see.' He points to the drink that he has seasoned with his most recent victims. 'You must be thirsty.'

'Not at the moment.' I can feel Adam trying to suppress a smile. 'Why should I believe you when you say you didn't take her?'

'Biscuit, Melanie?' I shake my head no. 'Please take one.' He picks up a plate of sugar cookies and offers it across the low table, set for a toddler's tea party—but for the small murdered guests. A wasp's wing falls onto snowy icing. 'The patients make them. Part of that occupational therapy our doctor friend thinks is so important. What a good man he is, our Dr Holderness.'

I choose a wasp-free biscuit in the shape of a star, so that Thorne smiles that hateful smile again. 'Perhaps I will be hungry later,' I say, accepting the napkin he graciously hands me. I put the biscuit on the napkin, beside the tumbler. Every move this man makes, every word out of his mouth, is a power game. 'You didn't answer my question, Mr Thorne.'

He shrugs, sighs, shakes his head in bewilderment as if he and I are unfairly persecuted victims together. 'I would like to help you,' he says.

'Why? Is Dr Holderness's treatment working so well that you have become selfless?'

He laughs. 'No compliments for the do-gooding doctor. Do you find do-gooders tedious? And pious? And exhausting? Because I do. But I am bored, Melanie. I seek amusement where I can.'

'I find it difficult to see how you can help me.'

'Insight, at least at first. Do you ever think about what he did with her body?'

I say nothing.

'I think you do think about this,' he says. 'I think you lose sleep thinking about it. But I can see it is painful to you. Do you like pigs?'

Again I say nothing.

'Ah. You must be vegetarian – you have already made it clear that you don't like violence. Good to know, in case I am ever able to entertain you.'

'One more remark like that and Miss Brooke will leave,' Adam says.

'An innocent comment, Dr Dire. Please accept my apologies, Melanie. I meant no offence. Quite the opposite.' He eats me up with his eyes and I refuse to shrink. 'I am a deeply creative person, you know,' he says. 'Everything I do, I do for art. I think I may have found my new muse in you.'

'You were talking about pigs, Mr Thorne?'

He makes a show of his patience with me. 'They'll eat anything. They'll make anything vanish.'

'I read a novel recently where the villain does that.' I shake my head in contempt. 'That's always happening in books and I always think it is silly. Are you trying to say you think that's what happened to my sister?' My anger is helping me. It is too big to let me properly imagine such a desecration. 'Can't you do better than that? Tell me the truth about why you want to help me, but don't waste my time.'

'I like company. I especially like your company. I like beautiful things, beautiful women. I used to like for them to become part of my vision, so I could make them even more beautiful. But they didn't want to. It was very sad. Not unless I persuaded them. Of course, this is not what I want any more.' The last sentence is uttered with such ironic insincerity it would be laughable if it were not so sickening.

'How did you persuade them?'

'Free carpentry. Wooden gifts. A visit to my workshop. In here, the only lure I have is information. Understanding.'

'And you have this information and understanding because of the things you yourself have done?'

'Not to your sister. But yes.' He glances at Adam and adds a quick, ostentatiously phoney, 'I am very sad to say.'

'Did you meet her?'

'Not in person. I spoke to her. She phoned me.' His eyes narrow. 'You didn't know, did you? Tell me the truth, Melanie.'

'I suspected recently.'

His face flushes. 'The tabloids, a few weeks ago?' he says.

'Yes.'

'Surely the police told you before then?'

'No.'

'It was on her phone records,' he says. 'The police checked them soon after they caught me. Went on and on about it in my interviews. Did you ask them about me?'

'My family did, but they wouldn't confirm any contact between you. Not when you were first arrested and not when we asked again last month.'

He nods and sighs. 'I can assure you the police have known all along. They are bastards, aren't they? Excuse my language. The journalists tell you more than they do. We see eye-to-eye on so many things, you and I, Melanie.'

'How many times did you speak to my sister?'

'Just one long telephone conversation. She started with a view to saying yes but ended with no.' He laughs. 'So often the case for me.'

'What exactly did she say no to?'

'My doing a carpentry job for her.'

'The telephone was your only means of communication?'

'Interesting question.'

'That isn't an answer.'

'Her only means of communication with me, yes.'

'What other means might there be, Mr Thorne? And with whom?'

'Good questions. I'd like to give you answers, Melanie. If I weren't trapped in this place, I'd find more of them for you – I'd do anything for you. Unfortunately, in the circumstances, you will need to do this yourself.' He shrugs tragically, and goes on. 'Something else for you to consider. She dealt in cash, your sister, didn't she?'

'Sometimes. But you're not telling me anything the

police don't already know. If you want my company you're going to need to do better. You said you'd find more answers. More implies you already have some.'

I can't decide if those amber eyes of his are actually small or if they appear that way because the rest of him is so big. There is a glint in one of them and he gives me a *Who Me?* shrug that looks absurd and obscene at once. 'I kept my business aboveboard. Everything recorded. Taxes paid. You get it, don't you?'

'You didn't want anyone looking at you carefully, uncovering the more serious dangers you posed.'

'Exactly. But your sister didn't want a paper trail of her payment to me. That's why she changed her mind. Got me wondering, after she disappeared, who was really paying for the work she wanted done?' He smiles. 'You've thought about that too. Your face is guarded, Melanie, but there are cracks in your armour.'

This is the second time he has said this. He has been right both times.

'By the way,' he says, 'do you like field hedges?'

'What?'

'Old English field hedges. Do you like them?'

I think of the countless family walks of my childhood, the earlier ones with you there too, and blackberry picking in September, and the quests for the dwindling nightingales that I still make with Luke in late spring. 'I do.'

'Are you any good at geometry?'

'I'm okay at it.'

'Forty-five-degree angles. I want you to visualise a forty-five-degree angle.'

'Sorry?' Immediately I am angry at myself for using this word to him.

'Please don't apologise.' He laughs at his own wit. He lowers his voice to a bedroom voice that I really, really do not want to hear. 'I never want you to be sorry with me.' Thorne picks up the biscuit with the wasp wing on it, licks the edge, takes a large bite, chews slowly.

Adam sits forward a little but his neutral expression doesn't change and he continues to scribble on his clipboard in writing that is so small and cramped I have to struggle to read even one word from where I'm sitting. I squint harder and my own name pops out.

Thorne downs a tumbler of orange squash in one gulp. 'I am ready to continue with your geometry lesson.

'Step 1. Dig a sloping hole that goes into the ground at a forty-five-degree angle, so that the hole finishes directly beneath the hedge. You want the hole to be the length of the body you need to bury.

'Step 2. Roll the body down. No detector is going to find that body. Not with that hedge above it. My bet is those hedges thrive because of the fertiliser. Some of them are hundreds of years old. Some of them are protected.'

He licks his lips. His tongue is fat too. He sighs. 'I miss the great outdoors. There is such a wonderful variety of plant life. Brambles, of course. Hawthorne. Ivy. All tangled together. All complex. Better yet, a hedge in a private field in the grounds of a private house, probably on private farmland, so he can keep her close.'

'Theory or experience, Mr Thorne?'

'Theory, of course, Melanie. But in my view it is the

strongest explanation there is as to your sister's where-abouts. I lived in a small house with no private hedges. The police searched it so thoroughly they practically demolished it. I promise you won't find her there.'

'So why should this matter to me?'

'Your sister was not the sort he would want to be entirely rid of. He would want to know where she is, to see that place whenever he wants. I can't tell you if she was his first, but whether or not she was, she won't be his last. She won't be enough. He will want another like her.'

'Why do you speak as if you are certain that she is dead?'

'It's difficult to imagine anything else, isn't it? You don't lie to others. Why do you lie to yourself?'

'What am I not seeing, Mr Thorne? What have the police missed?'

'You are thinking too much about type. About who *he* would choose. Which, yes, is you. And your sister. You would certainly be my choice. In many ways, though, you two were quite different, weren't you? You, I would want to keep. For a long time. I would want us to enjoy our time together.'

Adam shifts in his chair and begins to make another noise of protest, but Thorne brushes him away.

'You should be thinking about the type *she* would choose. That's a better starting point for you than the needle in the haystack of who would choose her.'

'Any ideas?'

'Yes, as a matter of fact.' He turns those tawny eyes on Adam. 'Someone like the good doctor.'

Adam doesn't react. He simply makes another note.

'Educated. Gentlemanly. Strong. The sort whose words are carefully chosen. And he would like her too. He certainly likes you.' Thorne glances at Adam and laughs. 'I've made the gooseberry blush. The only problem is that I don't think even Dr Dimwit would have been able to keep her in the style to which she wanted to grow accustomed.'

'Why are you so interested in my sister?'

'Missing women are my hobby. They are yours too. We have a lot in common, you and I. Everyone needs something to live for.'

'How do you know so much about her?'

'There's a lot in the newspapers. I have an eye for what might be true and what might not. I can find the real story hidden in the margins of what they don't say. I am like you, Melanie. I am good at interpretation. You find a small clue and you understand its significance while most would stick it in a file and let it moulder away. We should have been psychiatrists, you and I. Or detectives.'

'Has someone in here told you something specific?'

He shoos the question away with a hand, then swoops down on the biscuits, catching another and gulping it down in one bite. 'She liked nice things, didn't she? Expensive things. I could tell from talking to her. I never told the police what she wanted. Shall I tell you?'

'Yes.'

'You are very cold, Melanie. What would warm you up?'

Adam's eyes flick over me, quickly, as if he wonders about this too.

Thorne moves on, knowing there is no way I will dignify that question with a response. 'Shelves in her living room. She wanted roses carved into them. That is all. I thought she had a beautiful vision, if a bit limited. I also thought she was the sort of woman who knew what she wanted and would accept nothing less.'

'Did you visit her flat?'

'I told you I did not.' He sits up, shakes crumbs from his hands, catches sight of his bracelet when one of the flies falls off and onto his lap. 'It is ephemeral art, regrettably. Most of my creations are.' He smiles a terrible smile at Adam, the rictus smile of a snarling corpse in a horror film, and flicks the fly into the air with a finger, making me visibly startle, so that he fails to suppress a smile. The fly thuds onto Adam's clipboard with surprising weight. Adam's only reaction is to tip it onto the floor, calmly.

'I am afraid we need to say goodbye for now, Melanie. Time for my afternoon nap. The drugs they insist on giving me. When I refuse, well, they have ways of incentivising me to accept them, don't you, Doctor? Isn't incentivising the ugly word you sometimes use? *Comply with your treatment and you will be rewarded with a visit to the workshop, Jason.* I hope you will come and see me again, Melanie. I really enjoyed our little talk.'

I stand. My knees are wobbly. I grab the back of the chair to steady myself. 'Thank you for your time, Mr Thorne.'

'My true pleasure. I will consider you, Melanie. I will consider your sister. Shall I let you know if anything further occurs? Is that the only way I will see you again?'

'Yes,' I say, in answer to both questions.

'In that case, I will tell you that I have at least one fact at my disposal which will certainly interest you.' He sees me freeze. 'There will be a price to pay, for this little fact. Would you like to hear it?'

'You know I would.'

'You will need to play a game with me, then. A little game. A perfectly safe little game that Dr Dreamboat cannot possibly object to. Your wish to know will incentivise you – Ah, but it gives me pleasure to use that word to somebody else. Are you willing to play with me, Melanie? Are you sufficiently incentivised?'

I turn away, with Adam beside me and the nurse-guards watching.

As I am about to step through the door, Thorne calls out his parting shot. 'Lovely dress, Melanie.'

I inhale. My back arches. I stop short and the silky fabric gives a final swish against my legs before fluttering still. I do not know how long it is until I move again. I remind myself he could have seen the reconstruction. He did not necessarily see that dress on you. I do not look back. I do not answer him. For now, I have nothing more to say.

Wednesday, 16 November

The Cuckoo in the Nest

This is not a club that anyone would choose to be a member of. *Support Group for Family Members of Victims.* Christmas is still over a month away. The fact that it is already visible everywhere makes this gathering in the library meeting room especially challenging and important.

If you drew a line through the centre of this children's alphabet rug, Adam and I would be at opposite ends of it. I introduce him to the others, explaining that he is a consultant psychiatrist who works at the nearby secure mental hospital, and that he hopes to provide us with some alternative insights.

'Thank you for letting me come,' he says.

He is wearing black jeans and a dark grey jumper with a sliver of charcoal T-shirt at the neckline. There is a glimpse of orange socks. His model-handsome face is bristly with dark stubble. Perhaps he wasn't at work today? I find myself wondering what it would feel like to press my lips against his cheek. You better than anyone would understand these derailments. You would applaud them.

Concentrate, Ella, I tell myself.

Helen offers Adam a small nod of acknowledgement. She suffers from a neurological condition that causes any pain she feels, even a tiny twinge, to be amplified. The kindness of Helen's nod reminds me of where I am and why I am here and what I need to do, something I do not normally allow myself to forget.

Like a good teacher, Adam mirrors Helen and nods back. 'Would you like to tell me why you're here?' he asks her.

'My son was stabbed outside a nightclub,' she says. 'Early this year.'

Adam is regarding Helen with sympathetic calm. Thorne got nothing but a level stare, and only when looking at him could not be avoided. Yesterday's slouchy posture was clearly Adam's strategy for managing him.

'I'm not really in a talking mood,' Helen says. 'But thank you for asking.'

We sit for a minute, all of us sending our care to Helen. Then the door to the room opens and the man who sat in the corridor outside my risk assessment clinic steps inside.

'Hello,' I say. 'Are you here to join us?'

'If that's okay. I'm sorry I couldn't wait to see you last week. Something came up.' There is a tension around his eyes.

I rise to get another plastic folding chair. Two of the others, Betty and Patrick, move away from each other to make room, and the man with the once-broken nose squeezes the chair between them and sits down.

I pause to explain about the confidentiality of the group, and our guidelines and purpose. Then I ask if he would like to tell us about what brought him here.

He hesitates. 'My partner went missing.' He stretches out his long legs and crosses them at the ankles, as he did when I first saw him. He is dressed more casually today, in dark denim jeans and an aqua paisley shirt, which is untucked. His jaw stiffens. 'Perhaps I can say more later? Introduce myself properly then? I'm conscious of the fact that I've disrupted things.'

There are murmurs of 'Not at all' and 'We're very sorry about your partner'.

Helen turns to Adam. 'You asked why I'm here,' she says. 'It's important to be around people who understand. My friends find me depressing. They get tired of my going on about it all the time. Even Martin gets bored of it. But none of you do.'

Martin is Helen's husband. He rarely speaks at meetings, but he says, 'I don't get bored of it.'

I look at the newest member of the group, but he shakes his head to say, Not me, not yet, so I look instead at the man between him and Adam. 'Patrick?'

Patrick leans back and crosses his arms over his chest. He is chewing gum. Is it possible for cheeks to move aggressively? Because his seem to. His red hair sticks up as if he has put his finger into a socket.

Patrick is Ruby's father. His struggle to cope with the aftermath of her assault is heartbreaking. Ruby herself pressed him to join the group.

'How are you doing today?' I ask him.

I always ask about just one day. Never a general *How are you?* What is anybody in this room supposed to say to that one?

Patrick grunts and shoots a foul glance at Adam. 'Don't think you can swagger in here and expect all of us to start finding forgiveness.'

The new man has been looking sleepy, his chin so low his designer stubble is scratching his collar. His head shoots up to study Adam.

'I didn't say anything about forgiveness,' Adam says quietly. 'I am a psychiatrist, not a vicar.'

Patrick leans forward, slams a hand on each thigh, bends his knees so his feet are flat on the floor, and lifts one heel, then the other, in turn. 'Treating those men as if they were patients and not criminals. You make me sick.'

'I understand why you feel that,' Adam says.

'Don't fucking patronise me. You look after the evil cunt who took Ella's sister.' He turns to me. 'Why do you give this bastard the time of day, Ella?'

It flashes at me that I must visit Thorne again – a realisation that makes my breath so tight I feel as though I have been laced into a corset and sprayed with dead bugs.

'You're hurting Ella, spewing that tabloid rubbish.' Martin is glaring at Patrick. 'Look at her face. Look at what you've done.'

My voice is calm but my heart is beating too fast. 'This isn't supposed to be about me.'

Adam turns from Patrick, locking those black eyes of

his on mine. I am aware of the new man's eyes on me too. Everyone strains to listen above the small children singing outside the door. 'Why can't it be about you?' Adam says.

'I'm the leader of this group,' I say. 'I'm here to help others.'

'You do this because you're one of us.' Helen puts a light hand on my arm. 'You couldn't do what you do if you weren't. You deserve attention too.'

'She gets too much attention from the doctor,' Patrick says.

Martin throws his words at Patrick, seeming to throw a knife out of nowhere. 'At least your child isn't dead.'

Helen gasps and wraps her crooked fingers around Martin's elbow, as if by grabbing her husband she can undo what he has said. Her movement is too fast and hard, and she cries out in pain.

Patrick jumps out of his seat so violently it falls backwards with a crash. He makes a show of stepping over Adam's feet, stomps to the door, wrenches it open, and waits there as if deciding what to say before exiting. 'Silent Night' floats in, carried by sweet toddler voices.

But my attention is caught by something else. Or rather, someone else, standing by a rack of magazines she is clearly not interested in. She is ten feet away from the door. She sees me seeing her. She meets my gaze deliberately and holds it for a few seconds. Then she walks away as quickly as an elderly lady can. Mrs Buenrostro. I nearly pop out of my own chair to rush after her but the tornado I seem to be in the centre of is whirling too fiercely around me.

Helen tries to heave herself up to go to Patrick, but her body doesn't move quickly and before she can rise completely he holds out a traffic policeman's arm and she sinks back down, refusing Martin's attempts to help.

'Please don't leave us, Patrick,' she says. 'You belong here too. Martin didn't mean it.'

Something trickles down my cheek. I brush away a tear. 'This group is for anyone whose loved one has been the victim of a violent crime. It doesn't matter what type.' The Christmas carol has halted. I can hear a woman's voice, hushing a child. 'It isn't limited to families of murder victims. We all belong here.'

'Too fucking right, Ella. Except him.' Patrick jerks a thumb towards Adam. The partition walls of the little meeting room shake with his final slam of the door.

'Are you going to go after him?' The anger and distress of people she cares for have forced Betty out of the quiet invisibility that she wanted today. Her delicate hands are in such tight fists I am certain her nails will leave gouges in her flesh.

I reach out my right hand to touch the sleeve of her silky silver dress, then brush a speck of dust from her hair, which is silky and silver too. She slowly releases her fingers and gives me an almost-smile. I say, 'He is free to go, Betty. We all are. And he is free to come back if and when he wants to. I hope he will soon.'

The new man stands. He walks past Patrick's empty chair and somehow evades Adam's long legs without any theatricality or clumsiness. In seconds, he has the door open again. 'I find — I must go too. I hope to return sometime very soon. Thank you for making me welcome.'

I am only halfway through objecting that we do not even know his name before he is gone. I want to scream in frustration. This man has twice approached me, and twice bailed out. It takes courage, coming to a support group like this, or to the risk assessment clinic. He and I are both haunted by somebody who is missing. This makes me want to help him all the more.

'He obviously found us irresistible,' Betty says.

'It would be good to have a break,' I say. My cheeks are flaming. 'A few minutes for some water, and to catch our breath.' Already I am rising and moving towards the fake beech units at the back of the room, slipping five bright cups from the stack of child-safe drinkware on the draining board.

Adam is standing beside me, close enough for me to notice his soap, which smells of ginseng and citrus and black pepper. He takes the cups from me one at a time, filling them from the swan's-neck tap. My fingers are shaking. Visible evidence of my dissolving composure. Behind me, Adam is serving Helen, Martin and Betty their water as if they are his guests, as if he is not the visitor.

When I sit down again they all smile and I say, 'Well, that was interesting,' and everyone laughs, and Helen says, 'It's not a bad thing to change things, you know, Ella. Don't go home and regret asking Adam to come.'

Did I ask him? I am not sure which of us proposed the arrangement as we said goodbye at the hospital yesterday. I was still too dazed by my encounter with Thorne.

Helen looks directly in front of her. She says, 'I'd like to know how the last month has been for you, Betty.'

Betty gazes at her own feet, which are encased in silver ballet flats decorated with tiny crystal beads. Her toes must be freezing. 'My sister isn't talking to me,' Betty says.

'Why?' Adam doesn't move when he lets the word out.

'I said I couldn't go to my niece's wedding. The last time I went to a wedding I had to leave. Christenings too. I hate them. I hate celebrating these things. These young women having their lives, having the things Alice never got a chance to have.'

'I feel that way too,' says Helen.

'Of course you do,' Betty says. Her voice is even, gentle, as if talking to a small child to reassure them.

I rarely say anything about our family, but something in the last few minutes has torn down my usual rules and defences. I hear our mother's voice on Friday night. *I think of all the things she is missing*. And my anger towards her melts a little.

'My mother feels like that,' I say, and another tear leaks out.

Betty squeezes my hand. 'I wish my sister would understand. She says, "It's been two years." As if I should be over it.' Betty's words are not defensive. They are not edgy or angry. They are a little tired, though her voice is still lilting.

'No,' I say. 'Two years is not enough.' Ten years is not enough either. Is there ever a number of years that are enough?

'The man who did that to your daughter is a monster.'
Martin's eyes are bulging.

Betty is so calm, so quiet and soft. 'You won't understand him if you call him a monster. Your only chance
is to find his humanness. To find the ways that the two
of you are alike. That is the only way to predict and stop
him. The only way to find your own peace.'

I think of the grotesque monster I faced yesterday. Will
I get more out of Thorne if I try to see his humanness?
Try to understand him better? How dangerous would it
be to show him more kindness? What if I had lied and
told him I didn't find him repulsive, when he pointed to
his own body and asked me directly if I did? I remember
that flash of joy when I praised his rocking horse. A
blaze of pity for him rips through me at the thought,
taking me by surprise.

'There are no ways in which we are alike.' Martin
crosses his arms.

'When you were a child,' Adam says, 'did you ever pop
out at someone and say boo?'

Martin makes a barely visible 'of course' gesture.

'What you were doing then was taking pleasure in
someone else's fear. In feeling excited by scaring them.
My guess is that you enjoyed it as a child when your
friends, or maybe your sister or brother, booed out at
you in return. Don't you think it's evidence of the human
capacity to enjoy fear?' Alice and Betty are moving their
heads up and down in empathic we-agree-with-you-and-
are-listening gestures. 'It's a spectrum,' Adam says. 'We
are all on it.'

Adam goes on. 'Has anyone in this room ever found

297

out someone's email address or telephone number without asking them if they were happy for you to have it? How about you, Ella? Have you ever driven by the house of somebody you're interested in to see if their car is there? If their lights are on?'

I know this isn't a case of his turning to the teacher for help. He really wants to know if I have ever done this. And I have. I did exactly this to Ted last week. His lights were off. How is it that this man guesses so much about my secret ways of thinking and behaving? He even guessed that I talk to you. And that you talk back.

'No,' I say. 'I have never done anything like that.' My face must be giving me away with its change of colour.

He sits back in his chair. 'Ever phoned anyone to see who answered, then hung up without speaking?'

'No,' I say. This is another lie. I know what Ted's ex-wife sounds like. It was just once – I knew if I didn't stop immediately I never would.

I consider my indignation towards Sadie for making those blocked calls and feel a twinge of shame, though the thought of her coming anywhere near me or my family quickly makes it vanish.

'Who would do such a thing?' Helen asks.

Hanging above our heads is a green ribbon strung with holiday bunting, each triangle decorated by a child. I cannot take my eyes from a picture of a stick figure man chopping off the head of a stick figure woman. Why did they put that one up there, amongst the elves ringed in hearts and the smiling snowmen and red-nosed reindeer and fat Father Christmases and sparkly stars? Was it a small act of librarian sabotage, the failure not to dispose of this piece of toddler art made by a future psychopath?

'Anyone.' Adam's eyes seem to burn into my own. 'Anyone can do such a thing.'

Warning Signs

Adam lingers in his chair, looking at emails on his phone while I hug Betty goodbye, brush my lips against Helen's cheek so lightly they barely touch her, and beam the warmest smile I can manage at Martin.

As soon as the door closes behind them, Adam switches his phone off. 'Time for that coffee? We were cheated yesterday.'

I think of the text that came from Ted at lunchtime, still unanswered. *We should talk.* The sentence seems to be pulsing away through my blood, so that it moves through my veins faster, knowing what I am about to do, and gets faster still when I say, 'I'd love that, yes,' and watch Adam's eyes light up. They brighten more when I say, 'But can we make it something stronger?'

It comes to me in a rush that he was nervous to ask, anxious that I would say no. He smiles. Not his usual careful smile, but such a big smile that his face is not his usual careful face, but a shining face with crinkles around his eyes and mouth that I hadn't imagined were possible. I am not sure if my heart is hurting for Ted, or for the way I am using Adam's attraction to me. I think it is hurting for both.

That smile of his evaporates as we pass through the library's electronic security gates and a voice calls out your name.

I halt but don't say anything. At first, all I can see are warning signs. *No trespassing* in red. *CCTV in Operation* in yellow. Then I see a woman, standing before the glass of the semicircular window, lit by the street lamps below. She clearly belongs to the child who is bobbing up and down in the toy postal van, screaming that she wants another go.

'Miranda?' she says again.

I am not quite sure how, but my feet are slowly moving across a landing that is bigger than my entire upstairs, my fingers absently trailing the gilded bannister as I walk towards her, barely noticing that Adam is by my side.

She is shaking her head, as if in amazement. 'You look exactly the same.' She fumbles in her purse as the child's screams grow louder. She holds out some change. 'You don't happen to have a pound coin for this, do you?'

Adam passes over a coin and she drops several into his palm, then puts the pound in the slot of the toy van, which starts to jiggle and play a theme tune.

'You must have a painting in your attic,' she says.

'I'm not—'

She turns to Adam. 'And you're Miranda's partner?' She laughs and gives me a conspiratorial wink. 'You haven't changed your taste in men.' She looks at Adam and his frozen lack of response unnerves her.

Somehow, finally, I get the words out. 'I'm not Miranda. I'm her sister.'

The woman is hardly quick, especially with the child distracting her while she tries to recover her social self, but at last she is beginning to see that something is wrong and it isn't simply that she has mistaken my identity. 'But you look exactly like her.' She falters. 'Is she well?'

I am so used to the horror of everybody knowing. Of that being the only thing there is, the most important thing to know about me. That you are lost.

'You don't know?' Adam says.

She swallows several times. 'I've said something wrong. I can see that I have.'

'Miranda's been missing for the last ten years,' I say. 'We don't know what happened to her. It's been in the news. Everyone knows. People I don't know know.'

The ride is over again. 'Excuse me.' The woman tries to pluck the toddler out. The little girl clings to the wheel, but the mother manages to extract her and plop her onto a hip. The child clings on like a koala bear and this woman who knew you before you were snatched away strokes her child's golden hair, which matches hers.

'I can't imagine what you must be feeling.' Her face is blotchy.

Adam strokes his scalp. This isn't something I have ever seen him do. I think he is somehow taking the words out of my head and into his own, so he can form them for me. 'How is it that you didn't know?'

'My husband is South African. We moved there eleven years ago – the news didn't reach me. We've only recently returned to England.'

'And you know Miranda how?' I say.

'We worked together.'

'You're a nurse, too? Were you on the orthopaedic ward with her?' My shock is competing with my reflex impulse to gather intelligence.

She hushes the child. 'I was, yes. Your sister was a real heartbreaker, you know.'

Of course I know. But I don't confirm it to this stranger.

'And you are?' Adam is coldly polite.

'Veronica Skelton.' Veronica turns back to me. 'She was so beautiful,' she says. 'Like you,' she says.

It certainly wasn't an accident that Mrs Buenrostro came tonight. Is it really a coincidence that this woman who knew you is standing outside the library where I am running a publicly advertised group, in a position where I cannot fail to pass her on my way out? But if she has deliberately run into me, why go through the pretence of not knowing about you? Of striking up a conversation with me in this strange way?

And of bringing her child with her? The last factor is what makes me think her presence here probably is a fluke. Our mother would say that my wondering about this at all is yet more evidence that I am losing my mind, that I am a danger to everyone around me. Ted would agree that I am a paranoid conspiracy theorist.

'You say my sister was a heartbreaker. Did you notice any particular man whose heart she broke?'

She thinks for a few seconds. 'She didn't confide in me. I'm not sure she confided in anyone.'

This sounds like you.

'I wonder if there was a doctor, perhaps?' I look at

Adam, who returns my gaze steadily. 'Perhaps you knew Adam?' I say, presenting him to her with a gesture. 'He worked at the hospital, then.'

I know I am not being fair to him. Most of the consultants in Bath worked at that hospital at some point, including Brian, his brother, and Dr Blossom.

'Yes,' Adam says. 'In Psychiatry.' His face remains calm. He doesn't flush or twitch. There is no flicker of an eye upwards or to the left or right. There is no tell.

She pulls a biscuit from her bag and hands it to the little girl, a series of movements so quick and automatic she barely looks as she makes them.

She gives Adam an apologetic look. 'Sorry not to remember you.' There is no tell with her either as she says this. 'Did we meet?'

'Not that I can recall. You can't know everyone,' Adam says.

'Was there really nobody?' I am startled by the near-hysteria in my voice. 'No acquaintance ever that you noticed Miranda with?'

'Absolutely there was. But you were asking me about doctors and the man who comes to mind wasn't a doctor. He was a patient.'

'When? When was he a patient?'

'Maybe three years before I left.' She pauses to calculate. 'So about fourteen years ago.' She appears to be replaying a film reel inside her own head. 'He was really taken with her. I remember that. We all noticed.'

'Why was he in hospital? Do you remember that sort of thing with patients?'

'Not usually from so long ago, but this man was pretty

unforgettable. Incredibly charismatic and handsome, quite smooth and polished. He'd ruptured his Achilles' tendon. I don't recall how he did it, exactly. Only that he went to theatre for a surgical repair.'

I close my eyes and see the imprint of the boot in the woods, with the outsole worn so heavily. Could that be because its wearer was compensating for an old injury?

'Can you remember his name?'

'Not his surname. But I remember the first. Noah.' She looks dreamy, thinking of it. 'It's because I always loved the name. I'd always fantasised about having a little boy and naming him that.' She strokes her daughter's hair. 'But I got my lovely girl instead. Maybe next time.'

M + N + ?? My heart is hammering with excitement. 'Can you remember what he looked like?'

'Dark hair and eyes. Close-cut beard and moustache. Like that Spanish actor? God. Really famous. So frustrating . . . I can't think of his name . . . '

'That's more than fine. Thank you,' I say.

'I'm so sorry,' she says again, 'for the mix-up. That must have freaked you out.'

'I like it that seeing me brings her alive for someone else.' I look at Adam as I say this.

'You really do look like her, you know,' she says again.

I don't know what makes me say what I do next. 'Was it really an accident that you were here?'

Her face flushes red but I cannot be sure if it is because I have mortified her by making such an offensive suggestion or because I have confronted her with the truth.

'Do you want to tell me why you sought me out?' I

know as soon as the words are out of my mouth that I should have swallowed them back.

She shakes her head violently. 'I didn't seek you out.' Her phone rings. One ring, then nothing more. 'I have to go,' she says. 'That'll be my taxi.'

As she hurries away I rush after her. 'Can you give me your number so I can reach you again? I'd like to talk some more. Please.'

She shakes her head no. She clutches the child to her, fleeing from a baby-eating monster. I am following her down the stairs, though I glance briefly behind to see Adam staring after us in his measured way.

She halts in front of the glass double doors to the street. 'I've told you everything I can.' She pushes through the doors. There really is a taxi and she quickly gets in. Before it speeds away, I snap a picture of the beacon on top of it, with the company name and the car number. I know that data protection means I'll never get the taxi company to tell me where their car went. But it is possible there will come a time when I will need her as a witness, and if I give these details to the police they should be able to trace where the taxi took her.

I watch the taxi's rear lights until the small red dots are swallowed by darkness. Adam is beside me, his hand on my arm, lightly. 'You get home,' he says. 'We'll have that drink another time. It's been quite a night.'

'Just the usual.' I stand on my toes a little so that I can kiss his cheek, and watch him light up like a Christmas tree.

Thursday, 17 November

Guessing Games

There are at least a dozen empty parking spaces when I arrive at the circle of Georgian houses where Mrs Buenrostro lives. The sun has only just come up but I have a lot to do before Luke's football match this afternoon. It will not surprise you to know that I will be there. I have never broken a promise to Luke and I do not intend to start now.

For the hell of it, because I cannot resist an opportunity to try, I press the button for Flat 7, the Henrickson flat. There is no answer. Of course there is not. So I move my finger pad up an inch and plunge it onto Flat 6.

It isn't long before I hear white noise, then her voice. 'Who is it?'

She knows the answer to this already. She and I discussed the camera that is wrapped into the building's intercom system – she will be watching my grainy face on a small black-and-white screen inside her entry hall.

'It's Ella Brooke, Mrs Buenrostro. Are you going to let

me in, or do you prefer to lurk near the places where I'm working?'

'I wasn't lurking. I'd only arrived a minute before that man burst out. I'd thought to catch you afterwards, until I saw how things were.' She pauses for breath. 'How did you know my flat number?'

I lie easily, leaving our mother's detective work out of it. 'I planned to try them all but I got lucky with my first guess.'

She begins to give me elaborate directions for navigating the corridors of Henrietta Mansions and finding Flat 6.

I cut her off. 'I know the way.' I do not explain that this is because I have already looked at the floor plans using the land registry website. There is a buzz and the click of the lock releasing. With that, I am free to roam the building I could barely penetrate only a week ago.

When I reach the door to Flat 6, it is already open. Mrs Buenrostro stands inside. She is wearing another matchy-matchy trouser suit, this time powder blue. She has applied lipstick. Like our mother, this woman does not like to be seen in anything other than her best face. I do not bother to hide the fact that I am studying the L-shaped bend farther along the corridor that I know leads to Flat 7.

'Won't you come in?' she says.

I am practised at not looking at my watch, at not alerting anyone to the functions that circle my wrist. I have left a pre-alert voice message on my lone worker safety device, as well as an old-fashioned scrawled note on my own kitchen counter, detailing my plan to visit her. I am not expecting to disappear, but if I do, those who look for me will have a starting point. As long as I stay attached to the watch they will have real-time tracking too. I will throw the note away when I am safely home, and delete the message.

'Why did you seek me out last night, Mrs Buenrostro?'

'I needed to talk to you.'

'You have my telephone number.'

'In person.'

'Is Mrs Buenrostro your real name? Nothing comes up when I search for you on the internet.'

She looks behind me. She lowers her voice. 'It is a family name, my husband's great-grandmother's name. It is not carried in any written record that would lead to me.'

'That's why you chose it?'

She is actually whispering. 'Yes. To avoid leaving my footprint. I have had good advice in that regard.'

I think of you and your invisible internet life. I am fairly certain that you and Mrs Buenrostro had the same tutor.

'Please. Let's talk inside.' She motions for me to follow her, leads me into her beautifully proportioned living room. There are cornices and mouldings. There is a ceiling rose, high in the centre.

I choose a stiff-backed gold chair covered in fabric buttons, which poke into my spine. 'What do you want from me?'

What she says next is not the turn I expect the conversation to take. 'Do you know anything about undercover policing, Ella?'

'A little. I know about stealing the identities of dead

children. Sleeping with targets, deceiving them. Even having babies with them.'

She turns to look at a photograph on the chimney piece. She'd said she had no children. As far as I can judge from three metres away, the photograph is of a young boy. She wipes away a tear.

'Is that your son?' I say, as gently as I can. 'Did he die, Mrs Buenrostro? Did they take his identity? I'm very sorry for you.'

'You misunderstand.'

'Then help me to understand.'

'Not all undercover policemen do the terrible things you speak of. Do you know the term "deep swimmer"?'

I shake my head no.

'It's somebody who goes undercover for a long time, sometimes many years. Sometimes they can't go near their real life at all. Or only very occasionally.'

'I still don't understand.' But I am beginning to.

'We thought it would be easiest if we stayed as close to the truth as possible.'

She sounds like our mother. She sounds like you. And like me. She sounds like someone who has been coached in the methods and principles of covert policing.

I look again at the photo. Just the one. That is all. I am in no doubt that it is to remind her of who she is, what she is for, who she loves.

It is almost a physical pain not to inspect that photo. I do not want her to stop talking but I do want a closer look.

'You see, I must live discreetly. Someone close to me is working undercover. Very deeply and long term. He doesn't tell me much detail. I hardly see him and when I do, only secretly. It's never predictable.' Her voice catches. 'Family members make them vulnerable. They can expose them.'

'Why are you telling me? Isn't that dangerous for him? For you?'

'Only if you decide to speak of it. I think I know enough about you to feel confident that you would not put me at risk by doing so. It is your vocation to protect the vulnerable, Ella. Anyone can see that.'

'You don't know me at all. I'd throw you under a bus for my family, Mrs Buenrostro. I hope it never comes to that, but please consider yourself warned.'

She deliberately looks towards the photograph. I stand, but need to grab the back of the chair for a second to get my balance. My legs seem to have lost their very bones. Somehow, I walk with apparent steadiness to the chimney piece. She joins me. I stare at the picture while she stares at me, watching for a reaction that I am determined not to give.

The boy is sitting in the crook of an olive tree's trunk, the branches twisting off behind him and to both sides, so he seems to be cupped by them. He is grinning at his own daring, at being so high. It is a close-up, so there isn't enough landscape for me to be confident of my guess that he is in Spain or Greece. I can tell by the light that it is early summer, and by the sweet green of the leaves and olives. The picture was taken on the kind of instant camera that was popular several decades ago.

The boy is eight or nine. Not quite as old as Luke but not far behind him. His hair is the same near-black as

Luke's. His eyes are brown as opposed to the bright blue that I see when I look in the mirror or at Luke or our father or you. But what really strikes me is the familiar shape of the chin and the dimples I love so much on another face, as well as the honey tint of his skin from the sun, which he didn't get from you. There is the cowlick too, twirling itself into a little coil above the left temple.

I press my arms against my sides to stop them from visibly shaking. I keep my face unreactive. I make myself look at Mrs Buenrostro, brace myself to meet her gaze calmly.

She picks up the photograph, trails a finger over the smooth wood of the simple frame, which is overlaid with gold paint. 'Don't you imagine the other reason why I feel safe talking to you? Why I trust you not to throw me under a bus, as you so charmingly put it? Shall we sit, Ella? I get tired.'

'Let me get you a glass of water.' The offer is more for myself than for her. I need to be out of her sight for a minute.

She sinks onto a squishy sofa that is covered in country roses. She keeps the photograph on her lap. 'That would be kind,' she says. 'I suspect you know where the kitchen is.' She sounds faintly amused, as if it has occurred to her that I researched her floor plans.

Her flat is a square, with the kitchen in one corner, the living room in another, and bedrooms in the other two. The entry hall slices through the square's centre, with doors to the four rooms branching off and the bathroom at its end. The bedroom doors are closed. Mrs Buenrostro cannot see them from where she sits.

As quietly as I can, hoping there won't be a squeak, I open the first door. What do I expect? A man to be crouched behind it, waiting to spring out? And what kind of man? Criminal or undercover policeman? Do such people themselves forget which they are? There is nothing but a bed, prettily made with an ivory counterpane. There is a beautiful old wooden closet. My heart seems to stop when I pull the door open, but it is full of winter coats and makes me think of the *Narnia* books I read to Luke.

I try the second door. This must be where Mrs Buenrostro sleeps. It is furnished identically, but for the addition of a dressing table with her carefully arranged face creams and scents and an old-fashioned comb and brush set, made of engraved silver. Nobody is hiding in here either. The door squeaks when I shut it but I am beyond caring. She can probably feel where I am in the flat, anyway.

There is nothing remarkable in the kitchen. The walls are white porcelain, the floor is black slate, and it is filled with shiny expensive gadgets that appear never to be used. It is scrupulously neat and clean, like everything else about Mrs Buenrostro. She keeps nothing that might give her away, as if she herself were engaged in covert policing, too. Only the boy on the chimney piece.

She calls my name, so I hurriedly get the water and return to the living room. I put the glass in her hand, then sit once more in the uncomfortable chair.

'It wasn't true,' she says, 'when I said I had no child.'

I glance at the photograph on her lap. 'That much is clear now.'

'He was a much-wanted late-in-life baby. I was forty-two when he was born. We had given up hope.' She pauses at my quick inhalation of breath, but goes on. 'He works abroad. He is useful to them, because he speaks so many languages. Since I moved here I have hardly seen him. I don't know where he is, at any given time. He does visit, but very rarely. He never gives me advance notice. He has – ways – of letting me know.'

I look around this impersonal but expensive space in the centre of Bath. I think of your car and flat, your designer clothes, your cash-filled savings accounts. 'Are most covert policemen as rich as your son?'

'There is family money. My son does what he does because he thinks it's important. Like you, Ella.'

'So you were talking about your son, when you spoke of the man in Flat 7? When you spoke of Mr Henrickson?'

'Nobody has ever turned up asking about him. I can't tell you what a fright it gave me.' She almost smiles. 'But you don't look like an assassin or spy.'

'You'd be surprised,' I say.

'I remembered the woman who visited him as soon as I saw you.'

My back becomes clammy. My fingers start to tingle.

But she goes on, oblivious, caught up in her own story. 'That's the other reason I let you in. I thought at first you actually were her. You look so like her.'

'It didn't occur to you to go to the police when she disappeared shortly after you saw her with your son?'

'I didn't know who the woman was until you told me your sister's name and showed me her picture. As soon as you left I searched the internet. It left no doubt in my mind that your sister was the woman who visited Flat 7.'

I can't keep the sarcasm from my voice. 'Did you never pick up a paper or watch the news?'

'Somehow, I missed it.'

'You might have saved her. If you had come forward with this information, the police might have found something.'

'I am telling you the truth. I didn't know, then.'

Is she like our mother? Unable to climb down from a position once she takes it?

'And your son didn't tell you who she was? He didn't talk about the fact that this woman you saw him with had gone missing?'

She shakes her head. 'He made it clear he didn't want to talk about her or the baby when he left later that same day. That it wasn't safe to, for their sakes, and he didn't want me to raise the subject again.'

'Did he lie to my sister? Did she know who he really was? What he does?'

'He'd never have told her anything operational, but he'd never have let her involve herself with him unless she knew the bare bones of the truth. My son has integrity.'

'Did it occur to you that whoever took my sister might have done so because of her relationship with your son? That they were using her to get at him?'

She shakes her head more violently than a woman her age ought. 'It's not possible. He's far too careful. He would never let them find the people from his real life.'

'How could he even think of exposing someone else

to those dangers? How could he ask her to give up so much for him? To give up any chance of a normal life?'

'He had a rule not to let himself get involved. For exactly those reasons. He broke that rule for your sister.'

'It must have been unimaginably hard for her.'

'It would have been, yes. It wouldn't have been easy for her to trust him when he could say so little. He'd never be able to predict the times he could see her. Their contact would have been infrequent.'

'How often does he visit you?'

'I haven't seen him since the day he was here with your sister.'

'You don't think it's suspicious that he disappeared from view when she did?'

'It means he was deeply enmeshed in an operation. It doesn't mean he hurt her.'

'You really haven't seen your son for over ten years?'

'You don't ask questions of someone who does what my son does.'

'My sister would have.'

'I don't know how he even manages to remember who he actually is. You've no idea what he needs to see and do to keep other people safe. What a long-term prize he is after. You've no idea how much the families lose.'

'Poor you. Poor him.' I sound like our mother, with these bitter words. 'Do you think that someone, some-where stopped them looking properly at what happened to my sister to protect him from exposure? To make sure whatever he's doing isn't spoiled?'

'He wouldn't allow that.'

'I'm not sure it would be up to him.'

Tears fill her eyes, drip down her cheeks. 'Do you understand now why I had to see you again? Why I had to talk to you?'

'No,' I say. And I move my head from side to side too. But I do know why.

'I think your nephew is my grandson,' she says. 'I suspected it when your sister came that day with the baby.'

'Did you meet her? Did your son introduce you to her?'

'Everything I told you about what happened that day was true. She didn't look up, didn't acknowledge me, didn't want to see me. I don't think she had any idea who I was. I'm sure he didn't tell her. He wouldn't have risked telling anyone. He would have told her what she needed to know about him. But not about me. He would have been scrupulous about what he did and didn't say.'

'Why are you confessing all of this now?' My voice is icy icy cold, so cold it makes our mother seem warm when at her most brittle. I am her daughter. I am your sister. I have a vision of this woman and her son turning up on our doorstep and running away with Luke in the night. For the first time, our mother's terror is in my own bones.

'I don't know,' she says. 'I don't know what I want. Not anything that could hurt Luke.'

Don't say his name. I don't say this. As powerfully as I feel it, I can't strike her like that. But I can't stop myself from thinking, *Don't say his name again or I won't be able to stand it.*

'I wish – I long to see him. Please, you must have a photograph.'

'No.' The word seems to make a visible cut through the air.

'I know I asked last time and I didn't blame you for saying no then, before you knew – I thought you were right not to show his picture to strangers – but I know everyone has photographs on their phones these days. Please.'

'However strongly you believe in your son, the last time you saw him was a few weeks before my sister disappeared. Undercover policemen are as capable of murder as civilians. If that woman really was my sister – and you said the baby was very new, maybe a month or two old, so I can't discount the possibility – then your son is probably connected to what happened to her. Either because of what he does, or because he hurt her.'

'He wouldn't. He would never hurt a woman.'

'I don't want you near my nephew. I don't want your son sneaking back into the country and going anywhere near him.'

'Don't you see? Don't you see how much my son must have loved your sister? He put himself at unimaginable risk to see her, to have a child with her.'

'He put her at unimaginable risk,' I say.

'If harm came to her, it wasn't because of him. Think how much care he has taken. How much restraint and self-control he shows. Think of Luke. Noah left him with you and your parents, knowing that was the best thing for him.'

'Noah?' I say the word as if I am tasting it. *M + N + ??* Veronica Skelton remembered the name she loved. She witnessed an infatuation so strong between you and a patient she couldn't help but recall it.

'Yes.'

'Is that his real name?'

'Yes. Most undercover policemen use their given Christian names. It's safer that way. I don't know what surname he uses in his work. Lots of different ones, I should guess.'

'Presumably he goes by Henrickson in his personal life?'

'Yes. Noah chose it. His father was Enrique. You probably know that's Spanish for Henry? So son of Henry.'

I had wondered if Henrickson was a trick like the one you and Mum used to play with names, so that it would evoke the real person but at the same time disguise them. This man's trick had the same purpose as yours and Mum's, but it was his own invention.

'That way,' Mrs Buenrostro says, 'when Noah slips into England, there is a safe identity for him to wear.'

'How easy is it for him to slip in?'

There is contempt in her shrug. 'Think how easily the UK borders can be penetrated. It isn't hard if you know what you're doing. If you have money and help. Noah has both.'

I jump up. I walk to the window and look out of her filmy curtains. The fountain is bubbling as usual. My car's nose is inches away from the trunk of a hornbeam tree. Everything looks as it did yesterday and the day before and the day before that. But everything is different. 'How old is your son, Mrs Buenrostro?'

'Forty-six.'

Six years older than you would be. The kind of age difference you liked.

'And he has been – how do you put it – a deep swimmer the whole time?'

'For the last fifteen years. My husband died twenty-one years ago. Noah started covert policing soon after that, but only occasional jobs at first.'

She pauses. 'Noah loves football. Like his father. Does your nephew?'

'I understand that you want to believe your son is some kind of hero, and that you think you are doing the right thing.' She visibly flinches at my refusal to talk about Luke. 'You have spent many years doing that. But I have spent the last decade with a big fat hole in my life that is shaped exactly like my sister. I want you to go to the police and tell them everything you told me.'

'There's no point. There won't even be any evidence that Noah was in the country ten years ago. There won't be records of him. The ordinary police will hit a wall with any kind of enquiry about him.'

'Even undercover policemen aren't allowed to commit crimes. I can see they may be allowed to break the law when it involves drug lords or mafia leaders, when they're in character. But not in their real lives, not against inno-cent civilians. Your son may well have committed what for my family is the worst crime there has ever been.'

'I have told you the kind of man my son is. There is no way he did that.'

'Go to the police yourself or I'll do it for you. They might treat you more sympathetically that way, if you explain you didn't realise who she was until now.' I can't bring myself to speak your name to her. 'Maybe they won't be as sceptical as I am. I will give you until the end of the weekend.'

'You won't let me see your nephew's picture?'

I squint. 'I don't want to hurt you but I feel duty-bound to tell you that if you go anywhere near my nephew I will call the police. The *ordinary* police,' I say with bitter emphasis. 'And I will be instructing my parents to do the same.'

I feel a stab in my stomach, almost a physical blow. Our mother is right – it isn't safe for me to go near Luke until I have figured out every bit of this.

She actually smiles. 'I'm disappointed, but I'm glad too. That boy is lucky. You may not be his mother, but you act as if you are. You're as fierce as a lioness.'

Tell that to my mother, I think. I am astonished that Mrs Buenrostro has said one of the most beautiful things I have ever heard.

'Perhaps you really haven't seen your son in a decade. But I don't believe that the two of you didn't set up some emergency way you could get hold of him.'

She moves her head in the smallest, most reluctant concession, a gesture that refuses to admit much and leaves me uncertain as to whether I actually saw it.

'Do you think the police knew of his relationship with my sister?'

'He probably would have disclosed it to his handler.'

'Probably?'

'I can't be certain. Noah doesn't trust easily. He's a bit of a lone wolf, as they say.' Again she sounds proud. 'But I would be surprised if he failed to do that.'

'I am going to ask you this once more. Do you think

the police deliberately swept their knowledge of my sister under the carpet to protect your son, to protect his operation?'

'If they knew about her, they would know he didn't hurt her.'

'How could they possibly know that?'

'I can't tell you.'

'Can't or won't?'

Her only answer to this is a helpless shrug.

'Do you not see what I do? That they cared more about your son than they did about investigating my sister's disappearance properly?'

'My son is a very brave man. He is a good man.'

'Tell that to my sister,' I say.

White Lies

It is 10.30 when I park in front of our parents' house. Mum's car is gone but Dad's van is here. I slip my key into the lock and let myself in, ready to punch the code into the alarm panel, worried when I discover they haven't set it.

'Hello? Dad?'

There's the sound of a cough coming from our father's workroom. I walk in to find him lying on the dilapidated orange velvet sofa of our childhood that he will not let our mother get rid of. He is dressed in his favourite olive-green trousers and a thick navy jumper. There is a box of tissues on the plank of old wood he uses as a coffee table and an unfinished mug of tea that Mum must have made him before she left.

He scrambles up, still half-asleep, looking embarrassed. 'Hello, shining girl.' He holds out an arm and I cross the room quickly to take his hand and sit beside him.

'Hello, Daddy.'

'You haven't called me that for a long time.'

I nod my head. There is a lump in my throat. 'Why are you lying down when you just got up?'

'Ah.' He shakes his head in amusement. 'And you and your mother think you aren't alike. It's a cold, Ella.' He manages an extremely wet and convincing sniffle, then blows his nose loudly several times in a row. 'Don't tell your mother. I'm trying to hide it from her or she'll put me in quarantine.'

'Really?'

'Everyone gets colds. Let me be clear and say it. It's not my cancer.'

Does he look as though he has lost weight? I'm not sure. 'Okay,' I say. 'Colds are good. I'll take a cold over the other options.'

'To what do I owe this surprise visit from my favourite youngest daughter?' He gives me his sly look. 'I'm sure you forgot your mother's teaching her pre-school ballet class right now?'

'I may not have forgotten that.' I take one of the tissues and blow my own nose. 'But it's the third Thursday of the month, and tomorrow's the third Friday. You know we always keep those days free of charity activities. I have a little extra time.'

'Your mother fears you work too hard. It's her small way of trying to stop that.'

'Did she tell you about our fight?' My voice croaks on the last word.

He holds out his arms and I fall into them, burying my face on his chest. 'I was horrible to her. And she was right. Everything she said was right. I haven't been kind to her. I closed myself off to her feelings.'

He waits for me to calm down. After a few minutes he wordlessly gives me a handful of tissues and I blow my nose all over again. I try to smile. 'I got your jumper wet.'

'It's a good thing your mother made me wear wool today. She likes me to be warm and waterproof.'

'She said it's not safe for me to be near Luke. That I put him in danger. She's right.'

'Your mother doesn't really think that. She felt terrible after she last saw you. She regrets the things she said.'

'I do too. So much.'

'We both knew you would.'

'Will you tell her I'm sorry? Tell her I love her?'

He pushes a stray hair from my forehead. 'Tell her yourself. Come to Luke's football match this afternoon. We'll both be there. That's why I don't want your mother to notice my cold – she'll tell me not to go.'

'They can hear you sniffling over in France. You'll never fool her.'

'It would make your mother very happy if you came.'

I shake my head no. 'I can't. I've opened up so many things, so many unsettling things. I might draw these things to Luke if I go near him.'

'What things?'

I look at my lap and twiddle my thumbs as if I were five years old.

Dad puts a finger under my chin and makes me meet his eye. 'You and I have always been honest with each other.'

'Always.' And I spill out all of it. Jason Thorne. The visit you made to Mrs Buenrostro's son with Luke shortly before you disappeared. The likely identity of Luke's father and the possibility he had something to do with your disappearance. Sadie's newfound hatred of me. The rift with Ted and the photograph of him with Ruby. The anonymous phone calls and the email from Justice Administrator.

I don't mention your amniocentesis and my theory about why you had it. I'm clear about when the confidentiality clause applies. Our father does not need to know that you slept with two different men within weeks of each other.

I also leave out the fake policeman. That is one alarming thing too many. It is not necessary, anyway, given the fact that I actually reported it to the police myself. According to the call I made to them this morning, they have discovered absolutely nothing about who he is. *Our enquiries are ongoing*. That was all they had to say.

'You took so much on, so young, Ella. I never meant any of this for you. But you make me very proud. You're a better detective than any of the actual detectives.'

I puff out a bitter little laugh. 'Think of all the mess it's opened up. Mrs Buenrostro's going to want to see Luke. I'm scared of her. I'm scared of her son and the things he's doing. He's pretending to be a serious criminal.'

'Do you know what exactly?'

I shake my head. 'She wouldn't tell me. I can only guess. I'm thinking something major, some kind of organised crime or drug cartel he's infiltrated on the continent. She says it's a really long-term assignment and he speaks multiple languages. Deep swimming, she called it. Assuming she's telling the truth.'

'Do you believe her?'

'I think so.'

'Do you think she knows more than she's saying?'

'Definitely. But I'm not sure I want to know more than I already do. What if the people he's trying to bring down find out who he really is? And then find a connection to Luke?'

'It sounds like he's tried to build in layers of safety between his covert life and his real one. It appears he's put a lot of effort into protecting his family.'

'You're trying to comfort me.'

'I mean it.'

'But he and his mother have so much money, quite apart from his job. She says it's family money.'

He gives me his slant smile. 'Miranda would like that.'

'Yes,' I say. 'But that kind of money gives people power. If they can't find legal ways to get what they want, there are always alternatives.'

He considers for a few seconds. 'It explains a lot. Miranda's flat. Her car. The deposits in those accounts. Presumably they were all gifts from this man.'

'I was thinking that too.' I almost laugh but somehow do not. 'How can you seem so calm?'

He does actually laugh. 'It's my job as your father.'

I sit back and look hard at him. 'You put it all in motion. I was so angry at Mum. I told her you asked for Miranda's things from the police. I wanted to hurt her. I wanted to show her I knew something about you that she didn't. That she was wrong. That the rest of us aren't afraid to search for the truth.'

His skin goes paler.

'She intimated that she knew you did this,' I say. 'I didn't believe her.'

'She may well have guessed.' Our father will never betray our mother by suggesting she lied. 'Your mother is very perceptive. But I didn't tell her.'

'And she hasn't confronted you with it?'

'No.' He takes both of my hands in his. 'I was wrong to do it.'

'No you weren't. You were completely right. But why did you?'

'Miranda belongs to us all. I thought that if something could be done, it should be done.' He shakes his head as if disgusted with himself. 'A ten-year-old boy. I knew he was listening when your mother and I were talking about that box. I knew he'd tell you and I knew you'd never let it go. My thoughts were selfish.'

'They weren't. You're never selfish.'

'You can see no wrong in me. I'm a lucky father to have that.'

'It's because you deserve it.'

He swallows hard. 'I don't want to leave this world without knowing.'

A sob rushes out of my mouth. I am instantly, hysterically crying. 'Why do you say that? You're not about to leave this world.'

'No, Ella. No no no no no. Just the words and the world view of a man my age. Any father would feel this. It doesn't mean what you're thinking.'

It takes several minutes, a thick stack of tissues, and a glass of water before I can breathe again.

'Okay?'

I nod.

'What I was trying to say was that we've gone too long without knowing. But I didn't ever imagine the things in that box would lead you this far. I should have considered more carefully the position it would put you in. And Luke. You're going to go to the police, aren't you? You need to tell them everything you can about Mrs Buenrostro and her son.'

'Not yet. That's why I'm telling you. I promised Mrs Buenrostro I'd give her a chance to go to them herself first. She says it's pointless, but I still thought if she did it on her own terms it might help. It suits me to wait, anyway. There are some other things I have to do before I can get to the station. Which isn't exactly my favourite place.'

How is it that our father can read my mind? 'You're going back to see Jason Thorne.'

'He said there's something he can tell me.'

'Don't.'

'I can't not. I can't not follow it through. You know that about me – you said it yourself.'

'I wouldn't want you any different, however inconvenient it sometimes is.'

'Even if you didn't fully imagine what it would mean to look at Miranda's things, you must have known that following any trail wouldn't be comfortable.' I glance at my watch. 'I need to go.'

'You wouldn't make it to the football on time anyway.'

'No. And I need to have more of a measure of things before I go anywhere near Luke. Mum was right.'

'Do you remember Miss Pear, Ella?'

When Luke was four or five, he overheard a police-woman slip out the word *MisPer*, which is police shorthand for Missing Person. He knew the policewoman was talking about you. He misheard her, though.

'Why did she call Mummy "Miss Pear"?' he asked. 'Can I call her Miss Pear? I like pears,' he said.

There is another thing Luke used to say around then, usually prompted by strangers who assumed I was his mother. 'This is my Auntie Ella. My mummy got lost somewhere.' He would always go on to elaborate. 'My mummy got lost but sometimes you can find lost things.'

'Of course I do,' I say.

'Luke will survive without you for a few days,' Dad says, 'but not much longer. Your mother recognises how much he needs you.'

'Will you explain my absence to him? I don't like asking you to tell even a white lie for me. But can you say it's a work emergency? Tell him I'll call as soon as I can to see how the football went.'

'We know Luke's not a natural athlete.'

'Not exactly. But I like him that way.'

I remember when Luke was four and he'd just started school. I arrived to collect him from his first session of afternoon football club. He wasn't with the other boys, who were squealing and running after the ball in a pack.

Luke was lying on his tummy by a small square of earth that held a caged sapling. He was sifting for pebbles with his fingers so he could make a rock garden, entirely immersed in his own little contented world. I scooped him up in my arms and twirled round and tickled and kissed him. He giggled, not caring what anyone thought, not worrying about being seen as babyish.

Dad swallows. 'You know he does it because he wants to be strong for you, Ella. He hates sport. The football. The karate classes. All of it.' He smiles. 'I hear he can knock out three pull-ups in a row, now?'

'Something like that,' I say.

'He wants to be able to defend you. Because he couldn't help his mum.'

'Oh.' The word shoots from me more like a cry than language. 'Did he tell you that?'

'He didn't need to.'

'You know us all better than we know ourselves.' I put my arms around him and we stand like this for a full minute. I kiss his cheek. 'Can you call Ted? Tell him what's been happening? Ask him to check around here?'

'I'll do that as soon as you go.'

'Are you really sure it's a cold?'

'No question.' He laughs. 'I'm a lucky man, to have a wife and daughter who care so much.'

'You certainly are,' I say, feeling a pang that he has spoken of his children in the singular. 'I tease Mum too much. But I'm beginning to be convinced by her methods.' He walks me to the door, but then I remember one of the things I meant to do here. 'Give me one minute. I need some things of Miranda's.'

I run up to your childhood room. Mum keeps some of your favourite dresses and shoes in the wardrobe, to make sure they will be here for you the day you come home. I grab the things I want and stuff them into the tote bag I brought with me for this purpose.

'That was two minutes,' our father says as I run down the stairs. This is a routine of ours – I always take longer than I promise, and he always points it out but never really minds. He is still waiting by the front door.

'I'm sorry. I didn't mean for you to stand here.' His skin is slightly grey. There is sweat on his brow. I try to make myself believe it really is because he has a cold.

'It gives me pleasure to see you speeding down those stairs. How many times do you think I've watched you do that since you learned to walk?'

'Too many to count.' I point to the alarm panel. 'Promise me to use this?'

'You have my solemn promise.'

I set it myself and kiss him once more and gulp back a little sob that I hope he doesn't hear before I say goodbye.

The Girl Who Never Cries

I drive around our parents' village several times, checking my mirrors to make sure I am not being followed. Only then do I pull over, careful to choose a place that isn't overlooked. I squirm out of my jeans and sweater and boots and into your dress and shoes – even our shoe size is the same. Finally, I dial Adam Holderness's mobile.

All of my nerves seem to be exposed. You once called me the girl who never cries, but today I am able to do little else. My voice is husky in the face of Adam's kindness and concern, and his promise to get me in to see Thorne if I come straight to the hospital. He must hear that I am on the verge of weeping.

It rained in the night but now the sun is magically bright on the fields, turning them a wintry greeny-yellow that makes me think the next season is really on its way. The fields are so beautiful they make me want to cry too. Are you beneath them? Is that where you are? Beethoven's Symphony Number 7 is on the radio and I remember how you always loved it.

When I pull into the hospital car park I go through my usual routines, checking who else is around me, pulling in between two cars that have staff permits on their windscreens. I take off your locket and my watch. I stick them in the glovebox along with my phone before I step out of the car and turn on the alarm.

Just when I thought my emotions couldn't fluctuate any more wildly than they already have in one day, I halt, swallowing back a scream of absolute fury.

Ted is leaning against the low brick wall, standing in the gap that opens onto the path from the car park to the hospital's reception building. He is in uniform.

'What are you doing here?'

'Waiting for you.'

'Did you follow me? But you can't have followed me. I was checking the whole way. Nobody followed me.'

'Your father said you were coming here. He said you asked him to call me.'

'Yes. But that was so you could keep an eye on them. Not on me. Go away.'

'I'm afraid I can't do that.'

'I don't want to see you.'

'You're ignoring my texts. I've lost count of how many I've sent. You're not answering your phone to me.'

'I've been busy.'

He is searching my face. 'How was your meeting with Thorne?'

'Go practise your public safety duties on Ruby.' I have no anger towards Ruby, only concern for her. My bitterness is entirely directed at Ted.

'I told you it wasn't what you thought. I told you it was work.'

'So the police have started to do their work in cafés instead of stations?'

'The man who assaulted her has attacked three other women. He'll attack more if we don't put him away. We need her as a witness and she's reluctant. Ruby doesn't like the station.'

'Is that allowed?'

'If it keeps her safe and gets another scumbag off the streets I will sleep just fine at night.'

'I'm sorry I gave you such a hard time. I was blinded by—' I am about to say jealousy, but I stop myself.

'By what, Ella?'

'I'm not sure.'

He lets it go, almost certainly guessing the truth. 'I should have explained earlier. I can see how it looked, why you thought as you did.'

'It's sad how easily you and I get derailed, how quick we are to get angry with each other. That's what's staying with me in all this.'

He touches my cheek and I put my fingers over his. 'We're not as bad as you think,' he says.

A movement at the far end of the path catches my attention. When I look I see the door to the reception building swinging closed and Adam walking towards us.

Introducing these two men would suck away every last drop of my energy. 'I need to go, Ted. I have an appointment.' I turn to move away but before I do Ted's arm shoots out and his hand catches mine.

'Don't. You got away with it once. Don't go near Thorne again. You're not safe with him.'

'He's locked up and surrounded by guards. It's not as if the two of us are alone.' I snatch my hand away. My voice is as low as I can make it. I don't want Adam to hear but I want to be sure that Ted does. 'Why are you always trying to stop me? I can't live with that. Why don't you see how important this is to me?'

'I want to save you.'

'From what, exactly?'

But there is no time for Ted to answer, because Adam is at my side. He gives Ted his even look. 'Is there a problem?'

Ted glares at him. He is an inch shorter than Adam. 'No problem.'

'Good of you to stop by, but all is well inside.' Adam speaks to Ted as if Ted is a servant whose services are no longer required. It is subtle, an undercurrent, but it is definitely there. Ted hears it too and bristles.

Adam touches my arm, lightly, not lingeringly but long enough for Ted's eyes to narrow and his nostrils to flare. 'Are you ready to go in, Ella?'

I give a yes nod to Adam and a goodbye nod to Ted. Then I walk away, with Adam by my side. I do not turn to look behind me, but Ted's eyes are on my back, boring into me with such intensity I feel as if I'm being burned.

Truth or Dare

Jason Thorne is sitting on the same golden doll's house sofa in the same fake drawing room wearing the same jeans and lumberjack shirt I last saw him wear. He heaves himself up to greet me as I walk towards him. His face is practically splitting he is smiling so hard. For an instant, I see a vulnerable little boy beneath that face, wanting to be liked and admired as much as he likes and admires, but never being granted this wish.

'The delightful Melanie Brooke,' he says. 'I cannot tell you what pleasure it gives me to see you.'

I hear Betty's voice. *Your only chance is to find his humanness. To find the ways that the two of you are alike.*

I picture the scene I am in as if from outside and think of the families of the women Jason Thorne tortured and killed and stored in freezers in his basement. How would they feel to see me sitting in this fake drawing room playing at civility with this man? What would I feel in their place? I can only answer this question for myself, not for them, and I am unwaveringly clear in my answer.

I would give my blessing if it got them even the tiniest way towards the many answers they craved. I would countenance their doing anything they needed to for that purpose.

So I take my first step in Jason Thorne's game and I do the thing I could not possibly have done the last time. I touch him. I look him in the eye and smile and put out my hand and say 'I'm glad to see you too' and watch the briefest flutter of puzzlement and surprise in his face before he gains control of it.

He takes my hand in his and I can see the nurse-bodyguards stiffen to attention at the same close-by table as before. Adam stiffens too. Jason Thorne's hand feels like an ordinary hand. Yes, it is extra big. And yes it is extra sweaty and extra warm. But it is just skin. Did I expect it to be scaly, like a monster's? When I start to pull my own hand away, Thorne responds instantly and loosens his already-gentle hold, careful not to encroach. I resist the impulse to wipe my palms and fingers on your dress. They will dry, I tell myself. I can wash them later, I tell myself.

'Won't you sit down?' He has placed a chair exactly in the position I dragged it to last time, remembering my seating preference.

'Thank you very much.' I lower myself onto the chair, flattening my hands against the cushion, a natural move-ment which has the advantage of wiping away at least some of his sweat.

Thorne has not positioned a second chair for Adam, who calmly goes and gets one and puts it beside mine. Adam sits too, reverting to his previous slouchy posture.

I am surprised to notice that there are no dead blue-bottles or moths or slugs dangling from Thorne's wrists and buttonholes. 'No jewellery today?' I ask.

'I didn't realise you'd miss it. Do you miss it, Melanie?'

'I must confess I don't.'

'Then I must confess that I didn't want to wear something that made you think badly of me.'

I find this revelation a million times more disturbing than the moulting insect corpses. 'That was kind of you, Jason,' I say.

His smile is even wider. 'You used my first name.' But the smile falls away. 'Why are you being nice to me?'

'You haven't done anything to me that deserves less than that, have you?'

'I hope not.' He considers, then shakes his head, definite. 'I haven't.'

'And because I need you to help me – I believed you when you said there was something important you could tell me about my sister.'

'Ye-es.' He draws out the word, nods slowly. 'You're not here then because you find yourself strangely in love with me?'

'It would be a lie and a cruelty to tell you such a thing.'

'I told you last time that I could see you aren't a liar.'

And I remember thinking how wrong he was then. And continues to be. I am trained in the School of Miranda, with a particular speciality in omission.

He places each of his feet flatly on the floor, spreading his knees widely. 'I hope it doesn't make you uncomfortable when I sit like this? Difficult for a man my size to find the right position.'

341

Adam barely looks up. 'Change it now or she's leaving, Jason.'

'God you're tiresome. It was purely innocent. You're the one with the dirty mind, Doctor Do-Good.' Thorne makes a great show of gluing his thighs firmly together before turning back to me. 'I am sorry, Melanie, that you had to hear the ugly spin that man puts on everything.' He shakes his bald head sorrowfully.

For the first time, I wonder if his hair loss is natural. In the photographs from before his arrest his hair was short and wavy, the colour of lion fur. Surely even a disposable razor would be deadly in this man's hands. Or perhaps they allow him to use something battery-operated?

'Can you please call me Ella?' I say. 'I don't like Melanie.'

'You should have said. With pleasure. I appreciate the confidence.' He smiles so widely and naturally, even sweetly, that I am disconcerted. 'What are you thinking, Ella?'

I shrug my shoulders to dismiss the idea that I could possibly be thinking anything.

'I wish it could be otherwise, but I can only help you if you play a little game with me. I did mention it the last time we were together.'

We were together. Is he delusional? Despite Ted's cynicism, they were probably right to stick him in this place without trial.

It must be the recollection of Thorne's hair that makes me think of it, but do you remember that story Mum used to tell us, taken from an eighteenth-century novel she read long ago? The one about the very careful lady who accepts the gift of a lion?

This cautious lady soon tames the lion. After that, she pets it and strokes it and plays with it and brings it treats and feeds it from her own little golden plate with her own little hand. She lets it drink from her own little golden cup and even allows it to sleep at the foot of her very own silken bed. One morning, before breakfast, the lion tears the lady to pieces.

At the end, Mum would always ask us, Whose fault was it, the lady's or the lion's? As soon as I was old enough to talk, you would let me answer, and I would repeat what I learned from listening to you so many times. The lady's fault, I would say, because she changed her character but the lion did not.

'Will you play my game?' Jason Thorne asks.

What I am doing with this man is wrong in exactly the same way as the lady was wrong with the lion. 'It depends on what the game is.'

'The game is simple. You must answer any question I ask you with the truth. And you must accept and obey any command I give.'

'I won't accept those second terms. I won't do anything physical and I will never promise to obey anybody.'

He moves his head from side to side rapidly. 'No, no, no. I wouldn't expect that from you. I respect you too much for that, Ella. These would be verbal responses to verbal commands.'

'Okay,' I say. 'Then yes to both of those rules.'

'Aren't you worried I will make you play my game and then refuse to tell you what you want to know?'

'If you apply your rules unreasonably I will break them. And you can't make me play. I choose to. Plus, I trust

343

your word.' Somehow, against all reason, I actually do, despite your voice in my ear.

You are acting like the lady, you say.

'You are one of the few who can,' he says. 'I like your dress, by the way.' He tries – and I think it is a real try – not to look me up and down. But he fails.

'Thank you,' I say.

'Though perhaps it is a little loose?'

It is the black shirtdress you used to wear after you had Luke. It is silky and buttons up the front and that is why you loved it so much, so you could open it up to breastfeed him. You must have had it laundered more times than you could count, because you seemed to be wearing it whenever I saw you.

'It was my sister's,' I say.

'That's a personal thing for you to tell me, Ella.'

'Yes. It is.'

'I am – moved by – the confidences you are making. So I will make one in return. I believe I have seen that dress before.'

My throat goes dry. I feel Adam stiffen even though he doesn't break his supposedly indifferent slouch. 'But you said you never met her in person.' My words come out as a croak.

'Let me get you some water, Ella.' Thorne pours from the same jug as before into the same coloured plastic cup as before. 'You know, I love to say your name. I much prefer Ella, too.' This time, I drink, and he does his best to disguise his satisfaction with the change. 'Better?'

I nod.

'It is true that I never met her in person. The conversation I had with her was, as I said, by phone. But I didn't say I never *saw* her in person. I made some fascinating – observations.'

The pen scratches across Adam's page.

I open my mouth and close it several times before I manage to get any words out. 'But you didn't tell the police.'

'Have you momentarily forgotten who you are talking to?' He actually laughs. 'My findings on your sister were made before the police became interested in me. I hardly wanted to draw their attention by telling them I'd followed her.'

I open my mouth with more questions but he cuts me off. 'If you want to know more you will have to play my game.' He looks at Adam. 'The good doctor has taught me a great deal about inducements.'

'I already said I would do it,' I say.

'Ah. But once we start, you might find that you don't like it. I want to make sure you are in an unshakably cooperative state of mind. I don't want you quitting until we are finished, Ella.'

We. How many times has this man said *We* in the last few minutes? My instinct is to repudiate it. Silently, I recite a litany to remind myself. *See his humanness. See his humanness. He is human like me.*

'Be sure you play fairly, then.' I sit back, cross my legs, rest my hands on my knee. 'Whenever you are ready, Jason.'

Adam looks up from his notepad as if he has been busy with something else and only just decided to notice us. 'Miss Brooke may not quit, Jason, but if you cross a line I will quit for her and put a stop to it.'

'But I fully intend to cross several lines, *Adam*.' Thorne relishes his appropriation of the first name. 'I do suggest you think carefully before interrupting. *Miss Brooke* will not think well of you if you interfere before the end. Even a poor crazed psychopath like me can see that you would very much like *Miss Brooke* to think well of you.'

Adam doesn't react to a single word of this. He simply returns his attention to his clipboard to make several rapid notes.

'Let us begin,' Thorne says. 'First question. What would you say to your sister if you could?'

I think of Ted role-playing with me in the park, lying on top of me and making me remember the last time we made love.

'I don't know.' My voice is quiet.

'Pretend I'm her. Pretend she can hear you right now.'

'No.'

'Do it or you lose and I tell you nothing.'

'I will do it if I get to ask you a question or issue you with a command for each of yours. As we go. Taking turns.'

'Those are not the conditions you agreed to.'

'Now that we have begun I realise this is the only way I can do it. Take it or leave it.'

'I will take it. I think it is a fair development of the rules. I want it to be our game together, Ella, not mine alone.' He laces his fingers and rests his chin on them. 'Do you think I would have been a different man if I'd met you when I was young? I like to imagine I might have been.'

I think again of the story of the lion and the lady. 'My mother says you cannot change a person's nature.'

'Another intimate confidence and I didn't even ask for it.'

'I suppose that's true.' I consider for a minute. 'This isn't part of the game, but I can't help but wonder what brought you to do the things you did.'

'I look like a monster, don't I?'

'I have met some beautiful monsters. My mother says that it's how a person acts that can make them monstrous, not how they look.'

'Is that all you see in me? The monstrous things I have done?'

'It's the largest part of what I see. But I also see that you're intelligent and talented. What you do with wood is true art. You actually like people, don't you?'

He is blushing. 'Only selectively. They don't usually like me back. Unless I have inducements. That's the only reason you're here. Because I have induced you.'

'True. But I actually prefer you today to the last time we met. Perhaps you've got better with people, more imaginative about what they are thinking and feeling.'

'Empathic?' He says the word like a sneer. 'Dr Dismal certainly likes that term.'

'Perhaps Dr Holderness and his team really are helping you.'

'No more of this tiresome subject. If you want the sad story of my neglected childhood you will not get it.'

'That sounds boring,' I say. 'I'm happy to skip that.'

'Let's start over. Back to our little game. What would you say to your sister if she were sitting right where I am? No more trying to divert me, however good you are at it.'

'I thought you were diverting me, but okay,' I say. 'Here it is. *Why did you leave me?*' I am startled that of all the things that would come out, it is this.

'That is too polite and controlled. Say it like you mean it.'

'I'll do that after you tell me how many times you saw her and where and when.'

'That's too many questions in one. The answer you get is *Once*. I saw her once. If you want more say it again like you mean it. *Why did you leave me?*'

'Fine.' I sit back as if bracing for a performance, but what comes out is real. '*Why the fuck did you leave me?*' The third word is an explosion. Each of the others is a bullet.

He nods approval. 'Does that feel better?'

When I first told Ted I was going to see Thorne, Ted said I would be Thorne's entertainment. I told him I could live with that, and I see that I can, easily. 'Tell me when you saw her,' I say. 'That is one question.'

'And I have one answer. It is a big one. The day before she disappeared. And here is a bonus gift, thrown in because I like you far too much to stop myself. Saw her and heard her.'

There is a rustle of paper and the dull thump of Adam's clipboard hitting the floor. 'Time to stop this. Now.'

'No,' I say. 'Absolutely not.'

'I did warn you, Dr Dumb Dumb, that you would not impress Ella if you interfered.'

Adam stands. 'I am ending this visit. This is information that should be given to the police in a proper manner.' He looks to the door. 'Please come with me now, Ella.'

'No. This isn't a formal interview. He's perfectly entitled to disclose what he wishes to me. You have no reason to stop this.' I cross my arms. 'You have no right.'

Thorne smiles his ugly smile at Adam, which is not the same smile that he smiles at me. 'She will never forgive you if you drag her away now, Dr Dreary.' Thorne turns to me. 'Will you, Ella?' I say nothing. 'I'm speaking the truth, aren't I?'

'Yes,' I say. 'You are.'

Adam slowly sits down. He doesn't pick up the clip-board. He doesn't resume the fake slump. His back is absolutely straight and he looks ready to spring up again in an instant. The nurse-bodyguards, though maintaining their pretence of indifference to what is happening five feet away, also appear to be sitting straighter.

'Tell me what you saw that day, Jason,' I say. 'You have to tell me. And what you heard.'

'Not yet. My turn to issue a command. Remember? You promised, didn't you?'

'Yes.'

'Okay. Now I am going to repeat exactly what you said, and I want you to answer as if you were your sister. Role play. A little trick I learned here. Don't think about it. Just quickly say whatever comes into your head. On the count of three. One. Two. Three. *Why did you leave me?*'

Nothing comes out.

Thorne tries again. 'I am you. You are your sister. *Why did you leave me, Miranda?*'

Again nothing. My head is exploding with the need for Thorne to tell me what he saw. There is no room for anything else.

'One last time. Do it or I will never tell you what I saw and heard. *Why did you leave me?*' He bangs a fist so loud on the fake wood table Adam and the nurse-guards all rise a little in their chairs and I let out a small gasp.

'*I didn't leave you. I'd never have left you.*' I put my hand up to my mouth and then peel it away onto my lap and raise my head to look straight at Thorne. 'No more,' I say. 'No more games. I have played fairly and done as much as I can bear. If you get off on the truth of that I don't care. Just tell me.'

'All right, Ella. I will tell you. Remember, later, that you asked for this.'

What happens next happens so fast I can barely understand it. It is a series of small things that occur in such a smooth and uninterrupted sequence they seem to be all one action. Everything is a whizzing blur of colour with objects coming into sharp focus only fleetingly. Didn't you once tell me that this is how butterflies see?

Thorne leaps from his toy sofa with a speed I would not have thought possible for a man his size. He smashes the table out of his way, setting the plastic jug and tumblers flying as the table lands on its side, a barrier between me and Adam and an impediment to the nurse-bodyguards. There is no place for me to dive out of Thorne's path to evade him, sitting as I am in a kind of prison with the half-circle chair cupping my back and sides and Thorne's bulk towering over me. I cannot process what he wants, but somehow I manage to process that what he is doing is coming for me and before this thought is properly in my mind, before I can take any stance, before I can reach up to jab an eye or puncture an eardrum or break a finger, before my knee has moved even an inch upwards, before I can do any of the things I have practised and taught for years, Thorne has snatched me from the chair, crushing both of my arms to my sides and squeezing my whole body against his and pressing my face against his chest so that I can't breathe. He is a foot taller than I am. I must look like a rag doll in the arms of a giant.

'If you come near us I will break her neck,' he says, lumbering off with me towards a corner of the room. I go limp while I try to work out what to do, try to think of a move, but I am entirely immobilised, with my back against the wall, and my arms and legs pinned and my whole body flattened by his.

There is no shouting in the background. Whatever Adam is doing, it is not a noisy thing. Whatever the nurse-bodyguards are doing does not make noise either. In these first few seconds, there is just the rush of air in my ears and the smell of Thorne's sweat in my nose and the thrum of my own blood through my veins.

'It's the only way, Ella.' He is speaking into the top of my head. He kisses my hair. There is the sound of his lips smacking together. There is wetness on my scalp. I retch and swallow back sick. 'It's worth it, being able to touch you at least once. It's not as if they'll ever release me for good behaviour. Do you know how many years of pretend reformation I needed to earn these visits with you? How patient I had to be to lure you here? How much trouble I went to last month to let the press know about that phone call with your sister?' One of his hands moves along my side and I hear the fabric of your dress rip before I feel Thorne's fingers squeezing my bare thigh and he lets out a sigh. 'We don't have long. I want you to know that everything I have said to you, everything I am about to say, is true. The only lie was for them – I would never hurt you.'

He lifts me, so my face is level with his, holds my head still, and kisses my mouth wetly before moving his lips to my ear. My body has entirely frozen. All I can think is that I will never know what he saw. Now he will never tell me. That thought is louder than my horror. Louder than the message that I may be about to die.

Then another thought creeps in from far away, and the part of me that I have trained and nurtured since you disappeared wakes up. The thought is that he is distracted, pressing me into this corner as he is, and by his efforts to keep me still while trying to feel me. And though he has my back to the wall and he is blocking me from seeing the rest of the room, I sense quiet, careful movement behind him.

He doesn't kiss my ear. He inhales so deeply it sounds like thunder. I wonder if he is about to take a bite out of me. When his fingers creep higher over my skin I wonder if he is going to try to rape me against this wall, with these people watching. But there is only more of his sour breath, then a murmur of sentences so low that only I can hear them. How long does he whisper to me like this? Is it only a minute? Is it several? It must be several but I lose track of how long he goes on, punctuating his phrases with kisses against my temple as he tells me his story. It is long enough. It is too long. Nothing that he has done to me so far has made me cry out. But these words do, causing the men in the room to shout warnings at him that I cannot understand. And when Thorne has said it all, when I know he has finished, I scream the word *No* so loud it makes him falter just enough for me to slide my right leg out and do the only thing I can. I jab my heel into the back of his knee with every atom of force I have. I jab so hard he grunts and presses forward into me even harder, squashing my breath from my bones.

Everything goes black until I hit the ground with a bump and open my eyes to the sound of crashing metal and shouts.

Thorne is on his back. A squad of nurses have swarmed him, all of them wearing blue gloves, and I think of Gulliver surrounded by the Lilliputians. They must have slipped in silently while Thorne and I were caught up with each other. Someone must have pressed an alarm somewhere, silent in here but ringing and flashing red alert where it counted.

Thorne turns his eyes towards me but not his head, because there is a pair of blue gloves keeping his skull still. 'We did well, didn't we, Ella? You got what you needed from me. And me from you. Fair exchange. A game well played.' Each of the nurses has taken firm charge of a part of Thorne's body: his head, an upper or lower arm, a thigh or ankle, a side of his pelvis. Every bit of him is firmly pinned to the floor.

One of the nurses shifts and that is when I see Adam, on his knees, bending over Thorne, holding a syringe. Another nurse cuts through Thorne's jeans and Adam plunges the longest needle I have ever seen into Thorne's hip. Thorne screams like a wild animal. A second syringe materialises and Adam plunges that in too. Then a third before Adam jumps up and is by my side.

I am half-sitting, flopped against the wall, and Adam doesn't move me. He looks from the top of my head to the tips of my toes and wonders aloud about crush injuries and broken ribs. 'Don't move.' He holds my head. 'Does it hurt to breathe?'

I shake my head against his hands.

'Moving your head didn't hurt?' His fingers are pressing in intervals along the nape of my neck. 'Here? No pain? And here? Any pain here?'

'None.'

'That was an impressive kick.' He is concentrating on examining me even as he speaks, trying to distract me from watching Thorne. He is shining a light pen into each of my eyes. But it isn't working. I am still trying to look at Thorne whenever I can. 'You dropped him to the ground.'

'It would have been more impressive if I hadn't let him grab me in the first place.'

He nods, but I am not sure if it is because he agrees with me or because he is pleased that I am talking so easily. 'I don't see how even you could have avoided that. You certainly disabled him. He outmanoeuvred us all.'

'Too right, Dr Dopey.' Thorne's voice seems to come from far away.

Adam takes my wrist between his fingers to feel for my pulse, puts the metal disc of a stethoscope to my chest to listen to my breathing, gently presses his fingers behind my ears, asks me to lie on my back so he can do the same thing to my ribs and stomach. He commands me to move toes and fingers. He taps my knees. Still I turn my head to the side to watch Thorne, whose gaze meets mine. He and I have barely torn our eyes from each other's since we both fell.

'Enjoying that, are you, Dr Dishrag?' Thorne sounds like a child doing everything he can to resist an over-powering urge to sleep.

Adam pushes up the sleeves of your dress to examine my arms. 'No marks that I can see.' He shakes his head, perplexed. 'No visible injuries.'

'I said I wouldn't hurt her.' Thorne's voice is growing more slurred with each sentence.

'Excuse me, Jason, but the bruises can still emerge and I heard you threaten to break her neck.'

'Was to keep you away. Wouldn't have done it. Told her I wouldn't. Tried to keep my weight off her. Even when she took me down.' He pauses for a long time between each word.

Another blue-gloved nurse comes through the door. He is pushing a wheeled stretcher with restraints and accompanied by a second doctor. This man quickly comes over to crouch near Adam, who continues to sit beside me, watching me breathe and rechecking my pulse. Adam begins to murmur to the other doctor in a language I can barely understand, explaining the combination of anti-anxiety, anti-psychotic and anti-cholinergic medicines he used to achieve rapid tranquillisation. The names of the drugs sound beautiful when Adam says them, as if they are rare flowers. Lorazepam. Haloperidol. Procyclidine.

'We're going to get you onto the stretcher now, Jason.' The nurse speaks to Thorne as if he is giving him great news.

'Fuck off. Get off me.' Despite the words there is no fight in him. His eyes close but he jerks them open again, trying even harder to defy the cocktail of drugs Adam shot into his muscles.

'On my count,' the nurse says. Ten men lift Thorne onto the padded stretcher so effortlessly, with such clock-work coordination, I realise they must practise as hard as synchronised swimmers. Quickly, they strap down Thorne's legs and arms, but the chemical restraints are already working so powerfully they barely need the material ones.

The second doctor rises, telling Adam he will go with them to monitor Thorne.

'His knee will need to be examined,' Adam tells him. I can't tell if there is pride or alarm in the glance he throws at me. 'There will almost certainly be damage.'

As they begin to roll him away Thorne opens his eyes. Even half-dreaming, those eyes seek me out and lock into mine. Though his words are slurred I can hear every single one of them. 'Wish I had you alone in this bed, Ella,' he says.

What happens next is like something from a horror film. I shoot up and forward, catching myself with my palms on the floor so that I am on all fours. As I move, a gush of vomit rushes out of me so violently it sprays several feet. Adam grabs my hair out of my face and holds it like our mother used to as I retch and retch and retch some more. When I finally finish and lift my head and open my eyes, Thorne is gone.

Sleeping Potion

An electric shock goes through my skull when several policemen walk in. I make myself stare hard before I see that none of these men looks remotely like Ted. I am too drained to talk to them but I fob them off with a promise to come to the station over the weekend to give them a statement.

Adam takes me home, insisting that he cannot allow me to drive. I give him my address, close my eyes, and fall asleep, waking with a small scream when his car stops in front of my house. For a split second I think I am still in the Visitors' Centre with Thorne pressing me against the wall.

'I'd like to come in and make sure you're okay. Is there someone you can call to stay the night with you?'

I nod yes. My neck hurts when I move it. I sit in his passenger seat, unable to work out what to do next, so Adam gets out and comes round to my side of the car and opens the door and gently takes my hand to pull me out. He walks beside me, along my front path, then helps me with the locks because my hands are shaking too much and I keep dropping the keys.

I am not quite sure how we end up in my kitchen, but I open my eyes as if I have been asleep and realise that this is where we are. The downstairs telephone handset is on the table and Adam passes it to me.

Dialling is a reflex. As soon as I hear her voice I say, 'Mummy, I need you,' and I start to cry, and somewhere far in the back of my mind I realise I have gone from Mum to Mother and back to Mummy. She says, 'I'm on my way,' and I can hear how hard she is trying not to sound scared.

All I want is to take a shower. I leave Adam at my kitchen table to wait for her while I go upstairs to the bathroom.

Your dress is splattered in sick. When I slip it off a new wave of the smell hits me and I lean over the toilet to throw up again. I wipe my face with my arm, squirm out of my black underwear and bra, drop them on top of your dress and shoes. I take a plastic bag from the cupboard beneath the sink and swoop it down over this pile of foul things, wanting to quarantine anything and everything that could possibly have Thorne's sweat and germs on it. Then I climb into the shower.

I make the water as hot as I can stand and soap and rinse myself once, twice, three times, scrubbing Thorne from my skin until it is sore. I shampoo my hair three times too. I let the water pound on the back of my neck, waiting for the ache to diminish, but it doesn't. I brush and floss my teeth again and again and again, then throw the toothbrush away.

I shun Ted's old bathrobe. Instead, I wrap myself in a lilac-coloured one that I have never worn before, stuffed at the bottom of my wardrobe since Mum gave it to me last Christmas. There are matching fluffy slippers to go with it and I slip these on too.

I pad downstairs to see that Adam has made himself a cup of tea, and one for me. 'You look a little better,' he says.

It occurs to me that what I look like is a purple puff-ball, but I am beyond caring. 'I feel – much better.' My voice is hollow. I haven't even towel-dried my hair. It is dripping onto the floor tiles at the rate of a leaking tap, and so tangled I will probably have to cut it all off.

I open the door that leads out from the kitchen to the garden and put out the plastic bag of your ruined things, not wanting them in my house for another second. Before today, I never could have imagined throwing away something you wore and loved, something that connected you to Luke.

Adam points to a bottle of pills on the table. 'It's Diazepam,' he says. 'You may need to manage some anxiety symptoms after what happened.'

'I won't have anxiety. This afternoon was nothing.'

'I'm not sure many people would describe it that way. With your permission, I'd like to talk to your mother when she gets here. Explain what the pills are and how to use them. The possible side effects. In case you choose to take them. For sleep – just short-term. They aren't only for anxiety.'

'Okay.' I sink into a chair, pick up the tea, hold the mug for a few seconds before putting it down without sipping. I hardly take in the fact that I am sitting in my kitchen with Adam wearing an absurd dressing gown and nothing beneath it. I reach for the bottle of pills and try to read the label but the words are swimming.

'I have to ask this,' Adam says. 'There's no possibility you're pregnant, is there?'

I ought to laugh, a dark laugh, but I don't. 'No. Why?'

'Best to avoid Diazepam in pregnancy. You can take two, if you feel you need them tonight,' Adam says.

'Actually, I think I'll take them now. I need sleep. I want to go to bed.'

He finds a glass, fills it with water, puts it in front of me. 'I'm worried about you, Ella. Not as a doctor. As me.'

'I'm fine. I've washed it all away already.' But my hand is visibly juddering as I put the pills in my mouth and gulp them down.

'Would it help to talk about it?'

I shake my head No.

He slides a piece of paper across the table to me. 'I think I gave you my number the first time I met you. Here it is again. I've put my address on too. If you need anything, call.'

'Thank you,' I say, 'for everything.'

There is the sound of our mother's key in the lock.

I stand up, clutching the dressing gown around me even more tightly. 'Now you get to meet my mother. This isn't an experience you will ever forget.'

But my eyes are filling with tears again as I say this and before I can meet her at the door there is the rustle of her coat as she hurries in, crying out and rushing through the kitchen and practically knocking me over when she throws her arms around me, somehow knowing where I am without my even calling her name.

Friday, 18 November

The Long Morning

There is a hand holding mine. I open my eyes to our mother's face, looking down at my own, and realise I am in my own bed and she has drawn up a chair to sit beside me, watching over me until I wake. The curtains are closed. The room is lit only by the hall light outside.

Then it all comes flooding back to me.

I sit up but quickly take her hand again. 'I'm happy to see you. It makes me feel about ten.'

'I'm happy to see you too.' She sniffles and wipes an eye. 'You've made Luke's room lovely, Ella. I liked sleeping in there.' She leans over to switch on my little bedside lamp, awkwardly, because I do not want to let her go.

'I'm glad you think so.' I push aside the quilt and try to stand, still clutching her, but she stops me. I realise I never took off the lilac dressing gown. 'I need to go, Mum. There's something I need to do.'

She grips my hand harder. 'Haven't you done enough? Your doctor friend told me everything, after you'd gone to sleep. You were unimaginably tired. Unconscious before your head hit the pillow. Can't you let yourself rest some more?' She closes her eyes for a few seconds, opens them and shudders. 'That man could have snapped your neck. He could have done . . . worse.' It is her turn to cry. 'We could have lost you too.'

'But you didn't. He's in much worse shape than I am.' I try to smile but she doesn't smile back, either because she can't or because I haven't done it right and whatever shape I have tried to put my face into does not resemble a smile at all.

'So I'm told. I don't want to scold you again, Ella. Not ever again, if I can manage it. I don't want to fight with you. I want to try to support you.'

'I'm sorry I scared you. And I'm so, so sorry for all of the horrible things I said.' I put my arms around her and kiss her wet face. 'I didn't mean them.'

'I'm sorry too, my beautiful girl.'

'You don't need to be.' I pull back to look at her. When did her wrinkles deepen so much? I think they are my fault. 'There is something you can do to help.'

'Anything.'

'Can you and Dad go by the hospital to pick up my car?'

'Where are your keys?'

'Adam said he'd leave them in Reception. I need my phone and my watch – they're in the glovebox. My locket's in there too.'

'We'll do it after we pick up Luke, okay?' She grimaces, clearly grappling with a problem. 'But I don't want Luke setting even a foot in that place.'

'I don't either.'

She thinks about it some more. 'Luke and I will wait in the car while your father runs in to get your keys. Your father will drive your car back and Luke and I will follow him.'

'Perfect.'

Something occurs to me. Why do she and my father need to take Luke with them? Shouldn't he be in school? I jump out of bed and throw open the curtains.

The light. This isn't morning light. The shadows are all wrong. 'What time is it?' I grab the little clock on my bedside table. 'Oh my God.'

'Don't take His name in vain, Ella. Please.'

'Oh crap.' She lets this one go. 'It's three o'clock, Mum. How can it be three o'clock?'

'You had a trauma yesterday. That does funny things to the body. And – Adam – the doctor – he gave you those Diazepam. You needed to sleep. He said this might happen, that I shouldn't worry if you slept an extra-long time, that I should let you.'

'No, no, no. Oh no. I won't have time.'

'Ella?' There is that thing in her voice you can't ignore. 'Look at me.'

I look at her.

She puts her hands on both sides of my face and searches as if there is a specific material thing she will find in there and extract, whether I want her to or not. 'Won't have time for what?'

I don't answer.

'Something happened yesterday. Jason Thorne told you something, didn't he?'

'I can't talk about it.'

'Okay,' she says slowly.

'There's someone I need to see, Mum.'

'Okay,' she says again. 'Dad and Luke and I will let ourselves in and leave your things on your kitchen table if you're not here. You do what you need to do.' It is not her martyred voice. It is her loving voice. For our mother to say these words and mean them is a superhuman act of self-control that goes against every instinct she has ever had. But she is not quite finished. 'There is one condition.'

'What?'

She manages an almost-smile. 'You need to let me get the tangles out of your hair, first.'

The Ice Queen

I walk quickly into town through more mizzling grey, twisting through side streets and cut-throughs until I am two minutes from the river and standing in front of a row of red-brick Edwardian houses originally built for railway workers. As ever, your voice is hissing in my ear.

Show him what he is missing. What he will forever be missing. He threw you away. So put on a little black dress. Dust some sparkly powder over your chest and on your eyelids. Wear a shoe with a heel for once. Dab some scent behind your ears. Leave your hair down. A bit of mascara wouldn't hurt.

It has never been easier to tune out your scolding and ignore your commands. My outfit is the anti-Miranda. I am wearing faded jeans. My soft brown peasant top is loose and gypsy-like and you would hate it. My hair is in a high ponytail and I am wearing clunky boots that I can easily run in but you would call ugly and shout at me for. And that is just fine by me because I am not exactly thrilled with you either right now.

I bang on his door so hard my knuckles hurt. He opens it quickly, stepping back in surprise to see me standing here. But before his mouth can shape itself into a smile, something in my face freezes him.

'God, Ella. What's wrong?'

I push past him and along this narrow hallway I have never seen before. I glimpse the open door to his living room. An ugly carpet, threadbare and red, with a pair of scrunched and presumably dirty socks tossed onto it. Cast-off furniture that I recognise from the few times he actually let me visit his childhood house, always when his mother was out. There are no family photographs on the chimney piece, no pictures on the walls. There is little light. He bought this place after his divorce.

We have landed in his kitchen. The sink is full of dirty plates and crusted saucepans. Cups and cutlery and unrinsed tins of soup and baked beans litter the wooden counter, which is pitted with black rot. Everything is covered in food waste and coffee grinds and teabags and egg shells that he hasn't bothered to discard. There isn't even a twinge of my habitual concern for him.

He notices me looking around. 'I've only been up for an hour. I worked a double shift until seven this morning.'

'So you were on duty when I saw you yesterday at the hospital, in uniform?'

He ignores the question. 'Do you want a cup of tea?'

I glance at his oven clock. Five o'clock. 'Actually, I'd like something stronger. And less likely to give me food poisoning.'

He grabs two bottles of German beer from his fridge. 'Glass?' He glances at the sink as if such a thing would be an impossibility and I shake my head. We each take one of the tubular metal stools that sit side-by-side in front of their companion kitchen bar, which is sticky with butter and marmalade and crumbs.

I bend at the waist and squirm a hand into a boot to pull up one of my socks. When I straighten up Ted is frowning.

'There's a bruise on the nape of your neck.' He pushes aside the neckline of my blouse so that the trim on the cup of my black lace bra is exposed, and I see how easily he still presumes such intimacy. 'There's another one on your chest,' he says.

I thought my heart had frozen, since Thorne whispered in my ear yesterday. But now that I am here, now that I am about to say the words Thorne said, my heart is beating fast and my skin feels so hot I am sure my newly visible bruises are camouflaged by the red that has crept over every inch of my skin.

'Don't touch me.' I jerk away and Ted falls back as if punched by an invisible fist. For a second, I think his stool is going to tip over and crash down with him on it.

'At least the man who made these bruises has the excuse of being criminally insane. And he has never deliberately lied to me. Unlike you.'

He waits until I seem to be breathing again before he speaks. 'Are you comparing me to that psychopathic scumbag? You took him down. If you hadn't kicked his ass he'd have raped you and murdered you in front of your doctor friend and those nurses. He'd have enjoyed the audience.'

I swallow half the bottle of beer, then cough so violently I can see Ted having a three-way fight with himself, one part wanting to slap my back so I don't choke, a second part not daring to lay even a finger on me again, and a third part wanting to strangle me with his own hands.

Already I can feel alcohol making its way through my veins, probably speeded by a residue of Diazepam from last night. I come right out and say it. 'I know, Ted. I know the thing you never thought I'd find out.'

'What the hell are you talking about?'

'I'm talking about the thing you never wanted me to know.'

'You're not making sense.' There is a faint sheen of sweat on his brow but he continues to pretend not to understand me. 'Whatever happened to you in that hospital yesterday with Thorne must have resulted in a head injury.'

'My head was examined before I left.'

'By that quack who obviously wants to fuck your brains out?'

'He's not a quack. And there was no serious injury. The bruises will fade. As far as he was capable, Thorne tried to restrain himself and not hurt me.'

'Listen to yourself. You talk as if you actually admire him. As if you actually like him. Do you believe those fuckwits who say he's insane? Only someone equally insane would go near him.'

'At least he doesn't tell me I'm mad every time I say

something he doesn't like. I needed to hear what he could tell me and I knew exactly what I was risking.'

'I warned you he was dangerous.'

'I managed to figure that out without your help.' I shake my head as if by doing so I can shake the words to the surface so I can actually say them. 'Thorne saw you, Ted. He saw you with her the day before she disappeared. He heard what the two of you said. He worked out who you were to me from the nature of your conversation with her.'

I have read so many times of faces suddenly being drained of blood. I always wondered if it could really happen, that fast and all-at-once. And now I know that it can. Because I have just watched all of Ted's blood rush out of his head and down to his feet. Because now I have seen for myself that skin really can appear as white as paper. Those words are not empty, but to see them in action is rare.

'That's not possible,' he says.

'So you didn't meet her in the woods behind my parents' house, the day before she vanished? You didn't drive from her to me, as soon as you parted?'

Can it be that his face blanches even more?

'Tell me you didn't really spend half an hour talking to her there. Go on. Tell me that's not true.'

He says nothing.

'I even know what dress she was wearing that day. Do you want me to describe it or would you like to?'

For once he has nothing to say.

'The black one that buttons up the front, that she was always wearing for breastfeeding, in case you have forgotten. Have you forgotten? Or perhaps you didn't notice.'

At last he says, 'How?' It seems that one word is the best he can do.

'Thorne followed her to my parents' that morning. She caught his attention when she phoned him about that carpentry job. You know. That phone call between them you kept telling me she never made.'

'Ella—'

'Spare me. He was scouting for a new victim so he wanted to see her in person and decide if he'd target her. He was crouching behind foliage and he had excellent binoculars. He wasn't carrying extra weight then – the meds did that to him – he could move easily. He knows how to hide – it's one of his arts. And he can lip-read.'

'Please, Ella—'

I put up a hand. 'You need to hear this. Did you know the ability to lip-read is more common in people who have problems relating to others? Did they not teach you that in training school? Thorne deliberately honed this little talent of his. He found it incredibly useful.'

He staggers off his stool, careering it onto the filthy linoleum. He throws his arms around me, pulls me onto my feet and against him, burying his head in my shoulder. Great racking sobs are shuddering through his body, making mine shudder too. 'I love you, Ella. I've always loved you. It was only once and it meant nothing. It was years ago.'

I jerk out of his arms. 'Is that why you got that weekend off? Did you come down to spend it in Brighton with me to make sure she didn't? Because you were afraid of what she might tell me if we had some time alone together?'

'No.' He moves his head from side to side so furiously the tears he hasn't wiped fly from his face. 'You'd been alone with her countless times since. She was never going to tell you. We both planned to take it to our graves. We'd made a pact. Probably the only thing she and I ever agreed about. She was more terrified than I was of you finding out, and that's saying a lot.'

'Why do you think she did it?' I hate that I have to ask this of him. I hate that he is still the best person to answer this, without you here.

'I don't know.'

'You fucking well do.'

He shakes his head as if he is genuinely puzzled. 'A mix of things. Her constant need for attention. I got the feeling things weren't going the way she wanted with whoever her man of the moment was. I think our relationship looked perfect and easy to her – the opposite of whatever she had. She wanted to shatter it.'

'What we had *was* perfect. You shattered it.'

'Yes. I did. And I still don't understand myself well enough to know why. For her, though, I think she needed to prove that you were vulnerable too. That she could take what she wanted from you. But she couldn't, Ella. As soon as I sobered up, all I wanted was you.'

'You thought Luke was your son, didn't you?'

'Only briefly.'

'Is that why you've always loved him?'

'I think he's a great kid. I love him because you do. I love him for him. Miranda swore to me he wasn't mine.

It was one of the things we talked about that morning, but she'd already convinced me. Luke is yours. That's how I think of him.'

'You never told the police you met her the day before she vanished. That was evidence and you never told because you only thought of yourself. You of all people know you should have gone to them with that.' My temples are throbbing. I press the flats of my hands against them. 'Were you involved in some way?'

'I was in bed with you when she disappeared. You know that.'

'You could have arranged it. Got someone else to do it.'

'I'm not a criminal mastermind. I'm a policeman with one serious and literal fuck-up in his past.'

'If that's true then you won't try to persuade me not to tell your buddies at the station about your relationship with her, about your meeting.'

'It wasn't a relationship.' He grabs me, spins me round, pulls me hard against him, starts to plant small kisses on my breastbone. 'Please, please, please forgive me, Ella. I love you. Let me show you how much. Please. Let me take you to bed right now.'

I close my eyes and count to ten before I open them. His lips might as well be touching stone. I feel nothing. 'You've got to be kidding me. I don't want this with you. Ever again. Let go of me or I will make you.'

I wrench myself away and move as far from him as I can, to his kitchen window. I stare out into his bare little garden.

'Please at least look at me.'

'No.' There is a silhouette of an apple tree. Beneath it is the shadow of a picnic table covered in beer bottles. 'How did it happen?' I direct the question towards the moon, which is such a faint sliver it hardly makes any impression at all on the black sky.

With the dark outside and the light inside, I can see his reflection mirrored in the window. He shrugs, seeming to ponder the most mystifying thing in the world. I close my eyes to blot him from my view, as if responding to a physical pain.

'You'd just gone back to the university again. She and I bumped into each other in the supermarket after work, went for a drink, talked about how much we were missing you.' He makes a noise that is almost a laugh, though it is bitter and astonished. 'All we did was talk about you. We ended up back at the flat I was renting then. She didn't even stay the night. Five minutes after it happened she left. We were both horrified.'

I open my eyes and turn around, leaning against the edge of the sink. 'Why did you get married? Was it to hurt me?'

'Please don't take this the wrong way – I'm trying to be honest – I owe you that. But you changed so much, after she was gone. You wouldn't let me take care of you. I'd been doing that since we met, but then, poof, no more. Everything you are now is formed by what happened. You aren't what you would have been.'

'There's truth in that, but you didn't answer my question.'

'I wanted to try to be normal with somebody. To be in a relationship without a big cloud hanging over it. But you haunted my marriage. You haunted me. You made my marriage another big fuck-up.'

'So that's my fault. You've used that one before.'

'I didn't mean it that way. It came out wrong. Everything is coming out wrong.'

'What's your blood type, Ted?'

He looks baffled but he still answers. 'O.'

'You couldn't possibly be Luke's father. He has AB blood. You don't need to be a geneticist to figure that out.'

'Tell me you will forgive me.'

'For which thing? For fucking my sister? For withholding evidence that might have helped us to find her? For spending the last decade telling me I'm mad and unstable and paranoid for wanting to know what happened to her?'

'All of them. I was scared I'd lose you.'

'You have. You can consider me well and truly lost. We would have survived your marriage and we'd definitely have survived Ruby. But not this.'

'I told you – Ruby—'

'You'd better not hurt her – she's been through enough already. I don't believe a single word that comes out of your mouth.' I grab my bag and swing it over my shoulder.

'Are you going to tell the police I met her that day?'

'No. You are going to tell them that all by yourself. You have until the end of the weekend.' I imagine him and Mrs Buenrostro in next-door interview rooms as the station explodes with new interest in your case. The two of them can do the hard work for me.

'My meeting with Miranda is irrelevant. It was unlucky timing. You know I had nothing to do with her disappearance. You must still feel too much for me to ask me to do this.'

'My feelings for you are dead. You've killed them. You make me sick. All you think about is yourself.'

'At least you'll finally believe me that she's not perfect. That you shouldn't idolise her.'

'Wow, Ted. Gee thanks. You certainly went to a lot of trouble to make a point I had already discovered without your help.'

I begin to pull the door open but before it has swung an inch he slams it closed and pins me against it. I think of Thorne pressing me against the wall yesterday.

'I don't care about myself. I care about you. More than anyone. For twenty-six years we've loved each other. You can't go. You can't do this. You can't just walk away.'

My thoughts are quick. It is the first time I have ever wanted to hurt him and it goes against the instincts of my entire life.

I imagine myself lifting a knee hard between his legs and shoving his shoulders. The fantasy is so vivid I can actually see him drop to the hall floor and double over onto his side, his hands slapped over his lower body, moaning, rolling back and forth with his knees bent. It would be so easy.

But this isn't what I do. What I do is not expert. What I do happens with a noise that is something between a scream and a cry and a grunt, and I can feel tears on my cheeks when that animal noise comes out and I shove at him blindly, pounding my fists on his chest. He lets me go not because I have wounded him, but because he is stunned by my rawness.

'I can and I can and I can.' I leave without closing to close the door behind me.

The Old Friend

I walk home so fast I hardly remember the journey. My car is parked in front of the house next door. Sadie is standing beside it, hands on hips, an expression on her blotchy red face that is somewhere between glaring and woeful. I haven't seen her without flawless make-up since our early teens.

I have no time for Sadie. Sadie is nothing. 'Go away,' I say, as if she is a mere fly buzzing around and annoying me on a hot day. Her long hair is unwashed, an unbrushed rat's nest with grey roots showing. Sadie's hair is normally salon-polished.

My heart is frozen again. My heart is hard. Its beat is not disturbed by Sadie. How can anything hurt me after you? You and I are not what I thought we were to each other. You are not the you I have always known. You are dead, even if you are still somewhere in this world, breathing.

I turn onto my path. I can feel Sadie, starting to follow me.

'Bitch,' Sadie says. 'You ugly, boyfriend-thieving bitch.

You deserve to disappear like that vain pig of a sister of yours. She was a slut, like you.'

I turn to face her, put out a hand to stop her coming a step nearer. 'I said, *Go away.*'

'I don't take orders from you.' Sadie spits the words out with a great deal of saliva. There is some on her chin but she doesn't appear to notice.

'Are you sure, Sadie? The camera is trained on this path. Come a step closer to me and it will clearly be self-defence. You approaching me. You assaulting me. You invading my property.' The words are dramatic. The situation is dramatic. But I speak and move like an extremely convincing human robot, saying all the right lines, making all the right moves. Perhaps I have become a psychopath, devoid of empathy. I am devoid of pity, and of fear, too.

Sadie looks at the camera and cringes several steps back, off the path. She studies the lens, trying to decide if she is out of its eyeline. I watch her as if she is the object of a scientific experiment, though without a scientist's depth of curiosity.

'I've been waiting for you for an hour,' she says. 'I've been ringing the doorbell every five minutes. You can't hide from me.'

'Great. The camera will have that too. Ringing a doorbell every five minutes is nuisance behaviour. It's reportable. And you already know that I won't hesitate to report you.' How odd. I actually sound like I care about what I'm saying. Perhaps I should be an actress.

She scrunches her mouth like a toddler on the verge of a tantrum. 'You're evil. There is a chair in hell for you. After the devil tortures you.'

I laugh.

'You find that funny?'

'It would seem so. You've only got the tiniest taste of what I can do, if you push me. You really did choose to pick on the wrong woman. I suspect the police have paid you a visit?'

She wipes her nose with her bare hand. There is dirt beneath her nails, which are bitten so that the skin is raw and bleeding. I have never seen her nails without perfect varnish before. I ought to be concerned about these signs of Sadie's distress but I do not possess even a crumb of compassion. Perhaps I should be worried about my own indifference, but I am not.

'I told them all about you,' she says. 'They know everything about you.'

'Fine by me. I have nothing to hide. I would guess they warned you to stay away from me. Clearly not advice you are heeding.'

She swallows hard. 'You are going to deserve everything you get.'

'Great. Threats too. You're handing the police all the evidence they need for solid harassment and stalking charges. They can throw in some malicious communications too. Did you really think they wouldn't trace your little messages? Did you think I wouldn't hand each and every one of them over?'

She is biting her lip. She is balling her fists. She has wrapped her arms around her own body. She is swaying from side to side as if she is drunk. I register each of her actions with dispassionate detachment.

'Move on, Sadie,' I say. 'No texts or emails in your

name or Justice Administrator's name or any other name. No calls, blocked or otherwise. No photographs.'

'I don't know what you're talking about.'

'Don't waste your breath. Let me be completely clear. I don't want you near me. I don't want any communication or contact from you in any imaginable form. If you approach me in any way ever again you will get another visit from the police and a very uncomfortable bed for the night. For many nights, if you continue to get in my face. I am going to phone them now so that they can remove you. I am going to ask for a restraining order. Consider this your final warning, which is more than you deserve. So. *Leave. This. Instant.*'

I walk calmly into my house. I do not need to look behind me to make sure she is not following. I would feel it in the air if she were. I would hear.

When I am inside I pick up the landline and go to the living room window as I prepare to dial the police. But Sadie is already in her own car, tyres screaming along the road.

With her gone, there is no reason to call the police right now. I can give them the evidence of her visit later. More to the point, I have miles to go before I sleep and I do not want to waste any more of them on a Sadie detour. I move away from the living room window and into my kitchen to begin walking them.

Dressing Up

I drop the landline onto the table, unused, beside the handwritten note my mother has left for me. *Dad and I will bring Luke and lunch tomorrow. Love, Mum.* She has weighted the note in place with my keys and mobile and watch and locket.

I toss everything into my bag but the locket. For the first time since you gave it to me, I cannot bring myself to put it on. My numb heart seems to wake up. It seems to speed up as I turn the cool platinum over and over in my palm and choke back a sob. Even if I cannot put it around my neck, I can't leave it behind, either – I can't not have it near me. I throw the locket into my bag too.

What I do next I do for me. Entirely for me. Not for Mum and Dad. Not for Luke. Do you get it? Are you listening? For me. Above all not for you. For you less than anybody. Right now nobody counts but me.

I rush upstairs to shower and wash my hair with a different shampoo. Not the one with the scent of you. I brush my teeth. I even put on some mascara. But not because you are telling me to. Because it is what I want to do. I dab Chanel Number 5 behind my ears, between my breasts, on the nape of my neck. Again not because of you. Because it is my choice. Because I have always loved it even though you do not. I do not smell like you.

My bra and underwear and stockings are slippery silk and sheer, tinted the same colour as my skin. I pull a cap-sleeved sweater dress over my head and look in the mirror. The dress is short and fitted, though not tight, and it has jagged horizontal stripes of mustard and navy blue. I fluff my hair, stick the front into a clasp, and realise I look like I stepped out of a 1960s fashion plate, especially with my knee-high black boots. I study my reflection some more. I look hard and cruel and beautiful. I look like you.

I get in my car, telling myself it was only one beer, one much-needed beer. One beer won't put me over the limit. I can even add a glass of wine and still be fine. I haven't called, haven't checked that he is actually home. But I seem unable to stop moving and somehow I am winding around the twisty lane and turning onto his gravelled drive.

I leave the car in front of his blue painted garage and push the buzzer on the blue painted door beside it. Both doors are built into a stone wall that encases his garden. I am not wearing a coat but I am not cold. I am warm warm warm.

The door opens and Adam stands there. He blinks several times. His face flushes. He says, 'I think you are a daydream come true,' and takes my hand and pulls me against him and kisses me, which is exactly what I hoped he would do.

He leads me through a courtyard, then into his house. I have a vague impression of cream rugs over old stone floors, brown leather sofas, pale walls. He pulls me beside him onto one of the sofas and I am startled by how natural it feels, how easy. Is this the way it is supposed to be? Nothing with Ted has been easy since you disappeared, and now I know why.

Adam's breathing is going faster and so is mine. One of my hands finds its way to the top button of his shirt, unhooks it, trails a finger through the dark hairs on his chest. He has that same fresh soapy smell I noticed in the library. It makes me want to inhale him. My other hand slips beneath the jacket of his suit, presses into the muscles of his back.

That is when his clothes register. My eyes crease in puzzlement. 'You're in serious clothes. I've interrupted something. You're going out.'

'I'm on call tonight. If the hospital rings I'll need to go in.' He puts his face close to mine again. 'But you can wait for me here. I like the idea of coming back to you. Would you like that too?'

I have been ambushed. I know this is Adam's voice, telling me he wants to come back to me, and asking if I would like that, but somehow I hear Ted's, and he is saying these words not to me but to you.

I know it is Adam whose face is only inches from mine, but I am seeing Ted. It is as if I am watching a film. The camera pulls away and I can see you too.

You and Ted are in bed, the sheets a sweaty tangle. You are wrapped around each other, whispering against each other's lips as you make love. You say my name as if it is a joke, and the two of you laugh together at stupid, clue-less me. You have always been the one I really wanted, he tells you. You, Miranda, he says. Always you. Never Ella.

I take a huge racking breath. I don't let any sound come out because I am trying so hard to keep it in. But my body cannot hold the crying. The crying is going through my very bones, shaking me and shaking me and shaking me some more, and my face is twisted with grief that I cannot smooth away. The crying is coming out of my face too. It is like retching when there is no sick left. My tears have run dry but something somewhere still needs to be expelled. Adam's arms go round me. He says nothing. He holds me, absorbing the worst of my shud-dering, but the movement is so violent the top of my head keeps hitting his chin.

I don't know how long it is before I calm down and he pulls away to look at me. 'Not the effect I was hoping for,' he says.

I actually laugh, though it is pretty feeble as laughs go. 'Sorry,' I say. 'I'm so sorry. It wasn't you. It was nothing to do with you.'

'Don't be sorry. I'm worried about you, Ella. I don't think you're admitting to yourself quite what you went through yesterday.'

'It's not that. Really it isn't.'

He considers for a few seconds. 'Okay then. I know you'll tell me when you want to. If you want to.'

'Can we start over?' I say.

He nods, looking so worried and serious. Slowly, I pull his face towards mine. This time, his face stays his face. He isn't overlaid by Ted.

As our lips are about to touch, with near-comic timing, his mobile rings, making him curse.

He mumbles his first and last name into the handset instead of saying hello. Within a few seconds, he jumps up and walks to the other side of the room, where he listens and paces, occasionally contributing a low mono-syllable. After a minute he says, 'On my way,' and rings off.

He comes back to the sofa, kneels at my feet to look up at me. His face is drained of colour. His lips are pinched.

I touch his cheek. 'What's happened?'

'Ella—' He cuts himself off, seeming not to know what to say.

'Is it Thorne?'

'Yes.'

My hand falls into my lap. 'Tell me.'

There is another long pause before he is able to speak. 'He was moved to a specialist orthopaedic unit. They had to operate on his knee.'

'Did he die?'

'No.' He shakes his head. 'Nothing like that. But he isn't accounted for. He's been missing for nearly an hour.'

'Fuck. You're fucking joking.' He might as well learn the truth about my swearing now.

'Unfortunately I'm not,' he says. 'You're safe here though. You know that, don't you?'

'I'm not worried about that. He'd be more likely to hurt you. He really doesn't like you very much.'

'I've noticed.' He rises to sit beside me again, brushes a stray hair out of my eyes, tries to smile, but barely manages it. 'You, though, he likes quite a lot. He'd be like King Kong following Ann Darrow through New York City. But he has no idea where I live or where you live or where your parents live.'

'I wouldn't be so confident of that.'

'I am. But it's beside the point. They'll find him before he even gets out of the medical centre. He hasn't been spotted by any of the CCTV and there should be a camera at every exit – he's probably hiding in a storage room. He's not going to get far on that leg and he was under general anaesthetic only this morning.'

'That's reassuring. Sorry – the sarcasm isn't meant for you.'

'You don't need to be sorry – it's milder than they deserve. The police want to interview some of the patients, so I need to be there. I don't want you to worry.' He pulls me closer. 'Think about what we'll do to each other when I get back.'

'You trust me alone in your house?' I say this teasingly but I am watching carefully for his reaction.

'You trusted me in yours.'

'I was only upstairs in the shower.'

He traces a finger along my lips so lightly that I shiver. I feared Ted had turned me to stone, but he didn't. The hairs rise on my skin. I seem to be made of electricity.

'I love having you here,' he says.

'You love sobbing women.'

'I don't think you'll be doing much of that with me.' He kisses me again, harder this time, his tongue in my mouth, running his hands over my waist, slipping a hand beneath my dress, moving it over my silky underwear. I picture Ted seeing me with this man. The fantasy sends a spear of pure joy right through me. 'You don't make it easy to leave,' he says.

He pours a glass of red wine from a decanter sitting on a tray with overturned glasses, as if awaiting guests, and I wonder who actually arranged these things. I imagine him as the prince disguised as a beast from the fairy tale, with an invisible housekeeping crew.

He puts the glass in my hand. 'I can't drink tonight but you can.' I take a sip and he kisses me once more, inhaling the wine from my mouth. 'I'll get drunk if I don't leave now.' And with these words he goes.

The Builder's Daughter

At first I just sit, watching the wood crackle in the log fire, sipping the wine, giving myself goosebumps by tickling my own arm as you used to. But it never feels as lovely when I do it myself and I don't want to do anything that reminds me of you.

Plus, I am not very good at sitting and I can't stop thinking about Thorne. Only five minutes have passed before I put the wine glass on a low table and wander through the rooms, reminding myself that Adam said I should make myself at home.

This is not a house where Luke could ever be. There is no clutter. It is far too clean. When I switch on the kitchen light there are no dust motes. The kitchen looks unused, straight from the pages of a bespoke catalogue. Luke would smear those bone-painted solid oak cabinets in five seconds flat. With this thought, I wonder if Adam would like a boy in this house. I wonder if Adam would like a boy at all.

The other downstairs room is filled with gym equipment

that I could never afford let alone fit in my house, and I am startled to see the extent of his devotion to his own fitness. There is an exercise bike with a built-in tablet console, a treadmill with more electronic attachments for entertainment and monitoring, a cross trainer, and a rowing machine. There is a heavy-duty rubber mat beneath a bench press. There is an assortment of weights arranged on purpose-built shelves.

The only other thing I can find on the ground floor is the storage space below the stairs. He has turned it into a coat cupboard and it is more ordered than any coat cupboard I have ever seen. Our mother's appears chaotic by comparison. Coats for all seasons and occasions hang on matching wooden hangers. There is a bag of golf clubs, some wellies, a variety of sports shoes and a pair of tan leather walking boots.

I pick up one of the boots and turn it over to study the bottom. I am not sure why I do this. The first thing to hit me is how pristinely clean the boot is. Does this man really wash his boots each time he wears them? There isn't even a fleck of dried mud on the bottom. But what makes my heart catch is the familiarity of the pattern on the outsole. I look again, telling myself I am imagining it. It cannot be.

I run to get my phone so I can compare the shoe with the photos of the footprint and the plaster cast. When I turn the phone on I see that the battery is dead from the calls I made before I got to the hospital yesterday, probably not helped by the night it spent in my glovebox.

I pick up the walking boot again. The plaster cast could only capture the toe area, so I place my hand over the heel and arch of Adam's boot, leaving the anterior visible. Three moulded hexagons are stamped into the centre. Radiating out from these to the edge are small squares with ridges between them. The ridges are worn away so deeply on the outer side of the boot there are no squares at all, just smooth outsole.

You always said I had a strong visual memory. I close my eyes to try to call up the photograph of the partial imprint left in the woods. I see the same hexagons, the same ridges, the same areas smoothed by his individual tread. The pattern and wear are distinctive. But I am aware of the power of suggestion, and the likelihood that my mind is replicating the boot I have examined rather than recalling the photograph. A mere two days ago, I'd convinced myself that the sole's erosion could be evidence of a previously ruptured Achilles' tendon. I seesaw back and forth in doubt and certainty. I put the boots away, exactly as I found them.

I hurry to the stairs, which are old stone, ground down in the centre by centuries of feet. I rush up to do a quick survey of the rooms.

The first door I open reveals a study with shelves of medical books, all of the spines pulled to exactly the same distance from the edge. I touch one, examine my finger, and find that there isn't even a speck of dust.

A black leather chair sits in front of a huge mahogany desk. On the desk are a laptop and a small clock. I turn on the machine but immediately I am faced with the command to input a password and I don't have time even to begin to guess at what that might be so I switch it off again. The drawers contain papers and bills and invoices, all carefully organised in labelled folders, as well as a book full of medical notes and an old accounting ledger.

There is a stethoscope with his name engraved on the diaphragm. It is still pristine in its box and I wonder if it was a gift, because Adam is not a cardiologist and he does not strike me as the kind of man who would choose to have a heart carved on each side of his name. It is the kind of thing you would do. Lightly. Playfully. Perhaps even lovingly.

My eyes fly to the clock. He has been gone for fifteen minutes. It will take him twenty minutes to drive to the hospital, twenty minutes to get back, and surely he will spend at least an hour there, probably much longer. I decide on an ultra-conservative fifty minutes. This is the amount of time I will allow myself to snoop. It will leave me an extremely safe margin not to be caught.

All of the rooms are pitch-black until I switch on the lights. There is a bathroom, with marble-tiled floors and walls. Improbably white towels, perfectly folded, hang from stainless steel rails. There is a guest room with a platform bed covered by a white quilt.

Then there is Adam's room. At first I cannot figure out how to open the heavy blinds that shield his windows. Then I see there is a switch near each. When I press one, the blind rolls itself up slowly, like the ones we had in our hotel when Mum and Dad took us to Seville for your sixteenth birthday. The crescent moon casts enough light for me to see the hedgerow that encloses the sides and back of the house. It would be impossible to view this building from the other side of the shrubs and trees.

The window itself is locked. It opens with a key, but

that is not in any place I can see. I shake away the fear that the light will give me away in here, reminding myself that Adam cannot possibly be back this soon. I have forty-five minutes, by my ultra-safe estimates. My heart is beating fast and loud. I decide to scrunch that number into extra cautiousness and give myself thirty-five minutes before I flee. I close the blinds, leaving them as they were.

A door leads to a bathroom that looks much like the other, except that this one contains the essential things Adam needs every day. Shampoo and shower gel, toothbrush and toothpaste and dental floss. A brush and soap and razor remind me of how I used to shave Ted, how we would kiss as I rasped a potentially lethal cutthroat down his neck – not an experiment either of us would risk now. I am furious that I have let myself be ambushed by a happy memory of him.

Adam's bed is solid and simple, a matt black frame, a grey quilt. The only other furniture is a large reading chair in charcoal-coloured leather and a huge chest of drawers in the same wood as the bed frame. The chimney breast has been blocked up and smoothed over. The chest is set in the recess to the left of it. There is nothing of interest in the drawers. Just clothes, arranged with military neatness. This man really could not bear the inevitable mark another human being would make on his living space. Is this why he has never mentioned a previous girlfriend or wife? So far, I have found no real evidence that there has ever been one.

To the right of the chimney breast are panelled double-doors, presumably for a built-in wardrobe that makes use of the other recess in the wall. Above the doors are matching panels, but these are cupboard-sized. I cannot reach them without something to step on.

I look hard at the whole set-up, trying to figure out why my mind is registering something odd about it. Is it the size of the wardrobe doors? The cupboard above them? The scale of both together from the outside as opposed to the likely space on the inside?

I cannot pinpoint what is niggling me. I study the doors some more and it hits me. The problem is proportion. There is too much space between the top of the wardrobe doors and the bottom of the cupboard doors. Six or eight inches at most would look right, but there is well over a foot.

I pull open the wardrobe. Inside is a hanging rail with shirts on one side and suits on the other, all in dry cleaner's plastic and grouped by colour. There are several black shirts, but I am certain that if one was ever missing a button he has already had it replaced or thrown the whole thing away. Ted can congratulate himself on the pointlessness of that evidence bag.

Adam's perfectly polished shoes are arranged on a slatted bench. I drag the bench out. Instead of climbing on it to reach the cupboard, something makes me kneel down to examine the wardrobe's floor. There are small holes, drilled into it at four-inch intervals. The two holes at the front are bigger, so I hook my fingers into them and lift and let out a cry.

I have taken the lid off a hole the size and shape of a coffin. The wardrobe is four feet wide and two feet deep. Although this rectangle beneath the floor matches the wardrobe's depth, it stretches six feet. Inside is a foam mat covered in a sheet, a pillow in a case, and a single quilt, folded at the bottom as if awaiting a guest.

The room seems to be spinning and my blood is pulsing in my ears with such force I think Adam can hear it from the hospital. *Oh my God.* I actually say this aloud. I am breathing too fast. *Calm down, Ella.* I say this aloud too.

And then I hear you. *You don't have time to react to this. You don't have time to be mad at me and tune me out. You have twenty-five minutes before you get out. So get on your fucking feet and keep looking and then get the hell away.*

I try to think clearly. I let the false floor drop back into place so he won't know I found it. I climb onto the storage bench and pull open the high cupboard doors above the wardrobe. I have to clutch the cupboard doors for a few seconds to stop myself from falling. I throw the pillows I find in there onto the polished floorboards. I run my hand over every inch of the bottom of the now-empty cupboard until I stumble upon another set of holes, exactly right for hooking fingers. In an instant, I have pulled up what proves to be another false bottom, revealing a hollow space between the ceiling of the wardrobe and the floor of the high cupboard.

The space is not empty. Inside is a camouflage daypack he must have been given in the army. When I pull it out it nearly crashes onto my head. The hydration hose slaps my temple so hard I think it draws blood but I can't afford to worry about that right now. I sit on top of the pillows and unfasten one of the side compartments and slide my hand in.

Why is it that when you are looking for something you always assume it will be in the last place you check? The final hidden pocket? That tiny corner you missed at first?

Jason Thorne never lied to me but it wasn't the honour of a thief. It was the strange honour of a psychopathic serial killer who thinks I am his true love. Am I foolish enough to believe Thorne would never hurt me? No. I am certain he would like nothing better. What Thorne and I mean by love are very different things. Sexual violence is the only form of expression he knows, however passionately he tells me otherwise. But his insight, sickening as it may be, is still useful. His words are echoing in my head. *So he can keep her close.*

I know what it is before I look. I know what it is as soon as my fingers tangle in the familiar silky platinum that matches the chain in my handbag. Your locket is smoother than the stones your son and I left for you in the woods by our parents' house, where this man spied on us. I know this because the missing pink-stained stones are here too, in the other side pocket. I set the stones down.

I bring your locket to my lips and press it against them before I open it and look at my own photograph, taken over ten years ago. Taken by you. Opposite my image should be your baby son, snapped by me when he was so new he was like a sea creature, still curled, still wanting to swim. But that photograph is gone – he has ripped Luke out.

I imagine you in the hidden coffin and wrap my arms tightly around myself and rock back and forth. But you are shouting at me, telling me to move, to get out. There will be time for all this weeping and wailing later, because by my own conservative calculations I have twenty minutes left to leave. I listen to you. I start to move. I have only risen an inch before a stab of fire shoots through the top of my arm and everything goes black.

Evening Prayer

I try to open my eyes but my lids are so heavy. I manage a tiny slit before they slip closed again. My arms are heavy too, and my legs. There is a hand smoothing my hair, floating over my forehead.

It is you. I know it is you. I can smell honeysuckle. Only your hands are this soft. You take so much trouble over your hands, with those weekly manicures that I tease you about. I try to smile. I try again to open my eyes. I must be very ill and that is why you have finally come back from wherever you have been. You have come back to take care of me.

I try to say your name but only a slurry M comes out. I try to ask you to help me open my eyes so I can look at you. I want so badly to see you, after so long. I hear your voice, singing me the evening prayer from the *Hansel and Gretel* opera, just as you did when I was small. *When at night I go to sleep, Fourteen angels watch do keep.* You are one of the two angels guarding my head. You are whispering that you have found me. I want to tell you that I am so happy but it is too hard to control my mouth. My lips are shaking and my chin is trembling. My whole face is in tremors.

'Melanie?' My eyelid opens but I am not the one who makes it do this. You must be trying to help me and I try to tell you that I am so sorry but I cannot keep it open myself. I try to tell you that the light you are piercing into my eye hurts. But this problem with my mouth makes telling these things impossible. You say, 'Open your eyes, please, Melanie,' and even though it is my name, the only name you ever call me, it is not your voice.

Adam Holderness's face is close to mine. I blink. He looks so blurry. There are two of him. I don't want one of him, let alone two. I only want you, but you have blown away, back to wherever you are. There is only him. My arms are jerking. My legs are twitching so much they seem to be operated by invisible puppet strings. My head is twisting on my neck.

'Try to relax, Melanie.'

My back goes rigid. My head is jerking from side to side as if I am signalling No. Forever No. I cannot stop gesturing No.

Above me is white ceiling. Below me is? What is below me? My legs are bare. Where are my stockings? Something damp and smooth is against my skin. It squelches like a suction cup when I try to move. I am in the leather reading chair in his bedroom and my feet are elevated. He has put up some sort of footrest and tipped the back low so that I am reclining.

My hips are lifting up and down, up and down. My

back is arching and flattening, arching and flattening. My dress is riding up. I glimpse his face again. He is frowning. He looks worried but I cannot decide if this is because he wants to kill me or save me.

My legs are shuddering and when he runs a hand along the inside of my thigh it lurches so violently he takes his hand away and instead catches my wrist in it, counts my pulse.

'You're having a reaction to the drug you needed. I'm sorry. Normally Procyclidine would stop this happening but there wasn't any to hand. Antihistamine works too. Let's get some of that in you while you're a little calmer.' He tries to sit me up but I am a contorted board.

'No.' The word doesn't sound like a word.

'We have to stop the tremors and the muscle rigidity.'

We. I try to say No again but it sounds like I have a mouthful of sand.

'It's dangerous for you otherwise. Please, Melanie.'

I allow him to put something in my mouth, hold a water bottle to my lips, feel some of it spill over my chin. He rubs my throat as if I am a pet and though this induces my swallow reflex it is like gulping a rock. My throat feels bruised.

'Your sister had the same reaction.' He looks so sad I almost believe that he is. 'The infection made her symptoms challenging to manage.' He shakes his head. 'If she hadn't had that baby she would have been fine.'

You would not have been fine. He was never going to let you be fine and he is not going to let me be that way either. My head knows this but I cannot make myself scared enough to leap from the chair and run away. Despite what my head knows, I cannot properly feel these truths and what they mean. I am not ready to accept them.

He touches the neckline of my dress with one hand, picks up a stethoscope from somewhere with the other. 'May I?'

My head is vibrating from side to side as if he has stuck a motor in it and it isn't because the drugs have me in their grip. It is because you do.

Despite my attempt at no, he tugs the knitted fabric to expose more of my chest before he puts the cold metal against my skin. 'Your heart is strong, Melanie,' he says. 'Body and soul. Much stronger than your sister's.'

'Did she?' I remember Thorne's garbled voice after Adam injected him with the tranquillisers. That is how I sound.

He wrinkles his forehead, trying to understand me. 'Ah. The stethoscope.' He nods to confirm it, as if he has discovered a shared passion with a boss he wants to impress. 'Yes. She gave it to me. She would have been pleased by the idea that it could be used to care for you.'

The fuck I would, you say. Since you left you seem to say fuck a lot. Like me. Though I am not sure any more if you did that much while you were here. It is too easy to blame you for the things I do wrong.

He takes the stethoscope away with his right hand but leaves his left on my chest, so that some of his fingers trail over my breast.

'Don't.' I try to lift an arm to push him away but my arm has stopped being like a stick and is now being like a wet noodle. It moves only a few inches before flopping down again. I am a woman-sized rag doll.

'Are you sure? You came here to me. Your voice is saying no but not your body. Do you know what disinhibition is?'

I do but I am not about to waste what little voice I have admitting it.

'It's a side effect of the drug you needed. So is a sense of well-being. You look tranquil, Melanie, and you haven't looked tranquil since I met you. The antihistamine is starting to work already – it was a high dose. You have bedroom eyes. You always do but especially now that we're alone.'

I am thinking. I am trying so hard to think. Why is it so hard to think? What do I need to do? The answer comes almost as soon as I silently ask the question. I need to keep him talking until I can fight him off. That is what I must do. Whatever happens, I cannot let him put me in that coffin. I try to shake my head to wake up but it only makes my brain slop around in my skull like jelly.

'Why?'

'Why what?'

'Why Melanie?' I am not sure how comprehensible the second word is but somehow he is primed to hear it.

'She talked about you so much. She always called you that. I felt I knew you even before we met, because of her. I loved you before we met, because of her. She worshipped you.'

I must be moving my head to deny this could be possible. I was the worshipper. Not you. Of all people, I do not want this man to teach me about you. I would more cheerfully be taught by Ted.

'She did, Melanie. Whatever her faults – and there were plenty – she did. It's the only thing I'm still grateful to her for. But to answer your question, it's your real name and the one I like best. It's what I know you by.'

You would never have meant for him to use it. You didn't want to share my name with anybody, let alone him. I do not say this. I say a different true thing. 'Thirsty,' I say.

'Sadie? Why do you want to talk about her?' His lips turn down in a frown. 'She's not a real friend to you. Not someone who trusts you as you deserve.' He considers, as if unsure whether to go on with what he wants to say. 'Have you wondered what brought you to my notice, Melanie?'

'Yes.'

'It was that interview you did with the paper, and the photo. You look so much like your sister. I made it my business to learn everything I could about you, after I saw it. That included Sadie. I even helped her and Brian to discover each other. Brian wanted to make some extra money – the private clinic work was my idea. Sadie's place was on a list I gave him, the only realistic prospect on it.'

He manipulates people as if they were pieces on a game board. 'Why?'

'So you and I would be thrown together, somehow. Through them. I didn't imagine they'd end up seeing each other though. Not a very likely couple, were they? Still, it was useful. And it was so easy to make her hate you. She was nearly there. I just helped to speed things.'

'How?'

'Brian mentioned the party in passing to me at work. I said I'd like to come. When he phoned to give me the details, he told me about this friend of Sadie's, said she was beautiful and kind of extraordinary – which of course you are, Melanie – and he thought I'd like to meet her. Sadie was in the room with him and they started to talk to each other. Can you imagine the conversation, Melanie?'

'Yes.'

And the story he tells me is exactly what I think it will be.

'"Not Ella," Sadie said. "You don't want to inflict him with Ella."

'"Of course Ella," Brian said. "Ella is lovely."

'"You sound as if you wish you'd met her instead of me," she said.

'"Of course I don't," he said.

'"I don't believe you," she said, and for once I agreed with her. "It's been like this my whole life," she said, and that made perfect sense too.

'She grabbed the phone from him to talk to me directly, said you were a crazy mess and no real friend would wish you on anyone they cared about and you were still obsessed with your shitty ex-boyfriend, which we both know isn't true any more.

'Brian excused himself, then, told Sadie he was going out for a paper. She doesn't have much of a radar for when she annoys people, does she?'

I say nothing.

'She continued to talk to me. She asked if Brian and I saw much of each other at the hospital. I explained not really, we were in different fields. She went on to describe you – not that she did you justice – asked if I'd ever seen you with him.'

'Couldn't have.'

'I know every line of your face, Melanie, but I said it was possible I once saw Brian having coffee in the hospital café with a woman who sounded rather like the one she described. I said I couldn't be sure. I said I'd confirm after I saw you in person at the party. All it took was a small nod at her when the two of you passed the living room door, after you arrived.'

'Lie,' I say.

'Yes,' he says. 'Sometimes lies are needed.'

You would actually agree with this in principle. 'Cruel,' I say.

But he misunderstands who I am talking about. 'Yes. She is. She should know you better. Brian says she's fanatically jealous. I don't want her near you. She would do real harm to you if she could. I was scared when you found her at your house earlier.'

I don't quite take this in. My throat is so desperately dry it is all I can think of. 'Water,' I say.

His eyes move to the foot of the bed and I drag my own after them. There is a silver tray. On it are several glass ampules and syringes and a light pen. There is also a plastic bottle of water, half-full. He reaches for that, takes off the cap, lifts my head to help me drink. I am so parched my lips rip apart as if I have pulled off a plaster.

'Thorne?'

'Still not found.'

Thorne will tear this man apart, I think, if he gets hold of him.

'It won't be long,' he says. 'I'm not worried. He's not important.'

He sees me looking at the tray.

'You were so distressed. You seemed half-mad, sitting with that mess of things around you. It was necessary to sedate you, but you reacted too strongly to the drugs – you needed a higher than normal dose. The alcohol you'd taken heightened their effects.'

He writes himself out of decisions and actions, as if they were somebody else's.

'No more,' I say. This is a new art, this trying to make sentences with as few words as I can.

He runs his fingers down my neck, caresses my hair, moves it away from my face, puts it back. I realise my hair is completely loose. He must have removed the clasp I used to fasten it, thinking I might jab it in his eye. He was right to think that. The idea of it makes me happy.

'It would be best for you to be able to feel things,' he says. 'Not too sleepy. Not too awake. Just right.'

Chemical restraint. That is what they did to Thorne before he was physically restrained. Do I need to act drowsier or more alert to stop this man shooting more of it into me? The puzzle is too great but it is a puzzle only of the mind, not one I feel in the pit of my stomach as I should. He was telling the truth when he said the drug would make me feel safe and calm. It is against all reason but I do.

He leans over to kiss me and I don't try to stop him. He pulls away, frowning. 'Your mouth is still trembling.'

He has brought my bag up here. It is sitting on the bed by the tray. He stretches towards it to pull out my watch. 'This isn't working.' He must have figured out what it was and disabled it.

I think of my dead mobile. For a few seconds, I clutch at hope that Find My Phone or Send Last Location will lead the police here. But if the battery ran out in the hospital car park, then that is where the tracking will end, too. It is highly unlikely that phone will help me.

I try to say your name. It comes out sounding like Mermaid.

'I want to be honest with you. I want to tell you everything so we can go forward. The tranquillisers were just to keep you calm until I could explain.'

'Don't need.'

He nods agreement. 'After hearing you and Ted earlier, learning what the two of them did to you, I knew you would understand.'

'How?' I mean, how did he hear me and Ted. And didn't he say something suggesting he knew Sadie came to my house? How did he know that too? But again he ignores my question and says what he wants me to hear.

'You found her locket. Can you guess how many times I took it out and opened it and stared at your picture before we finally met? It's like looking at her, but with none of her faults.'

'No.'

He shakes his head mournfully. 'You're only proving I'm right. She slept with me a few times, came here to dinner when she was lonely. She certainly liked it when I gave her expensive presents. But she made me promise

410

never to tell anyone about us. There was somebody else – she never admitted it, but it was obvious.'

I remember the name you obliterated from your address book. H is for Holderness. I am in no doubt that Adam is the man whose name you blocked out, perhaps to hide his identity from Noah. Or perhaps because Adam became so odious you could no longer bear to see any evidence that he was in your life. Maybe both of these things were true.

'Then she got pregnant.' He closes his eyes as if even now it hurts him. 'She'd refused to see me for a few months, then she turns up and sleeps with me because she's needy or sad and wants some attention and WHAM, she's pregnant.'

Remember how Adam made you feel, when you first met him? Remember how he made you warm, before you knew what he really was?

I had wondered what could have brought you to sleep with two men so close together, never imagining that Ted could be one of them. But three? My poor love.

Stop being so pious. It was empowering. I took back my power. I was in control. And don't you 'poor love' me. I don't need your pity. I don't want it. Don't you dare judge me.

You are as fierce as ever. Your fierceness helps. You always yearned for a life of drama and adventure and excitement, and that's what you got, even if it did spiral out of control.

I can't argue with that one.

There is truth in what Adam says, even if he has no understanding. Luke's father hurt or disappointed you

411

in some major way, probably because he had to disappear again. You flew to Adam for refuge, and probably Ted too, but then you made up with the man you loved and dispensed with Ted and Adam.

'I thought it was mine,' Adam says. 'I was sure it was mine.'

It. That is what he calls your son. All these years later and he still cannot bear to admit Luke's humanness.

'She swore it wasn't mine, the timing was wrong. All that crap women say.'

He slips for an instant into talking as he must think. Women. Crap. Two words he easily puts together. He is a different man to the one I have known, not able to disguise his hatred entirely, the ugliness of how he thinks.

'Amnio,' I say.

'You know about that?'

'Yes.'

'It was to shut me up. I wanted it to be mine but there was no denying the paternity test. I never learned who the father actually was. He was too careful. Or she was.'

He gets up, straddles the chair so his lower body is pressing into mine and my hands are pinned beneath his thighs. With his weight on me like this I cannot breathe. I cannot get my arms free. I cannot turn my head with his hands on both sides of it. But I must be making enough of an attempt for him to know I am trying.

'I've wondered for so long what it would feel like, for us to be like this, to feel you moving beneath me. That's why I don't want to have to tie you up.'

'No need.' My voice is so weak.

He runs my hair through his fingers. 'I knew when

we finally met that you were as interested in me as I was in you.' He laughs. 'That performance of yours with Brian's brother. I can't tell you how much I enjoyed that. You were everything I hoped for. The chemistry was there from the start between us.'

'Yes,' I say.

His fingers are beneath my chin, tipping my head up. 'I never noticed this before. The last traces of a haemangioma. It's beautiful.' His mouth is on my birthmark, kissing away my magic, sucking it out of me like a vampire.

Stop thinking like that. Your magic is deep inside you. He can't get at it. It's still your secret weapon. So use it.

My breath is shallow, but he mistakes the reason and pulls back a little to study me. 'I don't want to risk getting you too excited until you've properly recovered. Caring for you is so important to me. You even told that bastard Ted to fuck off.'

How could he know this? Just. How? I manage to stammer out the word.

All at once, he gets up. He sits on a low stool he has put beside the chair. 'I saw you pull away from him when he touched you in the hospital car park. But when you went to his house — I don't want to say what I thought at first. How angry I was. It made me wonder if I'd got you wrong. Maybe you liked to string along multiple men. Maybe you couldn't turn away any scrap of admiration. Like her. But what you said to him. I can't tell you how it pleased me. And you were magnificent against Sadie.'

I am thinking of Thorne. Thinking how I got under his skin when I changed tack. When I tried to be extra

413

nice to him. It was a dangerous game, but it worked. Mostly. Can I bring myself to do that with this man too? Maybe the poisons he shot into my muscles are doing me an accidental favour, with their well-being side effect, shrinking my anger into a magically small kernel that is hidden so far away even I cannot feel it right now.

Thorne's name comes out of my mouth even though I do not mean it to, and Adam continues to talk to me as if I am his co-conspirator rather than his enemy.

'I was so close to stopping Thorne's game when he said he'd been watching her. I was near her too that day. I was certain Thorne was going to tell you he saw me, that he must have seen me, that that explained the extra degree of venom he has for me. I was within seconds of halting your visit when he grabbed you. There is something I have to apologise to you for, but I think you will understand.'

'Of course,' I say.

He takes my hand, kisses it, and I make myself smile. Tranquillisers really do make you tranquil. Fake smiling is easy and natural and almost feels real.

'After I brought you home from the hospital, I planted a listening device in your bag while you were showering. I needed to know what Thorne whispered to you out of my hearing. That's how I heard everything with Ted. And with Sadie. Do you forgive me?'

'Of course,' I say again.

He lifts my hand, turns it over, presses more kisses onto my palm. 'I never imagined she'd been with Ted. I never thought that badly of her. I know neither of us did. She didn't deserve you.'

I can be mad at you. I can scream at you. I can recite every fault you ever had, every wrong you ever did, and there have been some whoppers. But God help anyone else who does. You said this to me once but I didn't say it back. I should have said it back.

'Three different men within weeks of each other. What kind of woman was she? I didn't know about Ted until you did. I never even saw him until I watched you with him and the boy on Halloween.'

Watched. I realise now who sent me that photograph of Ted and Ruby in the café.

'Photo of Ted?' I say.

'You needed to know the truth about him.'

He tried to get rid of Ted. He probably would have continued that campaign if Ted hadn't turned my heart to ice without anybody else's help. Except yours.

I swallow hard and he feeds me another sip of water. 'A little at a time, Melanie,' he says.

'Blocked calls?' I say.

He looks puzzled. Given the terrible things he is prepared to admit, I am inclined to believe he didn't make them.

'Justice Administrator?' I say.

Again he looks perplexed, but I'm not sure if it is because I'm still slurring my words or because he really doesn't know what I'm talking about.

'Do you hate Ted now?' he says. 'Do you hate him and your sister?'

'I do.'

'How could she do that to you? You must be glad of what happened.'

What happened. Not what he did. He speaks as if external forces got you and your locket and the birthday stones into his house.

'What did happen, Adam?' I try to soften the question with his name.

I think he has wanted to tell this story for a long time. It is not a story I want to hear. It is a story I never wanted to hear. I wanted a different story.

'She was going to meet him, whoever he was.'

'How did you know?' I ask this as if I am impressed by his ingenuity.

'I knew she'd be driving along the lane and I knew when.' This isn't an answer. He doesn't want to admit to me – maybe not even to himself – that he had been stalking you. As he stalked me. He doesn't want to detail his methods. 'I parked my car with the bonnet slightly off road, against a tree.'

'Why?'

'It wasn't like me to be so careless, but I was shaken. I hadn't meant to park that way.'

Liar.

'A minute before she was due to pass me – I don't know why – I rested my head on top of the wheel. I didn't plan what happened next. All I wanted was to know she would stop for me. That she would do that much. The most basic test of whether she actually cared. That's all I wanted from her. Do you know what it is like to want that?'

'Yes.'

'Nobody came along the whole time. You know how deserted that road is. When she saw me, her tyres

416

screeched. She pulled part-way into a shallow ditch. She was crying my name. I suppose, looking back, I might have appeared injured. I didn't realise that then. At first I thought she stopped because she really did care.'

You did care. He got you because you were kind. He posed that way deliberately, whatever he says. Because you could never turn away from somebody hurt. You might sleep with their boyfriend after you fixed them, but you would never ignore anyone who needed fixing. You liked it when somebody was broken and you mended them and they called you a beautiful angel and told you how important and extraordinary you were, how only you could have done that for them. He didn't really know you, but he guessed at this essential thing and exploited it.

'She threw open my front passenger door, climbed in to check on me. The wind blew the door shut. When she saw I was fine she started to scream at me. Obscenities. Words you would never say, Melanie. How I'd inconvenienced her, slowed her, she had to be somewhere important and didn't have time for games. She said what I had done was cruel. She was so hysterical I was worried for her. Medically worried. I thought her hormones had triggered it. I took her hand to try to reason with her. Her skin was so clammy – she had a fever. She started to grab the door handle to get out but I was worried about her driving. She needed the same drug you needed last night. That helped. The passenger seat was flat so I laid her down to rest.'

He took your keys and purse from your car to make it look like you had some presence of mind, some unknown plan, but he left the little-used mobile phone that could have signalled where you were. He probably did something to hasten the battery drain too, because it was dead by the time the police found it. And he was careful about DNA. The DNA in your car was from known acquaintances, all of whom were eliminated as suspects.

'You took care of her,' I say, corroborating the spin he has put on things.

'I wanted to make sure she was calm and safe.'

He speaks as if all of it was an accident. As if he didn't happen to have a syringe of tranquillisers in his pocket, as if he hadn't flattened his front passenger seat in readiness. As if he hadn't hunted you and set you up. As if he hadn't planned any of it. As if there weren't a coffin-like box where he could hide you beneath his floor.

He rests the flat of his hand on my cheek. 'It's amazing how you can feel so much for somebody, then feel nothing. But if you actively hate her, you mustn't blame yourself. It's understandable. I had no idea, when it happened, how very much she deserved it.'

'What happened, Adam?'

'She had a seizure.'

'When?'

'She was too unwell to leave. She had an infection. A high temperature. Her reaction to the drug wouldn't reverse. You rebounded so quickly. That strong heart of yours, again. She didn't rebound at all.'

'When?'

'A week after she came here.'

'Did she . . . ?' I still must ask. I still must hear him say the word, though I cannot.

'There was nothing anyone could have done.'

Nothing anyone could have done. His doctor's euphemisms. As if kidnapping and drugging and probably raping you had nothing to do with him.

He doesn't say the word but he doesn't need to. The word is there. It is in the air.

'You see now, don't you, that you've been better without her? We all have. I'm going to hold your hand for a few minutes now, Ella. I can see you need that.'

Talking to you has been my way of keeping you alive, keeping you present even in your absence. But all along I have been talking to the dead. Your voice will dwindle away, until it is no louder than the cry of a gnat.

Except that I can still hear you. And you are no gnat. You are screaming in my ear. *Don't let him see you sad. Keep him thinking you are on his side. Dampen down your reaction. NOW.*

I squeeze his hand. 'I'm glad you're with me.'

'You're more loyal than she ever was.'

He is more right than he imagines.

He kisses my forehead. 'It's what I love about you.'

I swallow back the sick that comes up my throat when his lips touch my skin. 'And me you.' My voice trembles with the effort of pretending to return his feelings, but he seems to see this as passion. 'Did she—' I stop.

'What? Did she what?'

'Suffer?' My voice catches. I sound as if I am choking. I know it is ill-judged to ask but I cannot not.

'She was asleep whenever I went to work. She didn't ever wake until I got back. She was never aware of being alone. She was well cared for.'

As if your sleeping was natural. As if he didn't put you in a hole when he was out. But I know where you were.

'Did the police ever come here?'

He nods. 'I want to tell you everything. There were two of them. Two days after she arrived, as I was getting back from work. They said they were looking at all the houses in the area. I invited them in, made them welcome, poured coffee. One of them poked a head in the living room for a few seconds, but that was it. They said they were sorry to have troubled me. Then they left.'

I am imagining you, in that rectangular pit. Could those policemen have found you if they'd bothered to look? Rescue was within feet of you but didn't happen. I am praying you were unconscious. Praying you weren't aware of those buffoons in the house, so close to saving you. What would it have been like to know they were there without being able to cry for help? To hear the door close after they said goodbye?

He is so articulate, so calm and intelligent. This man, this doctor with his military-hero background, with his medical eminence. He doesn't exactly scream kidnapper. Wouldn't most policemen be fooled? Not the type who needs to steal a woman to keep her, they would think. He and Thorne are no different, though Thorne would find the comparison insulting.

'I'm worried that you are trying too hard to be brave. For my sake. Whatever she did, she was your sister.'

I try to lift an arm, testing, but I am still so woozy I can barely move. He studies me as though I am a human weapon he has deactivated, then he turns to fiddle with the tray on the bed.

I watch him as carefully as I can while his attention is diverted. There is something odd in his trouser pocket, sticking out a little. The puzzle of what it is comes to me all at once. A syringe, and I am seeing the tip. It is visible over the top of the pocket because it is completely extended. It is fully loaded, ready to plunge into me in an emergency, in case I recover my strength sooner than he anticipates.

He turns back to me and I stretch, as if content, and smile at him again. He climbs onto the chair beside me, on his side, kisses my ear, whispers into it. 'We'll talk more tomorrow. You're waking up too much when you need rest. In the morning you'll be better. I can't wait to wake up with you in my bed.'

'Me too.'

He turns me onto my side so we are face-to-face, body-to-body. 'We fit together so well.' He slides one arm under me, curls the other over me, bends a leg over my thigh. 'Goodnight, sweet Melanie.' He kisses me, pulling me harder against him, and I am so distracted by that kiss I barely have time to register that all in one movement he is pushing up my dress and something is burning deep into my hip before the world plunges into darkness.

Saturday, 19 November

The Colour Red

Whatever is holding me up seems to be swallowing me. Or am I sinking? I turn my head to the side and feel as if someone has banged the top of my skull with a mallet. The force of it is still reverberating behind my eyes. It takes several seconds of squeezing them shut before I can bring myself to open them again. I am in bed. Sheets are clinging to my skin.

I lift an arm, testing, and though it seems as if an invisible hand is trying to oppose the movement, I manage to do the same with the other arm too. Slow. Everything I do is slow. But at least I am moving. The tremors are gone but my body seems to be made of steel balls stuffed into a woman-shaped sack.

He isn't in bed beside me but he must have been at some point because there is a dent in the pillow from his head. He would have been sleeping close to me. I cannot afford to wonder now about what he might have done while I was unconscious. I listen as hard as I can. I can hear him, I think probably on the landing outside.

He must be talking on the phone. I consider screaming my lungs out to draw the attention of the person at the other end, but it's way too risky. They are unlikely to hear, but he certainly will, and then he will know I am against him and I will have lost the biggest card I have. When I push myself up onto my elbows the room rocks. My neck wobbles as if I have whiplash.

He is moving. I can hear his footsteps approaching the door, then pausing there. My stomach cramps so tightly I want to double over. I count in my head, waiting for him to come in, but he doesn't. He goes downstairs, quickly, enthusiastically, a man who cannot wait to start his happy new day. He is humming something from *Carmen* but my brain hurts too much to work out exactly what.

The peace I felt before has deserted me. Didn't he say that the drugs could cause contradictory symptoms? Last night's deluded sense of well-being is entirely gone. My head is too full and my terror is too big and I realise I have never properly understood the women I try to help. I have never properly grasped how fear immobilises.

I scan all around me for a phone, plotting to dial 999, but I cannot remember seeing one last night and if there was he has removed it. Of course he has. I manage something that is almost like standing, using the bed to lever myself up, but my legs are too wobbly to walk properly and too weak for me to risk the noise I would make if they were to give way and crash me down.

Not afraid. Awake. Ted's voice is as fierce as it has ever been. It hauls me up and lowers me to the floor as if I am a puppet. It forces me to drag myself towards the door even though the room is spinning.

My upper arm aches and my hip throbs too. I think of the tortoise and the hare. Today I am the tortoise. I am not sure how long it takes but at last I am struggling onto my knees so I can reach the handle. It doesn't turn. I put all my weight on the metal, pushing and pulling at the door at the same time, but the handle rattles and rattles and I am seeing stars and the rattles seem to vibrate right through me, making me draw in my breath at another cramp. He has locked me in.

Think. Think. Think. I move my head too quickly, trying to decide where to go next. Is there really a lag of several seconds before my brain catches up with my skull, snapping and slapping inside it? I'm progressing in my movement, because I'm managing to crawl on all fours now instead of sliding along like a serpent on its belly. This is faster.

There is something strange, something I cannot process. And then I do because I falter and fall flat and my nipple scrapes against a splinter in the wood as I pull myself up again. My heart thrums in my ears. My clothes are gone. I correct myself. He took off my clothes.

Not now Not now Not now. You are with me again. *Not now*, you say. *No time to think about that now.*

My knees are raw from the friction against the bare boards. There is a trickle of something between my legs. I have to pee but I don't think it is that. The bathroom door seems so far away. Every inch I manage to move seems impossible, but I am finally hauling myself up and turning another handle. At least this one isn't locked and I heave myself in.

I close the door as quietly as I can, plotting to lock it.

But I bite my lip and swear silently when I discover there is no lock. I fumble for a light. It seems miraculous that I find it, though I am so dazzled I have to open and close my eyes several times.

I strain my neck to examine my upper arm. It is blotched as if with sunburn, and I realise this must be bruising. I try to count the red dots left by the needles he shot into my muscles, but counting is so hard. I get to two and have to start over. I get to three and have to start over. I get to four. I keep losing track of what I have counted and what I have not. I try to be systematic, going roughly across from left to right, then down and across again. I get to four several times more, so I squirm around to inspect my hip, where there are two more red dots. That makes six in total. I try again and get the same number.

I struggle to understand what all of this means. *What it means is that he gave you more of the drugs during the night, topping up the dose before you woke.* I try to remember what happened with Thorne. There were three drugs, then, I am sure of it, but Adam said I had my reaction because there was something he couldn't get hold of. I am sure that's right because I can even remember that the missing drug started with a P. The likelihood is that he gave me two different things each time, so three doses in total of a tranquillising cocktail.

I pull myself to my feet, using the sink. I examine the window. It is made of privacy glass so nobody can see in and I can't work out if everything is blurry because of the glass or if it is my vision that is all wrong. The hedges and trees block my view beyond the garden. Not that there is anyone nearby to see. This place is so remote there would be no point signalling or shouting for help. I wonder if I could actually escape through this window. If I were to regain enough strength, is there a safe way down?

But all of these calculations are pointless. The window is locked. Like the others it is triple-glazed. I want to break the glass to flee or make a weapon, but there is nothing in this room to break it with.

Did you do all these things too? Make all of these hopeless discoveries? I try to push the questions out of my head. Because you didn't find a way out. All of the things you tried got you nowhere. And you were ill. Even before he told me you were clammy and fevered, before he told me you had an infection, I worried about a recurrence of your mastitis. To try to do all of this when you were feeling so wretched would have been doomed.

I think of a film I once watched even though I knew I shouldn't. I knew I was the last person on earth who ought to sit through the story of a man trying to discover what happened to his missing girlfriend. They have a fight while driving, stop at a station for petrol, and she goes off to the loo but never comes back. He finally learns the truth, but only by experiencing exactly what she did.

No No No No No. The words come out as one long murmur, in the lowest voice I can manage. But they release something.

I turn to the mirrored cupboard, glimpsing the face of the haggard woman who stares out at me, mascara streaking down her cheek, her hair tangled, her skin pale and blotchy and so yellow I wonder if the tranquillisers have produced some kind of instant jaundice. *You cannot possibly be my sister*, you say. *Not looking like that.*

I hold my breath when I open the cupboard door. I am dreaming of that cutthroat, picturing it on the glass shelf where I saw it yesterday night. But it is gone. Of course it is gone. I press my hands to my head and squeeze my temples and want to scream but I have to take my fingers away from my face and curl them around the edge of the sink when another cramp rips through me.

I think of Luke and all of the things Dad and I did to make the house safe for him after you vanished. No fire hazards or cutting hazards or tripping hazards or suffocation hazards or strangulation hazards or choking hazards. This man has carried out an obscene form of baby-proofing, though I know that cannot have been his primary reason for removing my clothes.

Since I managed to haul myself to my feet there has been an irregular splish splosh of drops hitting the floor. Something warm is creeping down my leg. There is a splatter of bright red on the cream-veined marble. More red smears the inside of my thighs. I touch my hand to the blood and it comes away sticky. As if I were a child terrified of a dare, my fingers slowly float to where the blood is coming from.

It doesn't hurt. If he raped me I would know. Wouldn't I? I would be sore. I would ache. It would sting. But none of these things are true. My upper arm hurts. My hip hurts. My head hurts. My belly hurts from the cramps. No other parts of me hurt.

Another thought rushes at me. All at once, I understand

the reason for the bleeding. I have been caught out and stumped like a thirteen-year-old. The thing that hasn't happened to me for ten years is actually happening right now, and I don't know whether to laugh or cry at the timing.

I address myself silently to him. *What a fucking mess I've made of your floor, you neat-freak bastard. Just you wait until you see what I'm going to do to your towels.* I grab a giant bath sheet and wrap it around me, twisting and knotting it above my breasts so it is like a strapless dress, the way you taught me, the way I still do every day when I get out of the shower, so automatically I do not need to think or look. I grab a hand towel and blot away as much blood as I can from my hands and thighs and between my legs.

My bladder is so full it burns. I heave myself onto the toilet and when I pee it is fierce red and when I wipe the paper turns crimson and I am stunned by the blood, as if ten years of it has come at once. Is this normal? I cannot remember if this is normal. Didn't you once tell me that it always looks like there is much more blood than there actually is? I don't press the flusher. I don't want him to hear so I leave the red pool in the bowl and quietly lower the lid and look around the bathroom again to try to see what else I can do.

There is a silver towel rail and I pull myself up by it, at the same time hoping to prise it out of the wall with my weight so I can use it as a weapon. I am examining it for hidden screws when I hear a key jiggling and then the bedroom door opening.

He says nothing at first, clearly looking around for

me, trying to work out if I am about to pop out at him. He approaches the bathroom, stands cautiously outside.

'I'm in here.' I say this as if I am eager for him to find me.

'Are you okay? There's blood on the floor.'

'I'm embarrassed.' I say this in the wimpiest voice I can manage with him still able to hear. Despite the circumstances, I can't help but feel the miracle of the two words I am about to say. 'My period,' I say, as if it were an ordinary occurrence. And then, 'Do you want to come in?'

I am slumped on the floor with the towel still around me and another beneath me, my back against the wall, my legs curled. 'I'm so sorry.'

He kneels down. 'You poor thing.'

'I'm feeling so weak. I thought if I rested here for a few minutes . . . ' I really do have so little strength and I absolutely must make him believe the truth of this. 'I look terrible. How can you stand to look at me?'

'Looking at you is all I want to do. And touching you. God, it was hard to stop myself last night. But I wanted us both awake. You were too sleepy.' He counts my pulse. 'The antihistamine did its job. The tremors have gone. But you're still frail.'

I hear your voice. *Gee whizz. I wonder why that is.* Your brave sarcasm helps. It is part of me. It is in my bones with you. And you are laughing, too, talking to me. *You're like Superman, baby sister, surrounded by Kryptonite. Show him that.*

I try to stretch out a hand, let it fall, try again. He takes it, covers it with kisses.

'You won't . . .' I say.

'Won't what? Tell me, Melanie.'

'You won't want me now.' I look stricken. 'The mess.'

'That doesn't bother me. You're worth it. We can't wait any longer, can we?'

'No.'

'We can take a bath together, after. Would you like that?'

I look right into his eyes and nod.

'I'm taking you to bed now.'

I let him lift me up, bundled in the towels. I wrap my arms around his neck and bury my face in his shoulder in my best imitation of a helpless maiden. His breathing is growing more rapid as he puts me on top of the sheets, pulls his black T-shirt off before he lies on his side next to me, pushes away the towels, runs his hand down my back and over my breasts, along my thighs, kneading with increasing force. All the time, his mouth is against mine.

'Sorry,' I say again.

'Why? Don't be.'

'I'm too weak to touch you much.'

'That was only necessary until things settle down for us.'

I manage to lift an arm to his waist. 'There,' I say proudly.

I press the other between his legs. 'And there,' I say even more proudly, when he lets out his breath.

I kiss him more deeply, and I really am panting. My heart really is beating so fast I am afraid it may stop. My skin really is flushing so hot I may just burn up. My stomach really is in a knot so tight I wonder if it will

433

drag the rest of me in after it, my whole body inside out in a contortion artist's ball. But I slide a hand down his side to his hip, as if wanting to pull him towards me. 'You really don't mind the blood?'

He only looks at me and shakes his head no and I whisper 'Good' and close my eyes and sigh and press his hips towards mine. I let out a sigh of pleasure. I curl a hand over the bulge at the front of his trousers and listen to him gasp. All the while I am manoeuvring the syringe I took from his pocket with my other hand, wiggling the cap off and letting it drop and praying he doesn't notice, trying to adjust the position between my fingers while my other palm continues to press against him, making him moan.

I can remember you explaining once about intra-muscular injections, proud after you did your first one, telling me you weren't embarrassed that it was a man and his trousers had to be partly down for you to do it.

I fly my hand up and around. I am aiming blind but I know I have a clear track to the outer part of his lower back. I dart the needle in and his eyes widen, confused for an instant about what is happening.

Perfect. Your voice is so clear I nearly turn to look for you.

I manage to press the plunger but the liquid in the syringe is thicker and much harder to squeeze out than I imagined. I have no idea how much has gone in. I only know he is shouting and swearing. The things he really feels about me are finally out.

He knocks my hand away and bulldozes me onto my back with the full weight of his body over mine. He presses one arm over my neck and reaches round with the other to pull the syringe out and examine it. 'You didn't get enough in. You're just like her.'

Too fucking right, I think, and I'm not sure if I am hearing myself or you but I manage to get one of my arms free to punch his hand so hard the syringe flies out of it and across the room.

He takes his arm from my neck and rises onto his knees to tug down his trousers. Is he fumbling? I really think he is. He is struggling. He is not as coordinated as he thinks. I am not either but I manage to sink a knee into his stomach. He falls to his side with an expulsion of air, all the while trying to avoid the kick I am aiming between his legs.

My power and aim are too poor to do more than bait a furious bear, but the half-life of the drug is in my favour. The potency is reducing in my body with every minute. The opposite is true for him after his recent dose. The tranquilliser has to be increasing its grip on his nervous system as the drug speeds through his blood. I cannot help but perceive that the fight is fairer.

Didn't get enough in, he said. But not enough still means some. Doesn't it?

Yes, you say. *Yes Yes Yes.*

The Man from Far Away

I try to roll away. Once, twice, three times, until I gain enough momentum to crash off the side of the bed. My spine is bruised into pins and needles and the back of my head smashes onto the floor.

Above me, he is swearing again. Is it possible there isn't as much force in his voice as the last time he spoke? He thumps off the bed and onto me, as if I am a full-length cushion, and whatever breath is left in my belly shoots out. A fist smashes so hard into the side of my jaw the world is awash with stars.

He is trying to nudge my legs open and I am trying with every ounce of strength I have left to resist. The opposing forces are equal, at last. I am sure of it. My skin is slippery with blood, which is making it more difficult for him.

If they find my body someday I want them to be able to tell Luke that there was forensic evidence that I fought hard. I don't want Adam Holderness to be able to face his colleagues easily. I want him to be so visibly damaged it will be impossible for him to look at anybody for weeks without their asking questions.

My parents will be turning up with Luke at my house soon, if they haven't already. They are going to raise hell until they discover where I am. This bastard will have some explaining to do. Missing woman. Known male acquaintance covered in injuries. He won't be able to hide the connection between us like he did with you.

My body remembers. My body wakes up. Adrenaline jets through me. Muscle memory. What Ted said. What Ted made me do. I let out a grunt and roll onto my side, rolling him with me like I did only a few weeks ago in the park with Ted, the same move I practised then even when I didn't want to. And I take this man who snatched you from us by surprise. In one continuous motion I knee his upper thigh once, twice, three times in quick succession. He pulls away and springs into a crouch like Ted did, so he can come at me again.

I heave myself into a sitting position with my legs in front of me, my back against the bed. I raise a leg into a bend and release it. I kick him hard in the face three times in a row with this motion. When he falls onto his back I scoot closer and bring my heel down on his nose. I can hear bone splintering and tissue squelching. He is not wearing a mask like Ted was. I lose count of how many times his face crunches beneath the blows.

Blood is coming from his nose and his forehead is split and his eyes are closed and something is oozing from his scalp and there is a voice somewhere, so quiet that at first I think I must be imagining it. It is not Adam

Holderness's voice. I am not sure Adam Holderness can use his voice at all right now.

'You've done a great job, Ella,' the voice says. It is a quiet voice. A man's voice. A stranger's voice? Or is it faintly familiar? 'I think you can stop now,' the voice says.

I don't stop. I kick again. I jut out my chin. My eyes are locked on Adam Holderness, searching for the faintest sign of movement, the tiniest twitch.

'Ella.' The man is kneeling beside me. 'Stop.' My leg falls to the floor.

The man drags the quilt off the bed, lifts me a little to wrap it around me. I have forgotten that I am naked, that I am covered in blood.

The man says, 'I thought maybe you needed help, but you did more than fine on your own.'

But I did need help. I did get help. You helped me. Your voice. Always your voice is what I hear when I am most in need. And Ted helped too. Ted finally did the thing he always wanted to do. He saved me. He made me practise those moves when I didn't want to and it made all the difference. I cannot lie to myself about that.

'Can you look at me, Ella?'

I shake my head no. I cannot look away from the man who tore you from us. His face does not look like his face any more, and there is so much blood I can barely see his features, but he isn't any less him.

The stranger turns my head towards him and away from the pulpy mess on the wooden floor.

My thoughts are not working like they usually do. I can only see in fragments. A man sitting in a corridor with his face behind a newspaper. The same man, coming to my support group only to leave within minutes. He said his partner was missing – I'm sure I am right to remember that.

Another man comes into the room. He is wearing gloves. I see that both men are wearing them. Both men have coverings over their shoes too. The second man crouches near Adam Holderness.

'Is he dead?' I say.

The second man looks at the one sitting beside me. His look is an unspoken question that I cannot understand. The man beside me seems to consider before he gives his answer, which comes as a negative shake of the head that is so brief I am not sure if I saw it at all.

'No,' the second man says. 'Unconscious but alive, though barely.' The second man's voice tugs at me too. Just a tone, but I have heard it before. Where? There is something in his features that I recognise. It is only a flash, but an image of that same face comes to me as if I were looking at a photograph. The fake policeman. But his hair is bottle-blond now instead of dark and the blueberry-sized mole below his eye is gone and so are the sideburns. With his face so naked I see he is younger than I guessed. Perhaps late twenties, early thirties at most.

I blink hard, wondering if I am imagining it.

The first man smooths my hair from my face but speaks to the second. 'Go,' he says. 'You know what to do.' And the fake policeman quickly leaves the room.

'I've seen him before,' I say.

'We don't have much time, Ella. You're badly hurt. I

don't know if it's your blood or his, but you're covered in it.'

'Who is he? He's not a policeman.'

'He is, but not one most members of the force would know. He's not usually in uniform.'

There is a buzz in my ears. I put my hands on them and press, as if that will make it stop, but it doesn't. 'Noah?' I say it like a question, even though I know the answer.

'Yes.'

'Why didn't you say who you were before?'

He shakes his head. 'We can talk later. You need medical treatment.'

'No. Now.'

'At least let me get you into the recovery position. You should be lying on your side.'

I look at Adam again. My breath quickens. 'No. No, no, no, no, no. I need to be upright. I need to watch him.'

'Okay. Okay. It's okay. I understand. But I want you to try not to worry – I don't think he's going to be waking up any time soon.'

'Tell me why.'

'I was going to tell you who I was the first time, when you were doing your walk-in clinic. That's why I came. But I was called away – not a call I could ignore.'

He lifts a corner of the quilt and blots my face with it. When he lets it fall, the grey is stained with red.

'Your undercover friend. Where have I heard his voice?'

'He knew how frustrated I was when my first attempt to talk to you was interrupted. So he left you a voicemail later that day, pretending to be a journalist. That's where you heard him. But you never got back to him.'

He smiles, a sad smile, and an appeasing one. 'Please, Ella. Try to understand.' It is a familiar smile, even in its woeful form. It is exactly the smile I love most in the world, with the same dimples.

'A few days later I sent him to you. He thought the uniform would persuade you to go with him – that was his own improvisation – he's learning.' His dark brows draw together in a straight line, like Luke's do when he is angry. 'When I heard what happened I came back to try again to see you. I only had a small window and it was during your discussion group. I told the truth there, about my circumstances.'

'Only the barest bones of truth.' I can see how much you and this man have in common. 'You wanted to spy on me. I'm told that's what you're good at.'

'You're trembling.' He tightens the quilt around me. 'We need to talk later.'

I try to shake my head but my brain rattles around, making me wince. 'It's already later. It's already much later than it should be. Years too late. You wanted to keep all the advantage for yourself. All the advantage of knowing everything and keeping us in the dark. All the advantage of watching us.'

He nods slowly. 'Yes, I wanted to see you in action, to get the measure of you. But there were practical reasons too.'

'Why did you leave the discussion group? Was it because you saw your mother lurking outside?'

'I didn't learn she was there until afterwards. We came separately. We missed each other by minutes. I couldn't see her from where I was in the room.'

'Then why?'

'The same reason as the guy who stormed out.' His jaw stiffens when he looks at Adam. He has spoken to me gently, touched me gently, but this new expression makes me see how extremely ungentle he can be. 'I didn't want to be in the same room with that piece of shit. I can read people or I wouldn't do what I do – I'd planned to find out more about him. I would have stayed if I'd thought I'd be able to get you alone but he obviously wasn't going to leave your side.'

'Why now? Why meet me now, after all this time?'

'I'm not trying to shut you down or avoid your questions but you can barely keep yourself upright and I need to leave. I shouldn't be in the country right now.'

'Doesn't your handler track you?'

He doesn't answer.

'Or is that only in theory?'

Again no answer, but there is a brief flash in his eyes as they meet mine.

'Tell me what made you get in touch with me at last,' I say.

'The messages to the Henrickson accounts.' His voice cracks. 'With the voicemail – I thought, for a few seconds I thought it was Miranda. She's the only one who had that number. It's the one I wrote down for her when we first met, along with my address and email. She used them until I told her the truth about what I did.'

'Would you have written a first initial instead of your Christian name?'

'Yes.'

'That's how she copied it in her address book.'

'She understood things before I explained them. She was always ahead of me. There's a note in your voices, you know, a strand that's the same in both of you. As soon as I listened I understood, but for an instant I thought she'd come back.'

Noah's forehead creases in exactly the way Luke's does when he is baffled. 'How did you find the Henrickson email address and number? What led you to those, after all this time?'

'The police finally returned her address book. She left them where I would find them.'

'That's like her. You're like her. You sound like her. She had eyes like yours. Not just literally. You see like her, too, don't you? You have her vision. You're pretty relentless, Ella Brooke. Next thing I know, my mother is sending message after message that you turned up on her doorstep and she's asking all over again about the woman and the baby she saw ten years ago.'

I look around the room, this blood-drenched mess of a room that was so disturbingly neat until I entered it. 'But you still haven't said why you're in this place. You still haven't said how you found me.'

'I put a tracker on your car.'

'That's not okay.'

'I knew you got here last night. I wanted to make sure there wasn't a sinister reason why you didn't go home.'

Should I give him credit for saying *I*? For not trying to disclaim responsibility with *We* or *They* or *You needed*?

'You can't do that to civilians,' I say. 'It's not allowed.'

'I'm sorry,' he says. 'There was no other way to follow you. The tracker's gone already.'

443

'Don't do that again.'

He doesn't reply. Doesn't nod. Doesn't do anything to show he agrees to this.

'Did you hear what I said, Noah? I won't say another word to you – ever – unless you promise me this. No surveillance of me or Luke or my parents. Not of any description. Not by any means or method.'

'I promise.'

I wipe a hand across my forehead. It is like touching treacle. 'When did you get here? What made you break in?'

'We arrived this morning. The tracker was saying your car was here but I couldn't see any sign of it. It didn't make sense that a guest would hide it away in the garage. Then Holderness came out, walked round the whole house before going back in – I told you I didn't trust him from the minute I clapped eyes on him.' He puts a gloved hand on mine. 'We're running out of time, Ella. I need to go.'

'Not yet.' I have ten years' worth of questions for this man.

The tabloid headlines spear me again. Some of them were close to the truth. Perhaps with their scattergun approach it was inevitable, though Adam himself may have found a way to feed them. Thorne too.

The next question I ask is for Luke – I know he will need the answer to it someday. 'Was she going to run away with you? Was she going to abandon Luke?'

'She would never do that. I wanted her with me but it wasn't possible. I could never keep her safe, keep Luke safe, doing what I do. The only way to work it is to keep the people I love far away.' He smiles. 'But your sister isn't the kind of woman to accept a lover who disappears for long periods and refuses to tell her why or where.'

'That's true. And she's right.'

'Yes. She is.' We flit in and out of speaking of you in the present tense, even though we both know that isn't what you are any more.

'There were ways she could contact me, but I couldn't always check. She was supposed to meet me the morning she vanished, to say goodbye. It was going to be a long stretch before I'd be able to get back. But she never arrived. She'd never not met me when she said she would. I did whatever I could to try to investigate, but she really did seem to have disappeared into thin air.' His voice tightens. 'All of my talents for burrowing deep, for discovering things, and I couldn't use them for her.'

I ask him the same question I asked his mother. 'Did they not look for her properly, because they wanted to protect what you were doing?'

'No. Absolutely not.'

I look hard at him. He meets my eye. He makes an effort to do this, and not to break the contact. I will never know if he is telling the truth, but I am not sure I can live with the pain of disbelieving it. Perhaps he cannot either.

'Ella?'

'Yes?'

'I knew she would never have gone if she had a choice.'

'I knew that too.' I tip forward over my legs as if an invisible force has punched me from behind and put me into a seated forward bend. I gulp. I try to swallow. I make a noise that is not speech, the noise of an animal in pain.

I am not sure how much time passes before Noah gently folds me back up, but almost as soon as he does I am slumping. I slide so low only my shoulders and head are propped against the bed frame. The rest of me is practically lying down, though my knees are bent. Noah lifts my upper back a little, so I am more upright, and I tip sideways into him. 'It's time to call for medical attention. Now.'

'No.' I put my other great fear into words. The fear Mum and I share. And Dad, though he never says it, partly because it is too much to bear for him and partly to try to keep Mum and me calm. 'I've always worried that you'd want Luke. That one day you would swoop in and take him.'

'I do want him but he wouldn't be safe with me. I couldn't look after him, doing what I do. I've always known where he is. I know you'll be angry but I've looked in on him sometimes. And you. He's so contented, so well loved and cared for. I wouldn't mess that up for him. I've seen enough of him to know he wouldn't allow it even if I were foolish enough to try.'

'Norfolk.' I manage to pull away from him, though he still holds me up. 'I took him there last summer. I felt watched. Was that you?'

'You're good, you know. Not many people would sense it, but I worried I'd spooked you. I was sorry about that but I loved seeing the two of you together.'

This last sentence makes my heart clutch. I can't stop myself repeating what I have already said. 'You can't follow us again. You can't spy on us.'

'I already promised you I wouldn't. I don't break promises.'

'Given what you do, I find that hard to believe.'

'Okay. I don't break promises to the people who know me as me.'

I look towards the covered window, as if somehow I can see through it, see through to the place where you are now. 'After I met your mother, I thought you had taken her.' I think again of what Thorne said. 'I'm certain he buried her here.'

He squints in disgust at the human lump on the floor. 'You need to be seen by a doctor and we need to get the police out here to deal with that scumbag.'

Scumbag. I'm trying to remember who else uses that word.

The second man comes back with a telephone in his gloved hand and hands it to Noah. He jerks his head towards the door to signal that they need to move, then leaves the room again.

'It's Holderness's landline,' Noah says. 'I want you to dial 999. Tell them everything you need to tell them. Can you do that?'

'Yes.'

'Miranda said if it ever came to it I should trust you.'

I manage a small nod. The movement makes my brain hurt.

'I wanted Miranda to be proud of me, and for our son to be.' He pauses. 'I'd like you to be. I'm not sure how much longer I can do what I do.'

I am seeing stars. I press the heels of my hands against my eyes to make them go away but it only makes more stars. 'There are probably cameras here.' My words seem to come out in slow motion. Does he hear them that way? 'He probably got you on film.'

'There are no cameras. He didn't want any evidence of who comes in and out of this place. He didn't want a record of what he says and does.' He wraps my fingers around the phone. 'I have to be gone before the emergency services arrive but I need to make sure you're safe.'

Noah moves to Adam's side, where he studies the rise and fall of his breathing. It is slight but regular. He presses a fist onto the centre of Adam's chest and slides it up and down several times, quickly, without pause. He grabs the muscle that runs between the top of Adam's shoulder and bottom of his neck, then squeezes and twists.

All the while, Noah is searching for even a twitch. But there is no reaction. Still not satisfied, he lifts one of Adam's wrists, holds it for several seconds above his battered face, and lets it drop. Adam does not move his head out of the way, or redirect his arm.

Noah seems to be talking to himself as he swaps his blood-smeared gloves with a clean pair from his pocket. 'He's completely unresponsive.' Adam continues to lie there, inert, as Noah considers him.

'If he wasn't dead before, he must be now,' I say.

'I don't want to leave you.'

'I'm fine,' I say. 'I'll be fine.' The buzz in my ears is turning into a roar.

Noah picks the syringe up from where it landed, examines it in a gloved hand, returns to my side. 'You're showing signs of being heavily drugged, you're covered in bruises and cuts, you're bleeding heavily, and you've hit your head. You need to be seen by a doctor.'

The phone falls out of my hand. I cannot tear my eyes

from the pile of raw flesh on the floor. 'I've seen enough of doctors.'

'You're not fine. Not medically. But you're more than fine in all other ways.' His eyes darken. 'You really are like your sister.'

I don't correct him. I won't ever correct him. Because you and I are so alike but also so different. I will keep that secret for you and Ted. It has no bearing on anything, now. The only person you hurt with that was me. And yourselves. I won't tell him that you slept with Adam either. I won't tell anyone. Noah can go to his grave believing you were faithful to him. But Luke will need to know about his father and grandmother someday, once all of us together have worked out when and how.

You see, Miranda? The confidentiality clause never expires. Not about the things that really count.

You must always forgive the people you love, Melanie.

Whatever your secret thoughts and motives, you were right. I forgive you. I only wish you were with me to hear me say the words.

I am with *you*, you say.

Noah takes off a glove, curves his bare hand against my cheek. His skin smells of latex. I stare straight into his brown eyes, realising he must have a blue recessive gene for Luke to have ended up with your eyes and mine.

'What's your blood type?' I say.

'A. Why?'

I press my hand to his cheek too. His designer stubble had masked his dimple before, but not today. I move a finger up to his temple, swirl it inside the little knotted cowlick. The last two times I saw him, he'd slicked his

449

hair back to hide it. Part of his disguise. 'You're so much like Luke,' I say.

'There's a bond between us, Ella. There's loyalty. Because of our resemblances to those we most love, because of our closeness to them.' He puts the glove back on, picks up the telephone handset, presses it into my palm once more.

I hold the phone for a few seconds before asking him one more thing. 'Why do you call me Ella and not Melanie?'

'She told me Melanie was for her alone. It would have been an intrusion to do anything else.'

That is the right answer. The perfect and only answer. I nod, the slightest nod, and wipe away tears.

I dial 999, press the button for speakerphone so Noah can hear. I say all the things I need to say. I tell them there is an unconscious man on the floor who I injured in self-defence. I tell them what he did to me. I tell them what he did to you. I tell them that I think they will find your body somewhere in the house's grounds.

Noah watches me as I speak, encouraging me with those intent brown eyes, nodding approval of the story I tell but clearly not prepared to leave until he is happy that I have said all that I need to.

They tell me not to put down the phone. I lean against Noah. I am in a kind of waking dream, though I keep murmuring that he is staying too long and cutting it too close, that he won't have time to escape before the ambulance arrives. When they say that help is only minutes away I jerk out of this twilight state for a final time and tell the man you loved above all others, the man who helped to make Luke, that he must go, that you'd be furious if he were caught here. He kisses the top of my head before rising swiftly but silently. He pauses once more over Adam to make sure he is still unconscious, then disappears from the room.

As soon as he is gone, my hand drops to my side and my grip on the phone loosens. There is a tinny voice, coming from somewhere far away, repeating my name, asking me what is happening, asking me to tell them I am all right. But my eyes close and I sink to the floor, knowing that I cannot possibly do a single thing more.

I open my eyes to a face. The face is a patchwork of oozing blood and red blotches and deep gouges. The face is only inches from my own and it is spitting at me. The words it is saying are a muddle and my head is pounding so hard I cannot understand what they mean.

I am stretched out on the floor and there is a monster on top of me with its hands around my throat. The hands are squeezing. The monster is calling me by your name. It thinks I am you. The ceiling is starting to spin. I am sure my face is blue.

A clear thought comes. It is that I know who the monster is. Then I have another thought. This one is about arms. It is that arms are weakest near the wrists. Arms are weaker the farther from the core of the body they are. Muscle memory comes too. Somehow I squeeze my own lower arms inside his and press outwards against him but he is barely releasing the pressure and if I don't do something quickly I am going to lose consciousness for what is likely to be the very last time.

He will put me in a coffin and I will never see light again. Just like the man in the movie. Just like you. I do not know how I know this but I do.

I want to get a kick in, but his weight is making it impossible for me to move. I need to get his body off mine and I need to get his hands off my throat.

I wiggle my arms out, arching my right arm over his left to jab two fingers into his trachea. The effect is instant. He lets go of my throat and wraps his hands around his own, gasping for air, tears running. I use the heel of my left hand to punch upwards and into his already-mangled nose. I pull my right arm back again, then release it like a spring, driving my thumb into his eye socket, my fingers splayed and braced against his temple, pressing as hard as I can. He lets out a strangled scream and moves his face away and rolls off me.

He is on his back, one hand clutching his neck, the other his eye, and I sit up, scoot away, shift along the floor to where I can hear that tinny voice again. I remember it from somewhere. I can hear it even over the monster's gurgling. It is coming from the telephone handset on the floor beside me. The tinny voice is louder, more frenzied, insisting that I speak. I pick the handset up. I stare at it for a few seconds, this strange piece of hissing plastic and metal, not sure what to do with it. I am supposed to talk and listen, I think. Yes, that is what I am supposed to do.

But I do not do this because the monster is growling and lumbering closer. What I do is adjust my grip. What I do is whack the monster's temple as if the handset is a bat and his head is a ball.

Monster. I remember somebody saying I needed to try to find his humanness. I needed not to see him as a monster. Who said that? Who were they talking about? I am not sure. But it doesn't matter because a monster is a monster and that is what this is.

I whack his head once more so hard that my whole body hums and the noise against his skull echoes in my own head. He seems suspended, for a few seconds, swaying back and forth. Then he falls straight down. That is when, finally, the police burst in.

Tuesday, 14 February

Valentine's Day

There was a frost last night. The world is magically dusted in white. It is like a fairy land, here in our little clearing in the woods. The sun is dazzling and bright and makes everything it touches beautiful as it pours through the leafless branches of our cherry tree.

The most beautiful thing of all is your son, who is standing beside me, clutching my hand so tightly it hurts. I do not ask him to loosen his grip. I lead him out of the clearing, through the woods, along the path to the village church.

Already the days are stretching. It seems a miracle for the world to be so light this early. There are other ordinary miracles too. I am having my fourth period in a row since I lost what seemed to be a decade's worth of blood in the space of a few hours. The gilded doctor smiled as if to say, I always knew it would happen one day.

Thorne was wrong and right. The monster did keep you close, in a place he could see, though you weren't beneath a hedge. That is where he kept the other two women. The police haven't identified them yet but they think he killed them after he took you, with a few years between each victim. Thorne predicted that too.

I know that many families will be waiting and wondering, dreading that one of the women belongs to them. I worried aloud that I have given them a curse, but our mother said that not knowing was the worst thing, and that finding out would be a gift, though a terrible one.

He put you under an apple tree, which he could see from his bedroom window. I got you out. I wish more than anything else in the world that I could have done more for you, but at least I did that.

Now Mum and Dad can be by your side in a few minutes, and Luke and me too. Your grave still isn't marked, but you have only been here for three days. It will take us time to choose the right stone and to decide what to write on it. Luke wants a phoenix. Mum wants a cross. Dad wants something simple and pure with just your name and dates. I think Dad is right with this one. No image or shape or word could ever begin to describe you. So why try? *Sister. Mother. Daughter. Lover.* All true, but nowhere near enough.

I cannot say what I feel about Jason Thorne. It is for the families of his victims to say. But I know exactly what I feel towards the man who ripped you away from us. It is a hatred so hot and deep I poked out his eye with my bare finger. I took away half his sight.

He took away your precious, beautiful, messy life. He stole you and drugged you and raped you and kept you in darkness before he murdered you. He put you beneath the bare soil of his garden as if you were a family pet. No box. Nothing. He buried you naked. He wrapped you in nothing and he must have burnt your clothes. He left you with – nothing. Again and again, nothing. They never even found your keys or purse or shoes.

He lied when he said you died from a seizure. There is a bone in the neck that can break when a person is strangled. The hyoid bone. Yours was fractured, like the other women's. The police are certain that he put his hands around your throat and squeezed the life out of you, as he tried to squeeze mine.

I make myself consider these things. I make myself see them in detail. Really see them. I promised I would never look away. I promised I would never let you go.

You are not wearing your locket. I asked them to entwine the chain through your fingers, with the platinum oval curled in your palm, so you can keep it close. But first I took Luke's little photograph out of my own locket and put it in yours.

I cannot wear anything around my own throat now. My locket is in Luke's room, with a copy of his baby picture in the place where the original used to be. He keeps my locket in a small box of treasures by his bed.

Luke and I have rimmed your grave with the stones from Norfolk, dismantling the M we left in the woods and carrying the pebbles here. We didn't use the ones that man stole. Luke and I will return to the seaside and choose new pinks to replace those. We will find new colours too, and make it so beautiful you would cry.

I want to stretch out over the cold ground where you are. The mound of dirt they have covered you with is like a bed. But I do not want Luke to see me do this, so the two of us crouch beside you. I take a handful of earth in my hand, let it run through my fingers, put my mud-stained skin to my mouth. Kissing this dirt is not like kissing you, but it is the best that I can do. It is all I have.

'I love you, Mummy,' Luke says to the earth. It makes my heart hurt to hear him call you Mummy again, as if the certainty of what has happened to you has at last frozen him in his relationship to you. There can be no changes now.

'Auntie Ella?'

'Yes, Luke?'

'Mummy doesn't want you not to do what you really want because of her.' He speaks as if he is translating what he hears your ghost saying to him, bringing your words from the underworld to those of us who are not magical enough to hear them.

'I think you're right. I feel that too. That's why I'm going to get that teaching certificate.'

'But Mummy wants the charity work to continue.'

'Granny and Grandpa and I will keep it going. We'll pay for some experts to do most of the things I used to do.'

An anonymous donation was made to the charity a week after I found you. The money will fund it for at least a decade. I don't need to ask to know it was Noah.

'They won't be as good as you.'

I try to steer the subject to something else. 'Granny and Grandpa want to have a little party at the end of the month.'

'For your birthday?'

'Yes. They are insisting. Will you help them plan it?'

'Definitely. It's my half-birthday too, don't forget. Can Ted come?'

I can't help the hesitation before I answer. 'You can ask him, Luke.'

'Okay.' He is still considering the soil that holds you. 'Maybe when you get a job as a teacher they'll let you start a self-defence club?'

'Brilliant idea.'

He is looking so hard at the ground I think he is trying to see through it, trying to see right down to you. 'Because we aren't sure you're going to like being trapped in a stuffy classroom all day.'

'We? Do you mean you and Granny and Grandpa?'

'No. Me and Mummy.'

'I see.' I ruffle his hair but he still doesn't tear his eyes from you. 'We need to choose a desk for your room, Ninja Warrior. We can look next weekend.'

'Do you think he's really going to come, Auntie Ella?'

I stand up, reach out an arm, pull your son to his feet, make him look at me, make him look away from you. Now that he knows where you are, I must be careful that he spends enough time with you, but not too much. You will be sad, but I think you will agree that he mustn't be too often with the dead. I flinch to think the word, but sometimes I must make myself.

'He's here, Luke. He was here when we arrived. I think he wanted to give us a little time.'

I look over my shoulder at the porch of the church. That is all it takes for Noah to leave the shadows and walk towards us. When he reaches the place where you are he crosses himself and bows his head. He falls to his knees and kisses the earth. Luke looks uncertain, but then he returns to the place I just pulled him from and does the same, a replica of his father.

Luke is arranging the yellow roses that Noah brought you. The two of them are bending their dark heads together. Can you hear what they are saying?

I quietly withdraw. I follow the little path that winds through the gravestones to the gap in the drystone wall that surrounds the churchyard. I want to give the two of them some time with each other, some time with you, before I have to drag Luke away from you and his father and take him to school.

I will wait here, by the wooden gate, in this puddle of winter sunshine that seems to be following me. In the pocket of my waxed jacket are three cards. I take them out and fan them and hold them in my hands, one green, one red, and one blue.

The first Valentine arrived yesterday and came to my house. I didn't guess at first what was inside the large brown envelope with its first-class stamp, posted from central London.

But as soon as I pulled out the pale green envelope I knew who it was from. It was bordered with roses that he had drawn himself. Perhaps he was remembering the design you wanted for the shelves he never made you, and thought it would please me. *I like beautiful things.* That is what he said. Perhaps he was reliving the flowers that some of the tabloids claimed he etched on the women. He had written *Ella* in the centre, ringed with a heart, and the words *To be opened on 14 February.*

I did not wait until today as directed. I opened it immediately, expecting several dead bluebottles to fall out, but none did. There was no greeting or signature on the handmade card. He plunged right in.

My favourite time to think of you is at night, as I fall asleep. Did you know that you smell of lily of the valley and taste of honey, and that your hair and skin feel like petals? I know these things. I know you.

I smiled to learn that you found your sister. I helped with that. I hope you think of me, if not yet in the way I would wish, at least – for now – with some affection and gratitude. Feelings can deepen over time, Ella. Yours will catch up with mine.

I was also glad of the treatment that Dr Devil met at your hands. I cherish the thought that his limited view is now of high walls and razor wire. I understand that he is likely to plead not guilty for the charges relating to your sister and the other women, and self-defence for the charges relating to you. Do not worry, my dearest Ella. He will lose on all counts. I have proved that you must trust in my insight.

Dr Demon would benefit from some occupational therapy. I think the table saw would suit his particular talents. What an honour it would be to tutor him myself, but I am engaged in other important work at present, and this will take quite some time to complete. Not to worry – I have numerous acquaintances who would be delighted to assist the doctor with his personal development.

Would you like me to arrange this? Alas, I suspect that you would not. You have power over me, Ella. Will you exercise that power? You can inspire me to do the right thing.

463

You can stop me from doing the wrong. You have only to say. But you must say.

The man we spoke of privately when you and I were last together is not worthy of you. I will not mention him to anybody, unless there comes a time when you would like me to. For his sake, let us hope he never again betrays you.

But here, Ella, is the real purpose of this card. Will you be my Valentine? I think I know what you will say. You will say nothing. At least for now. You see how well I understand you? But without the word No I will be encouraged. Whatever your answer, you are mine. And I am becoming the man you want me to be. My appearance is not what it was when we last met. I can say no more than that. Only — I think you will like what you see.

They will try to use you to find me, Ella. We are both much too smart for that.

I know where you are, as you will realise from the arrival of this card. Do not be alarmed by this. I would only ever protect you and those you love. I will do my best to act in ways that will make you proud, but you must give me some sign. Before long, I will find a way for us to be alone, so I can show you how I feel in person.

The card and the two envelopes will soon be with the police, though I am certain that Thorne has been careful to ensure he cannot be traced from them.

The police will question me, and I will answer carefully, as you would want me to, but balanced with my own conscience and the need to protect others. I am very good at this, now. I have had a lot of practice.

I will not let myself be scared that Thorne will find

me. I will not give him, or anyone, the power to control or threaten me. I will not hide or run. The last ten years of my life have been formed by my sense of fear and danger. I will not let the rest of it be. But if he does turn up on my doorstep, I will be ready.

The second Valentine was from Ted, who I haven't seen since he came to my hospital room the day after I found you. He'd deliberately waited until visiting hours were over, banking on the fact that the journalists would be gone by then. He also counted on his uniform getting him past the police officers guarding my door. They thought then that Thorne might be foolish enough to come crashing in. As if he would make it that easy.

Ted stared so hard at me. He scarcely blinked he stared so hard. At first I thought he was shocked by my appearance, by my white face splashed with purple bruises and criss-crossed in red gashes that they'd stuck together with glue.

I had made the nurse show me in a mirror. She didn't laugh when I said I would make a perfect bride of Frankenstein's monster. But unlike that bride, I am really alive. The glue washed away in a week or two. The bruises have faded and my cuts have almost healed. 'You were lucky,' the nurse said. I gave her your half-smile. I didn't contradict her. *It wasn't luck.* That is what you would have said if you were still talking to me.

But as Ted stared and stared and stared some more, I was confused about why he had come at all, only to be struck so entirely dumb. So I spoke instead. I told him I would keep his secrets about you. And then I told him to leave. He didn't move so I pressed the call button for somebody to make him.

'It will never be over between us. I will give you time, but I will be back.' His voice was hoarse as he choked out these words, the only words he had come to say.

Ted's card was the red one. *I will love you forever. I will wait until you forgive me.* I am not sure if the first thing is really possible. I do not know if the second will ever happen, though I want it to, because I do not like living with this splinter of ice in the part of my heart that was Ted's.

The third card was not signed. The third card was blue. The third card said simply, *Me and You*, with a drawing of a boy and his aunt. Can you guess who? Of course you can. It is the only card I will treasure. He has left one for you too, with a pencil sketch he did of you holding him as a baby. My hand rested on his shoulder as he buried it just beneath your blanket of earth.

I look up to see that your son and his father are walking away from you, walking towards me. So I slide the cards back into my huge jacket pocket and snap the flap to keep them secure while I wait for the two of them at the exit from this sad place.

They are holding hands, smiling their identical dimpled smiles, and I cannot help but smile too.

But Noah's smile soon disappears. He is looking so hard at me. Does he only see you? Or does he see me too? His forehead is creasing in worry and I think perhaps he is searching my face for scars. He pushes open the gate and he and I walk out of the churchyard with Luke between us.

I am waiting. I am listening. I am imagining what you would say to me. I do not see you and Ted together, now, when I close my eyes. I only see you. But you don't say anything. Not even a whisper. You are silent, and silent is the last thing I want you to be.

You will know that I forgive you. You will know that there is a hole in my soul that will never close up.

How strange that I spent my whole life thinking that I wanted everything you had, thinking that I wanted to be you, when all the time the opposite was also true. Ted once said that I was the good sister, but you are the good sister too. You are mine and I am yours and your son is the only Valentine I want. I have him because of you.

As ever, I strain to hear your voice. Your voice saved me, during that dark weekend in November. It can save me again. It is still the voice I want to hear above all others. That is why I will never stop talking to you, my love, my darling Miranda, my lost heart. That is why I will never stop listening for you. I am the sister of the sister. And that is why I will keep our secrets.

Acknowledgements

The statement, *this novel would not exist without*, has never been more powerful for me than it is with this one. My first and deepest thanks go to Bella, who taught me what it means to love a sister and be loved by one. The intensity of feeling that Ella and Miranda have for each other is the truest thing in this book.

My UK editor, Sarah Hodgson, gave inspiring and wise advice, coloured always by her loveliness and warmth. She had faith in *The Second Sister*, and in me, from the start, despite the tangle of my messy early drafts. My American editor, Laura Brown, offered superb insight and guidance. Her passion for the novel meant so much. Thanks also to Iris Tupholme, my Canadian editor, and to Jonathan Burnham of HarperCollins USA. My agent, Euan Thorneycroft, always knows exactly what to do. Having him on my side is a miraculous piece of luck. I am immensely grateful to everyone at A.M. Heath, especially Jennifer Custer, Hélène Ferey and Jo Thompson.

The team at HarperCollins UK is simply brilliant. In Editorial there is Julia Wisdom, Kathryn Cheshire and Finn Cotton; in Publicity, Felicity Denham. In Sales there is Sarah Collett and Anna Derkacz; in Marketing, Hannah Gamon, Katie Sadler and Louis Patel. In Export there is Damon Greeney and Rebecca Williams; in Production, Stefanie Kruszyk. Anne O'Brien worked her usual copy-editing magic. Micaela Alcaino designed the beautiful cover.

Richard Kerridge's comments on the third draft of this novel were vital. So too was his feedback on the short story I wrote about Ella and Miranda, 'The Sleepover'. His unsparing critical eye is an extraordinary thing to have, as is his love. My father reads every draft of everything I write. He and my mother never waver in their love and support. The two of them inspire me all the time and make me extremely proud. My brother Robert makes me laugh when I need to, even suggesting alternative titles (*The Brother of the Sister* is my personal favourite). He is a great ally and friend.

As ever, my three daughters make everything more meaningful and magical and beautiful. Lily is an amazing junior editor. She was *The Second Sister's* tireless first reader, of an early (censored!) draft that I read aloud to her – a special experience for us both. Imogen and Violet are patient and understanding in the face of my intense absorption in writing, and cheer me at every turn.

Many people have been generous with their time and expertise. Sergeant Steve Fraser, of Avon & Somerset Constabulary, was so professional and kind. He answered my endless questions with patience and detail, and invited me to Keynsham Custody Unit (one of the most fascinating episodes of novel research I've ever had). Matthew Wright talked to me about police radios. Mel Creton advised about self-defence. Alice Hervé shared her knowledge of doll's houses. Nathan Filer let me interrogate him about drug treatments for psychiatric patients. Gerard Woodward continues to offer his friendship and encouragement. All of these people made the book possible. Any mistakes are my own.

The epigraph from 'The Seven Ravens' is taken from *Grimm's Household Tales*, Edited and Translated by Margaret Hunt, London, George Bell and Sons, 1884, Volume I, pages 108-110.